From *Amaryllis* to *Obsidian Prey*, critics adore the electrifyingly passionate and suspense-charged novels of

Jayne Castle

"With her typical offbeat humor and flair, Castle takes a pair of powerful, unmatchable protagonists, sets them down in her innovative, synergistic world of St. Helen's, and gives them a mystery to solve, villains to outwit, and a passion to explore."

—*Library Journal*

"A fun, fast frolic on another metaphysical plane! The characters are fun and sexy. . . . A romance that will link your senses to the primitive side!"

—*The Literary Times*

"Classic sharp wit and unrivaled skill for creating captivating characters."

—*Booklist*

"A scintillating foray into love in another place and time [with] the heady charm of a great romance."

—*Romantic Times*

. . . and they are equally enamored of her irresistible page-turners written under her real name, the beloved *New York Times* bestselling author

Jayne Ann Krentz

"One of the hottest writers in romance today."

—*USA Today*

Turn the page for more rave reviews!

Also by Jayne Ann Krentz

Absolutely, Positively
Deep Waters
Eye of the Beholder
Family Man
Flash
The Golden Chance
Grand Passion
Hidden Talents
Perfect Partners
Sharp Edges
Silver Linings
Sweet Fortune
Trust Me
Wildest Hearts

Written under the name Jayne Castle
Amaryllis
Orchid
Zinnia

JAYNE ANN KRENTZ
writing as

Jayne Castle
Orchid

Pocket Books
New York   London   Toronto   Sydney

Pocket Books
A Division of Simon & Schuster, Inc.
1230 Avenue of the Americas
New York, NY 10020

First Pocket Books paperback edition May 1998

POCKET and colophon are registered trademarks of Simon & Schuster, Inc.

For information about special discounts for bulk purchases, please contact Simon & Schuster Special Sales at 1-866-506-1949 or business@simonandschuster.com

The Simon & Schuster Speakers Bureau can bring authors to your live event. For more information or to book an event contact the Simon & Schuster Speakers Bureau at 1-866-248-3049 or visit our website at www.simonspeakers.com.

Illustration by Craig White.

Manufactured in the United States of America

10 9 8

ISBN 978-0-6715-6902-0

Prologue

❖ ❖ ❖ ❖ ❖ ❖ ❖ ❖ ❖

"Time is running out, Mr. Batt." Rafe Stonebraker rose slowly from the massive, old-fashioned Later Expansion period chair. He was well aware of the effect his deliberate movement had on the man seated across from him. ·

Batt did not exactly flinch but the dapper little man definitely tensed. "Running out?"

"You've had three weeks to find me a wife. To date you have not produced a single possible match from your files. What seems to be the problem?"

"With all due respect, Mr. Stonebraker, you are not the easiest person to match." Hobart Batt produced a professional, placating smile but there was a cautious expression in his eyes. "I warned you when you first registered that it might take some time to find a suitable candidate."

"Synergistic Connections is supposed to be one of the most efficient matchmaking agencies in New Seattle." Rafe stood looking down into the flames that flared in the cavernous fireplace. "You advertise that you have a success rate exceeding ninety percent. I expected better service from your firm, Mr. Batt."

"Mr. Stonebraker, I assure you, we are doing our best. The thing is—"

"Yes?" Rafe turned his head to study Hobart's earnest, anxious features. "Just what *is* the thing?"

Hobart shifted uneasily under the scrutiny. He tweaked his pink bow tie and adjusted the sleeves of his expertly tailored pale gray suit jacket. "To be blunt, Mr. Stonebraker, your, shall we say, rather unique situation is proving to be a bit more difficult than I had anticipated. We face a number of serious challenges."

"I see. Are you saying that the resources of your matchmaking agency are not up to the task of finding me a wife?"

Hobart's neat brows came together in an offended line above the rims of his round, gold-framed glasses. "I assure you that we are doing everything possible to find a good match. But the combination of your rather unusual psychic talent and your somewhat rigid personal requirements constitutes a considerable stumbling block."

"When I registered you assured me that Synergistic Connections had established a reputation for its ability to match even unusual and rare high-class talents." Unusual and rare were among the more polite descriptors for those such as himself whose paranormal abilities did not fit into the normal range, Rafe reflected. *Exotic* was the popular term. His jaw tightened. As if he was some sort of strange, wild beast from one of the still-unexplored continents of St. Helens, he thought.

"Quite true, sir."

"You saw my para-talent certification papers. I'm only a class six. Mid-range. I fail to see why I should be a problem for your firm."

The certification papers were frauds, of course. He'd had them prepared by an expert forger several years ago. It had cost him a great deal of money, but money had not been a problem. It was never a problem for him.

ORCHID

Rafe made money the way a baker made cookies—
easily, quickly, and efficiently. With his particular type
of psychic talent it was no great trick to sit down in front
of the computer, analyze the financial markets, and
make decisions that produced quite predictable profits.

He had commissioned the false certification papers because he had no intention of allowing himself to be for-
mally tested in a syn-psych lab. Psychic talents were
common in the population. Almost everyone had some
degree of paranormal ability. But most people fell well
within the conventional, measurable spectrum, which
ranged from one to ten.

The vast majority went to a lab to obtain an exact
rating. Such testing was as routine as getting a driver's
license and took place at about the same time in life.
The full degree of individual psychic talent did not ma-
ture until the late teens.

Paranormal abilities had appeared early on in the
small population of colonists stranded on the planet St.
Helens two hundred years ago. Psychic powers took two
general forms. The majority of the population fell into
the category called talents, meaning that they possessed
a specific type of paranormal power that could be actively used. There were illusion-talents, hypno-talents,
horticultural-talents, diagnostic-talents, tech-talents, etc.

The psychic energy that talents produced endowed
them with a sixth sense. But unlike the other five senses,
it could not be accessed except in brief, unpredictable,
erratic bursts without the aid of a prism.

Prisms comprised the second, smaller category of people with psychic abilities. In them, paranormal energy
took a different form. Prisms possessed the ability to
focus the powers of a talent for an extended length of
time. The economics of the situation being what they
were, trained, high-class prisms often made good money
selling their focus services to talents who wished to use
their paranormal senses in a controlled, predictable manner for a lengthy period.

Neither talents nor prisms were distributed equally across the para-spectrum. The vast majority in both groups were bunched together in the lower and middle ranges. Very few people, talent or prism, possessed anything higher than a class-six level of psychic power.

By the time he was fifteen, Rafe had figured out that his talent was not only exotic, but much stronger than the average. His parents, both academics who held tenured professorships at the University of New Seattle, were disappointed that he had not inherited their gifts for teaching and research. Instead he had been born with a full measure and then some of his grandfather's rare para-sensitive strategic-awareness talent, commonly referred to as strat-talent.

To further complicate matters, he was obviously more than a class ten, although it was impossible to tell just how much more as the lab instruments could not measure energy levels higher than class ten.

Knowing the difficulties that lay ahead, his folks had urged him to conceal the full extent of his psychic abilities. Rafe had intuitively understood and complied. He did not need anyone to tell him that the strength of his paranormal powers placed him in the dark, unexplored regions that lay beyond the far end of the official psychic spectrum.

Like the handful of other people he knew who had a higher than normal degree of para-talent, his instinct was to keep the fact a closely guarded secret.

There was a name for people whose talent was so far off the charts that it could not be tested and quantified: psychic vampires.

The experts claimed that there was no such thing as a psychic vampire, of course. Given that true, off-the-chart talents seldom, if ever, volunteered for testing and current lab equipment could not measure anything higher than a class-ten talent, anyway, no one seriously argued the point. The current state of technology had created a classic scientific impasse. As far as the researchers were concerned, what could not be detected or measured did not exist.

But psychic vampires occupied a unique place in modern fiction and film. They were, after all, the stuff of legend. They fascinated and repelled. Rafe was well aware that books featuring handsome, sexy, super-talents who enslaved lovely, innocent prisms and forced said prisms to focus exclusively for them sold faster than iced coff-tea lattes in July.

The reality, however, was that even class-ten talents had a difficult time getting a date for Saturday night. People respected high-end talents, some were even a bit awed by them. But almost everyone was a little wary of anyone who possessed an extremely high degree of para-talent, especially when that talent was a particularly rare type. Strong power, in any form, made intelligent people cautious.

High-class talents were often difficult to match with a high probability of success. *Exotic* high-class talents were even more of a problem for matchmakers. Any talent who was fool enough to admit to possessing both an exotic talent coupled with an off-the-scale amount of psychic power would very likely have no sex life at all, Rafe reflected.

His own love life had certainly been nothing to write home about lately and he had a set of phony certification papers to prove he was not a psychic vampire.

"I must be frank, sir." Hobart fiddled with his elegant gold cuff links. "It's not the level of your psychic abilities which is causing the problem. As you say, a class six in most types of talents is well within the normal range."

"Then what, exactly, is the problem?"

"It's the, um, specific nature of your paranormal abilities which is making things a trifle awkward."

Rafe did not move. He gazed without speaking at Hobart until the syn-psych marriage counselor began to shift uneasily in his chair. A worried, vaguely desperate expression appeared in Hobart's eyes. He glanced around as if expecting to see that someone—or perhaps something—else had entered the room.

Rafe knew that a hunted feeling had just come over Hobart. A primal kind of wariness and the beginnings of the sort of fearful awareness that made the hair stir on the nape of the neck.

Rafe sighed and doused the small flash of psychic energy. It was a stupid parlor trick, but it worked every time. He supposed he ought to be ashamed of himself for using it on the hapless Hobart.

He watched Hobart relax and smiled slightly.

"I know that there are not a lot of strat-talents around," Rafe said. "But you assured me that you specialized in matching rare talents, Batt."

"Unfortunately," Hobart said earnestly, "It's proving to be more of a hurdle than I had anticipated. Perhaps my recent successes with unusual talents made me somewhat overconfident. The problem is that most folks have only a vague notion of what a strat-talent is. I'm afraid that the general impression that most people have of talents such as yourself is not a reassuring one."

"Are you saying that my para-profile is scaring off potential wives?"

"To be blunt, yes. I'm afraid that, although you are well within normal power ranges, you are considered something of an exotic, sir. I'm sorry to use the term, but there it is."

Rafe gazed deeply into the fire. "There are worse terms for exotics who happen to be strat-talents."

Hobart pursed his lips. "Yes, I know."

Primitive was one of them, Rafe thought. Another popular epithet was *throwback*.

He did not need Hobart to spell out the details of his problem. Para-sensitive strategic-awareness talent was believed to be a para-heightened version of ancient human hunting instincts. Strat-talents were perceived to be natural hunters who could, in essence, think like the quarry.

Many people, experts included, privately considered strat-talents to be paranormal throwbacks to the evolutionary past. The psychic energy they possessed was more synergistically linked to the basic senses—sight, smell, hearing, touch—than were other forms of paratalent. At least that was the theory.

Primitive. Rafe had learned to hate that word.

There was a commonly held belief that, due to the unsophisticated nature of their paranormal power, strat-talents faced a limited job market. A lot of people assumed that they generally pursued criminal careers.

The misconception was true as far as it went. But in reality strong strat-talents also tended to do spectacularly well in business. Their unique abilities allowed them to assess markets and the competition the way their primitive, earthbound ancestors had once assessed herds of large woolly beasts. A little nudge here, a small, judicious push there and the first thing you know you've got a whole bunch of large woolly beasts floundering helplessly in a swamp or dashing headlong over a cliff. Easy prey.

Rafe knew that he and his kind had a reputation for being ruthless. He preferred to think of himself as simply single-minded.

Hobart regarded him with a direct, not unsympathetic gaze. "I'm afraid the process of finding a good match for you is going to take a lot longer than I originally estimated, Mr. Stonebraker."

Rafe raised his brows. "Because most of the potential matches assume that I've got criminal inclinations?"

"I have done all of the appropriate background checks on you, sir. I will not hesitate to assure all potential candidates that you display no deviant or antisocial tendencies."

"I appreciate that, Batt."

Hobart appeared oblivious of the sarcasm. "The commonly held conviction that strat-talents frequently turn to crime is only one of the more unfortunate bits of conventional wisdom we must overcome. There is another popular myth which is equally difficult to dispel."

Rafe narrowed his eyes. "Five hells. Are you referring to that old notion about strat-talents being human lie detectors?"

"Well, yes, since you mention it."

"That's bat-snake shit and you know it."

Hobart winced. "Yes, Mr. Stonebraker, I am aware of that. However—"

"It's a complete misunderstanding of the nature of strat-talent. Probably left over from the days before the syn-psych experts had perfected their paranormal testing methods."

"Yes, of course, sir. Nevertheless—"

"Every intelligent, educated person knows that there's no such thing as a human lie-detector." Rafe moved one hand in a gesture of disgust. "If there were, there would be no need for courts and criminal trials."

Hobart coughed slightly. "You'd be surprised to learn what a strong grip some of the old notions have on the average man on the street."

"I'm not looking to marry the average man on the street."

"I understand, Mr. Stonebraker. But the bottom line is that we are dealing with a serious image problem here."

He was beset with image problems these days, Rafe thought. After all these years of living life on his own terms, he suddenly had to worry about how others saw him. It was damned annoying.

"Even if it were true that strat-talents can detect lies," he said patiently, "what is so off-putting about the idea? I assume that you would only match me with a reasonably honest wife."

"Think about it, Mr. Stonebraker." Hobart gave him a very level look. "Would you want to be married to someone whom you believed could detect even a tiny, polite, social lie? Would you want to live with a wife

8

who would know you were not telling the truth when you said she looked like a film star in a bathing suit? The occasional, graceful half-truth is vital to the conduct of a civilized life."

"Okay, okay, I see what you mean. But the fact is, I don't possess any magical ability to know if someone is telling me the truth."

Not exactly.

It was true that the same hunter's intuition that served him well in business and in his hobby of private investigation sometimes gave him warning signals when others tried to mislead him. But that was a far cry from being able to detect lies, he assured himself. It was certainly not the kind of personality flaw that should keep a woman from marrying him.

Hobart peered at him. "More people than you would believe have an aversion to the notion of marriage to a strat-talent. They are afraid there might be some truth in the old shibboleths. But even those outmoded misconceptions, difficult as they are to correct, are not our only serious challenges, Mr. Stonebraker."

Rafe folded his arms and propped one shoulder against the end of the bookcase. "You mean I've got other defects?"

"Well—"

"Tell me, Batt, have I got anything at all going for me in the marriage market?"

"Yes and no."

"What in five hells is that supposed to mean?"

"One of our most difficult challenges is not the nature of your talent. It is the fact that you are a Stonebraker."

Hell. He had been counting on his family name to overcome some of the complications posed by his talent. "I would have thought that was one of my few pluses."

"It is and it isn't."

"Damn it, Batt—"

"What I mean is, of course your family name speaks for itself. Everyone in the tri-city-states is aware of

Stonebraker Shipping. The Stonebraker name commands enormous respect in the highest social circles as well as in the business sphere. Your family has made great contributions to New Seattle."

"Get to the point, Batt."

"The point," Hobart said carefully, "is that you have chosen not to involve yourself with Stonebraker Shipping. You have not followed in your grandfather's footsteps. You did not even pursue a career in academia as your parents did. Instead, you have completely disassociated yourself from the source of the family fortune."

"Ah." Rafe closed his eyes in brief resignation. "I think I see the problem."

Hobart's mouth tightened with disapproval. "Matters would be greatly simplified if you had taken your place in the Stonebraker empire."

Hobart was right, Rafe thought. As challenges went, this one was probably among the more difficult for a professional matchmaker. Any woman who could be persuaded to overcome her aversion to marrying a strat-talent who happened to be a Stonebraker would naturally expect to move in the same elite social circles as the rest of the clan. He had turned his back on those circles and the family fortune at the age of nineteen.

Rafe considered the problem from a hunter's viewpoint. In a sense he was a victim of his own strategy.

As Hobart had just said, virtually everyone, at least everyone who had even the smallest connection to the business community, had heard of Stonebraker Shipping. Fortunately, Rafe thought, almost no one was aware of the current, highly precarious condition of the shipping dynasty his great-grandfather had founded.

There was still time to save the company and the livelihoods of the two thousand people, including the many members of his extended clan, who depended upon the firm. Rafe had been working night and day on the problem for weeks. He had only three more months to get all of the necessary duck-puffins in a row.

One of the most crucial duck-puffins was a wife. He needed one to present to the board of directors of Stonebraker Shipping at the annual board meeting when he made his bid to grab the C.E.O. position.

A wife was not merely a matter of window dressing in his case. Corporate tradition as well as the usual St. Helens social bias in favor of marriage dictated that only a married or seriously engaged person would be elected president and C.E.O. of Stonebraker Shipping.

His chief competition for the job was his ambitious cousin, Selby Culverthorpe, who had been respectably married for six years and had two kids to show for it. Selby's status as a family man as well as his long-term loyalty to the family business gave him a strong edge in the eyes of the conservative Stonebraker board. Selby fairly radiated trustworthiness, maturity, steadiness, and loyalty. All the characteristics of a good little Founders' scout.

Rafe, on the other hand, was all too aware that he had a reputation as the mysterious, unpredictable renegade of the clan. Although he was the great-grandson of old Stonefaced Stonebraker, himself, and the grandson of the present C.E.O., Alfred G. Stonebraker, he could not deny that he had walked away from his heritage a long time ago. Everyone in the clan had strongly disapproved of his decision to go his own way.

Alfred G.'s fury had been truly monumental. The battle between grandfather and grandson had assumed the proportions of family legend. Alfred G. had cut Rafe off without a penny. The two had not spoken for years following the explosive rift that had shattered what had been, until then, a close relationship.

Everyone who knew anything about Stonebraker family history knew that Rafe did not have access to the family fortune or social circles.

That was about to change. Unfortunately, Rafe could not advertise the fact. To do so would be to sacrifice his one edge in the coming war for the control of Stonebraker. He needed the element of surprise for several more weeks.

He also needed a wife or, at the very least, a fiancée to help him reshape his image.

But since marriage was for life on St. Helens, he intended to make his selection as carefully and as rationally as possible. He had assumed that meant using a good matchmaking agency, the way most intelligent people did. On the whole, everyone agreed, the first generation Founders had been right when they had established the matchmaking system and reinforced it with all the weight and force of law, custom, and social pressure at their disposal.

Occasionally marriages were contracted without the assistance of professional agencies, but those alliances were rare and generally frowned upon.

Theoretically, marriage agencies such as Synergistic Connections, with their scientific techniques and synergistic psychological tests gave individuals the best possible chance of contracting satisfactory marriages. Unfortunately, it looked as if the best agency in New Seattle was failing in his case, Rafe thought.

He had the sinking feeling that he had wasted the past three weeks concentrating on his other duck-puffins while he left the wife-hunting problem to Synergistic Connections.

He realized that Hobart was watching him with an expectant expression. But he could hardly announce that he fully intended to become the next C.E.O. of Stonebraker Shipping. Secrecy was critical at this juncture. His entire plan to save the family firm depended on it. If Selby were to discover too soon that Rafe was maneuvering to take control of the company, he would have three months to take action to prevent the coup.

Selby was only a tech-talent, Rafe thought, but lately the sneaky little bastard had shown a surprising flair for business strategy.

"It's not as if I'm not gainfully employed, Batt." Rafe

unfolded his arms, straightened and walked across the room to a low, heavily carved table. He plucked a small white card from the pile he kept in an ornate glass bowl. The embossed black letters read *The Synergy Fund*.

With a flick of his wrist Rafe sent the crisp business card sailing toward Hobart.

It landed on the immaculately pressed pleat of Hobart's pale gray trousers. He gingerly picked up the card and glanced at it. "Yes, yes, I'm well aware that you manage a very successful stock market mutual fund. I, myself, own some shares in it. I understand that your personal financial picture is extremely sound. That is not my point."

Hobart was obviously not impressed. Rafe decided not to make things worse by mentioning his evening hobby. After all, he only indulged himself in the off-the-books private investigation stuff when he was especially bored or restless.

"What is your point, Batt?"

Hobart cleared his throat. "Surely you understand that some of the image challenges we face could be greatly mitigated if you were employed in the executive branch of your family's firm."

Rafe smiled coldly. "You mean if it looked as though I'd finally seen the light, decided to join Stonebraker Shipping and henceforth start moving in the right social circles, some of your clients might be willing to overlook my strat-talent?"

"Frankly, yes." Hobart reddened but his expression remained professionally determined. "It would make my job a good deal easier if you gave the impression of being a, shall we say, more conventional Stonebraker."

Such an impression was exactly what he could not afford to give at this point, Rafe thought. "Let's try this from another angle, Batt. Perhaps you should introduce me to some less than ideal candidates. Who knows? I might be able to change my image in their eyes."

Hobart's eyes widened in alarm. "See here, I'm a professional, Mr. Stonebraker. I'm not about to allow you the opportunity to try to intimidate any of my clients."

"I wasn't talking about intimidation," Rafe said smoothly. "I was talking about persuasion."

"Persuasion?" Hobart looked skeptical.

"Give me the chance to convince some potential spouses that their preconceptions about people with my kind of talent are wrong."

A surprisingly steely gleam appeared in Hobart's eyes. "Before you consider trying to talk a lady out of her preconceptions about strat-talents, there is another course of action you might wish to consider. One that would greatly simplify things."

"What is that?"

"You could try dropping a few of your extremely narrow personal requirements."

Exasperation shot through Rafe. "I do not consider my personal requirements excessively narrow. I'm not choosy about eye or hair color or even bra size. I thought I made that clear."

"I refer to your insistence that your wife be a full-spectrum prism, among other things."

"I realize that a lot of matchmaking agencies don't think that full-spectrums and high-class talents make good matches, but as we just discussed, I'm only a class six. There should be no problem on that score."

"No, no, that's not the issue." Hobart flapped one beringed hand in a dismissive motion. "As it happens, I have recently confirmed two very successful matches involving full-spectrum prisms and very high-class talents. I no longer place much credence in the old theory that the two types never make good marital alliances."

Rafe raised one brow. "I'm acquainted with Lucas Trent and Nick Chastain. I attended both of their weddings."

"I see. Then you do understand."

"I understand that they each found their own bride but that you later verified the matches, Batt. You signed off on them even though many professional matchmakers would have hesitated because of the old thinking on the matching of unusual talents and prisms. That's one of the reasons I requested your services. You're supposed to be the best and you're willing to accept new data."

Hobart looked gratified. "I like to think that I'm good at what I do. Indeed, I consider my work a calling. And my experiences with Mr. Trent and Mr. Chastain did teach me to keep an open mind when it comes to some of the more traditional thinking on the subject of scientific matchmaking."

"So my request for a full-spectrum prism shouldn't bother you too much, Batt."

Hobart grimaced. "I might be able to find you a full-spectrum prism, although I confess I have no idea why it is so important to you."

It was important, Rafe thought, but he could not explain why to himself, let alone to Hobart. His inner certainty flew straight in the face of the results of all of the syn-psych research on the subject as well as conventional wisdom.

It was assumed, not without some evidence, that there was a natural antipathy between high-class talents and full-spectrum prisms. Powerful talents were vaguely resentful of full-spectrums. They did not appreciate the fact that nature had made them dependent on prisms for extended, full range use of their own, personal psychic energy.

Most full-spectrum prisms, on the other hand, found high-class talents arrogant, rigid, and demanding. In addition, full-spectrums were said to be extremely picky when it came to choosing spouses.

But for some time now, Rafe had become increasingly convinced that he needed a woman who could link with him on the metaphysical as well as the physical plane. All of his strat-talent instincts urged him to that conclusion. That was one of the reasons he had been driven, albeit reluctantly, into a state of celibacy for the past several months. He was tired of the self-enforced loneliness but he could not work up any enthusiasm for a casual affair. In some fundamental, *primitive* manner he did not want to investigate too deeply, he knew that it was time to find a mate.

It wasn't supposed to be this way. Paranormal abilities were supposed to be gender neutral. The rules of the metaphysical plane were different than the rules that applied to the physical plane. Any prism could focus for any talent without any sense of sexual or even personal intimacy on either side.

Or so the theory went.

But Rafe had long suspected that the exotic nature of his power made him different in this area, too. Perhaps it was because his psychic energy was so closely allied to his physical senses. He only knew that the yearning he felt for a mate extended into the metaphysical realm.

There was another, more pragmatic reason for insisting that his future wife be a full-spectrum prism. It was one thing to conceal his off-the-chart talent from business acquaintances, casual friends, marriage counselors, and even some members of his family. But there was no way he could hide the extended range of his paranormal abilities from a wife.

Bluntly put, he had to find a woman who would not completely freak out when she discovered that she was married to what some would call a psychic vampire. Based on the recent experience of his two friends, Nick Chastain and Lucas Trent, he had concluded that a full-spectrum prism was his best bet.

Rafe could not think of any diplomatic way of explaining that unique need to Hobart, however, so he focused on a different issue.

"What's wrong with having a few personal requirements in a wife?" he said. "After all, I'm going to have to spend the rest of my life with her, whoever she is."

Hobart gave him a look of polite reproof. "You don't

think it's just a bit limiting to demand that, in addition to being a full-spectrum prism, your future wife must be an admirer of meta-zen-syn philosophical poetry?"

"It seems perfectly reasonable to me that she share my literary tastes."

Hobart glared. "What about your requirement that she also be a practitioner of classic meta-zen-syn meditation and exercise? Few people outside of that ivory tower think-tank crowd up in Northville have even heard of meta-zen-syn."

"It's not that uncommon," Rafe said defensively.

"And then there's your demand that she be an admirer of Later Expansion period architecture." Hobart cast an exasperated glance around the firelit chamber. "No offense, Mr. Stonebraker, but very few people admire this particular style anymore."

"It's an acquired taste."

"Which almost no one acquires," Hobart retorted. "Any realtor will tell you that mansions such as this one are almost impossible to move when they come on the market."

Rafe followed Hobart's gaze around the room. It was true that the gothic elements that characterized Later Expansion period mansions were not to everyone's taste. He could not even explain why they were to his taste. He only knew that the arched doorways, the intricate patterns in the tile work, and the elaborately molded ceilings pleased something deep inside him. He had even gone so far as to restore the original jelly-ice candle fixtures and fireplaces, although he had also installed discreetly concealed modern lighting, heating, and air conditioning as well.

For a few seconds he tried to see his home through Hobart's eyes.

Fifty years ago the somber, overwrought architecture of the Later Expansion period had been extremely fashionable, an overreaction, perhaps, to the excessive ebullience of the Early Exploration period that preceded it. But the demand for the dark, brooding style had quickly faded.

Today many of the old houses in the district were shuttered and locked. Faded "For Sale" signs sagged from the massive gates that barred the long, elegant drives. Weeds sprouted where skilled horti-talents had once tended exotic gardens. Windows remained dark after the sun set. The sidewalks that lined the street were cracked.

No doubt about it, the neighborhood had gone into a slump.

Most of the dynasty-founding business families who had once made their homes on this particular hillside overlooking the city had moved to newer, more fashionable hills.

Hobart was right, Rafe thought. His home would not appeal to a modern, sophisticated woman.

"Okay," he said. "Maybe I could give a little on that last requirement. My future wife doesn't have to like this house."

Hobart raised his eyes briefly to the ornately decorated ceiling. "Very gracious of you, Mr. Stonebraker."

"Look, if you can't do the job, Batt, just say so. I'll register with another agency."

Hobart squared his discreetly padded shoulders and got to his feet. "There is no other matchmaking agency in New Seattle that could give you better service. You'll simply have to be patient. You must accept the fact that it will take time to find the right match for you."

But time was the one thing he did not have, Rafe thought. It was rapidly becoming clear that he could not depend upon Hobart Batt and Synergistic Connections to find him a suitable wife in the few weeks that he had left before the annual board meeting.

He had no choice but to take matters into his own hands. He would allow Hobart to continue to comb through the listings of registrants at Synergistic Connections. There was no harm in that and it made sense to cover every angle.

But while Batt fiddled around with his files of registered candidates, Rafe thought, he would go hunting on his own. He was a strat-talent, after all. Hunting was the one thing he did very well.

The first rule of the hunter was to go where the quarry was. Full-spectrum prisms were not exactly thick on the ground. Some worked in research labs and others held positions at the university. It would not be easy to meet and screen a lot of them in such a short amount of time.

But there was another place to find full-spectrums. Many of them worked at least part-time for focus agencies, where they commanded exorbitant rates for their services.

How hard could it be to arrange to hire and evaluate a bunch of unmarried full-spectrum prisms from a variety of local focus agencies? The natural optimism of the hunter rose within Rafe. Anticipation flowed across his senses.

He would hunt his own mate. *Wife*, he immediately corrected himself. He would hunt his own wife, not mate. *Mate* sounded so . . . primitive.

So did *hunt,* for that matter.

Okay, he would *search* for his own *wife*.

When he had narrowed the field to a handful of possible candidates, he would call Hobart in to help him choose the best match of the lot.

Chapter

1

❖ ❖ ❖ ❖ ❖ ❖ ❖ ❖ ❖

One month later . . .

"Stolen?" Stunned, Orchid Adams managed to keep her jaw from dropping in open-mouthed amazement, but it was not easy. She was still reeling. One thing she had to admit about focusing for Rafe Stonebraker, the jobs were never dull.

She turned on her heel in a slow circle and stared at the volumes housed in the rows of glass cabinets that lined the steel walls of the state-of-the-art, climate-controlled, underground gallery.

"You're kidding." She took a deep breath. "All of these old books are *stolen?*"

"Every last volume." Elvira Turlock smiled proudly. Light gleamed on her elegant silver chignon. "Including the one that brings you and Mr. Stonebraker here this afternoon."

"Good grief," Orchid whispered, awed in spite of herself. This was definitely Stonebraker's most bizarre case yet.

Elvira looked pleased by her reaction. "My new book of Morland poetry is quite spectacular, don't you think?"

Orchid studied the slim, leather-bound volume inside the glass case. She would not have it in her library, she thought, but she had been raised to be polite.

"Interesting," she said cautiously.

"Oh, dear." Elvira winced. "We all know what 'interesting' means, don't we?"

Rafe stirred in the shadows. "It's called *Three*."

Orchid did not exactly jump in surprise at the sound of his low, dark voice, but she did feel the hair lift on the nape of her neck.

She reminded herself that she had known he was there. He was, after all, the one who had brought her here today. But her new client was a strat-talent. He had an extremely annoying knack of sinking deep into the shadows.

She had almost refused to accept the first assignment earlier in the week. Only the combination of her boss's abject pleading and dire threats had finally convinced her to work with Rafe.

"I don't want to work with a strat-talent," Orchid had said when Clementine Malone had told her about the job. "They give me the creeps."

"Come on, how many have you worked with?"

"One." Orchid shuddered at the memory. "That was enough."

"Look, you know I'm trying to build an exclusive image for Psynergy, Inc. Stonebraker's an exotic. We want to attract exotic talents."

"There are other kinds of exotics."

"Yeah," Clementine said, "but not like strat-talents. You know how rare they are."

"Not rare enough as far as I'm concerned."

"Not to put too fine a point on this," Clementine said, "but you're not exactly one-hundred-percent normal yourself."

Orchid winced but she refused to take the bait. "Give

Stonebraker to one of the other full-spectrum prisms on the staff."

"They've all got assignments. Or a home life at night." Clementine grinned triumphantly. "Which you, being single, don't yet have. Besides, you know you always request evening assignments."

"Only because I need my days for my writing."

"Stonebraker apparently prefers to work at night."

"Right. Probably under full moons."

Some people viewed strat-talents the way they did wild jag-pards in zoos. Fascinating, but dangerously undomesticated. In a world where virtually everyone had some degree of paranormal talent and where such abilities were taken for granted as a naturally evolving aspect of the human species, para-sensitive strategic-awareness talent was considered very retrograde, evolutionarily speaking.

After meeting Rafe Stonebraker, Orchid was prepared to dismiss the throwback theories. Whatever else he might be, he was neither primitive nor unsophisticated, although she would not go so far as to call him domesticated.

He was well educated, well read, highly opinionated, and chillingly intolerant of those who failed to think as clearly and cogently as he did. Intelligence and awareness burned in him with the cold, powerful energy of jelly-ice.

But during the past week she had rediscovered why strat-talents were sometimes called hunters. They did have some distinctly unnerving habits. Hanging out with one was a bit like keeping company with a chameleon-cat.

She had discovered that if you took your eye off Rafe for even a moment it was easy to lose sight of him. He did not exactly disappear, but he had a natural affinity for whatever camouflage happened to be convenient. If he wished, he could fade right into the woodwork. His ability to become uncannily still made it possible to overlook him when he stood in any kind of shadow.

Until he moved a second ago, he had been blending quite nicely into the dark space created by two narrowly focused lights positioned above two of the glass cases.

"Percy Morland was one of the foremost stylists of sixth generation meta-zen-syn philosophical poetry," Rafe said.

His disapproval lapped at her like a dark sea in the windowless chamber.

"Yes, I know." With an effort of will, Orchid managed to keep her voice polite. Did he think she had never attended a basic lit class?

No doubt about it, as interesting as he was—and he was a far sight more fascinating than meta-zen-syn poetry—Rafe Stonebraker was starting to get on her nerves.

Orchid reminded herself that it never paid to offend the clients. Clementine would not be pleased if she was rude to this one in particular. *Think Exclusive* was Clementine's latest office slogan.

Orchid did not mind thinking exclusive, but she wondered if Clementine was aware of just how exotic her newest client really was. Rafe claimed to be a class-six strat-talent and he had the certification papers to prove it. But this was the third time she had worked with him in the past week and Orchid was willing to bet her next royalty check that he was far more powerful than his papers claimed.

When she focused for him she could literally feel the self-control he was forced to exert in order to hold his talent to a class-six level. She sensed the hunger in him to use the full range of his power. She knew that the powerful prism she projected for him whetted his appetite.

Three years ago she had known another strat-talent whose hunger had been just as powerful. Calvin Hyde's talent, however, had also been tainted with the dark hint of evil. But after the first very cautious focus session with Rafe, Orchid had known at once that he was no Calvin Hyde.

He could be irritating, arrogant, and maddening but there was no evil in his talent.

She could feel other things besides the hunger in him and that fact was making her increasingly uneasy. After all, everyone knew that the focus link was supposed to be completely neutral when it came to the personal side of things.

The indescribable rush of intimacy she experienced when she created a metaphysical prism for Rafe had to be a product of her own overactive imagination. There was no other logical explanation. But it was definitely not normal.

Thankfully, thus far Rafe appeared to be blithely unaware of the sensations she experienced during their focus sessions. As far as she could tell, he seemed completely unaffected. Nevertheless, even though she was not afraid of him, Orchid was beginning to think that it might not be a good idea to work with him again in the near future. Something about their link was definitely weird.

Suddenly Rafe moved closer to her, coming to stand directly behind her. He studied the book over her shoulder.

"Most experts believe that Percy Morland was a very high-class vision-talent who suffered from periodic bouts of unaligned synergy on the metaphysical plane," he said.

"I've heard that," Orchid murmured. She wondered if Rafe knew how irritating he was when he went into his lecture mode.

"He refused treatment," Elvira put in helpfully. "Apparently Morland was paranoid about the syn-psych labs. Seemed to think the experts might destroy his artistic visions if he allowed them to try to realign his metaphysical energy waves."

"Can't blame him for steering clear of the labs." Orchid reflected briefly on her own extremely unpleasant experiences in a synergistic psychology research lab three years earlier. Lately the old nightmares had returned in full force. She'd had two this week. "If I could make a fortune writing poetry like that, I wouldn't want anyone messing with my para-energy waves, either."

Elvira chuckled. "An excellent point, my dear. I take it you are not a great admirer of the meta-zen-syn philosophical poetry?"

"To be honest, no," Orchid admitted.

Rafe did not bother to conceal his exasperation. "Why not?"

She wondered, not for the first time, why her opinion mattered to him. "I consider it at best to be a dead-end in literature. More likely it was a huge joke foisted on the literary world."

"I see." Elvira raised her delicately arched silver brows. "How very intriguing to think that I risked so much just to steal a poetic joke."

"But I do admire the writers' financial sense," Orchid added. "Unlike most poets, they got rich. Their works still grace the shelves of every library in the tri-city-states and there was a time when they were the hottest thing in the bookstores. Everyone who was anyone read the stuff."

"I have three originals in my own collection," Rafe said in a dangerously neutral voice. "A Morland, a Jenkins, and a Singh."

Orchid told herself that she should not allow him to goad her. But the man had an attitude and it made her reckless. She'd always had this problem, she thought. She could already hear a distinct sucking sound but she could not resist putting her foot a little deeper into the jelly-quicksand.

"Got to hand it to those meta-zen-syn philosophical poets," she said cheerfully. "Morland and his pals were shrewd businesspeople, even if their poetry does sound like something a fifth grader might write."

There was a short, highly charged silence.

"I suppose it would be too much to expect you to appreciate the clear, strong visual strength of meta-zen-syn poetry," Rafe said in suspiciously civil tones.

The polished edge of his voice was so sharp Orchid was pretty sure it could have severed bone. She gave him her brightest smile.

"Yeah," she said. "A little too much to expect."

His eyes narrowed.

"You may as well give it up, Rafe, dear." An amused twinkle lit Elvira's merry blue eyes. "I don't think that you will be able to intimidate Miss Adams into pretending that she admires philosophical poetry."

"Obviously," Rafe said dryly.

She did not look at him but Orchid knew that, unlike Elvira, Rafe was not twinkling.

Orchid smiled blandly. " 'Synergy, confluence, harmony. Even chaos seeks balance'." She quoted smoothly.

Elvira's eyes widened in appreciation. "Why, that's lovely, dear. Which meta-zen-syn poet wrote those lines?"

"I did. Mrs. Kramer's fifth-grade class."

Elvira laughed. "Point taken."

Rafe did not laugh. She could feel the brooding stillness in him as surely as she could sense his aura of paranormal power. She was fairly certain that if she turned around to look at him she would risk a nasty cut from the knife-sharp edge of annoyance in his icy gray eyes.

Why did he care whether or not she admired the stolen volume of Morland poetry? she wondered. The question was just one more on the long list that she had been compiling on Rafe Stonebraker all week.

She did not know what to make of him. At times she had the disturbing impression that he was studying her.

Or perhaps testing her would be more accurate, she thought. Either way, the weird sensation was making her edgy.

Unfortunately, contrary to what she had predicted to Clementine, she was enjoying her assignments with Rafe. They had proved very different and far more interesting than her usual focus projects. She was beginning to think that she had a flair for the private investigation business.

In the course of the first two assignments she had assisted Rafe in the recovery of a lost third generation painting and helped him trace a highly prized racing pony-hound that a groom had taken from its stable.

It had become clear that Stonebraker Investigations handled only the most confidential of inquiries. Rafe was called in by clients who did not want publicity or the attention of the police.

This evening's assignment was the most unique yet. Orchid was still not sure why Rafe had even bothered to hire her. She was almost positive that he had known who had stolen his client's stolen volume even before he had phoned Psynergy, Inc., and asked for her.

To make matters even more curious, Elvira Turlock was not the least bit concerned about the fact that she had been caught redhanded with an extremely valuable stolen book. On the contrary, she obviously took great pride in displaying the volume to Orchid and Rafe.

Orchid got the impression that Elvira and Rafe were old acquaintances who had long ago established a quasi-professional relationship.

Elvira glanced at Rafe. "I suppose you feel you must return my Morland to George."

"He did hire me to find it." Rafe sounded mildly apologetic.

"Yes, of course," Elvira said.

Orchid cleared her throat discreetly. "George?"

"George Yeager." Elvira's smile was warm and tinged with an odd wistfulness. "An old friend of mine."

Orchid blinked. "You stole this book from a good friend?"

Elvira chuckled. "Why not? Six months ago he snatched my Kingsley. I had to even the score."

"I don't get it." Orchid glanced from Elvira to Rafe. "Is this some sort of game?"

Rafe shrugged but said nothing. There was almost no expression on his austere, bluntly carved features.

"George and I see it as more of a challenge," Elvira explained lightly. "Rather like a sailing regatta or a golf-tennis tournament. The goal, of course, is to make it appear that the theft was carried out by someone else."

"A challenge," Orchid repeated. A light went on somewhere in her brain. "I think I get it."

Elvira gave her a droll smile. "George and I are both widowed. Perhaps it would help if I explained that the two of us are more than merely good friends. Our little adventures serve to keep a certain zest in our relationship."

Elvira and the unknown George were lovers. Orchid grinned. "Why, Mrs. Turlock, that is incredibly romantic."

"Five hells." Rafe sounded thoroughly disgusted. "It's not romantic. It's a complete waste of everyone's time."

Orchid glowered at him. "Why are you complaining? You get paid to track down the thief, even though you obviously know who the culprit is before you even start. Sounds like easy money to me."

Rafe's jaw tightened. "It's not always quite that easy. George and Elvira go out of their way each time to fool me, too."

"Indeed we do," Elvira said. "Part of the game." She peered at Rafe. "Tell me, were you thrown off by any of the clues that I left behind this time?"

"The use of a miniature twin-blade saw to take apart the locked case gave me some pause."

"I hoped it would," Elvira sounded smugly satisfied. "It's Edison's trademark, not my own."

"Okay, I get the picture," Orchid said. "You and Mr. Yeager apparently have a longstanding competition going here, Mrs. Turlock. But what about the rest of these old books? You said that they were all stolen. Did you take them from Mr. Yeager's private collection, too?"

"Heavens, no, dear." Elvira smiled. "The rest of these were permanent acquisitions."

"Meaning she stole them from other private collections," Rafe muttered.

"I see. I think." Orchid eyed Elvira cautiously. "I take it that you are not unduly concerned about getting arrested, Mrs. Turlock?"

Elvira beamed. "Not bloody likely."

"May I ask why not?" Orchid glanced at Rafe. "I understand that Mr. Stonebraker contracted only to find Mr. Yeager's book, not to turn you over to the cops. He made that clear before we came here tonight. But what about the next private investigator or police detective who comes looking for a missing book?"

Elvira looked mildly astonished. "But, my dear, the only one I have to worry about is Stonebraker. No other private investigator or detective has ever discovered my little hobby of collecting old books. I'm a fine, upstanding member of the community. Who would suspect me? Except for Rafe, of course?"

She had a point. Orchid, herself, could hardly believe that the wealthy, socially prominent Elvira Turlock, who sat on the boards of most of the major philanthropic societies in New Seattle and whose brilliant parties were legendary, was a book thief.

"But sooner or later—" Orchid persisted.

"As she said, not likely." Rafe gave Elvira a knowing look. "Mrs. Turlock is careful to limit her acquisitions. She only steals from a highly select group of private collectors."

Orchid looked from Rafe to Elvira. "I don't understand."

"I acquire my books from collectors who are not in a position to go to the police." Elvira waved a graceful, heavily ringed hand at the volumes in the glass cases. "Every one of the volumes that you see here had been previously stolen from someone else before I took it."

Orchid raised her brows. "I get it. You steal from other thieves who can't go to the cops because they would have to admit they had stolen the books first."

"Precisely." Elvira nodded approvingly. "It limits my risk. However, I have many of the same security problems as the other collectors who dabble in stolen books and art."

"In other words," Rafe said, "she has to worry about thieves too. Mrs. Turlock is in no position to go to the police, either."

Orchid nodded. "Hence the state-of-the-art security system in this chamber?"

"Indeed." Elvira smiled at Rafe. "I've just had it updated again. You might want to have a look at some of the new features. Quite clever, if I do say so myself."

A gleam of what could only be professional interest appeared in Rafe's gaze. "Thanks. I'd like that."

"The least I can do. But first you both must join me for coff-tea and dessert before you leave. After you phoned this evening, I had my chef prepare a very nice pear-berry tart. You're quite fond of pear-berries, as I recall."

"My favorite," Rafe said. "Very thoughtful of you, Elvira."

Orchid could hardly believe her ears. Now they were discussing fruit tarts just as though they were not all standing in the midst of several million dollars worth of stolen books.

"Excuse me," she said crisply, "but if you're finished with me, Mr. Stonebraker, I really should be on my way."

Rafe looked at her with unwavering eyes. "But I'm not finished with you, Miss Adams."

A chill of awareness shot through her. It was suddenly very difficult to look away from that intent, icy stare. From out of nowhere, she was struck with an almost overwhelming urge to run but she did not think she could move if her life depended on it.

This was how a moose-deer that has just been singled out of the herd by a predator feels, she thought suddenly.

What was wrong with her? She was mildly claustrophobic but the underground gallery had not bothered her until now.

A tingling sensation wafted across the metaphysical plane, ruffling all her senses, psychic and otherwise.

Belatedly she recognized the faint shimmer of paranormal energy being actively projected. *Talent seeking a prism.*

An instant later, it vanished. But not before Orchid recognized Rafe's unique brand of psychic power. She did not know if he had meant to intimidate her with a flash of raw strat-talent or if the fleeting contact had been accidental. She strongly suspected the former.

Primal fear metamorphosed into outrage. "What do you think you're doing?"

"Sorry." Rafe turned his attention to the nearest bookcase. "It was an accident."

Elvira glanced quizzically from one to the other. "Something wrong?"

"Not at all." Orchid managed to summon what she hoped was a cool, professional smile. "Mr. Stonebraker let a bit of talent slip on the psychic plane. I thought perhaps he wanted to focus, but apparently he just lost control for a moment."

She glanced at Rafe out of the corner of her eye. *Touché,* she thought when she saw his stoic expression. She could have sworn that he blushed. She knew she had embarrassed him.

Any man endowed with Rafe's monumental degree of arrogant self-mastery would naturally be chagrined by the condescending assumption that he did not have complete control of his psychic talent. But he could hardly argue the point. If he denied it, he would be tacitly admitting that the flash of strat-talent had been deliberate. And that would mean that he had meant to intimidate her.

"I see." Elvira dismissed the event with a charming smile and turned to walk off down the gallery hall. "As long as you're here, why don't I show the two of you the rest of my collection? For obvious reasons, I rarely have the pleasure of allowing others to view it."

Orchid avoided Rafe's gaze. Perhaps the brief pulse of power had been an accident, she thought. Or perhaps she was overreacting. She was tired, she reminded herself. Anxiety dreams, punctuated by the two full-blown nightmares, had disrupted her sleep for the past several days. And then, this morning, Morgan Lambert had phoned her with the news of Theo Willis's death.

It had not been a good week.

"I'm especially proud of my Fay histories of the second generation." Elvira paused to indicate a row of leather-clad spines. "Aren't they lovely?"

Orchid smiled. "I like those. Read them in high school."

Elvira gave her a knowing look. "I'm not surprised they appealed to you, dear. Rafe, however, is of the opinion that Fay romanticized the second generation colonists. Isn't that right, Rafe?"

"I don't care for the romantic style," Rafe said.

"Figures," Orchid grinned. "I'll bet you've never read any of my books, have you?"

His brows drew together in a disapproving frown. "No."

"Don't bother. You wouldn't like them. Much too romantic."

"Personally, I love your books, Miss Adams," Elvira said. "Indeed, I am collecting them. Legally, of course. I was so excited when Rafe told me you would be coming with him today. I would be delighted if you would autograph a book before you leave."

"I'd be honored," Orchid said.

"Wonderful. Now, then, let me show you my little group of Espinosa mysteries." Elvira turned a corner and started down another stainless steel corridor. "Oh, by the way, Rafe, remind me to put in an order for another thousand shares of Synergy Fund stock before you go."

Orchid glanced at him. "Synergy Fund?"

"My day job," he muttered. "I'm the president and chief financial advisor."

Strat-talents were supposed to be good businesspeople, she reminded herself. "I see."

Who would have guessed, she thought. Stranger and stranger.

She was aware of Rafe pacing along beside her. If one discounted the subtle aura of power he radiated, there was nothing extraordinary about him. He was of medium height and he appeared to be in excellent physical shape. He looked lean and sleekly muscled in his dark sweater and trousers. His near-black hair was cut a little too short for current fashion.

It was, perhaps, unfortunate, given the nature of his particular psychic talent, that he had been endowed with the blunt, hard features and the intense eyes of a predator, she thought.

"Do take a look at my wonderful new Inchman, for me, Rafe." Elvira motioned toward a small volume. "I love it, but I have a nasty suspicion that it may be a forgery. I suppose there would be some ironic justice in that. Nevertheless, I would like to get a second opinion and I can hardly ask a professional—"

She broke off abruptly, interrupted by a high-pitched, electronic wail that oscillated suddenly through the steel gallery. The sound was not especially loud but it struck Orchid's nerves with an eerie intensity. She was abruptly dizzy.

An expression of acute dismay crossed Elvira's face. "Oh, dear."

Rafe winced as if in severe pain. He put his hands over his ears. "Five hells. The new security system, I assume?"

"I'm afraid so." Elvira closed her eyes and put her hand to her forehead. "The installer said there might be a few false alarms in the beginning. I'm afraid we have a problem."

"Do something." Orchid felt as if she were standing on the bow of a ship that was being tossed about by violent waves. She steadied herself with one hand against the wall. "Turn it off."

"That's the problem." Elvira swayed on her feet and gave Orchid a deeply apologetic look. "I can't. Not from in here. The lights will go next, unfortunately."

Rafe took his hands away from his ears and moved swiftly toward the door at the far end of the gallery. She caught a glimpse of his grim face and knew that he was as uncomfortable as everyone else.

Perhaps he was actually in more distress she thought, not without a pang of genuine sympathy. He was a strat-talent, after all. His kind were believed to have more acute physical senses than other people, even when they were not employing their psychic energy. She could only imagine what the strange, disorienting wail of the siren was doing to his ears and his equilibrium.

"Why doesn't one of your household staff stop it?" Rafe called out to Elvira as he went toward the door.

"I gave them the night off when I heard you would be dropping by for a visit." Elvira sounded weak. "There's no one here but us."

The lights over the bookcases winked out with startling abruptness, plunging the steel-lined room into stygian darkness.

"Wonderful." Rafe's voice echoed eerily in the tomb-like chamber. "Just what we needed to make the evening perfect."

"What is it about that siren?" Orchid shook her head, trying to clear it. "For some reason it makes me feel as if I'm about to pass out."

"It's designed to make you do just that. The sound waves it generates interfere with the natural synergy of ear-brain patterns to create a disorienting sensation." Elvira's voice was whisper-thin now. "In fact, I believe I'm about to faint, myself."

"Elvira." Rafe's voice sharpened. "The door's locked from the outside. We're trapped in this damn gallery of yours."

"The crypto-talent who installed the system designed it so that any thief who found his way inside would be locked in here and rendered unconscious."

"Good grief, we're caught in a fancy bug trap for burglars." Orchid massaged her forehead. At that moment unconsciousness held a distinct appeal. Anything was better than the feeling that she was going to be violently ill. "I don't do well in dark, enclosed spaces."

"Don't freak out on me," Rafe ordered. His voice sounded closer now. "I've got enough problems on my hands locating the other exit."

In spite of her growing nausea, Orchid was offended. "I never freak out." A flicker of hope went through her as his words finally registered. "What other exit?"

"There has to be one. Elvira?"

"Yes, dear?" She sounded half asleep.

"Pay attention. I know how crypto-talents think and I know how you think."

"Yes, of course you do, dear. You're a strat-talent."

"You and whoever designed the system must have planned for this kind of disaster. Where's the other exit?"

"You're right, there is one. Somewhere. Can't seem to think. So sorry, dear. This is very awkward. Quite embarrassing, in fact."

With a soft sigh, she fell against Orchid, who staggered under the unexpected weight.

"Oomph. Rafe, I've got her. I think she's unconscious."

"I'll take her."

She did not hear him move but a second later he brushed against her arm. He took the weight of Elvira from her.

"I'll leave her here on the floor for now," Rafe said.

Orchid's head was spinning faster in the endless night. "You'd better not get too close to me. I'm feeling a little sick. My boss will never forgive me if I throw up on a client's shoes."

"I won't be real thrilled either." He moved again in the fathomless dark. "Get a grip, Orchid."

"Easy for you to say. I can't seem to grip anything. I think I'm going to faint."

"If you do, I'll demand my money back from Clementine Malone. Come on, we've got to find that exit."

"You're the big-time strat-talent. Got any ideas?"

"Yeah. I just need to think clearly for a minute." There was raw pain in his voice now. "Damn. That siren is really doing a number on my ears."

An idea occurred to her. "Link."

"I'm not sure that's a good idea. No telling how that siren will affect a focus link."

"What have we got to lose?" she demanded. "I vote we try it."

"Okay, okay. You're right. Not much to lose."

When the questing tendril of raw power unfurled out on the psychic plane, Orchid greeted it with a great deal more enthusiasm than usual. Rafe's psychic energy burned, strong and steady, in the metaphysical realm where there was no day or night, no light or darkness.

The instant she projected the glittering crystal prism that could focus his power, everything steadied. The dreadful spinning ceased.

Strat-talent energy, a *lot* of it, more raw power, in fact, than she had ever focused in her entire career, slammed into the prism she had crafted.

"Better. Much, much better." Rafe's voice was hoarse with relief. "Definitely a good idea."

"Thanks. All part of the package of exclusive services available from Psynergy, Inc." Orchid let out the breath she had been holding. "Don't forget to tell my boss about this. I may be able to use it to get a raise."

The nausea faded as her sense of physical and spatial disorientation receded. She was still blinded by dense darkness and the obnoxious sound waves continued to assault her nerve endings but she found that she could now keep the nastier effects of the security system at bay by concentrating on holding the focus.

She studied the off-the-chart level of power pouring through the glittering crystal prism she had projected on the psychic plane.

"Class six, I believe your certification papers said," she murmured very politely.

There was a short, tense pause.

"You don't appear to be having any trouble dealing with my talent," Rafe pointed out dryly. "That makes you something more than a full-spectrum. A lot more. In fact, now that I've had a chance to focus at this level with you, I can see that there's something different about the kind of prism you project. What is it?"

Orchid was suddenly grateful for the enveloping darkness. It made it impossible for Rafe to see her blush. At least, she amended, thinking of his para-heightened senses, she hoped it made it impossible for him to notice the heat she felt in her cheeks.

"I'm an ice-prism," she mumbled. Until tonight there had been no reason to demonstrate the full range of her abilities to Rafe.

"A what?"

"An ice-prism."

There was another short silence. "I've heard of those. Never met one."

"There aren't very many of us around."

"Is it true what they say about ice-prisms?" He

sounded genuinely curious. "Can you really manipulate the prisms you project?"

"Mr. Stonebraker, do you have any immediate plans to get us out of here or are we going to hang around chatting all night?"

"Sure." An unexpected note of amusement laced his voice. "But you've got to admit that this is rather ironic. A couple of psychic vampires meeting in the dark. Just like something out of a novel. One of yours, perhaps?"

It was uncomfortably similar to a scene in her latest book, *Dark Desires,* but she had no intention of telling him that.

Out on the metaphysical plane, the raw chaos of energy pulsed through the prism, emerging in sharply controlled, brilliant bands of power. Orchid knew that, so long as she channeled the energy for him, Rafe could use it the way he used any of his other senses.

Strat-talent energy waves looked different from other kinds of paranormal power. The colors were deeper, stronger, less transparent. They vibrated on slightly different wavelengths, augmenting ancient hunting instincts and heightening senses that had long been lost to mankind. That was why the experts considered them more primitive in an evolutionary sense.

Rafe's psychic energy was fierce and powerful but it was clean, even at this level of intensity. It was not tainted with the muddy hues of evil and incipient madness that had shaded Calvin Hyde's talent.

She watched, enthralled as the energy surged across the metaphysical plane. It was exhilarating to focus at the highest ranges of her own power. This was what she had been born to do, she thought. It was akin to breaking into a run after walking all of her life.

She knew that she was not the only one savoring the experience. She could feel Rafe's exultant satisfaction. It occurred to her that he had probably seldom, if ever, had a chance to focus at this level for any extended period of time.

"Five hells." He sounded slightly dazed. "This is good. This is incredible."

She smiled to herself. The urge to show off overwhelmed common sense. She was an ice-prism, after all. One who rarely got to exercise the full range of her unique abilities.

You think this is good? she thought. *Watch this.*

She studied the nuances of Rafe's strat-talent, noting the rhythms of the waves, the subtle differences in hues, the texture of his surging power.

Using the exquisite control she wielded over her own psychic energy, she made minute adjustments in the focus. A gentle alteration here, a slight sharpening of power there . . .

The prism glittered as she went to work on its myriad crystal facets. When she was finished the metaphysical construct was so brilliantly clear that it seemed to glow with the light of an inner sun.

She heard Rafe groan. He drew in a deep, shuddering breath as he watched his powerful talent focused with preternatural clarity and precision. It was the kind of elemental sound he might make in the moment of sexual release, Orchid thought, fascinated. An answering rush of sensual heat flooded her stomach.

This was ridiculous. She took a couple of meta-zen-syn breaths to regain her self-control.

"It's as if you made that prism just for me," Rafe whispered.

"I did."

"A perfect focus."

"I told you, I'm an ice-prism."

"So it really is true . . . I never realized—" He broke off abruptly.

Orchid took a couple more controlled breaths and called on an old meta-zen-syn mantra. Balance and harmony, she chanted silently to herself. Balance and harmony was the key. The last thing she wanted to do was make a fool out of herself in front of Clementine's most exclusive client.

She had not felt anything that even remotely resembled physical attraction when she had focused for Calvin Hyde three years ago. All she had experienced on that occasion was complete and utter revulsion.

So why the sudden rush of yearning when she focused for Rafe?

Even now, in the midst of the crisis, she was aware of a passionate sense of intimacy, a wistful need for something more, something she could not describe. After her first focus assignment with him she had assured herself that the bizarre side effects of the focus link would disappear when she grew accustomed to working with his unusual talent.

But familiarity was definitely not leading to boredom or even to the customary, emotionally neutral state that defined the usual focus link.

"I'd rather not spend the rest of the night here," she said briskly. "Got any ideas of where the crypto-talent installed the second exit?"

"I'm a strat-talent, remember? I can find things."

"Even in the dark?"

"Especially in the dark. Why do you think I prefer to work at night?"

Chapter

2

❖❖❖❖❖❖❖❖❖

"Well? Did you find the seam you thought would be there?" Orchid's voice held a crisp edge of urgency.

"Yes." Rafe ran his fingertips along the wall. His focus-heightened sense of touch assured him that it was more than the place where two strips of steel had been joined. He could feel the faint trace of escaping air. "It's here. Right where I thought it would be."

"You're kidding?" A cautious relief bubbled in the words. "You actually found it?"

It occurred to him that she had not been terribly optimistic about his chances of locating the second exit. "Nice to know I had your confidence all along."

"Yes, well, I didn't mean to imply that I doubted your ability, it's just that—"

"Forget it."

"I've insulted you, haven't I?"

"I'll get over it."

"I'm glad to hear that," she said. "But you've got to admit, I had cause to be concerned. It's impossible to see my own hand in front of my face. The odds against your finding a hidden door were pretty dismal."

"No, they weren't. The odds were pretty damn good that I would locate it. Anything a crypto-talent can hide, I ought to be able to find."

The gallery was as dark as the inside of a sarcophagus but with his para-sharpened awareness, Rafe did not need light to see what he was doing.

He could make do without illumination, he thought. What he really needed at that moment was a cold shower. Orchid was standing much too close. Her unique, shatteringly feminine scent was distracting in the normal course of events. It became a heady drug to his paranormal-enhanced senses. He could feel the heat of her body even though she was not touching him. Hell, he could feel the heat of his own body. He was burning up with the crazy desire that always hit him when he linked with Orchid.

Primitive. The word seared through him. He was in control, he thought. He was not a beast.

He took a couple of meta-zen-syn breaths to steady himself. Then he shoved a bookcase away from the wall.

It had only taken a few minutes to find the telltale seam in the stainless steel panel. Now all he had to do was locate the release mechanism that would open the emergency exit.

A piece of cake-tart under normal circumstances.

A real challenge with Orchid breathing down his neck.

It worried him that he had overprojected a few minutes ago. Orchid now knew that he was no class six. He had not meant for her to discover that so soon in their still-prickly relationship. She did not seem unduly concerned about the fact that he was an off-the-chart talent, but that was almost beside the point.

The problem was that he had not been in full control of his power at that moment. The effects of the alarm system on his keen senses had been painful. He had been tense and edgy and increasingly desperate for escape. Orchid's incredible prism had come as a glorious, intoxicating relief.

But that was not the whole of it and he knew it.

He could blame the oscillating security siren and the urgency of the situation for his failure to moderate his power but he was well aware that was not the only reason he had shoved too much energy, too quickly out onto the psychic plane.

The truth was, the more he worked with Orchid the greedier he became for the experience. In his whole life, he'd never had an opportunity to project the full range of his talent through a prism. Few talents as powerful as himself got the chance because, even if they were willing to admit the level of their power, it was virtually impossible to find prisms who could handle it.

He had overshot the mark a few minutes ago, jacked up the power by accident, discovered that Orchid could deal with it and now all he could think about was going to the limit again the next time.

Preferably while he was making love to her. The image of her, naked and open and welcoming beneath him when they linked nearly shattered his hard-won concentration.

Control, he thought. Control was the key.

He breathed deeply, using the techniques of meta-zen-syn meditation to regain his self-mastery.

Finding a delicate seam in a steel wall behind a painting in the dark was a breeze compared to solving his more pressing problem, Rafe decided. It looked as though he had finally found a possible candidate for a wife and she was all wrong.

Other than the fact that she was an extremely powerful, indeed, breathtakingly strong, full-spectrum-plus ice-prism, Orchid Adams met virtually none of the criteria he had given to Hobart Batt.

In the beginning, she had been distinctly wary of him. He'd had the impression that if he made one wrong move, she would walk out in the middle of the focus assignment. But she had appeared to relax after their first link. It was as if he had passed a test of some kind. He had been cautiously optimistic.

However, it had quickly become obvious that they had almost nothing in common.

From her coff-tea house wardrobe, which, from what he had observed, consisted of nothing but faded jeans, slouchy blazers, and black T-shirts, to her love of the romantic, they clashed.

One of the most disturbing aspects of the situation was that he seemed to irritate her as much as she irritated him. But, as if he had, without warning, developed new, masochistic tendencies, he kept coming back for more.

Physically, she was striking, not pretty. She was slender and small-boned but she was definitely not pale, delicate, or sweet. She moved with energy and grace. Her witchy green eyes held a dangerous mix of cool self-confidence and mischief. Her black, shoulder-length hair framed a face that was animated with intelligence. She handled herself with the assurance that often characterized a full-spectrum prism. Everyone knew they tended to be arrogant.

The irony of it all was that, given her career as a novelist, she would probably prove to be the one woman in a million who actually liked his house. He had a nasty suspicion that it looked like the sort of place she imagined a psychic vampire would inhabit.

This was definitely not the mate he had set out to find.

So why in five hells did she feel so right?

For the past month he had haunted every focus agency in town in search of a full-spectrum who would make a promising candidate for a bride. He had spent a small fortune hiring one prism after another, only to discover that he felt nothing at all, either in or outside of the focus link.

Eventually he had worked his way through a variety

of agencies until he reached tiny Psynergy, Inc. When Clementine Malone had introduced him to Orchid at the beginning of the week, he had felt every instinct he possessed, strat-talent and otherwise, go to full alert. Something in him had throbbed with anticipation before the ink was dry on the agency contract.

That something was still throbbing. Which could prove embarrassing if he was not careful, he thought, thoroughly disgusted with his lack of self-control.

Choosing the right wife was too important a decision to be left to his hormones, he reminded himself.

He wished he knew if Orchid felt anything at all during the focus sessions. If she did, she managed to conceal it extremely well.

"What's going on?" Orchid asked sharply. "Are you making any progress?"

On top of everything else, she had a tendency to nag.

He used the ultrasensitive pads of his fingertips to search out the hidden lever in the floor. "Got it."

"Thank heavens. I don't think I could take another five minutes in this place."

"I'm not exactly having a great time, either."

Rafe decided it would not be smart to tell her that if he had to spend another five minutes in the dark alone with her he would probably start howling at the twin moons, Yakima and Chelan, even though he could not see them.

Definitely an uncool move. So very *primitive*. Bound to scare off a potential wife.

Damn. He was already starting to think of her as a mate. Things were moving too fast here. They were out of control. He had to step back from the brink and think about this before he took it any farther.

"You don't seem to be having any difficulty finding your way around in this tomb," Orchid observed thoughtfully.

"No."

"You know, there's enough contact through the link

for me to realize that you have a clear sense of where we are in this gallery, but it doesn't feel *visual*. At least, not to me. Can you actually see in the dark?"

"I have excellent night vision." He found the tiny switch that freed the mechanism. "One of my biggest assets." Although Hobart Batt did not seem to think it was a big selling point to a potential spouse, he thought.

"But can you really distinguish objects in this kind of total darkness?" Orchid sounded surprisingly curious all of a sudden.

"No, of course not. At least, not the way you mean. No one can see where there's a total absence of light." He hesitated. "I use . . . other senses."

"You mean like hearing? Touch? Smell?"

"Sort of—" He wondered where all this was going. "It's hard to explain. There's something else involved."

"Hmm. I'm not sure I'd like to have a better sense of smell." There was a delicate pause. "Doesn't it get to be a little overpowering when you're in a crowded room or when you take out the garbage?"

Rafe felt an uncomfortable warmth suffuse his face. It had been a lot of years since he had been acutely embarrassed by a woman. Luckily Orchid could not see his face at that moment.

"The sense of smell is different when it's augmented by paranormal energy," he said stiffly. "It doesn't translate quite the same way on the metaphysical plane."

"Oh. Well, what about that other sense you mentioned? The one you called *something else?*"

He hesitated, his fingers on the trap door release. He wondered why she had chosen that moment to start asking personal questions. "It doesn't have a name. I can't describe it except to say that it's a sort of awareness." *Hunter's intuition.*

"Interesting."

"Will there be any other questions before I try to open this damned trapdoor?"

"Sorry. Didn't mean to get personal."

He wrapped his hands around the lever and raised it cautiously. There was a squeak of steel hinges. A rush of air followed. An instant later, emergency lighting from a cramped stairwell flooded into the gallery.

"You did it." Orchid hurried to the opening. "My God, you really did it. You found the exit."

"Like they say, everyone has some talent, however small." Rafe got to his feet and moved past her into the stairwell. "If I know crypto-talents there will be an emergency switch for the siren right around here somewhere." He spotted the green lever immediately. "Right. Here we go."

He slammed the lever upward. The uncomfortable whine finally ceased.

"What a relief." Orchid gripped the edge of the steel door frame and sagged wearily against it. "Tell me, does this sort of thing happen a lot to you in the course of your private investigation work?"

"No." In the eerie green light of the emergency fixture he could see the tense, drawn expression in her eyes. He had been very careful to involve her only in cases that held little or no possibility of physical danger.

But after what had just happened, she might very well refuse to work with him again.

A frisson of dread swept through him. Maybe she wasn't exactly what he was looking for in a wife. But what if he never saw her again?

Rafe took a step forward. Reached out to touch her shoulder. "Orchid? Are you okay?"

"Yes, of course." She smiled weakly. "Just give me a minute. You'd better see to poor Mrs. Turlock."

"I'll get her." He made to step past Orchid and then hesitated. "Look, I'm sorry. I never thought anything like this would happen."

"Of course you didn't. Hey, don't give it another thought. I'm fine, really." She straightened and moved determinedly away from the door frame. "Actually, it was all quite fascinating. I must admit, working with you is never dull."

"I'm not sure that's a compliment."

Her smile brightened. Amusement replaced the strain in her smoky green eyes. "And you did rescue us from that horrible place."

"Least I could do."

"It was rather impressive, to tell you the truth. I was afraid we'd be trapped in there until someone from Mrs. Turlock's household staff returned."

"You don't have to remind me that you had your doubts about my ability to get us out."

She grinned. "Next time I promise to have a little more faith in your strat-talents."

Relief rushed through him. "Next time?"

"Sure. You know, I think I may have a flair for the private investigation business."

An hour later, Rafe drove home with the Icer's window down. He needed the brisk, bracing night air to clear his senses. He was still brooding over Orchid's remark.

A flair for the private investigation business.

What if the only thing she saw in him was an opportunity to play private detective?

He absently noted the small, dark compact parked at the curb as he waited for the gates to his driveway to swing wide. The vehicle did not belong to any of the few neighbors he had left.

The door of the unfamiliar compact slid up into the roof just as Rafe was about to drive through the open gates. The street lamp gleamed on the figure of a tall, thin, bird-boned man in a rumpled gray suit. Light winked on the lenses of his wire-rimmed glasses.

He waved frantically in an obvious effort to get Rafe's attention.

"Mr. Stonebraker, is that you, sir?" The thin man hurried toward the Icer. "I've been waiting for hours. I must speak with you."

Rafe quickly assessed the scene with a short burst of strat-talent. He sensed nothing amiss. No obvious trap, at any rate. Just an anxious-looking potential client.

The last thing he needed at that moment was a client.

"It's late," Rafe said.

"I'm afraid this can't wait." The bird-thin man stopped and peered at Rafe through the Icer's open window. "My name is Brizo. Dr. Alexander Brizo. I'm with the university."

"What do you want from me?"

"We desperately need you to find something for us, sir. Something that was stolen from one of our labs."

"Did you try the police?"

"Good lord, no." Alexander Brizo's eyes widened with horror. "The last thing we want to do is bring the authorities into this. There must be absolutely no publicity. Reputations are at stake. And the research contract, of course. Our lab fought hard for it. We don't want to lose it."

"What, exactly, was stolen from your lab, Dr. Brizo?"

Brizo blinked several times. "An object."

"Maybe you could be a bit more specific."

"An object sent back by the fourth Chastain Expedition. They're still in the field, you know, excavating the alien tomb that was discovered by the third Chastain Expedition."

"Yes, I know." Rafe frowned. "Are you telling me that one of the alien relics was taken from your lab?"

"That is exactly what I'm trying to tell you. You must find it for us, Mr. Stonebraker. Quickly. If word gets out that it was stolen while in our care, my colleagues and I will be in an extremely awkward situation. A great deal of grant money is at stake."

"Any idea who took the relic?"

Brizo looked uncomfortable. "Yes, we think it was a man named Willis. Theo Willis. He was a prism assigned to assist the psychometric-talent research team that is studying the most recent shipment of artifacts."

"Got any idea why he stole it?" Rafe asked patiently.

"No. Actually, we don't." Brizo looked baffled. "It's not as if one can use the relics in any way. None that have been found thus far still function. The researchers say they are much too old. And one can hardly sell an alien relic on the open market. They're easily recognized, after all. Any potential buyer would know it was stolen from a museum or a research lab."

"There are people who will collect almost anything that is rare or valuable, Dr. Brizo. That means that there is a market for anything rare or valuable."

"I see. You refer to an illicit, underground market. The sort that supposedly exists for works of art and such."

"Right."

"I hadn't thought of that. Yes, I suppose it's possible that Willis stole it with the intent of selling it to a collector. I certainly can't think of any other reason why he would have done such a thing. No other lab would want it unless it also got grant money to study it."

"You're sure this Theo Willis is the thief?"

"Virtually certain."

"Any idea where he is now?" Rafe asked.

Brizo's narrow face seemed to grow even thinner. "Well, yes. But I'm afraid that knowing where he is won't do us much good."

"Why not?"

"Because he's dead, Mr. Stonebraker. His body was found yesterday. He apparently drove his car off a cliff."

For the first time since Brizo had hailed him, Rafe felt the familiar stirring of his hunter's instincts. "Follow me to the house, Dr. Brizo. We can talk there."

Brizo cheered slightly. "You'll take the case?"

"Yes."

The scents of the night sharpened as Rafe drove through the gates. The light of the twin moons was so bright that he could make out each silver-tinged leaf on the looming oak-drona trees that lined the drive.

He knew this feeling, he thought. It was the sensation he always got when he became interested in a new case. The anticipation of the hunt.

But this time he was not responding to the prospect of the investigation itself. Finding something as unique as a stolen alien artifact would be simple. The underground market for such items was very small and his contacts in it were excellent.

No, it was not the case that aroused all his senses tonight. It was knowing that he now had an ideal excuse to hire Orchid Adams again.

Chapter

3

❖❖❖❖❖❖❖❖❖

Orchid smiled when her cousin, Veronica Adams, walked through the door of the restaurant. The effect on the other diners was predictable. She turned every head.

It was not just the fact that Veronica was a very blonde, very attractive woman who moved with the kind of grace and poise that captured attention. It was her stark white attire and her aura of serene composure that drew the eye.

Veronica was a Northviller, a member of the intellectually oriented Northville Community, and a devoted practitioner of the esoteric arts of the system of synergistic meditation and exercise known as meta-zen-syn.

Northville and the North Institute, the academic research center associated with it, were a two-hour drive from New Seattle. Both the community and the think tank were named for Patricia Thorncroft North, the philosopher who had set down the three principles of synergy. Everyone who lived in Northville worked directly or indirectly for the institute.

Almost everyone in Northville wore white except at their own weddings or funerals.

The North Institute attracted the most brilliant scientific and philosophical minds from the three city-states of New Vancouver, New Seattle, and New Portland. Over the years, it had developed a reputation for research and development in the field of synergistic theory that was second to none. It ran on corporate funds, private endowments, and grant money. The institute operated its own education system for the children of the academics who worked in the think tank.

Many of the people who were affiliated with the institute inevitably were attracted to the philosophical tenets of meta-zen-syn. The meditation exercises had great cachet with the intellectual crowd.

Orchid knew all about the think tank, its school system, and meta-zen-syn. She had been raised in Northville. Her parents were on the research staff at the institute. Her two older brothers had both pursued careers there.

Everyone had assumed that she would join the institute, marry, and raise another generation of Adams Northvillers. Instead, she had turned her back on her heritage and, at the age of twenty, she had fled to New Seattle to carve out a different life for herself.

In typical meta-zen-syn fashion, her family had accepted her decision, but Orchid still suffered occasional pangs of guilt. She was, after all, the first Adams in three generations to leave Northville.

The maître d' rushed forward to pull out the chair across from Orchid. He had not made such a grand production out of seating her a few minutes earlier, Orchid reflected. The effect of a stylish white suit, white scarf, and a pair of white heels was amazing.

Orchid was suddenly very conscious of her own faded jeans, rumpled jacket, black T-shirt, and loafers. She never had quite gotten the hang of wearing white. Five minutes after she put it on there was a spot somewhere on the front. It was almost a synergistic law of nature.

Nevertheless, she was happy to see her cousin.

"Hi, Veronica. How's the wedding shopping going?"

"Finished, thank goodness." Veronica smiled as she took her seat. "I must say, I had no idea that getting married would be so complicated. I'll be glad when it's all over."

"Only one more week to go."

The waiter materialized at the table. He whipped out his notepad and looked respectfully at Veronica.

"The fresh aspara-cado salad, please," Veronica said. "Dressing on the side. And a bottle of Baker-Hood spring water."

"Yes, ma'am." The waiter turned to Orchid.

"I'll have the salmon-tuna burger, extra mayo and extra relish, a large order of fries, and a jelly-cola, please," Orchid mumbled.

"Sorry," the waiter paused, pencil poised. "I didn't catch that. Did you say a large order of fries and a jelly-cola?"

Orchid felt herself turn red. She glared at the waiter. "That's right. And don't forget the hot sauce for the fries."

"Got it." The waiter shoved the notepad into the waistband of his black trousers. "Be right back, ladies."

He turned and sped off toward the kitchen.

Veronica regarded Orchid with a knowing eye. "What's wrong?"

Orchid grimaced. "How do you know something's wrong?"

"Don't be silly. We grew up together. Sometimes I think I know you better than your own parents do." Veronica's eyes filled with sympathy. "Is it the marriage registration thing? Have you had a call from your agency?"

Orchid rolled her eyes. "Of course not. I haven't had an agency date since I got matched with Preston Luce last year. And I'm sure that was not a real date. I'm almost positive that Preston rigged it."

"I still don't see how he could have done it." Veronica frowned. "He would have had to know the results of the multipsychic paranormal personality inventory you took when you registered as well as every detail of your para-profile. How could he have gotten that kind of information? It's all confidential."

"I think I've figured out how he did it." It had taken her a while to come up with a scenario that explained how Dr. Preston Luce had managed to get himself matched with her, but Orchid was convinced she had arrived at a probable explanation.

"Are you sure you're not just being a little paranoid here?" Veronica asked. "As good as the matchmaking process is these days, mistakes do happen once in a while. Fortunately, they almost always get corrected before things have gone too far."

"It wasn't my counselor at Affinity Associates who figured out that Luce was a sneaky, low-down, conniving little worm-snake. I was the one who realized after three dates that he only wanted to use me to get himself introduced into the right circles in Northville. And that's just what he did."

"Now, Orchid, you don't know that for certain."

"Yes, I do. And when I refused to go out with him again, he told my parents that he was heartbroken. Claimed he was willing to wait for me to come to my senses. They actually believed him for a while, even though I warned them that he was a user."

"Preston can be very charming."

"Of course he's charming." Orchid narrowed her eyes. "Sucker is a high-class charisma-talent, I'd bet my next royalty check on it. By the time my folks realized that he wasn't the nice guy he made himself out to be, it was too late. He had gotten himself hired into the department of synergistic studies at the institute."

"I'll admit that now that I've known him for a few

months, I'm very glad you didn't marry him," Veronica said slowly. "I don't think he's very popular with his research assistants, either. But there's no denying that he earns his keep at Northville."

"You mean he brings in the grant money."

Veronica chuckled wryly. "Never underestimate the power of a person who can pull in large corporate grants. The North Institute is an ivory tower. Those of us who live in it like to pretend we're above such grubby, mundane concerns. But everyone knows that it takes cold, hard cash to run the place."

Orchid sighed. "And whatever else he is, Preston Luce is a rainmaker."

"That he is. He landed two more major corporate sponsors just last month. Luce is golden at the institute."

Orchid wrinkled her nose as the waiter returned with a tray. "I suppose he'll be at the wedding?"

"Of course." Veronica paused while her salad was placed carefully in front of her. "You know how it is at the institute. It's a small world. One can hardly exclude a high-ranking member of the research faculty from a guest list."

"I guess not." Orchid eyed her platter of hot, greasy fries with moody resignation. "I'm not looking forward to seeing him, but don't worry. I won't make a scene."

"It never crossed my mind that you would." Veronica drizzled one tiny spoonful of dressing over the artfully arranged greens on her plate. "I know it's never easy for you to come back to Northville and Preston being there will only make it more awkward for you than usual."

Orchid bit into her dripping salmon-tuna burger. "I can handle it."

"I'm sure you can. But I know it will be a strain for you."

Orchid shrugged. Veronica was right. Going home was always a source of tension for her and it was getting more difficult as the years went by. All of the kids who had been her classmates in school had gone on to get

advanced degrees and doctorates in various fields related
to synergistic theory. Most had taken prestigious positions at the institute. Almost all of them were married
and had started their families.

In a world where getting married was considered a social
and moral obligation as well as a serious family responsibility, she had not even managed to find a husband.

When you got right down to it, Orchid thought, all
she had done thus far in life was publish three psychic
vampire romance novels. As accomplishments went, by
Northville standards, that did not add up to much.

Returning to Northville was a little like going back to
a high school reunion and discovering that you were the
only failure in the class, she reflected. The fact that
everyone believed that she had rejected a legitimate
match with Preston Luce simply because she liked to
rebel only made things worse.

Veronica looked thoughtful. "You know what you
ought to do?"

"What?" Orchid asked around a mouthful of burger.

"Bring an agency date to the wedding."

Orchid nearly choked. "Are you kidding?"

"I'm serious. It would make things so much easier
for you."

Orchid slowly put down her burger. "Veronica, I just
told you, I haven't had a single call from my marriage
agency since my counselor tried to match me with
Preston."

"So?"

Orchid scowled, exasperated. "To put it bluntly, I
can't get a date. At least, not an agency date and, at my
age, that's the only kind that counts."

Veronica smiled her serene smile. "You've got friends.
Bring one of them along and pass him off as an
agency date."

Orchid stared at her, goggle-eyed. "I can't believe you
just said that. Bring a fake date to your wedding?"

"Why not?"

"I'm already having anxiety dreams. I don't need any more problems, thank you very much."

Veronica frowned in concern. "Anxiety dreams? Why?"

Orchid pushed a fry through some hot sauce. "Probably because ParaSyn contacted me again. I got a letter from them a few days ago. They want me to return for a follow-up to that ice-prism study I was involved with three years ago."

"The one you walked out on because the researchers wanted you to focus for some criminally insane talents?"

"Yeah, that's the one." Orchid shuddered.

The psychic talents Dr. Gilbert Bracewell, the head of ParaSyn, had asked her to focus had not been just mentally disturbed. They'd had violent criminal tendencies. She had recoiled from the darkness in them. Morgan Lambert and Theo Willis had also been repulsed by the researchers' desire to see if ice-prisms could handle such deeply disturbed mental patients.

It was Orchid who had led the small revolt that had resulted in the termination of the project. She had walked out of ParaSyn in the middle of the study. Morgan and Theo had followed.

"I hated that place," Orchid said. "The last thing I'd ever do is go back for some stupid follow-up research."

"What about the other two ice-prisms who were part of that study?"

"I'm still friends with Morgan Lambert." Orchid put down her half-eaten fry, her appetite suddenly gone. "But I heard yesterday that Theo Willis died in a car crash recently. They say he drove himself off a cliff. Apparent suicide."

"How sad."

"Theo was not what you'd call a friend. I don't think he had any friends. But he and I and Morgan sort of bonded during our experience at ParaSyn. He was a little weird. Maybe even crazy. But, hey, he was an ice-prism, just like me. Everyone knows we're not exactly normal."

Chapter

4

❖ ❖ ❖ ❖ ❖ ❖ ❖ ❖ ❖

"About time you showed up." Byron Smyth-Jones, Psynergy, Inc.'s receptionist, secretary, and avant-garde fashion guru, glared at Orchid over the rims of a pair of glasses fitted with purple lenses. "The boss is having a fit."

Orchid raised her brows at the sight of Byron's latest wardrobe addition, a violet-colored, skin-tight suit styled with massive shoulder pads and wide cuffs.

"How can you tell if Clementine is having a fit?" she asked with grave interest.

"Very funny." Byron took a bunch of notepads out of a box and stacked them in a supply cupboard. "And completely beside the point. This time it's serious."

"It's always serious." Orchid glanced at the notepads. They were each neatly imprinted with the Psynergy, Inc. logo and the words "Think Exclusive" at the top of each page. "What's going on?"

Byron glanced over his shoulder. Orchid followed his gaze to a large poster featuring a photograph of an improbably huge chunk of extremely rare fire crystal. It was emblazoned with the logo and partially obscured the closed door of Clementine's office.

"Her new exotic is here to sign another contract." Byron lowered his voice to a hissing whisper. "He insists on using you."

"The new exotic?" In spite of herself, Orchid felt a tiny thrill go through her. "You mean Rafe Stonebraker asked for me again?"

"You got it. He's been here for the past half hour, signing papers. Clementine tried to get hold of you to confirm the assignment, but when she couldn't reach you, she went ahead and drew up the new contract anyway."

A fluttery sense of panic instantly wiped out Orchid's incipient excitement. Last night in the euphoria that had ensued when she and Rafe had escaped the gallery, she had thought it would be exciting to work with him again. Now, in the cold light of day, she was not quite so sure.

"I was thinking of talking to Clementine about using someone else the next time Stonebraker called. If he called, that is."

"He called, all right," Byron assured her.

"I wonder why. I got the feeling he was not overly pleased with my services."

"Whatever gave you that idea?" Rafe drawled softly behind her.

Orchid spun around and saw him standing in the doorway behind her. He wore a dark jacket over a dark shirt and a pair of dark trousers. There was a plastic cup of coff-tea in his left hand.

She narrowed her eyes. "Must you sneak up on people like that?"

He looked amused. "Sorry." He held up the cup in his hand. "I just went down the hall for coff-tea. You were here when I got back."

With an odd sense of desperation, Orchid glanced at

Clementine's closed door. "I, uh, thought you were in there with my boss."

"Ms. Malone and I finished our business a few minutes ago. She said you were due to stop by the office after lunch so I decided to wait."

"I see." Orchid tried to squelch the embarrassed heat that threatened to rise in her cheeks. She devoutly hoped that he had not overheard the reference to exotics, but something told her that he had. Rafe had extremely sharp hearing. She managed a cool, professional smile.

"I'm flattered that you asked for my services again so soon, Mr. Stonebraker. But when you dropped me off last night you didn't mention that you had another job in mind."

"I didn't get my new client until after I left you." He studied her with an unwavering gaze.

There was nothing overtly rude, threatening, or intimidating about his gaze. He simply watched her.

From out of nowhere, the familiar hunted feeling came over Orchid, just as it had last night in Elvira Turlock's gallery. She glowered at him. He blinked, frowned slightly. The sensation vanished.

If not for the fact that it had left every hair on the nape of her neck standing on end, she could have blamed the incident on her imagination.

"I'm a little busy at the moment," she said as the door of the inner office slammed open.

"No, you're not," Clementine announced. "I've canceled all of your other appointments. You're free to work with Mr. Stonebraker for the next month."

"A whole month?" Orchid whirled back around to stare at her boss.

"Yep." Clementine, built like her favorite form of transportation, an ice-cycle, bristled in her signature black leather and gleaming silver studs. Her stark white hair, styled in a short brush-cut, was set off by steel hoops in her ears. "Stonebraker says his new case may take a little longer than the others."

Orchid had no trouble seeing the dollar signs that glittered in Clementine's shrewd eyes.

"But I'm not free for a whole month." Orchid felt pressured. She needed to think about this, she decided. "I've got commitments."

"Nothing that can't be rescheduled," Clementine countered. "I checked."

"I'm talking about personal commitments, not Psynergy, Inc., commitments." Orchid was intensely aware of Rafe listening to the exchange. "I'm going to attend my cousin's wedding."

"That's a week off and you said you'd only be away overnight, anyway," Clementine said smoothly.

Orchid groped for another excuse. "Founders' Day is coming up soon. Only five days away."

"So?" Clementine shrugged one sturdy shoulder. "Have a beer, get a little crazy down in Founders' Square, sing the Founders' Anthem. Big deal. There's still plenty of time to work for Stonebraker."

"I do have another career, you know."

"You told me just the other day that you were on schedule with your writing."

"That's not the point."

Clementine planted her broad fists on her hips. "What, exactly, is the point?"

"Yes." Rafe gave her a curious look. "What is the point?"

There was no point and Orchid knew it. She had no excuse for turning down the focus assignment. She was not even certain that she wanted to turn it down. She was starting to enjoy the private investigation work Rafe did. But she did not like the feeling of being maneuvered into a neat little trap.

She turned back to Rafe. "When did you want to start?"

"Tonight."

"Impossible." A ridiculous sense of triumph soared through her. "I have a previous engagement."

"Cancel it," Clementine ordered.

"I can't do that." Orchid gave them all a somber look. "I'm meeting someone at the Volcano Club. We're going to hold a small wake for a friend of ours who died recently."

"Oh, yeah, that's right." Byron balanced another stack of notepads. "I remember. You and Morgan Lambert are going to drink a toast to that poor ice-prism you both worked with. The one you said was weird."

"Yes." Orchid challenged Rafe with another cool glare. "An acquaintance died a couple days ago. You know how it is."

"Sure," Rafe said. "I know how it is. I'll go with you to the Volcano Club. We can discuss the new assignment after you hold your mini-wake."

"Uh—" Orchid's brain shut down for an instant.

"I'll pick you up at eight." Rafe glided back out into the hall.

He was gone before Orchid could think of any more excuses.

A hush fell over the office. It was broken only by the sound of Clementine brushing her hands together in gloating satisfaction. Nothing made her glow like a newly signed focus contract.

"He may not be one of *the* Stonebrakers of Stonebraker Shipping, but he's certainly *a* Stonebraker," Clementine said. "I'll settle for that."

"What do you mean?" Orchid asked.

Clementine shrugged. "Gracie gave me the lowdown on him. Seems our client was in line to inherit control of Stonebraker Shipping at one time."

Orchid frowned. Gracie Proud was Clementine's permanent partner. They had been matched by a marriage agency several years ago. Sooner or later, gay or straight, almost everyone on St. Helens got married. The Malone-Proud relationship was, from all appearances, a blissful union.

On the surface the two women could not have been

more different, Orchid thought. Gracie was a petite, stylish woman with a knack for high fashion and social contacts. She owned and operated Proud Prisms, one of Psynergy, Inc.'s chief competitors. She was an unfailingly accurate source of gossip and information.

"Whew." Byron's eyes got very big behind his purple glasses. "We're talking about *those* Stonebrakers, are we?"

"Yeah." Clementine grimaced. "But our maybe not-too-bright client quarreled with his grandfather, old Alfred G. Stonebraker, years ago. Young Rafe lit out for the Western Islands to find himself, as they say. His grandfather never forgave him. Cut him off without a cent. Actually, Gracie says it was more like Rafe cut himself off. Apparently he refused to have anything to do with the family fortune or the company."

"But he's back in New Seattle," Byron pointed out. "Maybe he and his grandfather have been reconciled."

"Not likely," Clementine said. "Gracie knows about these things. She tells me that everyone who moves in the same ritzy circles as the Stonebrakers is aware that Rafe has no interest in the family business. Apparently Rafe's cousin is scheduled to take over control of the company in a few months."

"How sad," Orchid said.

"I'll say," Byron murmured. "Just imagine walking away from all that money and social clout. Clementine's right. Maybe our client isn't all that bright."

Orchid glared at him. "I was referring to the rift in the family. It's always sad when families are torn apart by a quarrel."

"Yeah, sure." Byron draped himself over the half empty box of notepads. He gave Orchid a deeply fascinated look. "So, tell me, is it true what they say about strat-talents? Can they really sense it if you lie to them?"

"That's just an old myth," Orchid said crisply. "Everyone knows that."

"Well, what about the other stuff?"

"What other stuff?"

"Are they really sort of, you know, *primitive?*"

Orchid picked up a stack of Think Exclusive notepads and sent them raining down on Byron's head.

At nine o'clock that evening the Volcano Club was only half full. Orchid, seated at a small table with Morgan Lambert and Rafe, studied the shadowed room. The place was a cross between a nightclub and a coff-tea house. It catered to a bohemian crowd of poets, artists, and assorted wannabes.

A young man on stage hunched over a microphone and growled the words of a poem he had written.

> Images burn in jelly-ice.
> Frozen forever in jelly-ice
> Shimmering in jelly-ice
> Dreams of synergy and orgasm
> In jelly-ice.

It may not have been deathless prose, but it beat the heck out of meta-zen-syn philosophical poetry, Orchid thought.

Tiny jelly-ice candles flickered on the tables. The small flames revealed an assortment of expressions, most of which fell into two categories, world-weary ennui and passionate intensity. The majority of the clientele was dressed in gray, the fashionable color of the moment among the artistic set.

Morgan Lambert fit well into the ambiance of the Volcano Club. He was a thin, intense man with sharp, ascetic features and the long, sensitive fingers of an artist. He looked at Rafe.

"Did you know Theo Willis?"

"No."

"He was sort of weird, but he was okay." Morgan glanced at Orchid. "Not much else you can say about poor old Theo, is there?"

"I guess not." Orchid slumped back in her chair and shoved her hands into the pockets of her jeans. "Never thought he'd kill himself, though. He didn't seem the type."

"They say it's hard to tell." Morgan sipped his weak green wine. "He'd been seeing a shrink for the past few months."

Orchid raised her brows. "I didn't know that."

"The only reason I know it is because he came by my place a couple of days before he drove his car off that cliff. We had a few drinks. He said he wanted to talk to someone, but in the end the only thing he told me was that he had been going to a syn-psych doctor."

"Did he tell you why?" Orchid asked.

"No. I got the impression he was under a lot of stress because of his new job at that university lab."

"Theo didn't handle stress well." Orchid pursed her lips. "But I wouldn't have thought it would make him suicidal. He would be far more likely to just quit the new job if it bothered him that much. He was always changing jobs."

"He needed the money this time, he said. He mentioned some crazy plan to start his own focus agency. One that would specialize in ice-prisms. He was trying to get financing for it but he wasn't having any luck."

Orchid sighed. "I can't see a bank giving Theo a pile of cash. He wouldn't have looked like a good risk."

"No," Morgan agreed.

Rafe contemplated Morgan with a surprisingly thoughtful expression. "Did Willis mention the source of his stress?"

Morgan shook his head. "No. But he was always under stress. He was sort of paranoid."

"How did the three of you meet?" Rafe asked.

Orchid wondered why he was so interested in the subject of Theo Willis. "Three years ago we were recruited for a study of ice-prisms. The researchers at ParaSyn wanted to see if prisms like us could be used to treat violently disturbed mental patients. They wanted to test a dippy theory Dr. Bracewell, the head of the lab, had concocted."

"What was the theory?"

"Bracewell thought that if criminally insane talents could be properly focused, the syn-psych shrinks might be able to realign the synergistic forces of their para-profiles."

"Regular prisms can't work with talents who are really over-the-edge crazy," Morgan explained. "There's just no way to get a good focus. Besides, it hurts. The usual result is temporary burnout for the prism."

"Probably just as well," Orchid put in. "Another one of nature's little tricks to keep dangerous talents from becoming too predatory. Synergy in action."

Rafe gave her an unreadable look. "What happened with the study?"

Morgan grinned briefly. "They didn't learn much. Orchid led a revolt right in the middle of the project. Got pissed off when they tried to make us focus some really bent talents. She had one session with a guy named Calvin Hyde and that was the end of it. Walked out of the lab. Theo and I followed right behind her."

"Calvin Hyde?" Rafe repeated. "He was one of the violently disturbed talents?"

"Bracewell said he was normal." Orchid shuddered, recalling the predatory hunger she had sensed in Calvin Hyde. "He claimed Hyde was one of the control subjects. And I think he believed it. Hyde could be very convincing. But as soon as I saw the energy waves of his talent, I knew he was a very dangerous, violently inclined man. The last thing I wanted to do was give him a focus."

Rafe watched her with unwavering intensity. "What did you do?"

She shrugged. "Pretended I couldn't get a sharp focus. Told Bracewell that Hyde was just too powerful for me and that I couldn't take anymore. I think Hyde really liked the idea that he was so strong I couldn't handle him. He was incredibly arrogant. Always had to be top, uh—" She broke off before she uttered the words *wolf-hound*.

"What kind of talent was Hyde?" Rafe asked.

Orchid hesitated.

It was Morgan who answered the question. "Calvin Hyde was a high-class exotic. A strat-talent. You know, one of those hunters. Very rare."

Orchid did not look at Rafe but she could feel him watching her.

"How strong?" he asked quietly.

She could not think of a diplomatic response to that query so she kept her mouth shut.

"She never did find out what his actual rating was," Morgan said. "Did you, Orchid?"

"No." Orchid refolded her small cocktail napkin with great precision. As diversions went, it was not much, but it gave her an excuse not to meet Rafe's eyes. "I didn't stick around long enough to find out. A class seven, maybe."

"I see," Rafe murmured.

"Bracewell was always running experiments with weird talents, as well as ice-prisms," Morgan explained. "Orchid said it was because he envied them."

"The talents?" Rafe glanced at Orchid.

"Yes. He's only a class-two hypno-talent."

Morgan chuckled. "Folks at the lab used to refer to him as Two-Watt Bracewell behind his back."

Anxious to change the topic, Orchid looked at Morgan. "Speaking of ParaSyn, did you get a letter from the lab recently asking you to come back for a follow-up study?"

"No." Morgan looked surprised. "Why? Did you?"

"Yes. I ignored it."

"If I get one, I'll do the same." Morgan lounged in his seat and raised his glass. "Well, here's to Theo. A fellow ice-prism. May he rest in peace on the other side of the Curtain."

Orchid hoisted her glass. "To Theo."

Rafe said nothing but he swallowed some of his coff-tea when the other two sipped their wine.

Morgan put down his glass and looked at Orchid. "Let's go on to a more cheerful subject. Any word from your marriage agency recently?"

"You call that cheerful?" Out of the corner of her eye, Orchid saw Rafe blink in what in another man might have been startled surprise. She ignored him. He had been acting weird all evening.

"All right, make that a more interesting subject," Morgan said.

Orchid wrinkled her nose. "Funny you should ask. I had lunch with my cousin, Veronica, this afternoon. She brought up the very same question. The answer is no. I still can't get a date."

Morgan whistled. "Sheesh. What is it now? A year since your last agency date?"

"A year and three days," Orchid said. "But who's counting?"

"Your folks, I imagine," Morgan said dryly.

"Don't remind me. I hate guilt trips."

Rafe folded his hands very tightly around his coff-tea cup. "You never mentioned that you were registered, Orchid."

Morgan's mouth curved faintly. "She postponed it as long as she could but a little over a year ago her family finally applied enough pressure to get her to a match-making agency. She's only had one date, though."

"And he doesn't count," Orchid said.

Morgan sighed. "Everyone knows ice-prisms are extremely hard to match."

"Try impossible," Orchid said.

"Still, I'd have thought your agency would have introduced you to more than one potential candidate by now." Morgan's eyes widened. "Hey, maybe Affinity Associates lost your registration paperwork."

"Not likely," Orchid said.

"You never know. Maybe you ought to give your counselor a call," Morgan urged. "It's possible there's been a screw-up."

"I doubt it. They're a very reputable agency."

"Things can happen in any office."

Orchid grinned. "You're telling me. I work for Psynergy, Inc., remember?"

The flaring light of the jelly-ice candle rendered Rafe's face into a saturnine mask. "Why haven't you called Affinity Associates to see what's going on?"

As if it was any of his business. Orchid decided it would be easier to slide out of the discussion with a small, white lie. "Okay, okay, I'll call this week."

Rafe's brows rose at that but he made no comment. The brief, knowing look that flashed in his eyes worried Orchid, however. She got the distinct impression that he did not believe her.

She recalled Byron's question. *Is it true what they say about strat-talents? Can they really sense it if you lie to them?*

Myths, she told herself. Nothing but rumors, gossip, and outdated speculation based on early, faulty, synpsych research test results. Strat-talents were not human lie-detectors. There was no such creature.

Theoretically it was no more difficult to lie to a strat-talent than it was to anyone else. But some people, regardless of their paranormal abilities, had an instinct for discerning the truth. Rafe might be one of those people. And she was not the most accomplished liar in the world, she reminded herself.

But what did it matter if Rafe believed her tonight? After all, her love life or lack thereof was none of his affair.

Orchid gave both men a determined smile. "I suggest

we abandon the subject of my marital prospects before we all expire from boredom."

"I don't find the subject boring," Rafe said softly.

Orchid glared at him and decided to turn the tables. "Are you registered?"

"Yes. Synergistic Connections."

For some reason the information hit her like a solid wall of jelly-ice. Rafe was actively looking for a wife. And he was doing it in the proper, appropriate, socially approved manner. Who would have guessed? She wondered why the news was so deflating.

"Good agency," she managed in what she hoped was a breezy tone.

"So I'm told. But I haven't been introduced to a single potential candidate yet."

Morgan gave him a commiserating look. "Sounds like you and Orchid have something in common. Neither one of you can get a date."

Chapter

5

❖ ❖ ❖ ❖ ❖ ❖ ❖ ❖ ❖

Orchid leaned forward to peer through the windshield when Rafe halted the Icer at the front gates.

"Where are we?" she asked.

"My place." He activated the remote control to open the gates. "I brought you here so that we could discuss our new job. You do remember that contract I signed in your boss's office this afternoon?"

"I remember."

The gates swung wide. Orchid sat beside him, wrapped in silence, as he drove through the trees that shielded the front of the big house.

He had not realized that he had braced himself for her reaction to his home until she spoke.

"Good grief. This is where you *live?*"

"Yes." He brought the Icer to a stop in front of the broad steps and deactivated the engine.

"It's incredible." She gazed at the dark, looming mansion with unmistakable delight. "What a fantastic place. I spent the entire amount of my first book advance on a genuine Later Expansion period sofa. You've got a whole *house* from that period."

He had been afraid this would happen, he told himself as he cracked open the Icer door and got out. She not only loved the damned house, it felt right bringing her here. Very right. All of his senses were pulsing in tempo with the invisible rhythms of the night.

He looked back through the open Icer door and watched Orchid as she watched his house.

"I'd give anything to live in a house like this," she whispered.

"Funny you should say that."

"But why would anyone want to steal an alien relic?" Orchid swirled the ridiculously expensive moontree brandy in her glass and watched Rafe as he stood in front of the fireplace.

She had found herself reluctantly fascinated by the tale he had just outlined. A stolen artifact, a mysteriously dead thief, and the client's request for absolute discretion. It sounded like one of her own plots.

"People steal things for a wide variety of reasons," Rafe said quietly.

"Yes, but there usually *is* a reason. I don't understand what it would be in this case. From what I've heard you can't do anything with the alien relics. No one knows what their tools were used for, if they were tools. None of them function any more. The experts don't even know how they were powered. All anyone seems sure of is that they're very, very old and that they aren't native to St. Helens."

The first small cache of alien artifacts had been discovered by Lucas Trent. He had found them in the course of a jelly-ice prospecting venture in the jungles of the Western Islands. Trent had given his finds to the New Seattle Art Museum which had, in turn, formed a research partnership with the science and history faculties of the University of New Seattle.

Another, much larger cache of relics had actually been located by the third Chastain Expedition several years earlier. The records of the find had been lost because all but one of the expedition team members had been murdered by a mad spec-talent before the reports could be filed. The "alien tomb," as the cache was referred to in the press, had been rediscovered by the fourth Chastain Expedition last year.

The huge collection of artifacts had caused a sensation.

Speculation ran rampant in the tabloids. Stories featuring women who claimed to have given birth to space alien babies were popular fare at the supermarket checkout counters. The Return cults, predictably, wove the relics into their ludicrous, quasireligious notions regarding the Curtain. Novels and films featuring the artifacts were popular.

But when all was said and done, Orchid knew, the experts had learned virtually nothing about the alien relics. They remained a fascinating enigma.

"You've worked with me often enough to know that people steal for some strange reasons," Rafe said. "Collectors are a unique breed."

Orchid thought of Elvira Turlock. "Do you think there's actually an underground market for alien artifacts?"

"It would not surprise me." Rafe took a thoughtful sip of his brandy. "But there are other possibilities."

"Such as?"

"The Return cults. Some of them have seized on the discovery of the alien relics to expand their crazy claims about the Curtain. It's conceivable that one of the more off-the-wall cult leaders arranged for the theft in order to get his or her hands on a genuine alien artifact."

"I see what you mean. Be great for show-and-tell at the next meeting of the believers, wouldn't it?"

"Yes." Rafe paused. "But the fact that the cult leader would have to display the stolen relic to his followers in order to get any mileage out of it makes me think that's a less likely scenario than it appears."

"Why do you say that?" Orchid waited expectantly. She knew that Rafe would have a reason for his deduction. He always backed up his leaps of strat-talent intuition with cold, hard logic.

"Because as soon as the cult leader starts to flash his own, personal alien artifact around at the temple meetings, he or she runs the risk that someone in the audience will mention the relic to outsiders. And sooner or later, someone will. It's inevitable."

"You're right." But then, he was always right, she thought. It was one of his less endearing traits. "People, even devout cult members, are bound to talk about something like that. Once the word got out that the leader had the artifact, everyone would know what happened to the stolen lab relic."

"All of which does not mean that some cult leader did not steal it. Crazy people do crazy things. But most of the leaders in the Return cults are businesspeople, first and foremost. They're in the racket to make a profit. They're not stupid or crazy. I doubt if any of them actually believe their own drivel. Why do something that would jeopardize the scam?"

"So, I take it you're leaning toward the theory that the relic was stolen by an eccentric collector?"

"At this point, it would seem to make the most sense." Rafe hesitated. "But I'm not sure. There's something about this that doesn't feel right, yet."

"Okay, you've got two possibilities so far, an eccentric collector or a mad cult leader. Any others?"

Rafe raised his gaze from the flames. His eyes were as enigmatic as any alien relic. "No. But I may come up with some after we pay a visit to the lab that lost the artifact."

"When are we going to do that?"

"Tomorrow evening after the staff has left for the day.

I've made arrangements with the lab's director, Dr. Alexander Brizo. He'll meet us there."

"We're going to visit the lab after hours?"

Rafe's mouth curved faintly. "I do my best work at night."

"Yes, I know, but I would have thought time was of the essence in this situation. If you wait until tomorrow night to start on the case, you'll have wasted a whole day."

"I've already started work and tomorrow won't be wasted, either. There's a lot of basic investigation to do before we go to the lab."

"Such as?"

"I contacted one of my sources on the street. A man named Whistler. He's got contacts into the underground art world. If there are any rumors about the artifact going into a private collection, he'll hear them."

"Sounds like a good start."

He arched one brow. "Thank you."

She blushed. It occurred to her that the remark had been the verbal equivalent of a pat on the head. "You know what I mean."

He ignored that. "I also spent today talking to some people who knew the lab technician Brizo believes stole the relic."

Orchid brightened. "There's a suspect?"

"Yes. But he's dead."

"Dead." She stared at him, astonished. "I don't understand. Who is this suspect?"

Rafe hesitated. "Theo Willis."

For a few seconds, Orchid could not even get her mouth closed, let alone speak. When she finally overcame her dumbfounded reaction, she slammed the glass of moontree brandy down with such force that several drops splashed on the table.

"That's impossible," she declared.

"It's what Brizo believes."

"Why didn't you say anything earlier?" Orchid leaped

to her feet. "You let Morgan and me blather on about Theo all evening and you never once mentioned that he was a suspect."

"Be reasonable, Orchid. I didn't know the name of the person for whom you and Morgan wanted to hold your little wake until we got to the Volcano Club. By then, it was too late. I couldn't say anything in front of Morgan. This is a highly confidential case."

"That's no excuse. You should have said something earlier."

"I wanted to lay out the whole case before I did that. I knew it would upset you to learn that a friend was involved."

"I'm not upset, I'm pissed off." She leveled a finger at him. "What's more, I've got a big clue for you, Mr. Investigator. You're headed down a dead-end trail if you think that Theo Willis was a thief. He was a trifle wacko, but he was not dishonest."

"All I'm saying at this point is that Brizo thinks he was involved in this thing."

"I refuse to believe that Theo stole that artifact. And I'm certainly not going to help you prove that he did."

"Orchid, wait—"

"I quit. Find yourself another prism. I'm going to call a cab. And then I'm going to call another private investigator."

"What the hell for?"

"To help me prove that Theo didn't steal that relic." She stalked to the massive, Later Expansion period table and snatched up the phone. "I'm going to clear his name."

"Damn it—" Rafe started toward her.

"Don't come near me." She punched out the number of the cab company she routinely used. Then she turned quickly, holding up a hand to ward him off. "Stay back."

His eyes darkened. "Stop giving me orders as if I were a cat-dog."

She felt the heat suffuse her face a second time. "I never meant—"

"Yes, you did." He snatched the phone out of her hand and slammed it back down into the cradle. "Calm down and listen to me. You can't walk out now."

"Watch me."

"I'm the one who's been hired to solve this case. If you really want to prove that Theo Willis did not steal that artifact, working with me is the most efficient way to do it."

His logic brought her up short. She drummed her fingers on the table, thinking quickly.

"I hate to admit it, but you've got a point," she said finally.

His jaw tightened. His expression was stark. "There's another reason why I want you to work with me on this case."

"Yeah, I know. You want me because I'm the best prism you've ever had."

"Because I want you. Period." His hands closed around her shoulders. "The only question I have at the moment is, do you want me?"

She stared at him, stunned into silence by the dark flames of sexual desire that leaped in his eyes. An answering heat stirred deep within her.

"Oh, my," she whispered. "So you feel it, too."

"If you're talking about what happens when we link, yes. I feel it. That's not a problem."

"It's not?"

"I could deal with that, if there wasn't anything more to it."

She could not look away from his intent face. "What is the problem?"

"The problem," he said very deliberately, "is that I go on wanting you after we cut off the focus link."

She was very close to him now. The heat of his body pulsed against her, drawing her nearer. "I see. That is a problem, isn't it?"

"I need to know if you have the same problem."

She drew an unsteady breath, violently aware of the sudden, exhilarating rush of her own pulse. "I'm sure it's just a superficial sort of thing. Some kind of weird, lingering after effect of the link."

"Think so?"

The flash of icy amusement in his eyes annoyed her.

"Well, it's not as if we have anything in common," she said.

"Don't," he said, "remind me."

He brought her up hard against his chest, wrapped one hand around the back of her head, and kissed her. A deep, hard, fiercely urgent kiss.

A driving thrill of need washed over her.

"Just call me superficial." She wrapped her arms around Rafe's neck.

It felt so right. Excitement and need rose within her. It shouldn't feel this good, but it did.

Rafe's low, hoarse groan induced a delicious, fluttery sensation in the pit of her stomach. He tightened his hold on her. She felt his hand close over her breast. The heat of his palm seeped through the fabric of her T-shirt. She sensed his pleasure when he discovered that she wore no bra. His satisfaction increased her own desire in some crazily synergistic fashion.

The contours of his heavily aroused body pressed against her. She could not get close enough to him.

Without warning, just when everything seemed to be going along quite nicely, she felt herself float up off the ground. She gasped and clung more tightly to Rafe. Surely the passion he was generating could not have triggered an illusion on the metaphysical plane. She was excited, but not *that* excited.

Admittedly there was a dreamlike quality to Rafe's kiss, but she was *not* hallucinating.

The world shifted around her.

She squeezed her eyes more tightly together. She was okay. Awake. Not dreaming.

So why the dazed sensation?

She opened her eyes part way, seeking to steady herself with a view of the solid, stable room.

There was nothing reassuring about the sight of the old-fashioned jelly-ice candles in the wall sconce spinning past her field of vision.

Before she could sort it all out she felt herself falling. Slowly, gently, she floated downward until she became aware of the thick rug beneath her.

It finally dawned on her that Rafe had swung her off her feet and lowered her to the carpet.

Laughter bubbled through her.

He came down on top of her, crushing her into the thick rug. He braced himself on his elbows. His eyes burned.

"Want to share the joke?" he muttered against her throat.

"If there's a joke, it's on me." She framed his face with her hands and pulled his mouth back down to hers. "I never dreamed it could feel like this."

He uttered a low, hoarse, hungry groan. His mouth closed over hers again. He wedged one leg between her thighs and pushed his hands up under the hem of her T-shirt.

She was fumbling with the edge of his pullover, trying to get her hands underneath it, when a measure of sanity returned. What was she doing? It was all happening much too quickly.

"Rafe. I'm not sure this is a good idea. It's too soon. We barely know each other. A superficial kiss is one thing. Superficial sex is something else."

"You may be right." Desire gleamed in his eyes. It was echoed in the faint curve of his mouth. "Maybe it will seem like a better idea if we do it this way."

She felt the familiar questing probe of his psychic talent seeking a prism. Automatically she responded. On the metaphysical plane a crystal clear prism took shape. Rafe eased power through it with seductive skill.

This time the accompanying flare of sexual awareness was so intense Orchid could not think. She could not even breathe. She felt as if she had just plunged over a waterfall.

And then she understood what Rafe was trying to do. Outrage slammed through her, dousing a good measure of the passion.

"Oh, no you don't, Stonebraker." She pushed against his looming shoulders as she tried to break off the psychic connection. "Stop it right now. Damned if I'll let you use a focus link to seduce me."

"No, wait," he whispered. "Don't let go. *Please.*"

Out on the psychic plane Rafe caged the prism she had created with shimmering bands of raw power.

Orchid was horrified to realize that she could not break the link. If she had not heard the tales from her friends at Psynergy, Inc., she would not have believed that it was possible to do what Rafe was doing.

Instinct and the self-defense tenets of meta-zen-syn took over. She stopped trying to resist. Instead, she sent more of her own power out onto the psychic plane. Swiftly she manipulated the facets of the prism, altering the focus until the energy waves scattered. It was as if they were refracted through a thousand glittering mirrors. Power ricocheted aimlessly across the psychic plane.

"What the hell?" Rafe's stunned surprise came through on both the physical and metaphysical planes. *"What are you doing?"*

"What do you think *you're* doing?" she retorted.

"Damn. I'm sorry." Rafe's reflexes on the metaphysical plane were even faster than they were in the physical world. He cut the flow of talent with devastating suddenness. "I'm sorry. Oh, shit, I never meant—"

Orchid quickly dissolved the prism. She watched warily as Rafe slowly sat up beside her. She did not know what to expect from him. He did not look angry or baffled or shocked.

He looked deeply mortified. A dull red stained his high cheekbones. Chagrin, embarrassment, and humiliation blazed in his eyes. There was something else there, too, she realized. Fear?

Why should Rafe be afraid?

"I'm sorry," he said again. He put out a hand as if to touch her and then withdrew it. "That was very . . . primitive of me, wasn't it?"

Relief flooded through Orchid. She suddenly understood the fear she had glimpsed in his eyes. "Hey, don't worry about it. I'm used to that kind of thing."

He blinked. "You are?"

"Sure. I write about psychic vampires all the time, remember?"

"I am not a vampire."

The tightly leashed fury in him brought her up short. She sat up slowly. "No, of course you're not. It's okay. I was only making a joke."

"I fail to see any humor in the situation."

"It might not be the funniest thing that's ever happened to me, but it certainly isn't the end of the world, either."

"Orchid, listen to me. I swear I never meant to do what I did."

"Lighten up, Stonebraker." She patted his knee. "You got a little carried away with the first prism who could focus your full range of power. No big deal. Next time you'll know what to expect. You won't go off the deep end a second time. You've got too much control for that."

His jaw was rigid. "I did not get carried away because of the focus link."

"No?"

"I got carried away because I didn't want to lose—" He broke off. "Forget it."

"I will," she assured him. And knew that she was lying through her teeth. She would never forget that kiss as long as she lived. "It was just a kiss that got a little out of hand. Probably happens all the time, right?"

He watched her closely. Dark curiosity lit his gaze first. It was followed by a flash of satisfaction.

He knew that she was lying.

Impossible. He couldn't be reading her mind. Strat-talents were *not* human lie-detectors, she reminded herself.

"You're wrong, you know," he said quietly. "That kind of thing does not happen very much to me. What about you?"

"Uh, no." She cleared her throat. "No, it doesn't happen much to me, either."

She held her breath, afraid he would pursue the point with the sort of single-minded intensity he applied to his investigation work.

But to her euphoric relief, he changed the topic.

"I knew you could create a near-perfect focus," Rafe said. "But I didn't realize you could manipulate it in a negative as well as a positive way. Before tonight, I would have said that what you just did was impossible."

Chapter

6

✧ ✧ ✧ ✧ ✧ ✧ ✧ ✧ ✧

Orchid was suddenly mildly embarrassed. "It's not that weird, you know. I have a friend named Zinnia who can manipulate the prism she projects to some extent. She can twist it. When that happens any power flowing through it is also twisted in a way that's painful for the talent."

"You did a hell of a lot more than twist the focus. You manipulated each individual facet of the prism."

"Yes."

"It's incredible."

"I'm glad you're impressed," she muttered.

Rafe shoved his fingers through his hair. His eyes were wary. "I didn't mean to jump your prism the way I did."

"I know."

"I didn't even realize I could jump a prism in that way," he admitted. "Didn't think it was possible."

"Happens all the time in psychic vampire romance novels."

He smiled ruefully. "Is that a fact? Maybe I'd better read one." He drew a breath. "Five hells. No wonder

85

the folks at ParaSyn wanted to run a few experiments on you."

Orchid fussed with her T-shirt while she collected herself. Then she drew her knees up to her chest and wrapped her arms around them. "I'll let you in on a little secret."

"What's that?"

"The ParaSyn researchers knew that I was an ice-prism, of course, but I never let them see how much I could do with my prism construct."

Rafe's gaze sharpened. "What do you mean?"

"I allowed myself to get talked into doing the study for the sake of science. But once I started I realized I didn't want to demonstrate the full range of my abilities. Some instinct made me limit what I showed the researchers."

"You don't have to explain. You're talking to an off-the-chart strat-talent, remember? I don't go around telling people how strong I am, either."

She smiled wryly. "No, I can understand that."

Rafe reached out to catch her chin on the edge of his hand. He turned her head so that her eyes met his. "The last thing I wanted to do was scare you so badly you had to resort to using your secrets."

Annoyed, she lifted her chin away from his hand. "Will you please stop apologizing? You didn't frighten me. You made me angry. Big difference."

"Right. Big difference. I'm sorry that I made you angry."

She raised her eyes to the ceiling. "If you say you're sorry one more time, I'll get really mad. I think you're only apologizing because you don't want to admit what really happened."

"What do you think really happened?"

"You lost control for a few seconds. Losing control bugs the heck out of you, doesn't it?"

His mouth thinned, but he said nothing.

She patted his knee again. "Don't fret about it. I'm sure it won't happen again."

His eyes gleamed. "It might if you continue to pat me as if I were a cat-dog."

She paused in mid-pat and hastily retrieved her hand. "Sorry."

He got to his feet with languid grace and stood looking down at her with a thoughtful expression. "You know, psychically, I'd say we're fairly well matched."

She rose, ignoring his outstretched hand. "I suppose this means that we do have something in common besides the fact that we can't get a date. Well, it's been an interesting evening, but it's getting late. I'd better be on my way."

She scooped up her jacket from the high back of the old Later Expansion period sofa and started toward the door.

"Where do you think you're going?" he asked.

"Home. Are you going to drive me or shall I call a cab?"

"What about Theo Willis?"

She stepped out into the hall and paused to look back at him. "I've decided that you're right."

"About what?"

"Working with you will be the most efficient way of proving that Theo didn't steal the missing relic."

"Willis is dead," Rafe said evenly. "He won't care whether or not you clear his name. From what I learned today, he doesn't even have any close family who will give a damn if he was guilty or innocent."

"I care. He was an ice-prism. There aren't very many of us. This sort of thing gives my kind a bad rap. Makes us look even more weird than we are. For the sake of ice-prisms everywhere, past and future, I'm going to prove that he was innocent."

"Damn," Rafe said as he followed her toward the door. "I hate it when this happens."

"When what happens?"

"When naïve, amateur investigators set out to solve a case for the sake of a principle."

"Really?" One hand on the doorknob, she glanced back at him over her shoulder. "Why do you set out to solve cases?"

"I do it for the money."

"Liar." She opened the door and walked out into the night.

The dream bore down on her with the relentless, heart-stopping power of a jungle storm.

The psychic vampire sent forth the questing probe from the heart of the night. Talons of strange, unnatural energy lanced across the metaphysical plane, seeking, groping, clawing for a prism.

All of her instincts, psychic and physical, fought the terrible summons. She knew that if she weakened, she would be trapped forever in the eerie embrace.

Darkness howled across the psychic realm. Paranormal power crackled like lightning. The vampire was closer, closer than the last time. She must awaken. If she did not, she would see the creature's face. She did not want to confront the predatory thing that sought to imprison her. Her only hope was to wake up before it was too late . . .

Orchid's eyes snapped open with shocking abruptness. She sat straight up in bed, aware that she was soaked to the skin with perspiration. Her nightgown clung to her breasts and the place between her shoulders, yet she was chilled to the bone.

This was the worst it had ever been. The vampire had been so close this time.

The jarring warble of the phone broke through the last remnants of dazed, mindless fear. Orchid blinked and reached out to turn on the bedside light. At the same time she forced herself to do some meta-zen-syn breathing exercises.

The phone rang again, an imperious summons. She realized that it had been ringing for some time. She glanced at the clock as she picked up the receiver. Nearly three in the morning. She had been asleep since shortly after Rafe had brought her home sometime after midnight.

"Hello?"

"Orchid?" Rafe's voice came through the line with the bracing impact of a bucket of cold water. "What's wrong? Are you all right?"

"Yes." Orchid fell back against the pillows with a sigh of relief that she sincerely hoped Rafe did not hear. It would probably not be a good idea for him to know how grateful she was for his call. "Yes, of course. I'm fine."

"You don't sound fine."

"You awakened me in the middle of a bad dream." It occurred to her that his timing could not have been better. "I'm all right now. Why in the world are you calling at this hour?"

"I don't know. You tell me."

"This is not a good time to go cryptic on me. I don't think very clearly at three in the morning."

"I'm telling you the truth. I woke up out of a sound sleep with the feeling that I had to call you right now. So I did."

Orchid shivered. "Weird."

"Yes."

"I'm glad you did," she confessed. "I've had that particular dream before. Several times during the past week, in fact. I don't like it very much."

"I could tell. What's the dream about?"

"I'm sure you've got better things to do than listen to me tell you about my stupid nightmare."

"No, as a matter of fact, I don't have anything better to do. I'm just lying here looking up at the sky."

"The sky?"

"I've got a window in my bedroom ceiling. Both moons are out tonight."

"Oh." She had a sudden, disturbing image of what it

would be like to be in his bed gazing up at the twin moons.

"Tell me about your dream."

Orchid knew that she should say goodnight and hang up the phone. Dreams were very personal. Much too intimate to discuss with a business client.

But the impulse to confide in him was overwhelming. Perhaps it was the hour. Three in the morning was a very dark time of night. Or maybe it was because her pulse had not yet settled down to its normal pace. Maybe it was simply because Rafe had crossed the invisible barrier between client and something else earlier in the evening when he kissed her. Whatever it was, Orchid could not resist the urge to talk to him now.

"Promise you won't laugh, but it's as if I'm being stalked by a psychic vampire. Every night he gets a little closer."

"Psychic vampire, huh? I take it this is not one of the romantic kind that you put into *Dark Desire?*"

She blinked. "You've read it?"

"Curiosity got the better of me. I picked it up earlier today. Started it tonight after I took you home."

"You don't have to give me a book report," she said.

"The plot is interesting." He sounded as if he were choosing his words with exquisite care. "I like the mystery element. And the descriptions of the focus link between the hero and heroine was intriguing."

"Thanks."

"Reminded me a lot of what happened between us earlier tonight."

"I have an excellent imagination," she said.

"Obviously. Maybe it's connected to the fact that you're an ice-prism."

"Hmm. I hadn't thought of that. You may be right. I don't know very many other ice-prisms but the ones I've met all have a strongly creative side to their natures. Morgan is an artist."

"What about Theo Willis?"

"Theo loved music. It was his passion. He wrote it and he played the vio-piano."

There was a short silence.

"Tell me more about your dream," Rafe said again.

There was a cozy intimacy in this conversation that was oddly comforting, Orchid thought. "There's not much else to tell. I've been having the same dream or a very similar one every night for almost a week. Tonight was the worst one yet."

"What's the vampire like?"

"I can't see his face but I can feel the power of his talent."

"Strong?"

"Very, but that's not the scariest part."

"What is the scariest part?"

"The talent doesn't feel normal."

"That's logical, isn't it? If you're having nightmares about a very powerful talent, it stands to reason the talent would not feel normal."

"You're strong," she said. "In fact, you're the most powerful talent I've ever focused. But you feel normal." *Not like Calvin Hyde.*

There was an acute pause on the other end of the line. "Normal?"

"Okay, maybe *normal* isn't quite the right word. I can't say your kind of power is what anyone would call commonplace."

"I was afraid of that," Rafe said.

"But you don't feel *unnatural,* if you see what I mean." There is no evil in you, she added silently.

"What you're really trying to say is that I feel primitive."

"Damn it, don't put words in my mouth. That is not what I mean at all." Orchid glowered at the phone. "For your information, your talent does not feel primitive."

"No?"

She frowned, thinking about it. "Actually, from a synergistic point of view, your para-energy and your physical senses are far better integrated than those of most talents. Evolutionarily speaking, you may represent the wave of the future."

"I'm not sure I like the word *evolution* any more than the word *primitive.*"

"Too bad, you're stuck with it. We all are. Any scientist will tell you that paranormal powers are evolving very swiftly among humans here on St. Helens. No one knows what the future holds, but chances are we'll see increasing variations and mutations."

"So now I'm a mutant?" But his tone was lighter now, almost amused.

"You and me both. Ice-prisms aren't exactly thick on the ground."

"True. Let's get back to your dream. What does this talent in your nightmare feel like?"

Orchid looked down and saw that she had crumpled a fistful of sheet in one hand. "It feels . . . crazy."

"I think I'm getting the picture at last."

"What do you mean?"

"You're starting to wonder if the dreams are a sign that you're going off the deep end, aren't you?"

She closed her eyes. "It occurred to me that the dreams might be some form of psychic hallucination. Maybe something generated by whatever it is that makes me an ice-prism."

"You can forget that theory."

She opened her eyes and glared at her own image in the mirror. "What are you? A syn-psych expert?"

"I don't need to be a syn-psych expert to tell you that I didn't feel anything crazy when we linked tonight. Not even after you manipulated that prism to fracture my talent. You surprised the hell out of me but you didn't *scare* the hell out of me. For the record that's an important distinction."

She smiled weakly. "I don't think there's much that would scare you, Rafe."

"Everyone is scared of something. Are you okay now?"

"Yes. Thanks." It was true, more or less. At least her breathing had returned to normal.

"You don't need me to come over there and comfort you in person?"

She grinned. "I don't think so. Thanks, anyway."

"I was afraid you'd say that. Go back to sleep. We've got a big night ahead of us tomorrow."

"I suppose you want your money's worth out of me."

"Damn right. Clementine Malone charged me a fortune for your services. Goodnight, Orchid."

"Goodnight. Oh, and Rafe?"

"Yeah?"

"Thanks for calling when you did."

"Maybe we're developing some kind of mental telepathy."

Orchid chuckled. "Don't be ridiculous. Everyone knows there's no such thing as telepathy."

In a world where the list of normal paranormal skills spanned a broad and growing spectrum, telepathy had never appeared in the population. Like psychic vampires, it showed up frequently in novels and films, but those were the only places one could find them.

Just as well, Orchid thought as she hung up the phone. It would not have been a good idea for Rafe to be able to read her mind at that moment. She was not certain she wanted to read it herself. Her thoughts were a jumble of vague uncertainties and distant possibilities.

That was the problem with waking up at three in the morning. Things looked different at that hour.

She left the light on and leaned against the pillows. For a while she thought about trying to go back to sleep. But now that she no longer had the reassuring sound of Rafe's voice to buoy her, she sensed the return of the cold, edgy unease that was swiftly becoming her constant nighttime companion.

She pushed aside the covers and padded into the

kitchen, turning on lights as she went. She opened the icerator door and took out some leftover pasta casserole.

The second letter from ParaSyn was still on the kitchen table where she had left it that afternoon after opening it. The content was similar to that of the one that had arrived earlier in the week. But this time, in addition to the authoritative tone, a hint of a threat had been added.

> . . . We sincerely hope you will agree to return to ParaSyn for this important follow-up research. In the three years since the first study was terminated prematurely, our researchers have discovered some disturbing facts about the nature of ice-prisms. We do not wish to alarm you, however, our experts feel that these findings could impact the long-term parapsychological health of people with your type of psychic energy.
>
> You owe it to yourself and to others with your kind of paranormal power to complete the study. Please contact my office at your earliest convenience.
>
> Sincerely,
> Gilbert Bracewell, Ph.D.
> Director of Research

"You can't scare me, Two-Watt." Orchid crumpled the crisp sheet of stationery in one hand. "I'm so tough, I hang out with a real psychic vampire these days."

She tossed the letter into the trash.

Immediately, she felt much better.

Chapter
7

❖❖❖❖❖❖❖❖❖

"Take it easy, Al," Rafe said. "I've got everything under control."

"Under control? *Under control?* Is that what you call it?"

Alfred G. Stonebraker's frosty gray eyes glinted with the sort of fierceness that made hardened business executives and ruthless competitors alike tremble. He thumped the top of the small garden table with an exasperated fist. "Stonebraker Shipping is teetering on the top of a cliff, about to be pushed over the edge by that conniving little twerp, Culverthorpe, and you tell me you've got everything under control?"

"Yes." With the ease of long practice and natural inclination, Rafe ignored his grandfather's icy glare. Alfred G. was a businessman of the old school. He did a lot of yelling when he was not happy.

His own techniques were different, Rafe thought as he stretched out his legs and crossed his feet at the ankles. Much quieter.

He lounged back in his chair and contemplated the

elaborately terraced gardens spread out before him. From his position on the terrace he could see all the way to the arbor.

As a child he had spent a lot of time in this horticultural fantasy land. His parents had brought him here often to visit his grandparents. Some of his earliest memories were of exploring the maze and sailing small boats on the pond.

He and Alfred G. had been good buddies in those days. That, of course, had been during the period when his grandfather had blithely assumed that Rafe would follow in his footsteps.

The rift between them had not occurred until Alfred G. had tried to coerce Rafe into joining Stonebraker Shipping. Rafe had known from the beginning that he could never work for his grandfather. Intuitively he had understood that they were too much alike. Besides, Rafe did not take orders well. Alfred G. was very fond of giving orders.

The ensuing battle of wills between the two had been watched from a wary, respectful distance by the various members of the family. No one, not even Rafe's parents, had dared to intervene, much less tried to mediate.

As Rafe's mother had wryly pointed out, a smart person did not step between two quarreling predators.

Fifteen years ago, there had been only one possible conclusion to the confrontation. In crude terms, Alfred G. had still been the alpha male of the clan. Rafe had understood that. He had packed his bags and left for the Western Islands.

When he returned he had been seasoned by several years of living on the edge of a jungle and by the violent episode known as the Western Islands Action.

Rafe had staked out his own territory in New Seattle, careful to avoid trespassing into his grandfather's realm. But he had kept tabs on the family firm and he had watched with brooding anger as Alfred G.'s old-fashioned business methods led Stonebraker Shipping into perilous waters.

The day had finally come when Alfred G. had accepted the fact that it was time for him to step down. He had summoned Rafe to a warrior's summit, prepared to hand over control of the faltering firm to the only other member of the clan who could save it.

Unfortunately, he had waited a little too long.

What Alfred G. had not realized until too late was that his ambitious nephew, Selby Culverthorpe, had been biding his time, awaiting a moment of weakness. With the savvy, stealthy cunning of a hyena-jackal, Selby had slipped past Alfred G.'s guard.

Working behind the scenes, Selby had laid the groundwork that he hoped would enable him to steal the prize of Stonebraker Shipping from under the protective paws of Alfred G.

Overnight, the orderly transfer of power which Alfred G. had envisioned was transformed into a desperate, secret effort to save the company. The threat to Stonebraker Shipping had united Rafe and Alfred G. as nothing else could have done.

Alfred G. picked up a knife and sliced a muffin in half with a slashing motion. "As far as I can tell, you haven't made any progress at all. The annual board meeting is less than two months away and you haven't even found yourself a wife, damn it."

"I'll have one lined up by the time the board meets. Everything else is in place."

"Humph." Alfred G. looked unconvinced. "Did you convince Taylor and Crawford to back off until you take control of the company?"

"Yes. Steve Taylor worked for me for a while in the Islands. We came to an understanding a few weeks ago. He gave me his word that Taylor and Crawford will wait until after the board meeting before they respond to the proposal to spin off the container division."

"Well, that's something at least. What about the distribution problems at the New Portland warehouse?"

"The problem has been resolved."

"How?"

"The new inventory control system had a glitch. It's fixed. I've also had a talk with Kimiyo Takanishi at Takanishi Freight. I convinced her that she would get a better contract from me than she would from Selby."

"She'll wait until after the board meeting to negotiate?"

Rafe picked up his cup of coff-tea. "She'll wait."

Alfred G. sank his teeth into a slice of muffin. His eyes narrowed. "Why can't you find yourself a nice young woman like Kimiyo?"

Rafe grinned. "Mrs. Takanishi is old enough to be my mother. I'll admit she's very charming and a brilliant businesswoman, but even if she was willing to marry me, we'd have a small problem with the fact that she's married. It wouldn't be easy to get rid of Ray Takanishi. He's as tough as you are."

"True." Alfred G. glumly munched his muffin. "Has that damned marriage agency sent you out on any dates yet?"

"Back off, Al. I told you, everything's under control."

"Sonovabitch, Rafe. Time is running out. Haven't you got a single possibility lined up yet?"

Rafe hesitated. "As a matter of fact, I have."

A hopeful look gleamed in Alfred G.'s predatory gaze. "Why the hell didn't you tell me?"

Rafe braced his elbows on the arms of the lawn chair. He steepled his fingers and regarded the maze in the center of the garden. "Because it's far from being a done deal."

"Why not?"

"We don't have much in common. And apparently she's as difficult to match as I am."

"How do you know that?" Alfred G. asked sharply.

"She's been registered even longer than I have. A full year, in fact. She's only had one date during that time."

"Sounds to me like you both have more in common than you think."

"What the hell do you mean?"

Alfred G. chuckled. "Neither of you can get a date for Saturday night. Tell you what. Bring her to my birthday party. Let me have a look at her. I'll tell you whether or not she'll suit."

Rafe tried to envision Alfred G. and Orchid socializing here in the gardens at what was considered one of the city's most important social events of the year. "Serve you right if I did bring her."

Alfred G. stopped smiling. "You are coming to the party, aren't you?"

It would be the first time he had attended since he had walked out on his heritage fifteen years ago, Rafe reflected. It would send a signal to his cousin that he could expect a fight over Stonebraker Shipping.

Attending Alfred G.'s birthday party would be the first shot over Selby's bow. An announcement that war had been declared.

"Wouldn't miss it," Rafe said.

"The relic was similar to the others that you see in that case." Alexander Brizo gestured toward the locked glass cabinet at the end of a row of laboratory workbenches. "Made of the same material. A bit longer and narrower in shape than the object on the left."

Orchid walked to the cabinet and gazed, fascinated, at the collection of alien artifacts. It was clear from their odd designs that they had not been made to fit human hands. They were all fashioned from a silvery alloy that defied analysis.

"This is the first time I've seen any of the relics outside the museum," Orchid said. "They really are strange, aren't they?"

"Very." Brizo sighed. "We don't know much more

about them now than we did when Lucas Trent brought in the first batch. We can't even identify the components of the alloy the aliens used to make these objects. All we know is that the items were not made of anything found here on St. Helens."

Rafe came to stand behind Orchid. He studied the objects in the case. "Whatever it is, it must be something incredibly different from anything the first generation colonists brought with them from Earth."

"Quite true." Brizo's brows came together in a sober frown. "The fact that the alloy did not disintegrate within months after it was exposed to St. Helens' atmosphere the way the Founders' Earth-based materials did, means that it is alien in every sense of the word."

"Any idea yet how old the relics are?" Orchid asked.

"Our best psychometric-talents estimate that they're at least a thousand years old. Maybe more."

"Too bad the fourth Chastain Expedition hasn't found any biological remains in that so-called alien tomb they're excavating," Rafe said.

"Not a trace," Brizo said. "If there ever were any bodies inside, they decomposed eons ago. The archeologists have not found so much as a bone fragment."

"Maybe the aliens didn't have bones," Orchid said. "Maybe they were as different from us physically as this alloy is from our metals."

"Or maybe they escaped St. Helens after all, but had to do it in a hurry," Rafe suggested. "That would explain why they left a lot of their equipment behind."

"It's certainly possible," Brizo said. "The most popular hypothesis at the moment is that the aliens came to St. Helens the same way the first generation colonists from Earth did, through the Curtain. We assumed that they got stranded here when the Curtain closed without warning, just as the Founders were stranded. But perhaps the Curtain opened again long enough to allow the aliens to escape."

Orchid stared at the strangely shaped relics behind the

glass. Every schoolchild knew the history of the colonization of St. Helens. A little more than two hundred years earlier a mysterious Curtain of energy had materialized in space very near Earth. It had proved to be an interstellar gate between the home planet and a hospitable new world the colonists named St. Helens.

But shortly after the first generation settlers had arrived the Curtain had closed without warning. Cut off from the home planet, the small population of humans had been left to fend for themselves. A desperate battle for survival had ensued. The green world of St. Helens had welcomed the humans but it did not tolerate their Earth-based technology. Something in the very air and soil of the planet was anathema to the machines and materials of Earth.

The aliens had had better luck so far as their technology was concerned, but they, themselves, had disappeared.

"You have no idea at all why Theo Willis would have stolen that one particular relic?" Rafe asked.

"No." Brizo shrugged. "It wasn't any more unusual or interesting than the others except for the fact that it was found outside the tomb, rather than inside."

"Outside?"

"It was imbedded in a small deposit of jelly-ice. Must have fallen into it a thousand years ago and just sat there until the expedition team discovered it."

"What did it look like?"

"It was a simple narrow rod about a foot long. A bit like a thin flashlight except that there was no visible means of generating light."

Orchid looked at him. "You said Theo Willis was found at the bottom of the cliff the day after the relic disappeared?"

"Yes. The police ruled it a suicide, but I'm more inclined to think it must have been an accident. I don't see why Willis would have killed himself right after stealing the relic. The problem is that the artifact was not found at the scene of the crash. It has disappeared.''

Orchid frowned. "What makes you so sure that Willis took the relic in the first place?"

"Because he seemed keenly interested in that one item in the collection," Brizo explained. "In fact, a few days before it disappeared, Theo asked to be assigned to the team that was responsible for conducting the analytical tests on it. He often stayed late to work on his projects and he was alone here the night the artifact disappeared."

"There was no sign of a break-in?" Rafe asked.

"None." Brizo gazed at the case full of relics with a deeply troubled expression. "Whoever took the artifact had the code to the jelly-ice lock."

Orchid studied the case. "Theo had that code?"

"Yes." Brizo looked at Rafe with a puzzled expression. "The only thing I don't understand is why he took that particular artifact. If he was going to steal one for a collector, as you suggested, why not take one of the more interestingly shaped items?"

"Good question," Rafe said. "My, ah, associate, Ms. Adams, and I will find out."

Half an hour later Orchid stood beside Rafe on the sidewalk in front of the small, depressing little house that had belonged to Theo Willis.

"You're sure it's all right to just go in and look around?" she asked uneasily.

"I wouldn't have invited you to come along if I thought we'd get arrested," Rafe assured her. "I know I'd never hear the end of it."

"Are you implying that I have a tendency to nag?"

"I would never be so crass as to suggest such a possibility. Ready?"

"As ready as I'll ever be."

It occurred to Orchid that Rafe was enjoying himself. She could hardly complain. She was tense and somewhat anxious because of what they were about to do, but she was also undeniably excited. There were answers to be found. Tonight she and Rafe might discover some of them.

She followed warily as he led the way around to the back of the darkened house.

There was a chill in the midnight air. Fog had gathered on the bay and was slowly, methodically swallowing the city. Long, wispy tendrils curled in the street behind Orchid. The streetlight at the end of the block glowed beneath a shroud of mist. The reflected glare did little to illuminate the scene.

Rafe seemed to have no problem navigating the foggy night. He did not even require a focus link. Orchid figured that finding Theo's back door was probably a snap compared to locating a secret exit in the utter darkness of Elvira Turlock's rare book gallery.

When Rafe disappeared around the back porch, she hurried to catch up. She did not want to lose sight of him in the fog.

She rounded the corner and experienced a moment of alarm when she could not see him.

"Rafe?"

"Over here."

She peered closely and saw him move, a dark shadow against even deeper blackness. "Has anyone ever told you that you have a way of fading into the background?"

"Is that a polite way of telling me that I don't have a scintillating personality?" A soft click sounded in the darkness. "Here we go."

"Did you break the lock?"

"No. I picked it. There's a difference." The door squeaked on its hinges. "Come on. We haven't got all night."

She made her way cautiously to the rear door and gazed into the darkened kitchen. She glimpsed another shadowy movement and realized that Rafe was already inside. She started to join him.

And promptly stubbed her toe on the concrete step she had not noticed.

"Ouch. Darn it."

"Watch the step," Rafe said from out of the darkness.

"Now you tell me." She flexed her toes inside her sneakers and decided that nothing was broken. Gingerly she entered the house.

It smelled musty and stale, as if it had been closed for several days. Which it no doubt had been, she reminded herself.

"Any reason we can't turn on the flashlight?" she asked as she trailed after Rafe down a narrow hall.

"Sorry. Forgot you couldn't see as well as I do in the dark." There was a soft snick as Rafe clicked on the small flashlight he had brought along. "Better?"

"Much." Orchid trailed after him down a short hall into the sparsely furnished parlor. The lovingly polished vio-piano in the corner was the only object in the room that had any personality. "Theo didn't get out a lot. He was either at work or here, playing his precious vio-piano."

Rafe's face was unreadable behind the narrow beam of the flashlight. "I'd gathered that much. Let's see what else we can find."

There was nothing on the walls except a calendar. When Rafe aimed the flashlight at it Orchid saw that it was the cheap kind traditionally handed out as advertising by insurance companies.

"He didn't even hang any pictures," she said.

"Probably just as well." Rafe skimmed the flashlight across a small, neat row of technical magazines. "I hate to think of the kind of taste in art a guy like Willis would have had."

Orchid smiled sweetly. "Come now. Surely it couldn't have been any worse than my taste in poetry."

There was a beat of silence from Rafe.

"You did make your opinion of my literary tastes very

clear when we were in Mrs. Turlock's gallery, you know," she said.

"They're not quite the same as mine." He paused meaningfully. "On the other hand we do share similar tastes in architecture."

"Okay, so I like your house. But it's probably just a bizarre fluke that we both have a thing for Later Expansion period architecture."

"Probably." Rafe opened a cupboard door and aimed the flashlight inside. "What happens if Affinity Associates comes up with a match for you who likes meta-zen-syn philosophical poetry?"

"I'll use it as an excuse to reject him," she said lightly.

Rafe swung around so quickly she jumped in surprise.

"You'd reject a potential agency match just because he doesn't share your taste in poetry?"

"Why not? I rejected the one match they got me because I didn't like his psychic talent. Hey, when it comes to shallow, I can outdo anyone."

Rafe pinned her in the glare of the light. "What kind of talent was he?"

"A charisma-talent." She held up a hand. "I know, I know, charisma is not supposed to be a talent. It's a personality characteristic. But trust me, Preston Luce has a talent for charisma. What's more, he uses it to get what he wants. He's a worm-snake with really great teeth."

"Preston Luce?"

"*Dr.* Preston Luce, if you please. Look, are we going to search this place or stand around all night discussing my one and only agency date?"

"At least you got one."

"You want the truth?" she said. "I'm scared to death that Affinity Associates will send me another very nice candidate one of these days. Maybe they'll send someone who actually appreciates the same books that I appreciate. Someone who likes to eat leftover pasta casserole at midnight. Someone who won't interrupt me when I'm writing. Heck, I'm terrified that the agency will send me Mr. Right."

"Why does that scare you?"

She exhaled slowly. "Because I don't trust any marriage agency to find Mr. Right for me."

"Why not?"

"Because I'm an ice-prism. I don't think the syn-psych people know enough about ice-prisms yet to match them properly."

"You don't trust their para-profiling capabilities?"

"No. Heck, they couldn't even weed out Preston Luce, professional charmer and all-around bastard."

"I wouldn't hold that against Affinity Associates. You said he was a charisma-talent. I met one once, a politician. They're hard to detect."

"All the same, I'm not looking forward to getting a second call from the agency."

Rafe looked as if he wanted to argue the point. She wondered why her marriage prospects or lack of same interested him. But before she could ask, he turned and splashed the beam of the flashlight across a chest of drawers.

"It would probably be a good idea if we finished our business here and got out. No sense arousing the curiosity of a neighbor."

Orchid thought about the nearly deserted street of darkened houses outside. "I don't think anyone in this neighborhood signed up for the local block watch."

"Probably not." Rafe began to go through the dresser drawers in a methodical fashion. "You take the closet."

Obediently she opened the door to reveal a small collection of precisely hung slacks and shirts. "What am I looking for?"

"Anything that looks like it doesn't belong there."

It did not take long to go through Theo Willis's limited wardrobe. Ten minutes after she had started work, Orchid closed the closet door and looked at Rafe.

"Nothing," she said.

"Nothing here, either." He started back toward the hall. "There must be something. There's *always* something."

"You didn't know Theo," she muttered as she followed him back into the living room. "He was a man of limited interests."

Rafe paused half way down the hall when the flashlight played across the wall calendar. "Hang on a second."

"What is it?"

"Morgan Lambert said Willis was seeing a syn-psych shrink."

"So?"

"So he must have had regular appointments. Maybe he noted them on the calendar." Rafe took a closer look at the little squares around each day. "Here we go. Looks like he had several appointments during the last couple of weeks with a Dr. Q.A."

Orchid was intrigued. "How do we find out who Dr. Q.A. is?"

"There are three possible ways to find out the doctor's name. We can go through the phonebook and call every syn-psych shrink with those initials. Or we can look for Willis's bank book to see if he paid for the visits with a check."

"What's the third method?"

"The easy way." Rafe flipped the pages on the calendar. "We go back to the day Willis made the first appointment and hope that he wrote out the doctor's full name the first time he noted it down the way most people do."

Orchid edged closer. She scanned the little boxes as Rafe turned the pages. A thrill of discovery raced through her when she spotted a name. "There. The fifteenth, two months ago. Dr. Quentin Austen. That must be it."

"It would be very interesting to talk to Dr. Austen," Rafe mused.

"Yes. He could tell us something about Theo's state

of mind in the days before he died.'' Orchid's excitement subsided. "But it's not likely Austen will give us much information about a former patient, even if that patient is dead."

"I'm sure we can convince Dr. Austen to help us," Rafe said a little too smoothly.

Orchid opened her mouth to ask him what made him so certain he could get Austen to talk. She closed it again when he suddenly raised a hand to hush her.

She saw him go very still in the shadows, as though he was listening to sounds she could not hear. He turned toward the draped window.

A chill shot through Orchid. "What is it? What's wrong?"

"I'm not sure. Something's not right."

"How do you know?"

"I just know." Rafe's words were no more than a whisper. He clicked off the flashlight, reached for her hand and pulled her toward the back door. "Time to leave."

Orchid did not argue. A million questions seethed in her brain but she decided this was not the time to ask them. She allowed Rafe to haul her down the hall far more quickly than she would have liked. She could scarcely make out the vague shapes around her but Rafe was as sure-footed as a cat-dog.

He led her swiftly to the back door but there he paused once more. Orchid peered through the window at what appeared to be a solid wall of gray mist. The vapor glowed eerily with the reflected light of the street lamp it had recently devoured.

"The fog's gotten worse," she said softly. "A lot worse. It's going to be a miserable drive home."

"We'll be all right."

"I've never seen it quite this bad." Orchid's unease grew stronger. "I can't even see the house next door."

It was true. The fog had swallowed up the house and everything else in the vicinity.

"We can't stay here." Rafe unlatched the door and stepped outside. "Be careful. Remember the step."

She wanted to ask him why they were whispering but she forgot the question the instant the door closed behind her. The strange mist seemed to thicken as they made their way around the side of the small house and started across the unkempt lawn to where the Icer was parked at the curb.

Orchid judged that they were halfway back to the car when Rafe jerked hard on her hand.

"This isn't real fog. *Get down.*"

"What the—?"

Rafe used his foot to trip her. Then he pushed her down, hard. Orchid sprawled ignominiously on the ground. She was wondering if he'd gone crazy when she sensed the rush of booted feet across the lawn.

"Link," Rafe ordered.

The questing probe of his talent roared out of the darkness at full psychic vampire strength. Orchid hastily constructed a prism, manipulating the facets for optimum power. An instant later the first of the attackers plunged out of the mist.

Chapter

8

❖ ❖ ❖ ❖ ❖ ❖ ❖ ❖ ❖

The very texture of the fog-bound night altered abruptly for Rafe as his psychically sharpened senses steadied with the aid of the focus link. Scent, sound, and that indescribable sensation, *awareness,* oriented him as easily in the darkness as sunlight did in daylight.

The mist was as thick as it had been a few seconds earlier, but it no longer mattered that he was partially blinded by it. He had other ways of seeing now.

There were two of them. He located them precisely in the fog. They closed in simultaneously from opposite directions. Experienced predators.

The first man swam out of the fog with the lethal intent of a shark-cuda. He wore a black ski mask. Rafe saw the glint of mist-refracted light on the blade of a knife.

The case had taken a serious turn. Next time he would bring along the pistol he sometimes wore in an ankle holster.

He shifted to the side, briefly concealing himself in the fog.

"Bat-snake shit." The knifeman whirled, seeking his prey.

"Where'd he go?" The second man emerged from the mist. He, too, wore a ski mask and gripped a knife. "Cut some of the damn fog, Jink. I can't see a thing."

Rafe went in low. He crashed into the first man. The impact took them both to the ground.

The uncanny, blinding mist vanished in a heartbeat, leaving behind only the natural, wispy tendrils of fog that had cloaked the city all evening. Rafe felt Orchid's startled surprise even through the focus link, but the crystal clear prism she had crafted did not waver.

Out of the corner of his eye he saw that she was still on the ground, propped on her elbow. She turned to stare at the violent scene unfolding in front of her.

Rafe ignored the shock on her face. She was holding the focus and at the moment, that was all that mattered.

The man Rafe had brought down was an expert. He heaved himself to the side, managing to partially free himself. The knife in his hand sliced out in a short, vicious trajectory aimed at Rafe's midsection.

Rafe spun away, leaping to his feet in the same motion. He kicked out at the hand that held the knife. There was a dull crunch. The man on the ground yelled in pain. His weapon flew off into the darkness.

"Get him."

The second man threw himself forward, knife arm outstretched. But he had to jump over Orchid's prone form in order to get to his quarry. Rafe saw Orchid's foot lash out in a curiously graceful, well-aimed movement that connected with the man's thigh.

The unexpected blow threw the assailant off balance. His legs snarled. He toppled, staggered, and went down.

Rafe leaped for him.

"Fog." The second man steadied himself, scrambled back to his feet and whirled to face Rafe. "Damn it, Jink, give me some fog. He's coming right at me."

The first man lurched to his feet. The mist thickened

abruptly. Rafe ignored it, concentrating with his other senses.

"Shit, it's like he can see right through this stuff," the second man yelled.

"Let's get out of here." The first man pounded off into the darkness.

The second man did not argue. He was already running after his friend.

Power still surged through the prism. Rafe's para-heightened senses strained eagerly. Every instinct urged him to pursue his prey. It would be so easy to bring down at least one of the fleeing men.

"Rafe. I can't see you. Where are you?"

Rafe wrestled with his natural strat-talent inclinations. He could not leave Orchid. She was his first priority.

The artificial fog dissolved as quickly as it had reappeared. Orchid started to climb to her feet. She looked around in wonder as the mist cleared.

"Are you all right?" she demanded.

"Yes." Rafe cut the flow of his talent through the prism.

He assessed her mood quickly. She was badly shaken, but she was in control. It occurred to him that a lot of people, male or female, who had just survived a knife assault would be in hysterics about now. "What about you?"

"I'm okay." She fumbled around on the ground for her fallen purse. "My God, Rafe, they tried to kill you. It was two against one."

The outrage in her voice made him grin. "No, the odds were even. Two against two. I had you for backup."

"Kind of you to give me some credit." Orchid brushed off the knees of her jeans as she got to her feet. "But I don't think I was a whole lot of help. Psynergy, Inc., employees are trained to handle a wide variety of focus situations. But I don't think this kind of thing fits into the more sophisticated, upscale image that Clementine is going for."

"Then she probably shouldn't sign contracts with strat-talents. We're not exactly up-market clients." He listened to the fading footsteps of his fleeing prey as he took Orchid's arm.

Adrenaline still pounded through his veins. He knew from past experience that it would take a while to dissipate. Even though he was no longer focusing his talent, he was still intensely aware of the myriad sensations of the night.

He was also acutely aware of the very smooth skin of Orchid's hand. He could feel the warmth of her, the slight, unmistakable, utterly unique scent that was hers alone. A restless hunger hummed in his gut.

Adrenaline aftermath, he reminded himself. A natural chemical cocktail created by violence had flooded his bloodstream. The fact that the potion had a powerful synergistic affinity for the chemicals of sexual desire was a well-documented, scientific fact.

The difference between man and beast, he reflected grimly as he put Orchid into the car, was not as great as many people liked to think.

Orchid looked at him as he got behind the Icer's steering bar. "One of those two men was an illusion-talent, wasn't he?"

"Yeah. Probably a little higher than mid-range. Class six or seven, maybe. That mist he generated was a very strong illusion."

"He had help from the natural fog that was already in the vicinity," Orchid murmured. "My friend, Amaryllis, works frequently with a very strong illusion-talent."

"That would be her husband, Lucas Trent." Rafe eased the Icer away from the curb.

Orchid shot him a quick, searching glance. "You know Lucas very well, I take it?"

"Well enough." Rafe had a fleeting memory of a night in the Western Island jungles when he and Lucas and

Nick Chastain had tracked a band of pirates to their lair. It had been Lucas's incredibly real illusion of driving rain which had given the three men the edge they needed to herd the renegades into a trap.

"I see. Well, Amaryllis says that it's always easier to graft an illusion onto an already existing chunk of reality than it is to create it from scratch."

"In other words, it's simpler to produce an illusion of fog when there's already a lot of fog around."

"Something to do with the fact that the human eye sees what it expects to see." Orchid gazed through the windshield at the misty street. "On a fog-bound night, you expect to see a lot of fog. A bit more comes as no big surprise."

"You were the surprise tonight."

"Me?"

He glanced at her. "That kick you used to topple the second man. That was meta-zen-syn."

"So?"

"You never mentioned that you were a practitioner."

She made a face. "I was raised in Northville. I was taught meta-zen-syn exercises before I could walk. But I don't think of myself as a practitioner. Practitioners are obsessive-compulsive about their exercises and they wear a lot of white."

"I see."

She shot him a quick, speculative glance. "You were using a form of meta-zen-syn, too."

"Yes." Rafe flexed his hands on the steering wheel. "My father is a practitioner. He taught me. Said I'd need the exercises to help control my talent."

"Well, at least you don't run around in white."

Rafe smiled slightly. "No, I don't wear much white."

"It's very hard to wear white, you know. I never could understand how everybody in Northville except me managed to keep their clothes so spotless. Mine always got dirty five minutes after I put them on."

Rafe suddenly felt extraordinarily cheerful. "Did they?"

"Yes." She frowned down at her hands. "Unfortunately, I don't know how to use meta-zen-syn to make my fingers stop shaking."

"It's the adrenaline. It will fade in a few minutes. If it's any consolation, I'm feeling the after effects, myself." *And how.*

"You don't have to be condescending about it."

"What?" Her sarcasm startled him. "Who's being condescending? I told you the truth. I am feeling the effects."

"Hah." She glared at him. "Look at the way you're driving."

"What's wrong with my driving?"

"Nothing." She sounded seriously aggrieved. "That's the whole point. You're as steady as a rock."

"Don't try to tell me what I'm feeling. I know damn well what I'm feeling. The fact that I can drive this car does not mean that I am not experiencing the same adrenaline effects that you're experiencing."

"Don't shout at me. I've had a very difficult evening."

"I'm not shouting at you."

"Your voice is rising."

He started to defend himself, then shook his head when he realized she was right. "Damn. Listen to us. This is a really stupid argument we're having."

"Yes, it is." She scowled. "Why are we having it?"

He sighed. "It's all part of the adrenaline jag. This, too, shall pass."

"Don't," she warned, "start up again." But there was a rueful smile in her voice.

He glanced at her. In the light from the dash he could see the very sensual, very soft curve of her mouth.

Desire tugged at him. It was growing stronger, not weaker. He used every ounce of self-control he possessed to squelch it. This was most definitely not the right time or place. Orchid had been through a very traumatic experience. He had to respect that fact.

"You know," he said thoughtfully, "we made a pretty good team."

"Yeah. We did." She paused. "Now that we are no longer arguing, I have a question. What, exactly, do you think was going on back there?"

"Isn't it obvious?" He exhaled slowly. "Someone doesn't want us asking questions about Theo Willis."

"I was afraid you were going to say that."

Half an hour later, Orchid sat curled on the massive, elegantly curved Later Expansion period sofa in Rafe's library. She watched him with serious, troubled eyes as she sipped moontree brandy.

"What do we do next?" she asked.

"You mean, what do *I* do next." He poured a second glass of brandy. "You're out of it as of tonight."

"Wait a second, I thought you said we were a team?"

He was surprised by her glowering look. "This thing has turned nasty." He carried his glass across the room and lowered himself into the massive, ornately carved reading chair. "I don't want you involved any deeper."

"You mean, now that it's no longer some sort of game, you want to go hunting alone."

"It's no game. It never was a game." He watched her, brooding over the satisfaction he felt having her here in his home.

The decision to bring her back to his big house on the hill overlooking the city had been a simple one. He had an excellent excuse, he told himself. Orchid should not be left alone after what she had just been through tonight.

"Damn it, I've had enough." She put her glass down with grim precision. "I think it's about time you told me what this is all about."

"What do you mean?"

"It's perfectly obvious that, until things got serious

tonight, this business of chasing down the lost alien artifact was just another excuse to hire me. You haven't
really needed my services at all in any of your cases. At
least not until tonight when those two men jumped us."

"That's not true."

"Don't lie to me, Stonebraker. Now, when it's obvious
you've got a real case that may take talent-focus team-
work, the first thing you want to do is fire me."

"I just think it would be a whole lot safer for you if
you got out of this before it gets any rougher."

"I'm not going anywhere until you tell me what's
going on. I think, after what I've been through tonight,
I've got a right to know. Why did you insist on hiring
me so frequently this past week?"

He closed his eyes and leaned back in the chair. What
the hell could he say to her? He had run out of glib
excuses. "You've got a point. Maybe it's time I put my
cards on the table."

"Past time."

He opened his eyes and looked at her. "Okay, the
fact is, I need a wife, or at least a fiancée, in less than
two months. Synergistic Connections doesn't seem to be
able to come up with a suitable candidate, so I decided
to go hunt—uh, *looking* for one on my own."

"A wife?" Her voice was a mere squeak of sound but
her eyes were huge.

"I knew that, among other things, I wanted a full-
spectrum prism who wouldn't faint when she discovered
that I'm an off-the-chart strat-talent. So I went out and
hired a lot of full-spectrums until I met you."

Orchid shook her head in disbelief. "This is a joke,
right?"

"Believe me," he put his brandy glass down very deliberately, "whatever else it is, it's no joke."

She stared at him. "You just decided to try out a lot
of full-spectrum prisms until you found one you thought
might work out as a wife?"

"I'm a little desperate at the moment."

"How very flattering. Lovely to know that you've been driven to checking me out as a potential wife because you're a little desperate."

Rafe began to feel cornered. "Well, it's not as if you've got a dozen potential husbands beating a path to your door, either. You told me yourself that Affinity Associates hasn't turned up a single candidate the whole time you've been registered. Why shouldn't we take a second look at each other? There doesn't seem to be anyone else around for either of us."

"You said you've got two months to produce a wife or a fiancée?"

He gripped the arms of his chair and shoved himself to his feet. He stalked to the fireplace. "That's right."

"Mind if I ask why?"

"It's a family thing." The ever-popular, all-purpose, unarguable, excuse on St. Helens. *A family thing.*

Orchid glared at him. "You're serious, aren't you?"

"Very."

"Good grief." She shook her head in stunned amazement. "This is like that old ice-fairy tale, the one in which Prince Charming takes a glass slipper around the kingdom until he finds a woman whose foot fits into it."

"I don't exactly envision myself as Prince Charming."

"Neither," she said, "do I."

He winced. "This is probably not a good time to discuss this."

She gave him a steely smile. "I can tell you right now, there won't be a better time. Is there anything else about this bizarre situation that I should know?"

He rubbed his jaw. "No, that's pretty much the whole of it."

"Tell me, please, I can't leave without knowing. How in five hells did I make the cut? Out of all the full-spectrum prisms you must have hired from all the focus firms in New Seattle, why me?"

"I don't know." That sounded weak. He sought for a more logical response. "Why not you?"

"You're right. Prince Charming, you're not."

Rafe spun around to face her. "Look, I'm trying to be honest here."

"Oh, great. No wonder Synergistic Connections is having a hard time finding a match for you. That kind of honesty probably has an extremely limited appeal."

"Yeah? Well, what about you? Your appeal must be somewhat limited, too, if Affinity Associates can't come up with a match after all this time."

She leaped to her feet. "I don't care if they never find me a match."

"Well, I'm not real keen on the idea of being saddled with a deadline for finding a wife."

"I can certainly understand that. Talk about pressure. Well, I wouldn't want you to waste any more of your valuable time on me." She whirled and started toward the door.

She was leaving. Desperation rolled over him in a wave.

"Orchid. Please. Don't go."

Something in his voice must have pierced her outrage. She stopped but she did not turn around. She reached out to grip the door jamb with one hand. Her spine was an elegant, unyielding line.

"I don't think it would be a good idea for me to stay," she said starkly.

"I've made a hash of this. I'm sorry." He took a breath. "But I was under the impression that you're at least mildly attracted to me."

"So?"

"So I'm more than mildly attracted to you. A lot more."

"That," she said brusquely, "is not a good enough reason for marriage, especially marriage without a confirming match from a proper marriage agency."

"I know." He hesitated. "But it's a good enough reason for an affair, isn't it?"

Her hand tightened visibly on the door jamb. Her

knuckles went white. "You don't have time to waste on an affair. You need a wife."

"Tonight I need you."

She turned slowly around to face him. Her eyes were shadowy pools that veiled a thousand secrets. "Do you?"

"Yes." This was a fine time to get the shakes. He had not felt this unsteady after the brawl in Theo Willis's front yard, he reflected. "But it's no good if you don't want me, too."

"As you said earlier, we're a good team when it comes to some things."

"Is this one of those things?"

"Yes," she said slowly. "I think it is."

A joyous relief that he had no business feeling at that moment swept away every other sensation except desire.

Rafe covered the short distance that separated him from Orchid in three long strides. He lifted her up into his arms and carried her through the doorway and down the hall.

She smiled tremulously and put one arm around his neck as he started up the broad staircase that led to the darkened floor above. "I could walk, you know."

"Somehow I get the feeling that none of your heroes would allow your heroines to walk up the stairs to the bedroom before they made love for the first time."

"You really did read one of my books, didn't you?"

"Yes."

Rafe reached the landing and paused long enough to kiss her again. Hunger surged through him. He hoped he was not actually panting with lust. So very primitive.

He carried her down the hall to the shadowed doorway at the far end.

"Oh, my," Orchid whispered when he walked into the room with her in his arms. "You said you had a window in the ceiling. This is incredible."

He smiled as she tilted her head back to gaze in wonder at the glass dome above the bed. The fog that blanketed the city had not climbed this hillside. Overhead their private night sky was clear. Stars glittered in the velvety darkness.

The bed had come with the house. It was a massive circular creation with an elaborately carved base of gold-enleaf wood. Rafe stepped up onto the dais with a sense of impending destiny. He set Orchid down on the spider-frog silk quilt.

For a few seconds he simply stared at her, adjusting to the reality of having her here in his bedroom.

"Something wrong?" she asked.

"No."

"Are you having second thoughts?"

"I can't think at all at the moment," he said.

A troubled expression passed across her face. "We're not doing this because of that adrenaline rush we got during the fight with those two men at Theo's house, are we?"

"No." Who cared why they were doing it? he thought. They were doing it. That was all that mattered.

"I've heard that the synergistic reaction that some-times occurs in the human bloodstream after a fight is not very different, chemically speaking, from the reac-tion caused by sexual attraction."

"I would take it as a great favor," Rafe said, "if you would save the lecture on synergistic blood chemistry until later. I don't think I can follow it at the moment."

Her eyes gleamed with sensual amusement. "Sorry."

With a groan he lowered himself to the bed and gath-ered her into his arms.

Orchid's soft laughter floated up to the domed ceiling, as weightless and bright as the starlight overhead. Rafe leaned over her, caging her between his hands, and kissed her until she stopped laughing.

Her mouth opened beneath his. With a soft, muffled exclamation, she wrapped her arms around him. He felt her sudden fierce need all the way to the bone.

She wanted him.

His own smoldering hunger leaped into full flame. An

exultant sensation stormed through him. Tonight she was his.

In an exuberant frenzy of happy lust he rolled with her across the wide bed, rumpling the quilt and the sheets until all was chaos. When they at last came to a halt, Rafe was once more stretched out on top of her. Her jean-clad legs framed his. She looked up at him, breathless. Her eyes were brilliant, starlit pools in which he would willingly drown, in which he could not wait to drown.

He could feel the heat of her body through the denim. It carried her scent, which was mingled now with the unmistakable fragrance of feminine desire. The night, the time when his senses were sharpest, when he was most keenly aware of that other part of himself, called to him. He was alive as he had never been before in his life.

He lifted himself off Orchid long enough to get a grip on the hem of her T-shirt. He managed to shove it up above her breasts and then over her head. Her soft hair got whipped into a wild tangle in the process. One silken lock fell across her face, giving her a sultry, mysterious look.

He looked down at her elegantly curved breasts. It crossed his mind that he had never seen anything more beautiful than the spill of starlight on her skin.

She fumbled with the buttons of his shirt. Impatient with her slow progress, he reached down and finished the job himself. He closed his eyes and shuddered when he felt her fingers on his bare chest.

"Rafe." Her voice throbbed with emotion.

He opened his eyes and bent his head to kiss her. While he held her mouth captive, he unfastened her jeans. Then he worked his way down her body, freeing her from the denim. When he rose over her again she was clad in nothing but a small triangle of silk.

Deliberately he put his hand between her legs. The crotch of her dainty panties was already wet. A heady sense of pleasure shot through him, leaving him slightly dazed. He pressed gently against the silk that shielded her.

Orchid sucked in her breath at his touch, gave a wordless cry and twisted restlessly beneath his hand. When he stroked her she clenched her thighs together, forcing herself more firmly against his palm. Her breathing quickened in the darkness.

After a moment she hesitantly reached out to touch him as intimately as he had touched her and sighed impatiently when she discovered his trousers in the way.

Her touch was curiously awkward, but it was eager. Her hands tortured him deliciously while she sought and found the fastening at the waistband of his pants, undid it, and finally managed to lower his zipper.

He fell heavily into her waiting hand. When she cupped him gently he thought he might go mad. He squeezed his eyes closed for a few seconds and fought a desperate battle with his self-control.

He won the battle, at least for a few minutes. When he managed to open his eyes again he saw that Orchid was gazing at his rigid erection with an expression of wonder and intense fascination.

"You are incredible," she whispered.

He did not answer. He could not. He was too close to the edge. If he did not take her now, he would surely shatter.

He jerked her sodden panties aside, lowered himself to her once more and fitted himself to her. He caught and held her gaze. He needed to look into her eyes when he claimed her.

She watched him with an odd intensity, as though waiting for something important to happen. He prayed he would not disappoint her.

He thrust heavily into her. Felt small, delicate muscles resist, give way, and then close snugly around him. Something else gave way, too. He heard her quick, sharp breath. For a moment she went rigid. She was hot and wet and very, very tight. Too tight.

He raised his head swiftly.

"Orchid?"

"It's all right." She framed his face with her hands. "I've waited a long time for this."

"But, *why?*"

"It never felt right before."

A profound sense of wonder and an exultant satisfaction mingled with the potent chemical mix in his veins. He knew exactly what she meant. Nothing had ever felt this right. He lowered his head to kiss her throat.

"Link."

She did not hesitate. Out on the metaphysical plane a brilliant crystal took shape. Rafe slammed talent through the prism as he eased himself deeper into Orchid's body.

He reached down to find her small, firm clitoris. At the first touch she cried out and pressed her face against his chest. He thought he felt her teeth. The sensation was almost unbearably exciting.

He stroked gently as he rocked against her. The elemental rhythms of desire established themselves in the oldest of synergistic harmonies.

Eons later, when the effort to hold himself back had become exquisitely painful, Orchid's fingers suddenly dug into his shoulders.

"Oh, yes," she whispered as if she had just made an incredible discovery. *"Yes."*

He raised his head so that he could see her face when she climaxed beneath him. The tiny convulsions shimmered through her. He felt them deep inside where he was securely lodged.

Orchid's release triggered his own. A dazzling mix of physical and paranormal energy poured through him. All of his senses were riveted by the sensation. He was swept away by the glorious wildness that seized him.

Nothing had ever felt so whole, so right, so perfect.

*   *   *

Rafe opened his eyes a long time later. He gazed up through the glass dome and contemplated the stars. Orchid stirred and stretched beside him. Then she propped herself on her elbow and leaned over him.

"Mind if I ask you a personal question?"

He studied her gleaming eyes and tangled his fingers in her hair. "At this particular moment, I wouldn't mind if you asked me to fly or go over a waterfall in a barrel."

"In a good mood, are you?"

"Very."

She folded her arms on his chest and rested her chin on her hand. "This is sort of a professional question."

"Go for it."

"Is it true that strat-talents can tell if a person is lying to them?"

He stilled. And then he started to laugh. He laughed so hard he had to sit up and wrap his arms around his midsection. He doubled over with laughter. He howled with laughter. The room rang with the sound of it.

"I didn't think the question was that funny," Orchid said.

Rafe's laughter finally faded into a grin. He sprawled on his back and pulled Orchid down on top of him.

"Let me put it this way." He thrust his fingers through her hair. "I'll know if you ever try to fake an orgasm."

Chapter

9

❖❖❖❖❖❖❖❖❖

She did not dream.

Or, to be more specific, Orchid thought, when she awoke alone in the massive round bed, she did not dream of being stalked by a psychic vampire, even though some would say she had gone to bed with one.

She felt remarkably refreshed, given her energetic activities during the night. High overhead morning light blazed through the glass domed ceiling. It poured over the bed like warm honey-syrup and puddled around her in a delicious pool.

No nightmares last night. Not one.

The extent of her euphoria told her more clearly than anything else could just how much she had come to dread the stalking dream. For the first time she realized how it had nibbled away at the edges of her nerves during the past few days.

She wondered if great sex always had such a revitalizing affect. The only way to test the hypothesis would be to do it again, she thought. Soon.

She did not know why she had waited until last night

to lose her virginity. Heaven knew that in her wild and reckless teenage years she'd done her share of climbing into backseats with the handful of young men who had the courage to date the daughter of one of Northville's most important academics. Her curiosity had been as strong as that of any other healthy adolescent.

But, perhaps owing to the fact that Northville suffered a serious shortage of interesting "bad boys" or because she was, at heart, a romantic bent on waiting for Mr. Right, she had never gone all the way.

By the time she had left Northville for the city, she was twenty years old and no longer quite so wild or reckless. She'd had goals and plans and none of the men she had met fit into them. She had male friends, but she did not have many boyfriends. None of the few men who had come into her life in the past few years had been Mr. Right.

Rafe might not be Mr. Right, she told herself, but he certainly was Mr. Exciting.

She wiggled her toes beneath the turquoise blue sheet and listened to the sounds of Rafe in the shower. The sounds of her lover, she corrected herself.

Who was registered at a marriage agency because he was desperately seeking a bride for family reasons.

That thought brought her exuberance down several notches. She sat up, pushed aside the blue-green sheets, and rose from the giant circular bed.

Halfway to the door of the bathroom she paused, turned, and glanced back over her shoulder at the rumpled bed. The old Later Expansion period piece had not been fashioned for frivolous sexual encounters, she thought. It had the weighty, portentous look of a bed that had been designed for founding dynasties. If she tried, she could almost make herself feel a little guilty for having such a good time in it last night.

Almost.

*   *   *

Half an hour later, showered and dressed in her jeans and T-shirt, she ran Rafe's comb through her damp hair and headed downstairs.

At the top of the elaborately carved staircase she paused, remembering how Rafe had carried her up the steps in his arms. A little thrill of pleasure shot through her.

Definitely Mr. Exciting.

The enticing aroma of freshly brewed coff-tea drew her down a hall to a small glass-walled sunroom that overlooked the garden. Rafe was seated at the table near the floor-to-ceiling windows. He had the morning edition of the *New Seattle Times* spread out in front of him.

He looked up when she walked into the room. His mouth curved with lazy satisfaction when he saw her.

"Good morning," he said.

"Hi." Brilliant conversation opener, she thought. Never let it be said that she, Orchid Adams, author of psychic vampire romance novels, did not know how to greet a lover first thing in the morning.

She suppressed the crazy little thrill of happiness mixed with trepidation she felt and made herself walk very casually to the table. When she got there, she was not quite certain what to do next.

What was the socially correct thing, she wondered, a little frantically. Should she just act really cool and help herself to the coff-tea? Give Rafe a brisk little peck on the cheek as if they had been lovers for ages? Make some jaunty remark about his being an early riser for a man who claimed to be a night person?

The heroines in her novels never had these problems she thought.

Rafe came to her rescue. He held out one hand. When she took it, he pulled her close against his side and urged her down for a kiss.

"You taste good," he said when she raised her head.

"I used your toothpaste," she blurted. *Cool, very cool, Orchid.* "But not your toothbrush. Honest. I just used

my fingers." Great. She'd moved from sounding gauche
to sounding like a blithering idiot.

"You can use my toothbrush anytime you want," he
said very seriously.

She could not tell if he was teasing her so she decided
to change the subject. She glanced down at the newspaper for inspiration and saw that he had been reading
an article in the business section. The headline made
her blink.

Reports of Pending Changes
at Stonebraker Persist

She frowned and bent her head to read the rest of
the article.

> Rumors that Alfred G. Stonebraker, longtime president and C.E.O. of Stonebraker Shipping, will soon step down continue to circulate
> in business circles. If true, they raise troubling
> questions about the future of the company. Hit
> hard by last year's brief economic downturn, the
> firm compounded its problems by failing to adjust to the recent technological shifts in the shipping industry.
>
> It is no secret that Stonebraker's Board of
> Directors is sharply divided on several issues.
> The strongest faction, led by A.G. Stonebraker's
> nephew and probable heir apparent, Selby
> Culverthorpe, is said to favor a merger with TriMark Consolidated. Such a move, while potentially favorable to Stonebraker shareholders in
> the short term, would no doubt result in the
> ultimate demise of the company as an independent entity.

"How sad," Orchid said without thinking.
Rafe's brows rose quizzically. "Why do you say that?"

"Misplaced sentimentality, I suppose." She sat down and reached for the coff-tea pot. "It's none of my business. I don't have any shares in Stonebraker. And I realize that you're not involved in your family's company. But won't you find it a little depressing to stand by and watch it get swallowed up by a competitor?"

His eyes met hers with riveting intensity. "Yes."

She reached for a slice of toast. "Do you ever regret that you didn't follow in your grandfather's footsteps?"

"You seem to know a lot about my family history."

She shrugged and took a bite of the toast. "Clementine filled me in on some of the background. She said rumor has it that years ago there was a big rift between you and your grandfather."

"Ms. Malone is right. My grandfather wanted me to join the company. It was impossible."

"Of course. You could never work for anyone else. You would have to be the boss, regardless of what you did."

Rafe regarded her with an enigmatic expression. "You sound very sure of that."

"It's obvious. Probably goes with being a strat-talent." She chewed reflectively on her bite of toast. "Or maybe it just goes with being you. Did you and your grandfather ever repair the rift?"

"We've talked," Rafe said deliberately.

Orchid smiled. "That's great. I take it he's mellowed over the years?"

"You've obviously never met my grandfather. *Mellow* is not a word that could ever be applied to him."

"I see. Did he ever forgive you for failing to join the family firm?"

"No."

"Oh." She hesitated. "He must be terribly upset about the possibility that Stonebraker might get bought out by Tri-Mark."

"He's not happy about it."

"Does he blame you for the fact that the company i in trouble now?" she asked gently.

"Yes. Says if I'd taken over five years ago, when he originally planned to retire, Stonebraker wouldn't be having the kind of problems it's having today. He's right."

She sighed. "Only to be expected he'd try to put a guilt trip on you, I suppose. It's one of the things families do best."

"I know."

"Still, a family rift is always unfortunate. Is there anything you can do to mend the breach with your grandfather?"

"Sure." Rafe folded his arms on top of the newspaper and regarded her with gleaming eyes. "I could get myself appointed C.E.O. of Stonebraker, stop cousin Selby's attempt to take control of the company, force the board of directors to get in line, modernize the firm's way of doing business, and renegotiate contracts with our subcontractors and suppliers."

Orchid stared at him, stunned. She slowly lowered her half-eaten slice of toast. "Good lord, that's exactly what you're going to do, isn't it?"

"Yes." He picked up his mug of coff-tea. "That's what I'm going to do."

She swallowed a bite of toast. "Mind if I ask why?"

Rafe hesitated. "The company's been in the family for four generations. It supports a couple of thousand people, including most of the members of the Stonebraker clan. If cousin Selby has his way, a lot of good, hardworking people, not just my relatives, are going to lose their jobs. It's always that way in a merger."

"So it's your sense of responsibility to the family that's motivating you to save the company?"

"There are other reasons." Rafe looked out into the garden. "Stonebraker has made some real contributions in the past. Until a few years ago, it was an innovative leader in developing new technology in the shipping and transportation fields. It's spawned any number of smaller businesses."

She smiled at the pride that underscored his words. It was not just a sense of family responsibility that drove him. Rafe had a strong sense of commitment to the community, too, although he would probably be reluctant to admit it.

"There's one other reason why I'm going to save Stonebraker," he added.

"What's that?" Orchid asked.

"Cousin Selby is a two-faced, conniving little twerp whose only goal is to get rich by dismembering Stonebraker. He wants revenge on the whole Stonebraker family. Damned if I'll let the little weasel-snake get away with it."

"Why on St. Helens does he want to bring down the whole family and the company, too?"

Rafe raised one shoulder in a dismissive shrug. "It's a long story. The bottom line is that he resents the fact that the real power in the firm has always been in the hands of those who descended through my branch of the family tree."

"I see."

"It would be one thing if Selby wanted to take control of the company in order to save it. But his only goal is to destroy it." Rafe's hand flexed around the mug. "I won't let that happen."

"I understand." The crisis had aroused all of Rafe's protective instincts, she realized. He would do whatever it took to save the company and defend those who were dependent on it. Nothing would be allowed to get in his way.

"There's just one little problem," Rafe said slowly.

"Only one?"

He gave her a level look. "The Stonebraker board of directors is very conservative. There's no way I can pull off my plans unless I convince them that I intend to marry and settle down. I need to look like a good, responsible family man in their eyes."

The toast point got lodged in Orchid's throat. She swallowed heavily to force it on down. "That's why you need a wife."

"Yes."

With a monumental effort of will, she managed what she hoped was a bright smile. "Good luck."

"So far I'm not having any."

"Sorry to hear that." She cast about desperately for a change of topic. "I guess the question now, is, what happens next?"

"Yes."

"Well? You're the expert," she said.

"Me?"

She raised her eyes briefly to the ceiling. "Good thing your clients can't see you with that blank look on your face. They'd think twice about hiring you. Fortunately, I know that deep down you're a really sharp guy or I'd be having a few doubts myself."

"I'm not any more of an authority on what happens next than you are."

"I beg your pardon?"

He moved one hand in a vague gesture. "It's not like I do this all the time."

"You don't?"

"Five hells, what do you think I am?"

"A businessman who amuses himself by playing private investigator on the side?"

His gaze narrowed. "What does my business or my hobby have to do with what happens next in our relationship?"

Somewhere a jelly-ice light went off in Orchid's brain. She plunked her mug down on the table and clapped a hand over her mouth. "Oh, dear."

Rafe's jaw tightened. "What the hell does *oh, dear* mean in this context?"

Orchid kept her hand over her mouth in an attempt to conceal her grin. "Nothing," she mumbled.

"Damn it, Orchid—"

"I wasn't talking about our relationship." She gulped down more giggles. "I was talking about our investigation. What's our next step?"

"You weren't talking about us?"

"No." She tried to look blasé. "I should think you'd be relieved to hear that. I'm told men hate relationship discussions."

"I am." He frowned. "I do."

"So, about our investigation?"

He refolded the newspaper with grim, precise movements. "It's not *our* investigation any longer, Orchid. I thought I explained that last night."

She braced herself for the battle. "You need me. I know you want to keep me out of this, but after last night, you have to admit that you need my focus services."

"I'll admit your services were useful during that fight, but I'm accustomed to working alone. I'll get by without you."

"Rafe, you can't just cancel the contract like this."

He looked amused. "Of course I can."

"But I'm involved in this thing. I can't walk away from it."

"That's exactly what you're going to do."

"No, it is not what I'm going to do. I want to find out what happened to Theo Willis."

"You don't seem to get the point here, Orchid. I'm firing you."

She raised her chin. "If you insist, I guess there's not much I can do to stop you."

"I insist."

"Very well, then, if that's the way you feel about it." She got to her feet and picked up the empty toast dish. "I certainly can't force you to allow me to assist you."

"I'm glad you understand that." Rafe's expression gentled. "I promise I'll keep you informed of my progress."

She paused at the doorway of the breakfast room and nodded. "Thank you. That would be extremely helpful."

"Helpful?"

"Yes. I haven't had a lot of experience with this kind of thing and I'll probably need all the scraps of information you condescend to toss my way."

"Scraps?"

"If you're really nice to me, I'll return the favor. I'll let you know what I find out, too."

Rafe surged to his feet. "What the hell are you talking about?"

"I thought I'd made myself clear. I'm going to continue the investigation." She walked into the kitchen. "With or without your help."

"Come back here, damn it."

Orchid allowed the kitchen door to swing closed behind her.

It slammed open again just as she set the dishes in the sink. Rafe loomed in the entrance.

"You wouldn't dare," he said.

"You don't know me very well, do you?" She rinsed the toast dish and reached for a towel. "I've made up my mind. Obviously, I'd rather have you as a partner because you know a lot more about investigative work than I do. But since you insist on firing me, I'll just have to go it alone."

He took a step toward her. "This is blackmail."

"Well, I suppose if you want to get technical about it—"

He planted his hands on his hips. "I don't like being manipulated."

"I'm negotiating, not manipulating. As a businessman, you should know the difference."

"Orchid, if you think you can get away with this—"

"Don't you dare threaten me. You're the one who hired me under false pretenses." She flung the towel aside. "But I'm prepared to overlook that if you'll take me on as a full partner."

"And if I don't you'll start messing around in this thing on your own, is that it?"

"You got it." She stretched her arms out on each side and grasped the edge of the counter with both hands. "What do you say? Have we got a deal?"

Rafe did not reply. He gazed at her for a long moment.

Orchid felt the stirring of his talent. The hair on the back of her neck lifted. The hunted sensation flitted across her nerves.

"Try that again and I'll treat you to a real surprise the next time you focus with me," she said.

"What makes you think I'll ever focus with you again?"

"How can you resist? I'm the best prism you've ever had. Admit it."

He stalked across the kitchen and pinned her against the counter. "You're right." His eyes gleamed as he cradled her face between his hands. "You are the best prism I've ever had."

The blatant, predatory sexuality in his eyes sent a shiver through her.

"You were pretty good, yourself," she managed.

"I love it when you talk dirty. You know something? I think you're going to drive me crazy before this is all over."

"The feeling is mutual."

"Should be interesting, if nothing else." The hunted sensation faded but the glitter in Rafe's eyes did not. "So you want to be partners?"

"Yes."

"Okay, *partner*, I need a date for tomorrow night. The least you can do is help me out."

She touched the tip of her tongue to the corner of her mouth. Every instinct she possessed was on full alert. "A date?"

"For my grandfather's birthday party."

Orchid relaxed slightly. "Oh, a birthday party."

"Don't get the wrong idea here. We're not talking a cake and some jelly-ice candles. Alfred G.'s party is a very big deal. Every member of the family will be there, including cousin Selby. Also, every politician in the city-state who wants a campaign contribution will attend. As will most of Stonebraker's business associates and a sizable portion of the membership of the Founders' Club."

"And you can't get a *real* date for a major social event like that?"

"You're real enough." He bent his head. His mouth hovered an inch above hers.

"Okay, partner. I'll go as your date. But only if you agree to do the same favor for me."

His eyes darkened. "You need a date?"

"In five days' time. For a family wedding in Northville."

"Deal." His mouth closed over hers.

She felt the fierce, prowling, hungry passion in him. It was as strong as it had been last night, but this morning it was all mixed up with anger, seething frustration, and some other emotions she could not name.

But she knew that she had won. They were partners now. She put her arms around his neck and kissed him back, just as fiercely.

Two hours later, after taking his new *partner* back to her apartment, Rafe stalked back into his own house. He went immediately into his study, grabbed the phone, and punched out Hobart Batt's number.

Hobart came on the line at once, sounding anxious. "Good morning, Mr. Stonebraker. I realize you're calling to check on progress. Unfortunately I still have not been able to come up with a good match. But rest assured, I'm working on the problem."

"You told me that through the matchmakers' multiple listing service Synergistic Connections had access to the files of everyone who is currently registered in New Seattle."

"We do. Believe me, Mr. Stonebraker, I've checked the MLS listings several times. I've also thoroughly checked the computer files of our offices in New Vancouver and New Portland. I regret to inform you—"

"Have you heard of a marriage agency called Affinity Associates?"

"Affinity?" A note of alarm entered Hobart's voice. "Yes. It's located here in New Seattle. But it's a very small operation, Mr. Stonebraker. If you're thinking of switching your registration to Affinity, I must warn you that, even though they have access to the MLS, they lack the resources and extensive expertise of a large agency such as ours."

"Listen, Batt—"

"Given your rather extraordinary paranormal profile, I feel that we are far better equipped to handle you."

Rafe hung on to his patience with an effort. "I'm not talking about moving my account to Affinity. I want you to check with them about one of their clients, Miss Orchid Adams. She registered with Affinity a little over a year ago."

"I see. In that case, I'm sure she would be in the multiple listing service. If you're thinking that we might have somehow overlooked her as a potential match for you, I can assure you—"

"She's got a very unusual paranormal profile. It's possible that Affinity did not properly assess her." Rafe paused deliberately. "Lacking the resources and expertise of a big firm such as Synergistic Connections and all, maybe they just screwed up her whole damn registration."

Hobart heaved a stoic sigh. "I'll look into it, sir."

"You do that, Batt. Or I *will* start thinking about switching my registration to another agency." Rafe tossed the phone back into its cradle.

He leaned back in his chair and stared at the darkened

screen of his computer. The silence of the big house settled around him.

He had set out to hunt himself a wife and he had found the one he wanted. He could not believe that they were not a good match. Affinity Associates had fouled up the registration. It was the only possible answer.

In the meantime, he had other problems. He picked up the phone again and dialed Dr. Quentin Austen's office number. The receptionist sounded bored. He could hear the occasional snap of her gum.

"I'm sorry, Dr. Austen is not available. If this is an emergency, I can recommend another syn-psych doctor."

"I don't want a professional consultation. This is a business matter."

Gum snapped loudly. "What kind of business?"

"Tell Dr. Austen that it concerns one of his recent investments."

He hung up the phone before the receptionist could ask any more questions. He was satisfied that Quentin Austen would call soon. He had discovered long ago that people tended to return phone calls that involved money.

That thought reminded him that he still had a business to run. He reached out, switched on the computer, and settled down to brood over the Synergy Fund's extensive stock market portfolio.

The technology sector was doing well, but it was time to unload some of the fund's retail stocks. He could sense a coming shift in the market. The dip would be minor, but he did not want to be caught in it.

Chapter

10

❖❖❖❖❖❖❖❖❖

At ten o'clock the following evening Orchid allowed Rafe to lead her out onto one of many terraces that surrounded Stonebraker House. She took a deep breath of the scented air and popped a flaky little pastry stuffed with spiced crab-ster into her mouth. It was her third in ten minutes.

She had discovered the pastries a short while ago after having worked her way through a buffet table filled with exquisitely prepared hors d'oeuvres. At first she had worried that she did not have any room left for the spicy crab-ster tidbits, but she had managed, with a serious effort of willpower, to find space.

All in all, Orchid was surprised to discover that she felt right at home at Alfred G. Stonebraker's birthday party. It was not all that different from the faculty receptions her parents used to drag her to back in Northville. She sensed the same subtle, behind-the-scenes maneuvering, the same political machinations, and the same family tensions hovering just beneath the surface.

The biggest difference here was that almost no one wore white.

The glass-walled room behind her was filled with elegantly dressed men and women who sipped expensive blue champagne while they discussed social gossip, business, and fashionable gallery openings. The strains of a tango-waltz played gently in the background. Down below the terrace a series of artfully arranged colored lanterns had turned the expansive gardens into a shadow-filled wonderland.

She glanced at Rafe. He was a solid shadow beside her. She had to admit that the man looked incredibly sexy in his formal black evening clothes. The austere style emphasized the aura of quiet power, both physical and paranormal, that was so much a part of him. The light from a jelly-ice lantern gleamed on his near-black hair and highlighted the fascinating sweep of his cheekbones. His eyes gleamed with the lazily watchful, enigmatic expression that betrayed the depths of his strat-talent nature.

His mouth quirked as he watched her munch the stuffed pastry. "Having a good time?"

"Food's great. And I like your parents. Remind me a little of my own. It's easy to see why they both wound up in the academic world. I can't envision your father working in a corporate environment."

"My father is a strong math-talent. I'm told that it was obvious from the start that he was not cut out to take over Stonebraker. That was why my grandfather put the pressure on me."

Orchid nodded. She had been introduced to Sarah and Glen Stonebraker shortly after they had arrived. They were a striking couple who wore the mantle of their education and intelligence with unselfconscious patrician ease, just as her own parents did. They had clearly been surprised by Orchid, but they had both been gracious and charming. There had been a lot of thoughtful speculation and even some relief in their eyes, but neither had been so rude as to grill their son's "agency date."

"You look much more like your grandfather than you do your father," Orchid remarked.

"I told you, the family considers me a throwback," Rafe said. "In more ways than one."

"I wish you wouldn't use that word."

"Throwback? Why not? Everyone else does." He put one foot on the terrace and leaned forward to rest his forearm on his thigh. "It's not entirely inaccurate. My grandfather and I are alike in a lot of ways. That's why we couldn't work together."

"Rafe, get real. You couldn't take orders from anyone, let alone your grandfather."

"That's the damn truth," said a deep, gravely voice from the direction of the open door behind Rafe. "Boy was as hard-headed, independent, and stubborn as an ox-mule from the day he was born. Always had to do things his way."

"Hello, Al." Rafe took his foot down off the low terrace wall and turned to look at his grandfather. "Enjoying your birthday party?"

"What's to enjoy?" Alfred G. strolled toward them. "So far I've been hit up for campaign contributions by three different Founders' Values party candidates. Your grandmother tells me I've got to dance the tango-waltz with her at midnight and Selby is acting like he already runs Stonebraker."

"Just another typical birthday party celebration for you," Rafe said.

Alfred G. narrowed his eyes in a calculating expression that reminded Orchid of his grandson. "Why don't you go mingle or something, Rafe? Give me a chance to get to know your friend, Orchid, here."

An extremely cautious expression crossed Rafe's face. "I'm not sure it's a good idea to leave you alone with Orchid."

Alfred G.'s perfect white teeth flashed in a charmingly dangerous smile. "She's not afraid of me, are you, Orchid?"

"Of course not, Mr. Stonebraker," Orchid said politely.

"There, you see?" Alfred G. beamed triumphantly at Rafe. "Run along. Let me have a little chat with your agency date."

Rafe looked at Orchid, brows raised in silent inquiry. When Orchid nodded in equally silent agreement, he gave an "on your head be it" shrug and started toward the door.

"Good luck," he said as he walked past his grandfather. "But don't come whining to me if the little chat doesn't turn out quite the way you expect."

Fifteen minutes later Rafe noticed that neither Alfred G. nor Orchid had come in from the terrace. A trickle of unease slithered across his nerve endings. He broke off a conversation with a sixteen-year-old cousin who yearned to go to the Western Islands. Turning, he made his way back through the crowd to the open glass doors.

Alfred G.'s voice boomed out of the shadows.

"What the hell do you mean, you're going to vote for Christine Bellows? She'll run this city-state straight into the ground with her tax-and-spend ways. Daria Gardener is the woman for the job."

"Gardener is a Founders' Values candidate," Orchid said crisply. "I wouldn't vote for her if she was the last politician on St. Helens."

"Anyone who doesn't vote a straight Founders' Values ticket is an idiot and a radical to boot."

"Anyone who votes only for Founders' Values candidates is a narrow-minded, hidebound, short-sighted traditionalist."

"What's wrong with being a traditionalist?" Alfred G. roared. "This planet was colonized by traditionalists."

"We can't go back to the time of the first generation Founders, no matter how much some folks would like to return to the good old days of no jelly-ice and no paranormal abilities. We have to move forward. It's the only path for a civilization that intends to survive. And that means we have to think about the future, not the past."

"Now, you listen to me, young woman. I've had a lot more experience in the real world than you have and I'm here to tell you—"

Rafe winced and moved swiftly away from the door. He had no inclination whatsoever to go out onto the terrace.

When he turned to retreat back into the crowd, he found Selby blocking his path.

"Hello, cousin." Selby's blue eyes were calculating behind the lenses of his glasses. "I must say, I'm surprised to see you here tonight. This is the first Alfred G. birthday party you've attended since you left for the Western Islands."

Rafe eyed him thoughtfully. He and Selby were less than a year apart in age but Selby had always been a little taller and more heavily built. His light brown hair was cut by an expensive stylist at one of the city's most exclusive salons. He had the pleasant, open, rugged features that characterized the males on the Culverthorpe side of the family.

Selby had the sort of face that made people want to trust him within five seconds of meeting him. Sometimes it seemed to Rafe that he and his grandfather were the only ones who ever noticed the razor-sharp glint of vengeful bitterness in Selby's eyes.

It was not the sort of observation one could make aloud to others, Rafe reflected. He knew exactly what would happen if he told the rest of the family or the Stonebraker Board that loyal, hardworking cousin Selby was bent on destroying the company. If he tried, Rafe knew that he would probably get a stern lecture warning him not to let his primitive strat-talent nature influence his common sense and family bonds. Selby, unlike certain other ungrateful members of the clan, had devoted his entire career to Stonebraker.

"Hello, Selby."

Selby cast an ironic glance toward the terrace. "Is Uncle Al terrorizing your date?"

"My date can take care of herself."

Selby chuckled, but there was no amusement in his eyes. "You must be picking tough ones these days."

He had never liked Selby, Rafe reflected. Not even when they had been young playmates together. Selby was a tech-talent. He had been the kind of kid who could construct a miniature catapult with the new erector set he had received for Christmas before Rafe could figure out what *insert part A into slot B* meant. And then, after Rafe had finally succeeded in building a small, rather shaky fort with his own erector set, Selby had used his catapult to knock down the walls.

Things had not improved when they got to high school where Selby had always outshone Rafe in math and science. Underneath the uneven rivalry had been a simmering resentment on Selby's part. Rafe had not understood why his cousin disliked him so much until his parents told him what had happened to Selby's father. By then it was too late to mend the breach. In any event, Rafe had already made plans to head for the Western Islands. He and Selby had seen almost nothing of each other in the intervening years.

Selby swirled the vintage blue champagne in his glass and cast a speculative eye toward the door. "You don't seem overly concerned about defending your companion."

"When did you develop such a keen interest in my private life, Selby?"

"The whole family has an interest in your private life. Especially since you surprised everyone by showing up here tonight with an agency date in tow."

Rafe did not bother to correct the small misunderstanding. He wanted everyone to believe that Orchid was from a marriage agency, not a focus agency. "Why does that come as such a big surprise?"

Selby took a long swallow of champagne and then

slowly lowered the glass. "There are some who think you may have decided to play the prodigal grandson. They have a quaint vision of you returning to the fold to take control of Stonebraker."

"Don't worry about it."

"I won't." Selby's mouth curved with cool certainty. "It's too late to stop me, cousin. I've got everything in place. In two months I'll be the new C.E.O. of Stonebraker."

"You sound very sure of yourself."

"I am."

Selby's conviction resonated on the metaphysical plane. Rafe had no trouble picking up traces of it. His cousin believed every word he was saying.

Selby's wife, Briana, appeared at her husband's side. She was an attractive blonde with a social polish refined by three generations of family money. She smiled politely at Rafe but he could see the troubled look in her eyes.

"Hello, Briana." Rafe inclined his head. "Nice to see you again."

"How are you, Rafe?" Briana took Selby's arm in a gesture that was curiously protective. "It was good of you to come tonight. I know your grandmother is very happy."

"I'm glad someone is," Rafe said.

Briana slanted a glance toward the terrace. "Is this your first agency date with Miss Adams?"

"No," Rafe said. "We've gone out together several times this week. The agency thinks it's a good match. We've got a lot in common."

Ten minutes later Rafe drifted past the open terrace doors a second time. The argument outside still raged, although the subject had shifted.

"Why in five hells should Stonebraker increase the size of its charitable endowment arm?" Alfred G. snarled.

"Companies the size of Stonebraker have obligations to the community," Orchid said crisply. "The Stonebraker Foundation is puny, given the size of Stonebraker Shipping."

"Our only obligation is to stay profitable."

"Nonsense. You are a part of the community. Your precious profits are made possible because of it and you, in turn, have responsibilities to it."

"I'm not going to give away any more money than I already do."

"Talk about your basic first generation values," Orchid retorted. "The Founders understood that if a society is to be successful there must be a harmonious, synergistic balance between corporate profits and civic philanthropy. Why they even went so far as to—"

Rafe started to slink off toward the buffet table. What was taking place out on the terrace was an accident waiting to happen. He did not want to be the first one on the scene.

"Rafe?" Alfred G. bellowed. "Is that you? Come on out here. I'm having trouble talking sense into your agency date."

Alfred G.'s booming command stopped Rafe in midslink. So much for trying to slip away unnoticed. He occasionally forgot that his grandfather was also a strattalent, albeit not as strong as himself.

Reluctantly, he went through the doorway. He did not need the lantern glow to see the bright gleam in his grandfather's eyes. Alfred G. practically hummed with energy. He was enjoying himself.

Orchid smiled cheerfully. There was a sparkle in her eyes, too, Rafe noticed.

"Didn't want to interrupt your conversation," Rafe said warily.

"What conversation?" Alfred G. snapped. "We're arguing like a couple of cat-dogs. Where in blazes did you find her, Rafe?"

"I told you. An agency."

"Which agency?" Alfred G. demanded.

"It's called Psynergy, Inc.," Orchid murmured.

Rafe gave her a warning look. She shrugged one shoulder and munched another canapé.

"Never heard of it," Alfred G. said.

"That's hardly surprising," Rafe said smoothly, "given the fact that you've been married for over fifty years to grandmother. You haven't needed a matchmaking agency."

"True."

"Which reminds me, grandmother is looking for you. She said something about you having promised her a dance."

"Don't remind me." Alfred G.'s gaze slitted. "What have you been up to while Orchid and I chatted out here?"

"Selby and I renewed our childhood acquaintance."

"I'll bet seeing you here tonight gave the little twerp a jolt, eh? He must know now that you've come back to save Stonebraker from his confounded merger plans. Give him something to sweat about for the next few weeks."

The fact that Alfred G. spoke so freely in front of Orchid gave Rafe considerable pause. He glanced quickly at her and saw that she was completely unfazed.

She probably did not realize the significance of what had just happened, he thought. Alfred G. had as good as announced aloud that he had accepted her as a suitable bride for Rafe.

Waves of energy the color of old blood slashed across the psychic plane, questing for a prism with the relentless ferocity of a true predator. The vampire was close, so close.

Tonight was the night. He would find her this time. She could no longer hide. There was no point resisting any longer. She would only exhaust herself.

Fear lanced her. She knew that if even a flicker of her

*own power revealed itself the creature would seize it in
jaws of raw energy. She would be trapped forever.*

*Closer. Closer. Why not have done with this terrible
game of hide-and-seek? Why not surrender to her fate?
It would be so much easier that way.*

*She felt the powerful draw of the vampire's talent. It
reached into the smallest hiding places on the metaphysical plane, searching for prey. She saw one of the tentacles
of para-energy unfurl toward her with hungry intent.*

Tonight was the night.

She screamed.

"Orchid. Damn it, wake up. Now."

Rafe's voice cut through the unnatural darkness of
the dream, cleaving impossible shadows with the blazing
efficiency of a sword.

Orchid opened her eyes to the natural shades of night
that filled her bedroom. Moonlight spilled across the
bed. She could feel the dampness of perspiration under
her breasts and on the back of her neck.

She looked up into Rafe's taut face. His hands were
clamped fiercely around her shoulders.

"Sorry." Her voice sounded thick. She swallowed a
couple of times and tried again. "The dream. Bad.
Very bad."

He hauled her into his arms, cradling her against his
bare chest. "The same one?"

"Yes."

"Damn." She dashed the back of her hand across her
eyes to get rid of the tears of frustration that welled
there. "I didn't have it last night at your house. I was
so sure that the stupid dream had finally finished."

Rafe rocked her gently. "I guess this blows my theory
that great sex is a sure cure for nightmares."

She gave a choked cry, half laugh, half sob, and
wrapped her arms around his hard, warm body. "It was
a good theory while it lasted."

"Yes, it was. One of my best." He stroked his fingers through her hair. "Maybe it's time to see a doctor."

Orchid tensed. "No."

He eased away from her and searched her face. "Why are you so averse to getting some help?"

"Two reasons. The first is that I don't think there's much a syn-psych shrink can do about weird dreams."

"What's the second reason?"

She bit her lip. "I think I know the advice I'd get. I wouldn't follow it, anyway, so there's no sense listening to it in the first place."

"What advice would you get?"

"The first thing a doctor would do is consult my para-psych profile."

"So?"

"As soon as he or she discovered that I'm an ice-prism, I'd be referred back to that research lab where Theo and Morgan and I went through all those stupid tests."

Rafe framed her face in his hands. "What makes you so sure of that?"

"It's only logical. No one knows much about ice-prisms. The folks at that lab are considered the leading experts in New Seattle. They've got all my old records. Any syn-psych doctor worth his or her diploma would suggest that I go back there for help."

"And you won't go back there, not even as a last resort to get rid of the nightmares?"

"No." She curled her hands very tightly until she could feel her nails biting into her palms. "I wouldn't go back there if my life depended on it."

"Take it easy." Rafe held her head still and kissed her.

It was a gentling caress, not a passionate overture. Orchid felt some of the cold evaporate from her chilled body. She relaxed slightly.

"How do you feel about eating leftovers at three o'clock in the morning?" she said against his mouth.

"I can eat leftovers at any time."

She smiled. "I think I have some lasagna in the freezer. We can thaw it in the ice-wave."

"I'm drooling already. But then, I do that a lot around you."

The following afternoon Orchid stood on the gently bobbing dock that functioned as a front walk for Morgan Lambert's shabby houseboat and leaned on the front doorbell. There was no answer.

She stepped back and glanced around at the small, floating community. The neighboring houseboat was several yards away. There was no sign that anyone was home there, either.

Beneath her feet the dock heaved. Overhead gull-fins wheeled and soared ahead of the approaching storm. Heavy, dark clouds pressed down on the city.

Orchid could see a sheet of rain sweeping across the downtown highrises. It would reach this sheltered section of Curtain Lake in a few minutes. She wanted very much to be inside Morgan's houseboat before the deluge struck.

She pressed the doorbell again.

Still no answer. To ward off a sense of growing unease, she reminded herself that Morgan was an artist. He kept strange hours. Chances were good he was sound asleep inside.

She knocked loudly. "Morgan? Are you in there? It's me, Orchid. I got your message."

She had found it waiting for her on her answering machine when she walked through her front door forty-five minutes ago. He had left it earlier in the day while she had been out grocery shopping. After watching Rafe polish off her leftover lasagna last night, it dawned on her that she ought to keep more food in the icerator while he was around.

Morgan's message had been short and to the point and it had sent a jolt of alarm through her.

Orchid, this is Morgan. Listen, something kinda weird just happened. I picked up my mail on the way in a few minutes ago. You aren't going to believe it, but there's a letter from Theo. It's dated the same day that he drove off that cliff but the postmark is from yesterday. It says in the letter that he left it with a neighbor. Told the guy to mail it if he didn't contact him in a couple of days.

I'm not sure what to make of it. It's sort of typical Theo, you know, a little paranoid. Maybe I should turn it over to the police or something. But before I do anything like that I need to talk to you. Maybe I'm overreacting.

Give me a call when you get in. I don't care what time it is. Feel free to wake me up.

But awakening Morgan Lambert was proving difficult. Orchid wondered if any of his neighbors had a key. There was a deserted feel to the small houseboat marina. It was a few minutes past two o'clock in the afternoon. Everyone was either at work or out running errands.

She rapped sharply one last time.

"Morgan?"

Still no response. Tentatively she put her hand on the doorknob. It would be too much to expect that Morgan had forgotten to lock his door.

The knob turned easily.

Cautiously, half expecting an alarm to sound, she pushed open the door. "Don't panic, Morgan. It's me, Orchid."

She put her head around the edge of the door.

And caught her breath at the sight of the small, cluttered living room.

It was a shambles. Ripped cushions were scattered on the floor. Books had been pulled willy-nilly from the shelves. They lay in a small heap next to an overturned lamp. The drawers of the desk had been yanked out and emptied on the carpet.

"Oh, my God."

Orchid started to step quickly back out onto the dock. She froze when she noticed a shoe lying in the short hall that connected the living room with the kitchen.

It was a man's shoe. There was a foot in it. The leg disappeared around the corner.

"Morgan."

Ignoring all the sound advice she had ever heard about entering a residence that had been recently burglarized, she hurtled through the door.

It was Morgan who was sprawled on the kitchen floor. A small plastic envelope half-filled with gritty gray crystals lay on the table. Next to the envelope was an empty glass. There was a filthy gray residue at the bottom.

She knelt beside Morgan and fumbled desperately for a pulse.

He was still alive. She glanced up, saw the phone on the wall near the icerator, and started to get to her feet.

Before she could move something scraped in the hallway behind her. She whirled around and found herself confronting a man in a black ski mask. He held a burning jelly-ice candle. As she watched, he casually tossed aside the ice-match he had just used to light it.

"So you wanna play with fire, do you, bitch?"

Orchid opened her mouth to scream, but at that moment the walls of the hall and kitchen twisted in an impossible manner, curving and bending around her. The floor sank away beneath her feet. Her stomach reeled. She reached out to clutch the table to steady herself, but it was not where her eyes told her it should be. Instead it was tilted at a wildly improbable angle. She could not reach it.

It was as though she had stepped into a bizarre carnival funhouse. Or another universe. Voices came out of the spinning void that was the kitchen hall.

"Shit, Jink, it's her. The one who was with that guy at the house we were watching. The one who kicked me."

"It's all right. She's alone today. She won't give us

any trouble. The illusion will keep her occupied while we finish the job.''

Orchid thought she heard a man's laughter. She could not be certain. Her world had narrowed down to the small, horribly convulsing kitchen. She felt as if she were on a roller coaster. Every time she tried to orient herself, the place shifted around her.

"Watch this," someone said out of the void in the hall.

She saw the flame of the jelly-ice candle grow larger. It was the only thing in her field of vision that did not waver. She stared at it with desperate concentration. For an instant she thought the world steadied. Her hand finally made contact with the edge of the table.

Then the flame exploded into a great conflagration. Fire filled the void. Waves of brilliant orange flames lapped at the kitchen.

Panic seared her senses. She had to get out. Now. Fire blocked the hall. That left only the window.

She groped for and finally found Morgan's ankle. She tried to tug his unconscious body across the undulating kitchen toward the window. It was impossible to make any progress. The walls flowed into new configurations every time she took a step.

She thought she heard more laughter. It was followed by a woman's scream. She thought it was her own but in that wild, chaotic kitchen-universe, she could no longer be certain of anything.

Chapter

11

✧✧✧✧✧✧✧✧✧

*S*he *could not smell the smoke.*

The realization struck her with blinding clarity. Flames billowed toward her, consuming the hallway, but she could not smell any smoke. It was thick in the air around her, but if she concentrated, she had no trouble filling her lungs with clear air.

Orchid released Morgan's ankle and forced herself to think. An old adage reverberated again and again in her brain. Where there's smoke, there's fire.

But what if there was no smoke? At least, none that you could smell?

Orchid closed her eyes. Instantly the room stilled. She could feel the kitchen floor beneath her knees, right where it should have been.

She was right. There was no smoke in the kitchen. Nor could she hear the roar of the flames in the hallway.

Illusion.

She kept her eyes closed, cutting off the vision of an inferno in the hall. Gradually her jangled nerves stabilized. In the absence of visual input, her other senses began to convey logical information once more.

She became aware of the sound of rain pounding on the roof. The storm had struck. Voices came from the front room. The same voices she had heard last night when she and Rafe had encountered the two men in the unnatural fog outside Theo Willis's house.

"It has to be here somewhere."

"We've turned the place upside down, Jink. Come on, we gotta get out of here."

"Keep looking. He won't like it if we don't find it. Let's check the bedroom."

"What about the woman?"

"Forget her. She won't give us any trouble. She's too busy having a nervous breakdown out there in the kitchen."

Orchid listened to the footsteps of the two men as they receded in the direction of Morgan's bedroom. Very cautiously she opened one eye.

The flames still consumed the hall. The kitchen writhed.

Orchid quickly closed her eye. The illusion-talent was strong. So was his prism. Together they were powerful enough to maintain the vision here in the kitchen while they searched the bedroom.

There was no way she could get down the hall and across the living room without the two men noticing. Her only option was the wall phone.

Unable to trust her visual sense, she kept her eyes firmly closed and tried to recall the exact location of the icerator. Directly behind her and a little to the right.

She turned, crouched, and began to crawl blindly across the floor. Thuds echoed from the bedroom. It sounded as if the intruders were pulling drawers out of a dresser.

Orchid knew she had found the icerator when she banged her head against it. *Damn, damn, damn.* But she managed not to cry out.

She used her sense of touch to guide her to her feet.

The icerator handle was reassuringly firm in her grasp. She clung to it with one hand and groped for the wall phone with the other.

A jolt of unwarranted relief raced through her when her fingers touched the receiver. Then she realized she would have to punch out the numbers without opening her eyes.

Where were the numbers on the phone?

Think. The number one was at the top on the left. The nine had to be last. No, that wasn't right. There were all those other little buttons. The pound key. The star button.

She risked opening her eyes long enough to squint at the number pad. A mistake. The keys swam before her, each digit moving in meaningless circles.

Hastily she closed her eye and stabbed at the key she thought might be the nine. Then she fumbled for the number one key. She punched it twice. Nothing happened. How hard could it be to dial 911 without sight? she wondered.

The answer was very hard. It took her two more tries before she got it right.

"New Seattle Emergency Center."

"Fire," Orchid whispered. She hoped that the driving rain would keep the men in the other room from overhearing her. "Shelter Cove Marina."

"Please speak up, ma'am. I can barely hear you."

Orchid raised her voice slightly, listening all the while for sounds from the bedroom. "There's a fire. At Shelter Cove Marina. Houseboat number four. Hurry, please."

"I'm dispatching help right now. Can you stay on the line?"

"No." Orchid fumbled the phone back into the wall cradle.

"Sonovabitch, Jink, she got to the phone. Probably called the cops. We gotta get outa here."

"Don't worry about it. We got what we came for. Let's go."

"Shit. I thought you said the illusion would hold her."

"Don't worry, she can't tell the cops a damn thing. She never saw our faces. Come on. Move it, man. I can hear a siren."

Orchid crouched on the kitchen floor and listened to the two men run from the apartment. When she heard their footsteps outside on the dock she opened her eyes very carefully.

The kitchen was back in the right universe. The hallway was no longer filled with fire. She drew a deep breath, trying to quell the tide of adrenaline that was sending chill after chill down her spine.

She straightened slowly and picked up the phone a second time to dial the emergency number.

"New Seattle Emergency Center."

"This is number four, Shelter Cove Marina again. We need an ambulance, too."

Then she called the one person she wanted to call most of all.

Rafe.

Fifteen minutes later, Rafe stood on the dock in front of Morgan Lambert's houseboat. He had one arm locked so tightly around Orchid that it was a wonder she could breathe. He was certain that he had set a record for the short trip from his hillside house to Curtain Lake.

Her phone call had come as both a relief and a terrible confirmation of the increasing unease he had been experiencing for the past hour. He had called her home phone every five minutes after the first trickle of restlessness had hit.

At first he had felt foolish. He knew as well as everyone else that there was no such thing as telepathy. But after the night he had felt the consuming need to phone Orchid and had awakened her from one of her psychic vampire nightmares, he had not been so quick to shrug off his intuition when it concerned her.

He watched the grim scene unfolding on the street

above the marina. The rain had stopped a few minutes ago, leaving a damp sheen on the pavement. The medics were in the process of trundling the still unconscious Morgan into an ambulance. Two police cruisers were parked at odd angles. The uniformed officers were inside Lambert's apartment, taking notes.

"Are you sure you don't want to go to the emergency room?" Rafe asked Orchid for the third, possibly the fourth time. He had lost count.

"No, I'm all right, really. Just a little shaken. Rafe, the cops are going to want to talk to us after they finish inside the houseboat. You heard the officers. They're working on the assumption that Morgan overdosed himself on dirty-ice and got ripped off by some drug-dealing friends. What are we going to say?"

"There's not much we can tell them. As far as we know, that may have been exactly what happened."

She turned in the circle of his arm. Her eyes were steely green. "Morgan did not do hard drugs. He would never touch something as dangerous as dirty-ice."

"You want to tell that to the medics who just pumped out his stomach? One of them said it's a wonder he's still alive."

Her mouth tightened mutinously. "Those two intruders must have forced him to swallow the stuff. Maybe the illusion-talent made the drug look like milk or wine or something." She shivered. "It had to be the same talent-prism team we ran into the other night at Theo's house. I'm sure of it."

The bastards would pay for scaring her, he thought. But he had a hunch she would not want to hear about his plans for retribution just now. She was too busy worrying about her friend, Morgan.

"You said you think that the two men were after a letter Theo Willis sent to Lambert?"

"I heard enough to know that they were searching for something. It had to be the letter Morgan mentioned in the phone message he left on my answering machine.

Unfortunately, I think they found it. We won't know what was in it until Morgan wakes up."

"In other words, we don't have any hard facts to give to the cops."

"No. But we have to protect Morgan. Those two men wanted him dead. What if they try to get at him while he's in the hospital?"

Rafe considered the matter briefly. "I doubt that they'll risk attempted murder in a hospital. After all, Lambert can't identify them. But just in case, I know someone who will keep an eye on him. For a price."

"Who?"

"Whistler."

"Your street source? Is he also a bodyguard?"

"If the price is right."

Orchid brightened immediately. "Good idea. But that still leaves us with the problem of what to tell the cops. I know Dr. Brizo asked us to keep the stolen relic a secret, but how can we do that after what's happened?"

Easy, Rafe thought. He'd had years of experience keeping secrets. He did business under a long-established policy of protecting his clients' privacy. Furthermore, he knew only too well that if news of the missing relic hit the press, his small handful of leads would vanish. People who might know things would panic and drop out of sight. Time would be lost dealing with questions for which he did not yet have any answers.

"We've got nothing concrete to give the cops at this point," he said. "If we tell them what's going on, they'll probably assume that your friend, Lambert, is involved."

"But Morgan doesn't have anything to do with this. He's just an innocent bystander."

"Maybe, but how do you prove that? Given the few facts we have, it would be very easy to come up with a scenario in which Lambert plays a major role."

"What do you mean?"

"He was a relatively close acquaintance of Theo Willis's. One of the few friends Willis had, apparently. It would be reasonable to assume that Lambert helped Willis stage the theft of the relic."

"No. Absolutely impossible."

"I'm not so sure." Rafe warmed to his own logic. "Maybe they had a buyer for it. Maybe Lambert got greedy and decided he no longer needed Willis. Maybe he killed Willis and then tried to do the deal on his own. Hell, maybe he tried to raise the price and the buyer got pissed and sent that talent-prism team to get the relic."

"That's ridiculous. If Morgan was involved in something shady regarding the relic, why would he call me to tell me he had a letter from Theo?"

"Maybe he was trying to draw you into a trap. He may have suspected that you knew too much."

"Rafe, that's just plain crazy."

"The bottom line is, there's no hard evidence that Willis's letter even exists."

Orchid groaned and reached up to massage her temples. "Good lord, I never thought of that. You're right. If I tell them what I know, the cops might leap to the conclusion that Morgan is mixed up in this."

"He is mixed up in it." Rafe watched a medic close the ambulance door. "We just don't know how, yet."

"I refuse to believe that Morgan had anything to do with—" She broke off as one of the medics walked toward them.

He was a young man with earnest eyes and a crisp, clean-cut appearance. The name stitched on the pocket of his uniform was Paulsen. He gave Orchid a reassuring smile.

"I think your friend will be all right, ma'am. Lucky you found him when you did, though. Judging by that half-empty packet of dirty-ice, he took a major overdose. Another hour or two and he'd have been gone."

"Dead," Orchid whispered.

"Yeah." The medic nodded. "As it is, he won't wake up for at least twenty-four, maybe thirty-six hours and he'll be pretty groggy for a while after that. But with luck, he'll make it. Hope he has the sense to get himself into syn-psych drug rehab. Next time he may not be fortunate enough to have you around to save him."

The medic turned and walked back to the ambulance. Orchid stared at his retreating figure. Then she looked at Rafe.

"They really did mean to kill him," she said.

"Maybe," Rafe agreed quietly. He did not share her conviction that Morgan Lambert did not do hard drugs.

Orchid clenched her hands at her sides. "I'll bet they're the same ones who murdered Theo."

"Willis's death is still an open question. Don't forget, the police have ruled it an accident."

"It was murder. I'm sure of that now." She clenched her hands at her sides. "Rafe, I don't like the fact that two of my old crowd from the ice-prism research group got tangled up with this missing relic thing."

"Three," he corrected softly.

"What?" She shot him a quizzical glance.

"All three members of your old research study group got mixed up with the case. Willis, Lambert, and you."

"I see what you mean." Her brows drew together in a troubled frown. "It is sort of a weird coincidence, isn't it?"

"Very weird. And given the fact that one of the old gang is now dead and the second nearly got himself iced today, I think I'm going to keep a very close eye on you, partner."

Rafe left two more messages with Quentin Austen's gum-snapping secretary, but Austen returned none of the calls. The investment ploy was not working as well as it usually did. Time to try a different approach.

He was working on the new angle when the phone finally rang.

It was not Austen. It was Hobart Batt.

"I contacted Affinity Associates, Mr. Stonebraker," Hobart said stiffly. "Apparently you were misinformed.

There is no Miss Orchid Adams registered with that agency."

Rafe tightened his grip on the phone. "Are you positive?"

"Absolutely. I spoke with one of the counselors. He very kindly double-checked the firm's files. He assured me that he has no record of her registration. None of the three counselors who work there remember her, although—"

"Although, what?"

Hobart sighed. "One of the counselors who was with the firm until a couple of months ago left to take a position in New Vancouver. It's possible, I suppose, that she was the one who worked with your Miss Orchid. But even if that were the case, the file would have remained with Affinity Associates after she left. Someone else would have been assigned to handle Miss Adams."

"Handling Miss Adams is easier said than done," Rafe said before hanging up the phone.

Interesting, he thought. What were the odds of Orchid's file getting lost in a small agency such as Affinity Associates? Probably vanishingly small. Unless, of course, someone had deliberately seen to it that the file went missing.

As far as he could tell, the only person who had a reason to lose Orchid's marriage registration file was Orchid herself.

He was still mulling over the problem of Orchid's mysteriously missing file that night as he stood in the darkened hall outside the offices of Dr. Quentin Austen.

Orchid watched as he used a pick to deactivate the ice lock on the glass-paned door. "Are you sure Dr. Austen is out of town?"

"I found out late this afternoon that he suddenly canceled all his appointments for the next couple of weeks and took an impromptu vacation. His receptionist doesn't know where he went."

"Hmm." She glanced up and down the hall again. "What if there's an alarm?"

"There isn't. I checked."

"How?"

"Called the building manager's office this afternoon. Pretended to be a sales rep for an alarm company. Said I'd make it worth his while if he'd supply me with the names of tenants in the building who might be potential clients. Austen's name was on the list."

"Meaning that he did not already have a system?"

"That was the obvious assumption."

"What if your assumption is wrong?" she asked.

"I'll think of something."

"My, this is an exciting hobby you've found for yourself."

"Beats the heck out of stamp collecting."

He heard the faint hiss as the jelly-ice dissolved temporarily inside the lock, releasing the bolt.

He eased the door open and waited for a few seconds, listening with all his senses.

Nothing. Austen's offices were deserted for the night.

"All right, here we go," he said softly. "Watch your step. We don't want to make any noise that would attract the night janitor's attention."

"I'm surprised there is a night janitor. This isn't exactly a high-rent office building. Guess Austen isn't the world's most successful syn-psych shrink."

Orchid followed him into the outer office and gently closed the door behind her. "What, exactly, are we going to look for in here?"

"I'm not sure. I'll know it when I see it."

There were two sets of file cabinets in the outer office. The drawers in the one nearest the receptionist's desk were not locked. Those in the larger cabinet on the other side of the room were. Rafe started with them.

There was no trick to deactivating the simple drawer locks. He opened the one that contained the files of patients whose last names began with Q through Z. He played the narrow beam of the flashlight over the names on the folders.

There was no file for Theo Willis.

Orchid peered over his shoulder. "I suppose that would have been too easy."

"Probably."

He closed the drawer and walked into the inner office. It was furnished with two padded leather chairs, one of which had a side table standing next to it. There was a box of tissue on the table. The client's chair, Rafe decided. The prints on the walls were nondescript designs in pale pastels. Probably intended to be soothing, he thought. They looked dull and lifeless to him. The rug was the shade of discreet gray that was guaranteed not to show stains for years. The desk was a cheap reproduction of an Early Exploration period piece.

Rafe aimed the flashlight at the top of the desk. The only items on it were a telephone, a leather blotter, and a fountain pen in a wooden stand.

"A little too neat, if you ask me," Orchid said. "I never trust anyone who maintains a perfectly clear desk."

"I'll remember that. Here, hold the flashlight while I go through it."

She stood over him and aimed the light while he quickly went through the desk's four drawers. Nothing caught his eye until he opened the last one on the bottom left-hand side and discovered a stack of garishly colored magazines.

"Well, well, well." Orchid bent down for a closer look.

Rafe glanced at the bulging nude breasts that filled virtually the entire cover of the first magazine in the stack. He lifted it and looked at the second one. It contained an enlarged closeup of a woman's naked buttocks.

"Looks like Austen has a few fixations of his own," Rafe said.

"Do you suppose the good doctor uses these magazines for therapy?" Orchid asked.

"More likely he uses them to jack off with in the men's room down the hall when he gets a break between clients." Rafe closed the drawer. "Damn. They've got to be here somewhere."

"What?"

"The billing records."

Ten minutes later he found what he was looking for in one of the unlocked file cabinet drawers next to the receptionist's desk. Satisfaction stirred in his gut when he found a file labeled *Willis, T.* There was a partially filled out billing log inside.

"We're in luck. Whoever removed the patient file on Theo Willis did not remember to take the financial stuff," he said.

"Or didn't think that there was anything important in that file." Orchid studied the log as Rafe removed it from the cabinet. "After all, what can you tell from it except that Theo was one of Dr. Austen's clients? We already know that."

"But this is our proof. And the fact that Willis's patient file is missing is a good indication that someone, probably Austen, did not want us to be able to link him to this office."

"In other words, the fact that there's no file on Theo tells us more than if we had found one."

"That's it in a nutshell. You know, I think you're getting the hang of this detective business."

"I told you, I have a flair for it."

Rafe scanned the list of payments. "Two months of therapy. It fits with what we saw on his calendar. He was going five times a week during the last two weeks before he died."

"Poor Theo. He must have been in really bad shape there at the end."

"Looks like it." Rafe started to drop the billing record back into the drawer. Something caught on the edge of the file folder. He turned the record over and saw a small, pink sticky note.

"What is it?" Orchid stood on tiptoe, trying to see over his shoulder. "What did you find?"

"Nothing much. Looks like someone, Austen's receptionist, probably, jotted a note to remind herself to send a thank-you for the patient referral. It's common practice for one doctor to thank another who refers a patient to him."

"Oh, right." Orchid dropped down off her toes and turned away. "Well, that's that. We know that Theo was getting some very intensive therapy shortly before he died. Looks like we'd better find Austen, doesn't it?"

"Yes." Rafe dropped the log into the file and shut the cabinet door. "I think the doctor will be able to tell us a great deal. The fact that he decided to take a sudden vacation today makes me even more interested in what he has to say about Willis."

"Rafe?"

He glanced over his shoulder and saw that Orchid had walked back into the inner office. She had her small flashlight aimed at a row of framed certificates that hung on the paneled wall.

"What is it?"

"Dr. Austen's diploma and professional certificates."

"What about them?" He went to stand in the doorway. "Most doctors hang their credentials on the walls of their offices."

"One of these papers is his paranormal talent certificate," she said slowly. "Rafe, Austen is a class-seven hypno-talent."

He frowned. "That's rather high for paranormal hypnotic ability, isn't it?"

"Extremely high. As a professional prism, I can tell you that it's almost unheard of to have such a high level of hypnotic talent. A lot of syn-psych therapists have some hypno-talent, of course. It's one of the things that makes them suited to the field of synergistic psychology. But the normal range is class three or four, at the most.

Austen is no off-the-chart vampire, but he is exceptionally powerful."

"Strong enough to have manipulated Theo Willis with hypnosis?"

Orchid lowered her flashlight and turned to look at him. Her expression was shadowed. "Theoretically, no one can be hypnotized into doing something against his will. But Theo had a lot of syn-psych problems. He was fragile."

"In other words, there's no telling what a clever, powerful, trained hypno-talent could do once he got his hands on Theo's para-psych history and figured out which buttons to push."

"Yes. Even working without a prism, a class-seven hypno-talent could do a lot of damage to a person as delicate as Theo." Orchid's eyes grew bleak. "I've been saying all along that Theo was no thief. But I hadn't considered the possibility that he could have been hypnotized into stealing the relic."

"So now we have a means." Rafe said. "Austen may well have hypnotized Willis and convinced him to steal the relic."

"We don't know that for certain."

Rafe ignored her caveat. Things were finally starting to feel right. He had long ago learned to trust his hunter's instincts at times like this. "What we need to do next is nail down the motive. I see a couple of possibilities."

"Austen either had Theo steal the artifact for him, which means the doctor is a secret, eccentric collector of alien relics—

"Or Austen acted as a broker. He could have arranged for Willis to steal the relic for someone else."

"There's a third possibility," Orchid pointed out.

"What's that?"

"Dr. Austen has got an even more screwed-up para-profile than Theo had."

"Believe me, the fact that Quentin Austen may be crazy has not escaped me."

Chapter

12

❖❖❖❖❖❖❖❖❖

Orchid rolled onto her side, propped herself up on one elbow, and looked down at Rafe, who was sprawled on his back beside her. "Are you awake?"

"I am now." He curved one hand behind his head. The light of the twin moons pouring down through the glass dome revealed the faint curve of his mouth. "So are you, obviously."

"I've been thinking."

"By an odd coincidence, so have I."

She settled herself more comfortably. "You're thinking about Quentin Austen, aren't you?"

"Among other things. I've been wondering all day why he chose to take a sudden, mysterious vacation. Now I think it's safe to assume that he's in this up to his syn-psych diploma."

"Do you think he might have arranged to have poor Theo murdered?"

"I can't say for certain yet." Rafe drew one fingertip along the curve of her shoulder. "But my instincts tell me Austen is probably not the killer."

"What makes you so certain?"

"Austen appears to be a novice at this kind of thing. If he had more experience, he would have done a more thorough job of getting rid of anything that linked him to Theo Willis."

"You're saying he isn't the brains behind the operation?"

"I'm not sure yet. He was smart enough to panic when he got a call out of the blue from someone who wanted to talk to him about some so-called investments. And he did think to yank Willis's file before he took off on vacation."

"What about that illusion-talent and prism team we keep running into?"

"They're not operating under hypnotic instruction," he said with grave certainty. "They're hired pros."

Orchid shuddered. "Yes."

"Austen must have sent them to keep watch on Theo Willis's house and then ordered them to find Willis's letter and get rid of your friend, Morgan Lambert."

"This is getting more complicated by the minute."

"No, we're finally getting somewhere. We've got some firm leads to follow."

She felt the strat-talent energy vibrating through him. The hunter had caught the scent of the prey. She wondered if this aspect of his nature ought to disturb her. It did not. Perhaps because she could sense the control he wielded over his talent.

"I'd like to know what it was in Theo's file that made Austen think he needed to remove it," she said.

"Speaking of missing files," Rafe said softly.

"Hmm?"

"Theo Willis's is not the only one that seems to have disappeared recently."

Something in the low tenor of his voice alerted her. Orchid dragged her thoughts back from the problem of Theo's connection to Quentin Austen and the missing relic.

"What are you talking about?"

Rafe turned onto his side, levered himself up on his elbow, and gently but firmly pushed her onto her back. He leaned over her, eyes gleaming in the darkness. "Your file at Affinity Associates is gone."

She was so surprised she could only gape for a few seconds. When she finally got her jaw working again, she swallowed twice before she asked very cautiously, "How do you know that?"

"I checked."

"Why?"

"Call it professional curiosity."

"Professional curiosity, my foot."

He ignored that. "Did you take it?"

"Huh? Me?"

"Yeah, you. Did you steal your own file so that you wouldn't run the risk of a bad match?"

"Steal my file? Are you nuts? Until I met you, I didn't even know how to do stuff like that. There must be some mistake." Orchid broke off when she caught the all but imperceptible trace of invisible psychic energy shimmering in the air between them. "Stop that this instant."

"Stop what?"

"You're trying to use your strat-talent to see if I'm telling the truth. Admit it."

"Everyone knows that there's nothing to those old stories about strat-talents being human lie-detectors." He lowered his mouth to hers.

Orchid hesitated briefly, tempted to continue the argument. But when she felt the hard outline of his thigh against hers, she groaned and put her arms around his neck. She would save the lecture until later, she thought. And the mystery of her missing file could wait, too.

Right now the heat of Rafe's aroused body was warming her through the sheet that separated them. She was suddenly, desperately aware of his fingertips on her nipple.

No one had ever touched her the way Rafe did. No one had ever aroused the exquisite, almost painfully intense sensations in her that he aroused. She shivered and felt his immediate response.

When they came together like this it was as if they had been made for each other.

The joy of knowing that she had the same passionate effect on him infused her with a heady excitement. She kneaded the sleek contours of his shoulders.

His mouth moved to her throat and then to her breast. She arched in his arms. His hand slipped beneath her. He clenched his fingers around her hip, squeezed gently, and then found the impossibly sensitive places between her legs.

Heat swelled.

"Rafe."

He rolled onto his back and pulled her down on top of him. When she opened her eyes she saw that his face was set in unrelenting lines of fierce desire. She cradled the rigid length of him in her palm.

"You don't know what you do to me," he whispered.

When his hand moved up the inside of her leg she cried out and stiffened. His finger, wet and slick with her own moisture, moved across her straining clitoris. A great tightness seized her. She sank her nails into his shoulders and gripped him with her thighs.

He did not thrust into her until the first ripples of her climax began. And then, just when she thought she was at the pinnacle, he entered her, deeply, fully.

The feel of him stretching her and filling her so completely at that moment was almost too much to handle on top of the already effervescent sensations that were sweeping through her.

And then she felt his questing talent searching for her on the psychic plane. She responded to it instinctively, joyously, with a sense of absolute rightness.

Power crashed through the perfectly tuned prism.

She heard Rafe's hoarse shout of release, but she

could no longer even open her eyes. She was lost in the synergistic vortex of energy and sensation that engulfed her.

Rafe lay awake for a long time after Orchid fell asleep in his arms. He watched the twin moons move across the arc of the glass dome until they disappeared. His mind teemed with mysteries. He had encountered a great number of them lately. One way or another, they all seemed to revolve around Orchid.

But the biggest mystery of all was Orchid herself.

No, he thought. The most enigmatic mystery in all this was his own reaction to her. He had never experienced anything like it before in his life. So how was it that he could sense the rightness in it?

The following afternoon Orchid drove into downtown with the vaguely guilty exhilaration of a young truant skipping school. It had not been easy escaping from Rafe for even an hour. After the attack on Morgan Lambert he had scarcely let her out of his sight. It seemed to her that he was always prowling nearby, watching over her.

But she had finally managed to convince him that it would be reasonably safe for her to drive to Psynergy, Inc., alone to collect her check.

"Nothing's going to happen in broad daylight on Founders' Day," she had assured him. "Whoever these people are, they obviously prefer to do things in secret. A couple of guys wearing ski masks in downtown New Seattle won't go unnoticed. You've got stuff to do here. There's no need to chaperone me."

Rafe had been reluctant, but in the end he had conceded that she had a point. He stood on the front steps and watched her drive out through the high gates. In the rearview mirror the grim expression of concern on his face was clear. She knew that he was already regretting his decision to let her go into town by herself. She put her foot down very hard on the gas, half afraid that he would find some way to stop her at the last minute.

A peculiar mix of relief and anxiety plagued her as she drove down First Avenue. This business of sharing space with Rafe was turning out to be more complicated than she had anticipated. She was not accustomed to having a man underfoot all the time. The experience left her with mixed feelings. On the one hand, she was grateful to have his strat-talent expertise on her side while they worked to untangle the mysteries surrounding Theo's death and the missing relic.

But her own emotions concerning her lover-client were rapidly becoming more convoluted and complex than the case itself.

She had an unnerving suspicion that this was how it felt to fall in love.

The downtown section of New Seattle was festively decorated for Founders' Day. Banners snapped in the breeze. Restaurants advertised first generation–style beer and old-fashioned Founders' burgers and traditional pear-berry pie. Signs were posted warning that the streets were to be cleared of all parked vehicles two hours before the evening parade began.

The Friends of the Library had erected a display of a huge book made entirely of various colored flowers in front of the public library. It represented one of the first generation hand-made books that the colonists crafted in their desperate attempt to preserve some of the knowledge trapped in their disintegrating computer data bases. Orchid was forced to blink rapidly for a few seconds as she drove past the inspiring flower sculpture. Everyone was entitled to a few tears of pride on Founders' Day, she told herself.

Fifteen minutes later she walked through the door of Psynergy, Inc.

"Happy Founders' Day, Byron. Got my check?"

Byron looked up from the gossip column of his favorite tabloid, *Synsation*. He stared at her over the rims of

his purple spectacles. His expression was one of fascinated horror.

"*Run*. Run while you still can," he hissed as he
glanced wildly over his shoulder toward the closed door
of Clementine's office. "Run for your life. Save yourself."

"I'm not running anywhere until I get my paycheck."
Orchid walked to the desk, pushed aside a stack of
"Think Exclusive" posters, and glanced down at the
open page of *Synsation*. "What's the big news today?
Any more alien abductions reported?"

"Nothing so tame and ordinary." He stabbed at a picture on the page. "Take a good look."

Orchid studied the grainy photo. It showed a couple
getting out of a car in front of a large, sprawling mansion. The picture had obviously been shot from a long
distance. Nevertheless, the car looked vaguely familiar.
So did the sleek set of the shoulders of the man whose
face was turned partially away from the camera. When
she looked closer she was almost certain she recognized the
vee that dipped to the waist of the slim-fitting gown the
woman wore.

"Good heavens, that isn't—?"

"You and Rafe Stonebraker?" Byron grinned malevo-
lently. "Indeed it is, my dear. The Stonebraker birthday
party is one of *the* social events of the year and," he
paused for emphasis, *"you were there."*

Orchid grimaced. "I can't imagine why anyone bothered to take a picture of me."

"I hate to be crass about it, but I doubt if anyone
would have bothered to get a shot of you had you not
been on the arm of the heir apparent to the Stonebraker dynasty."

"Oh, yeah. Right. I forgot about that part." Orchid
straightened, chuckling. "Thanks, Byron. You do know
how to put a person in her place. Got my check?"

"Yes, but I don't think there's any big rush to give it
to you."

"Why not, pray tell?"

Byron winced as Clementine's door crashed open. "Because the boss is going to murder you long before you ever reach the bank."

"What?" Orchid looked across the room, straight into the face of a charging buzz-saw. "Uh oh."

"Five hells, Orchid Adams, I ought to fire your ass," Clementine slapped a copy of the *New Seattle Times* against her leather-clad thigh. "How could you do this to me? After all I've done for you."

"All you ever did for me was give me a part-time job, Clementine. You were in desperate need of a full-spectrum ice-prism, as I recall. So were a number of other focus agencies in town." Orchid glanced at the newspaper. "What seems to be the problem here?"

"Problem?" Clementine's voice rose. "I'll tell you what the problem is. You went to the hottest social event in town last night and the damn newspapers got everything wrong. You screwed up the single most important opportunity anyone at Psynergy, Inc., has had in recent memory to project our new exclusive image, that's what's wrong."

"The real question," Byron murmured behind his newspaper, "is did she also screw the single, most important client Psynergy, Inc., happens to have at the moment. Enquiring minds—"

Orchid glared at him. "Shut up, Byron, or I will personally stuff every single one of those 'Think Exclusive' posters down your throat."

"Yes, ma'am." He buried his nose in *Synsation*.

Orchid turned back to Clementine. "What do you mean the newspapers got everything wrong?"

"You're identified as Rafe Stonebraker's agency date," Clementine said in ominous tones.

"So?"

"The damned society reporter makes it sound as though you were from a matchmaking agency, not a focus agency. What's more, he didn't even get Psynergy, Inc.'s name into the article."

Orchid exhaled deeply. "Clementine, I'm working undercover, remember? Rafe wanted to pass me off as a marriage agency date last night. He doesn't want anyone to know I'm working with him on a professional basis."

"But it was such a perfect opportunity to promote Psynergy, Inc., as an exclusive focus agency."

She looked so woebegone that Orchid felt sorry for her. She crossed the room to pat Clementine's broad shoulder.

"There, there. I promise that when this is all over, I'll get Rafe to mention Psynergy, Inc., to some of his friends. Okay?"

"I guess that's the best we can hope for now that you've wasted this incredible opportunity."

"That's the spirit. Now, can I please have my check?"

"Sure, sure. Give her the check, Byron." Clementine eyed Orchid closely. "Uh, there's just one other small thing."

Orchid took the envelope Byron handed to her. "What's that?"

"All that stuff in the paper about Rafe Stonebraker parading his so-called agency date in front of his family and the members of the board of directors of Stonebraker Shipping—?"

"What about it?"

"That was just part of the cover you and Stonebraker established, right? There wasn't any truth in it, was there?"

"Don't be ridiculous." Orchid walked very quickly toward the door. "Have a great Founders' Day."

She flung the door open and fled down the hall to the elevator.

By the time she reached the street, she had herself firmly under control. The sign above the entrance to the espresso shop across the street caught her eye.

The decision to waste a few minutes having a coff-tea latte by herself was an impromptu one. As soon as she sat down at one of the small tables however, she knew she had done the right thing.

She needed to think about Rafe. She could not do that very clearly when he was in the vicinity.

Unfortunately, she discovered as she sipped her latte and stared at the poster-covered wall, it was not easy to think clearly about him when he was safely out of sight, either.

A shadow fell across her tiny table. Visions of ski-masked men flashed before her eyes. She jerked, spilling several drops of her latte.

"Sorry," Selby Culverthorpe gave her a cool smile. "Didn't mean to startle you."

She composed herself and carefully set down her cup. "Did you follow me, Mr. Culverthorpe?"

"I did some checking this morning. There was some confusion last night about which matchmaking agency you're registered with."

"Is that so?"

"In the process of sorting it out, I discovered that you work part-time at Psynergy, Inc. I was on my way there to see if the staff would help me contact you when I saw you walk out the door and head for this espresso bar."

"Mr. Culverthorpe—"

"Call me Selby. After all, we were properly introduced last night. Mind if I sit down?"

She could not come up with any reason to refuse. The introduction to Selby and his wife, Briana, at the party had been fleeting at best but it had been made by Rafe's grandmother. Orchid knew she could not be rude without a very good excuse, which she did not yet have.

"Of course not." She indicated the seat on the other side of the tiny table. "Why were you looking for me?"

"Because you and I need to talk, Ms. Adams." Selby sat down across from her. "We have a mutual problem."

"What problem is that?"

"My cousin Rafe." Selby smiled again. His eyes glinted behind the lenses of his stylish glasses. "Fortunately, I have a solution."

"I don't understand."

"I'll get right to the point. The Stonebraker board is a very conservative bunch, Ms. Adams. They would never appoint a C.E.O. who was not married or, at the very least, engaged to be married."

"Is that a fact?"

"Yes," Selby said. "It's a fact. But I strongly suspect that you are already aware of it. I admit that, until recently, I've been working under the assumption that my cousin has no interest in Stonebraker. But I may have figured wrong."

"What changed your mind?"

"Seeing you with Rafe at Uncle Alfred G.'s birthday party last night. I can think of only one reason why my cousin would suddenly spring an agency date on the family. I think he's decided to try to take back what he walked away from all those years ago when he quarreled with Alfred G."

"Why are you telling me all this, Mr. Culverthorpe?"

"Because I don't think you know what you're getting into, Ms. Adams. Rafe may have found you through a matchmaking agency, although, I have some doubts on that score. But even if it's true, I'm willing to bet that it's not a high-probability match."

"What do you mean?"

"If it's a real match, my guess is that he applied pressure to his agency counselor to force him to come up with a candidate." Selby paused deliberately. "But it's equally possible that Rafe found one for himself and bribed her to play the role."

"Are you implying that Rafe would resort to intimidation or bribery?"

Icy amusement flared in Selby's gaze. "Don't look so shocked. I know my cousin. Rafe will do whatever it takes to get what he wants, if he wants it badly enough."

"What makes you so certain Rafe and I might not be a good match?"

"Give me a break, Ms. Adams. I'm not a fool. My cousin is a strat-talent."

"So?"

"He's an exotic. A high-class one at that. The agencies don't have much luck matching people like him. Even if you were told that you might be a halfway reasonable match, I'm surprised you'd considered it at all. Very few intelligent women want to risk marriage to a hunter. Too many unknowns. Marriage is a life sentence, Ms. Adams."

"I'm well aware of that. But Rafe's grandfather is a strat-talent and from what I saw last night he appears to be happily married."

"Uncle Alfred G. is only a class-four strat-talent. Rafe is a six. I suspect he may even be much higher." Selby's eyes narrowed. "Furthermore, I'll let you in on a little family secret. Uncle Alfred G. and Aunt Ellen were not introduced through an agency."

"Is that true?"

"It was a marriage of convenience that took place over fifty years ago. Aunt Ellen's father owned a company that Uncle Alfred G. wanted. Ellen's father wanted his daughter to marry into the Stonebraker family. They struck a deal. Aunt Ellen went along with it."

"It looked like a good match to me."

Selby dismissed that with a casual lift of one shoulder. "Occasionally unmatched arrangements do work out. Hell, if legend is to be believed, that's the way marriages were routinely handled back on Earth in the old days before colonization. They say divorce was routine, also."

"And families were routinely destroyed because of the system. Fortunately our Founders were smart enough to establish a different way of doing things here on St. Helens," she murmured piously.

"Exactly my point, Ms. Adams." Selby leaned back in his chair and gave her a meaningful look. "The risk factor is huge in an unmatched marriage. And there is no escape through divorce here on St. Helens."

"Everyone knows that."

"You'd better think twice about a low-probability match, too, Ms. Adams. Even if your prospective groom is rich."

"You're so sure that Rafe and I are a bad match."

"You may think it's worth the risk. Maybe you're assuming that if things don't work out after the wedding, you and my cousin can live separate lives. Maybe you think you can have it all, the Stonebraker money, social position, and a few discreet affairs on the side. But it won't work that way."

"Why not?"

Selby smiled grimly. "Because my cousin is a strat-talent. Take it from me, strat-talents aren't real sophisticated and modern-thinking when it comes to matters of wifely fidelity. There's a reason they're called throwbacks, Ms. Adams."

"I beg your pardon?"

"I would have thought you'd know all this. You're a trained, professional prism, after all. Strat-talents are primitive in more than just the paranormal sense. If you're planning on a marriage of convenience, think again."

"Is this a warning?"

"Yes, Ms. Adams, it is." Selby leaned forward. "I've got nothing against you, personally, but I've worked too hard and planned too long to let you or anyone else get in my way. I'm going to destroy Stonebraker. If you don't step aside, you'll get hurt."

"Tell me," Orchid said gently, "why are you so determined to destroy the company? You're part of the family, after all."

"My reasons are none of your business."

"I disagree. I think I've got a right to know why I'm being threatened by a rich and powerful man such as yourself."

Selby frowned. "I'm not threatening you. I'm simply telling you how things are."

"I feel threatened. I want to know why before I make any decisions."

Selby drew back, scowling. "I'm sure as hell not going to tell you a lot of private family information."

Orchid stirred her latte with a tiny stick. "Tell me, Selby, what did Rafe's side of the family do to your side to make you so angry?"

It was as if she had pulled a sandbag out of a dike that held back a wall of flood water. Selby's face contorted with sudden fury. Sharp, short bursts of energy came and went quickly on the psychic plane. A sure sign of paranormal power not under firm control. Orchid recalled Rafe telling her that his cousin was a tech-talent.

"Maybe I should tell you what happened," Selby said. "Maybe the truth will convince you of just how dangerous a strat-talent can be, especially if he also happens to be very wealthy and powerful."

"I'm listening."

"Uncle Alfred G. is responsible for my father's death. That's what the Stonebraker side of the family did to my side. Satisfied, Ms. Adams?"

Orchid's hand froze on the latte stick. "That's a very serious accusation."

"Unfortunately it's one I can't make in a court of law because there is no evidence. Alfred G. saw to that. But I have crafted my own justice, Ms. Adams. Don't get in the way."

"What makes you think your father was deliberately killed?"

Selby hesitated. Orchid watched him as he visibly reasserted his self-control. She sensed that he already regretted the fierce outburst.

"My mother told me the whole story when I was a child."

"What did she say? What happened to your father?"

Selby shook his head once, as though ridding himself of the last remnants of a spell. "This is none of your affair. You don't need to know the details. All you need to know is that men like Rafe and Alfred G. Stonebraker are dangerous."

"I only want to understand."

"You don't need to understand anything except that if you don't get out of this thing while the getting is good, you'll be hurt." He pushed back his chair with an abrupt movement and surged to his feet. "There won't be any more warnings, Ms. Adams."

"Wait, please."

Selby had himself back in hand now. The seething emotion that had blazed briefly in his face was gone. He looked down at her with cool speculation. "You appear to be a smart woman. I would have thought you'd know better than to get involved with a strat-talent. If you're in this for the money, I sympathize. But there are other ways to get rich without risking marriage to my cousin."

"What are you talking about?"

"I'm a wealthy man now, but I'm going to be far richer after I carry out my plans for Stonebraker. I'll make it worth your while to drop out of the picture."

"Oh, wow." She opened her eyes very wide. "No one's ever tried to buy me off before."

Selby's jaw jerked. "Think about my offer, Ms. Adams. Think about it very carefully. Because one way or another, I'm going to win."

He turned and walked out of the espresso bar without another word. An invisible wake of old rage and pain churned in the air behind him. Orchid picked up traces of it on both the physical and the metaphysical planes.

Chapter

13

❖❖❖❖❖❖❖❖❖

Rafe grabbed the phone before it had a chance to ring a second time. "Orchid, where the hell are you?"

There was a short, baffled pause on the other end.

"Uh, it's me, Whistler, Mr. Stonebraker. Here at the hospital guarding Mr. Lambert, remember?"

Rafe closed his eyes briefly and willed patience and control. This was insane. He was getting downright jumpy where Orchid was concerned. She was only a few minutes late, after all. She'd probably stopped to do some shopping or collect her mail.

"Sorry, Whistler. I was expecting someone else. What have you got for me?"

"Nothing's happening here but, y'know those guys you asked about? An illusion-talent and prism team who might do odd jobs if the money was right?"

"Did you find them?"

"Maybe. There's a talent-prism magic act working at a low-rent club in Founders' Square. They use knives in the show. Word is, the talent is pretty good with them.

The special effects aren't all illusions, if you see what I mean."

"What about the odd jobs?"

"I hear that, for a price, you can hire them to do some rough work. A man I know says he thinks they've been working off the books a lot lately."

"Did your associate tell you who hired them?"

"He doesn't know who the employer is. Fact is, he didn't know much of anything. Whatever is going on, it's real hush-hush."

"What's the name of the club?"

"Place is called the Icy Dicey Casino." Whistler lowered his voice. "I'm not sure if these are your guys, but I can't turn up any other talent-prism team that fits the description you gave me."

"This sounds promising." Rafe heard a car in the drive. He got to his feet. "I'll check it out. Thanks, Whistler."

"What about my money?"

"The usual arrangements. You'll have it tomorrow morning. In the meantime, stay with Lambert."

"You got it."

Rafe slammed down the phone and went to stand in the door of the study. He would remain calm, he promised himself. Poised. Serene. Casual. He would not demand explanations for the fact that she was twenty minutes late. She would get nervous if he leaped down her throat every time she walked through the front door. The last thing he wanted to do was make her nervous.

The door opened. Orchid stepped across the threshold. She smiled wanly when she saw him.

"Hello, Rafe."

"Where the hell have you been?" He winced at the sound of his own harsh voice. So much for serene and casual.

"Charming greeting." She tossed her purse down on a side table. "Good thing we're business associates, not

185

an engaged couple or else I might be tempted to walk back out the door."

The tension shimmered like an aura around her. He started forward. "What happened?"

"Nothing."

"Don't give me that. I know something happened. What was it?"

"Take it easy, Rafe. I had a short, informative conversation with your cousin, that's all."

He wasn't sure he had heard correctly. "No."

"No?"

"Selby wouldn't have dared." But he could see in her eyes that he had dared. "Sonovabitch. What did he say?"

"Among other things he said he doubted that you and I were a high-probability match. In fact, he's not altogether sure we're even a legitimate agency match. Can you imagine? Oh, yes, he also warned me against the risks of marriage to a strat-talent. And then he tried to buy me off."

Rafe was startled by the wildfire heat of his own anger. "Bastard." He did not realize he had lost control of his talent until he felt the familiar slight disorientation that occurred whenever he initiated a quest for a prism. His instincts revved to full throttle.

"Calm down, Rafe." Orchid watched him. She did not offer him a prism.

Rafe felt the uncomfortable heat rise in his face. Instantly he clamped down on his unquiet psychic energy. Until Orchid had entered his life, he had never had these problems. He had always been in full control of himself and his talent.

"I'll talk to Selby," he vowed. "He won't bother you again."

"He didn't actually bother me. He made me very curious, however. He's obviously as determined to wreck Stonebraker as you are to save it." She folded her arms and leaned back against the table. "Mind telling me what actually did happen to his father back when Selby was a kid?"

Rafe gripped the edge of the door. "He told you that old story about how my grandfather is responsible for his father's death?"

"He wouldn't give me the entire tale. Just enough to, shall we say, pique my interest."

Rafe felt as if the floor had fallen away beneath his feet. "You didn't believe him, did you?"

"I don't know what to believe. That's why I'm asking you for the truth."

Rafe watched her. "You're serious, aren't you?"

"I'm assuming there's a logical explanation here. I'd like to have it."

He stilled. "It's a family thing."

She gave him a humorless smile. "Yes, of course. It always is, isn't it? And I'm not family."

"It's not that." He broke off. "Okay, it is that."

"If you want my help on this *family thing*, you'd better tell me the whole story."

He hesitated and then made an executive decision. "I don't know the whole story, myself. My grandfather has never talked about it. But a few years ago, I got curious. I did some checking."

"What did you discover?"

Rafe shoved a hand through his hair, turned, and walked into the library. He heard Orchid's footsteps behind him. When he stopped and glanced back at her he saw that she was watching him very closely. Too closely.

It occurred to him that she had no real reason to trust him on this or anything else. He was surprised by how restless the knowledge made him. He had no claim on her loyalty, he reminded himself. As far as she was concerned, he was only a business associate and a temporary lover.

Depressed by that thought, he sank into one of the deep chairs in front of the cold hearth.

"Selby's father was named Perry Culverthorpe. The Culverthorpes are cousins on my grandmother's side."

"I figured that much out for myself." Orchid took the seat across from him. "Go on."

"At one time the Culverthorpes were a lot more powerful than the Stonebrakers. But things changed. Perry Culverthorpe never really accepted the reversal of fortunes that gave the Stonebrakers the more prominent role in the New Seattle shipping business. He felt he'd been somehow cheated of his rightful heritage."

"What happened?"

Rafe met her eyes. "My grandfather put him in charge of the New Vancouver office. There were some problems. A series of thefts occurred. It became obvious that someone was bypassing the jelly-ice seals on the cargo containers. The only one who had the code was Perry Culverthorpe."

"Did your grandfather accuse him of stealing valuable freight?"

"Not exactly. From what I was able to discover, Alfred G. went to New Vancouver to find out what the hell was going on. Perry was furious. He felt he'd been humiliated by my grandfather's lack of trust. He and Alfred G. had a major blow-up. Alfred G. removed Perry from his position as head of the New Vancouver office."

"Perry must have been enraged."

"Yes. In an effort to prove that he was innocent of the thefts, he set a trap for the thieves. He succeeded in surprising them, but he was killed in the process."

"How awful."

"When it was all over, the real thieves were caught, but Perry's wife never forgave my grandfather. She blamed him for Perry's death."

"And she taught Selby to blame him, too."

Rafe shrugged. "She taught him to blame all the men on my side of the family. Aunt Elizabeth was very ill for a long time. It affected her mind. By the time she died, she had convinced herself that if Perry had lived, he would have taken my grandfather's place at the helm of Stonebraker Shipping and Selby, ultimately, would have followed in his father's footsteps. Selby grew up believing that."

"I see."

Silence descended. Rafe listened to it while he watched the play of emotions across Orchid's face. It should not have mattered so much that she believe him, but it did.

It did.

"How sad," Orchid said eventually.

Rafe relaxed slightly. "From Selby's point of view, maybe it's sad. From mine, it's a major pain in the ass."

She startled him with a grin. "Rafe, you were born to deal with major pains in the ass. In fact, I'll bet you're bored stiff when you're between pains in the ass. What do you do to amuse yourself when you don't have a pain in the ass to keep you busy?"

"Recently I've experimented with having an affair with an ice-prism."

She gave him an ingenuous look. "Talk about a major pain in the ass."

"On the plus side, I'm never bored."

"Sounds a bit like dating a strat-talent. What did you accomplish on the home front today?"

Rafe's spirits were rising so quickly that he spoke before he considered his words. "I think I found the talent-prism team who tried to kill your friend Lambert yesterday."

Her eyes widened. "Really?"

"Yes." Rafe was chagrined to realize how much he enjoyed the blatant admiration in her eyes.

"That's fantastic." Orchid leaped out of her chair and tumbled into his lap. She wrapped her arms around his neck. "Brilliant work. You really are good at this kind of thing. Tell me everything."

He grunted as her soft weight settled on his thighs.

She made an extremely pleasant lap-full but her enthusiasm warned him that he had possibly made a serious miscalculation. He had intended to handle the illusion-talent and the prism accomplice by himself. Now, he suspected, that was going to prove difficult.

"Whistler called a few minutes ago. He says there are a couple of guys who could be the ones we want working at a club in Founders' Square. I, uh, thought I'd go down tonight and catch their act. See if they're the right ones."

"Good idea. When do we leave?"

"Not we," he said deliberately. "Me."

"You'll need me," she said complacently. Then she frowned as a thought apparently struck her. "We've only seen these guys in their ski masks. How will we recognize them on a stage?"

"That won't be a problem," Rafe said. "I'm a strat-talent, remember? I'll recognize them."

The Icy Dicey Casino was located on one of the darker side streets of Founders' Square, well away from the brightly lit strip. On an average night Rafe would have had serious misgivings about escorting a lady into this part of town. But tonight the Founders' Day celebration was in full swing in the square. The maze of seedy lanes and shadowy alleys were unusually crowded with loud, raucous revelers.

A street band played bad ice rock on the corner. More music poured from the open doors of a nearby syn-sex club. Clusters of people dressed in first generation costumes thronged the street, making their way from one bar to the next.

As he guided Orchid through the milling crowds, he automatically assessed the attire of those around them. Without consciously thinking about it, he checked to be certain that he and Orchid fit into their surroundings. His strat-talent instincts favored camouflage and shadows.

Neither he nor Orchid wore the homespun, colonial

ORCHID

costumes many of the revelers favored, but Rafe was
satisfied that he, at least, did not stand out in the crowd.
In his dark jacket, black open-throated shirt, and black
trousers he knew that he could fade into the shadows of
any convenient alley on a second's notice.

He was less content with Orchid's appearance. Theoretically she should have been as unobtrusive as himself
in her jeans, black T-shirt, and rumpled blazer. But he
knew that he could never overlook her in a crowd or an
alley and he worried that no one else could either.

He brought Orchid to a halt in front of the casino and
glanced at the poster advertising the magic act of one
Mr. Amazing. It was a full-color shot of a man with the
too-pretty look of a fashion model. He was dressed in a
snug-fitting, blue, spangled body suit and a red
satin–lined cape.

The magician's flowing hair fell in rippling waves to
his shoulders. Rafe figured he probably went to a high-
priced hair salon. There was no way that particular
shade of blonde could be natural on a man.

"Hmm." Orchid peered closely at the center portion
of the larger-than-life picture. "Mr. Amazing is pretty
amazing, all right."

Rafe realized that her attention was on the large bulge
clearly revealed by Mr. Amazing's skintight blue pants.
"Don't forget, he's billed as the Master of Illusion."

"You mean I can't believe everything I see?" she
asked innocently.

Rafe chose to ignore the amusement in her eyes.
"We're here on business, if you will recall. I want your
word of honor that you will do exactly what I tell you
to do."

"Sure."

The too-glib response worried him. "We have an
agreement, remember?" he said as he shoved open the
glass doors of the casino.

"Sheesh, calm down, will you? I've promised you
three times already that I'd let you take the lead to-

night." She gave him a sidelong glare. "What's the matter with you? You sound nervous."

"I am not nervous." The sensation he was experiencing at the moment was merely a wholly justifiable sense of caution, Rafe told himself.

There was no reason to expect any trouble tonight. This was, in effect, a simple reconnaissance mission. They would be here only long enough for him to identify the illusion-talent and the prism while both were safely occupied on stage.

Rafe eased Orchid through the mob that clogged the gaming floor. The artificially cheerful clang and tinkle of gambling machines mingled with the reverberating throb of the music.

When they reached the entrance to the shabby show lounge, Rafe tipped the usher enough to ensure that he and Orchid would get seats reasonably close to the stage, but not in the front row. The darkness of the chamber as well as the fact that the magicians on stage would be working with the lights in their eyes would provide ample concealment, he decided.

"Do you suppose this will be one of those magic acts in which the magician chooses someone out of the audience to assist in the show?" Orchid whispered.

"Do me a favor. Don't volunteer for anything. Things could get a little awkward if the illusion-talent selects you from the audience, realizes who you are, and decides to make you disappear."

She smiled demurely. "Would you look for me?"

"Yes. But you would not be happy to see me when I found you. I would not be in a good mood."

The show lounge filled quickly. When Rafe took the seat next to Orchid on the aisle he could feel the excitement simmering in her. He was mildly annoyed to feel echoes of that same excitement in himself.

Orchid leaned close to murmur in his ear. "I can see why the illusion-talent and his pal are taking on part-time work. Judging from the looks of this place, they aren't making their fortunes in the magic business."

Rafe briefly surveyed the theater. The jelly-ice lights were turned down low for reasons other than atmosphere. The gloom hid some of the threadbare quality of the curtain and disguised the fading paint on the walls. The thin velvet cushions on the seats were stained with several years' worth of spilled drinks. He did not need para-sharpened senses to smell the underlying odor of stale beer, cheap green wine, and the unique aura of frenzied desperation that seeped in from the gambling floor.

The lights faded all the way to black. A spot blazed in the center of the red and gold curtain. An expectant hush settled over the audience. The small band struck up a brisk musical introduction. A man garbed in a flashy tux trotted out from an opening on the left-hand side of the stage.

"Happy Founders' Day, everyone," the announcer roared at the small crowd. "The Icy Dicey Casino is proud to present our own master of illusion, Mr. Amazing with his special Founders' Day extravaganza. Ladies and gentlemen, prepare to be . . . *amazed.*"

The spotlight winked out. When it came back on a few seconds later it revealed Mr. Amazing in all his spangled glory. His long hair cascaded in thick waves to the high standing collar of his sparkling red cape.

Rafe leaned forward and rested his folded arms on his thighs. *Right size, right build. He even moved the right way.*

"Rafe? Can you tell if it's him?"

He did not look at her. He was too intent on studying his quarry. "Got to be certain. Link."

He sent out a short, probing pulse of psychic energy. His strat-talent senses fluttered. He felt the familiar wave of brief disorientation that always accompanied an initial quest.

Orchid said nothing but out on the psychic plane the

very special prism took shape. Crystal clear. Powerful. Unique. Made just for him.

With an intense feeling of satisfaction that was equaled only by the sensations he felt when he made love to Orchid, Rafe sent power through the prism.

Psychic energy sharpened all of his senses. The quality of the atmosphere around him altered. Suddenly he could see in ways that he could not explain, ways that felt utterly natural.

Ways that he had never been able to savor for more than a few seconds at a time before he met Orchid.

The darkened showroom assumed countless new dimensions. Objects that had been little more than shadows in the gloom could now be clearly discerned, not just through sight but in another, less easily described fashion. Smells sharpened and separated, revealing subtle nuances. The perfume worn by the woman in the next row made Rafe wrinkle his nose. He tuned it out. At the same time he was intensely aware of Orchid's nearness. It felt right to have her at his side, not just because they were temporarily linked on the metaphysical plane but because . . .

Because it felt right.

Rafe made himself push the awareness of Orchid and all of the other sensation in the lounge into the background. He concentrated on his quarry.

On stage Mr. Amazing raised his gloved hands high in a dramatic gesture, lowered them quickly and suddenly a curtain of what appeared to be crackling bands of energy materialized on the stage behind him. It shimmered grandly in an invisible breeze. Sparks snapped in the darkness.

"Ladies and gentlemen," Mr. Amazing announced in a deep voice augmented by a hidden microphone, "I give you, the Curtain as it must have looked to our noble Founders just before it closed forever."

The semi-inebriated audience was suitably awed. *Oohs* and *aahs* rippled across the rows of seats.

Rafe listened to the voice of Mr. Amazing with para-sensitive hearing. He filtered out the distortion created by the microphone.

The same voice. He was sure of it.

"And now," Mr. Amazing intoned, "let us see what our Curtain reveals."

The magician moved his hands in a melodramatic gesture. A woman with long green hair materialized out of the Curtain. She wore only a silver thong and a matching bra made of translucent silver mesh. The audience was treated to the sight of a pair of enormous breasts tipped with gaily painted nipples.

"Talk about an illusion," Orchid muttered.

Rafe ignored the comment. The woman's breasts did not interest him. His quarry was the only thing that mattered. He sifted through the scents that flowed around him in a vast sea, searching for one that was familiar.

In the world of para-heightened awareness, scent was one of the most reliable of all stimuli—easily identified, virtually impossible to disguise. The magician was already sweating in the glare of the stage lights.

A second later Rafe caught the unmistakable taint of an illusion-talent. A talent that was strikingly similar to the one he had fought the other night outside Theo Willis's house. It had to be the same man who had trapped Orchid in Morgan Lambert's kitchen with the fire illusion.

This was the enemy.

Eagerness coursed through Rafe. A deep yearning to give chase came over him. He recognized the instinct and squelched it quickly. It probably would not be a good idea to bound up onto the stage and pound Mr. Amazing into the floor in front of Orchid and the rest of the crowd. A little too primitive.

"Rafe?"

He sensed the aura of Orchid's sudden unease and knew that she had picked up some sense of his elemental desire to bring down his quarry. He hoped she wouldn't hold it against him. She was more understanding than anyone else he had ever met when it came to the nature of his psychic talent. Nevertheless, he was pretty sure she would take a dim view of him entertaining himself with a little happy mayhem.

"It's him," he muttered, feeling somewhat defensive.

"You're sure?"

"Of course I'm sure."

"You don't have to snap at me."

"I didn't snap at you."

"Yes, you did."

Before Rafe could think of a suitable rejoinder another assistant walked out on stage. A man this time. He was slightly shorter and not as solidly built as Mr. Amazing. His features were thin and sharp. He wore his dark, curly hair cropped close, and his costume resembled formal black evening wear.

Rafe concentrated intently for a few seconds. A sigh of anticipation escaped him when he caught the telltale traces of a familiar scent.

"The prism," he said very softly.

The music swelled as the assistant displayed a case of throwing knives. The lady in the translucent brassiere arranged herself in an artful pose against a colorful target. Mr. Amazing selected a knife and threw it with confident skill. The point sank into the target near her head. The audience gasped. The woman smiled.

Mr. Amazing selected another knife.

Rafe cut the focus link.

"What do we do now?" Orchid whispered.

"We leave."

Under cover of a burst of applause, Rafe reached out, took her hand, and got to his feet. He led Orchid back up the aisle to the curtained entrance of the show lounge.

They stepped out into the frenetic activity of the gaming floor.

"We're going to follow Mr. Amazing after he finishes the show, aren't we?" Orchid asked.

Rafe smiled at the enthusiasm in her voice. She was not a strat-talent, but she definitely had a few primitive instincts of her own. "The thought had crossed my mind."

"Then what?"

"Depends." Rafe drew her through the throng of eager gamblers toward the front of the casino. "The dressing room entrance is in the alley. We can keep an eye on it from outside."

The street in front of the Icy Dicey was even more crowded now than it had been earlier. The few cars that had ventured into it were trapped by the milling revelers. No one seemed to mind.

The decibel level had escalated. Another street band had joined the ice rock group on the corner. Rafe heard Orchid crunch a discarded noisemaker underfoot. Streamers drifted through the night.

He found a spot near a doorway that offered shelter from the jostling crowd and a good view of the alley entrance. A street vendor dressed in a Founders' Day costume held out a large paper bag.

"Popped nut-corn. Get 'em while they're nice and hot."

"Sounds good." Orchid fished in her pocket, found some change, and handed it to the vendor.

She accepted the brimming bag, took a handful of popped nut-corn for herself, and offered some to Rafe.

He scooped up a fistful of the salted nut-corn and shoved it into his mouth. Using his talent for extended periods of time heightened all of his appetites, he reflected.

"I love Founders' Day." Orchid surveyed the cheerful crowds as she dug into the bag for more nut-corn. "I know we're here on serious business, but it's actually turning into a fun evening. You know how to show a girl a good time, Mr. Stonebraker."

"Glad you're enjoying yourself."

"Are you going to give up this private investigation

hobby of yours when you take control of your family's firm?"

The question stopped him cold. "I hadn't thought about it, to tell you the truth."

"You probably won't have time for this kind of thing once you start running a big company like Stonebraker," Orchid said conversationally. "But I think maybe I'll start specializing."

"I beg your pardon?"

"I like this kind of work," she explained. "There must be other private investigators, maybe some who actually have a license, who need the services of an ice-prism. I think I'll tell Clementine that I want to limit my practice to working with them."

Rafe's gut tightened. "You intend to work with other private investigators?"

"Why not? Clementine wants us to think exclusive. What could be more exclusive than a full-spectrum ice-prism who helps conduct discrete private investigations?"

The thought of Orchid working in a dangerous situation with another talent sent a chill through Rafe. He had a sudden, clear vision of her standing on a street corner on a warm summer night munching popped nut-corn with another man while staking out a person of interest. A fierce sense of denial raced through him.

She was his. They were meant for each other. Didn't she understand that?

"I don't think that would be a good idea," he managed in what he hoped was a reasonable tone.

Her brows rose as she took another handful of nut-corn. "Why not?"

"Uh, because you don't really have any experience in investigation work."

"Sure I do, thanks to you." She shrugged. "And I'll get more as I go along."

"Orchid, this is not the kind of work you go into on a casual basis."

"You're the one who called it a hobby." She munched nut-corn. "How did you get started, anyway?"

"I did a favor for a friend shortly after I returned from the Western Islands. Found something that had been lost, something valuable. A few weeks later one of his friends called. Asked me to find something else. One thing sort of led to another."

"Sounds pretty casual to me. No training, no apprenticeship with a private investigation firm, no license. You only take referrals. You only take jobs that interest you. You only work for people who, for one reason or another, can't or won't go to the police."

"Damn it, Orchid, if you think you can just blithely go to work as a prism who does private investigations—" He broke off as he caught sight of a shadow emerging from the alley. "There he is."

"Mr. Amazing?" She spun around to stare at the alley entrance. "I don't see him."

"Not Mr. Amazing. His prism. But he'll do." Rafe took the half-full bag of popped nut-corn out of Orchid's hand and tossed it into a nearby garbage can. "In fact, the more I think about it, the more I think it would be a good idea to start with him."

"Why?"

Rafe smiled as he took her arm and plunged into the crowd. "Because he's the weaker one."

Easy prey.

"Do you think he's headed back to his car?" Orchid asked.

"I doubt it." Rafe kept his eye on the curly haired man. "He's acting as if he's late for an appointment."

There was something nervous and hurried about the prism's movements. He did not glance back over his shoulder, however, so whatever he anticipated lay ahead, not behind.

Rafe found it simple to pursue his quarry through the crowd. The prism was the only one who was walking purposefully along the sidewalk. Everyone else was either strolling, ambling, or dancing.

Rafe and Orchid followed the prism at a discreet distance. After a block and a half they passed the last tavern on the street. The crowd thinned rapidly.

Rafe dropped back a few more paces. The prism had yet to look over his shoulder, but if he chose to do so now that there were fewer people about, there was a chance he would notice his tail.

In the middle of the next block, the magician's assistant slowed his pace. Rafe got the impression that whatever the appointment was, it was not one the prism wanted to keep.

Something was wrong. The nervousness Rafe had detected in his quarry was increasing. He looked more agitated. There was a stiff, tense set to his shoulders. His strides became almost jerky. He began to fiddle with something under his coat. A knife?

Rafe's driving curiosity was suddenly tempered with caution.

"Link," he ordered softly.

"What's wrong?" Orchid supplied the prism even as she asked the question.

"I don't know." He shoved power through the crystal prism. "I just want all the information I can get."

The night shifted around him. Awareness infused his senses. He sorted through the new array of sounds, smells, and sights.

He picked up the mix of sweat, unwholesome, adrenaline-fed excitement, and a trace of anxiety and recognized the indefinable essence of bloodlust.

Not the prism, Rafe thought. Someone else. A predator waited in the darkness of a side street up ahead.

He saw that his quarry was moving even more slowly now than he had been a moment ago. But the prism kept going forward.

Rafe realized the curly haired man was going to turn down the side street where the predator was waiting.

"Oh, shit." Rafe released Orchid's hand. He shoved her into the shadows of a darkened doorway. "Stay here. Don't follow."

"What is it? What are you going to do?" she whispered.

"Just hold the focus for me. Whatever you do, don't lose it."

He broke into a silent, loping run. His para-heightened instincts told him he had only seconds to catch up with his quarry.

The prism was *his* prey, damn it. He would not give him up to the other hunter who lay in wait in the shadows.

Chapter

14

❖❖❖❖❖❖❖❖❖

Time ran out a heartbeat later. Rafe launched himself at the prism just as he reached the corner and started to turn down the street where the predator waited.

At the last instant, the curly haired man apparently sensed Rafe bearing down on him. He jerked around, his face a mask of startled fear. He threw up one hand in a reflexive gesture while he struggled to bring an object out from beneath his jacket with the other.

"Christ, no. Don't—"

The prism's scream halted abruptly as Rafe slammed into him. The jarring impact sent both men crashing to the sidewalk.

A figure came around the corner. Rafe did not need the weak streetlight or his paranormal senses to see the pistol in his hand.

There was a flash of icy flame when the gun roared. The bullet crashed into a brick wall above Rafe's head. He rolled and pulled the stunned prism deep into the cover of the doorway.

Rafe released the prism, got to his feet, and reached

down to yank a small pistol out of his ankle holster. He raised the gun and fired in one single motion.

But the predator who had been waiting for the prism had either lost his nerve or concluded that he did not like the new odds. He had apparently braced himself to shoot one man in cold blood. He was not prepared to deal with two, one of whom was also armed with a pistol.

He whirled and fled back into the darkness of the side street. Rafe tasted the fear in the other man. It had swamped the bloodlust.

"Rafe." Orchid's shout rang from her doorway. "Are you all right?"

"Stay where you are," he yelled back. She had to know he was in reasonably good condition, he thought. They were still firmly linked on the psychic plane.

For once, she obeyed orders.

He waited another few seconds, listening to the gunman's retreating footsteps.

"It's okay," he called. "You can come out now."

When he heard her start toward him, he broke the link. The night world dimmed, shifted, returned to normal.

Rafe became aware of the shaking man he had pinned against the wall with one arm.

"What's your name?" he asked very softly.

"Let me go."

"What's your name?"

"Uh, Crowder. Phil Crowder. Look, I don't know who you are, mister—"

"Sure, you do. We met the other night outside of Theo Willis's house."

'No," the man licked his lips. "That wasn't me."

"It was you, all right. I never forget a—" Rafe broke off before he said *scent.* "Forget it. You're the prism. Mr. Amazing is the illusion-talent who was with you that night." It was not a question.

Orchid came to a halt a short distance away. "Are you sure you're all right, Rafe?"

"Yes." He did not look at her. "But our friend, here, is not all right. Someone just tried to kill him. Who was it, Crowder?"

"I don't know."

Rafe pushed him harder against the wall. "Try again."

"I swear, I don't know. I was supposed to meet my bookie here. I owe him some money. Got a little behind at the tables. But that wasn't him. It was someone else."

"Someone the bookie sent, maybe?"

"Shit, no. Murphy wouldn't have sent someone to kill me. I'm not that far behind in my payments."

"Then who was it?"

"I don't know, I tell you."

Rafe concentrated intensely for a few seconds. He only needed a short burst of strat-talent awareness to assure him that the man was not lying. "Got any ideas?"

"No."

"I do," Rafe said very gently. "I think maybe whoever hired you to watch Theo Willis's house and get rid of Morgan Lambert has decided that you've become a liability. He came here tonight to get rid of you."

"Oh, Christ." There was fear and weary defeat in Crowder's voice. "I never wanted to do those jobs. But I needed the money real bad. For my bookie, y'know? He was threatening to send his knee man after me. Shit, I knew this was gonna be trouble. I knew it right from the start."

"Tell me about it." Rafe could feel Orchid watching him question Crowder. Her tension was palpable. He reminded himself to be careful. He didn't want to do anything too primitive in front of her. "Start with who hired you."

"Jink hired me. That's all I know, I tell you."

"Jink?"

"Mr. Amazing. I don't know the rest of his real name. He goes by Jink off-stage. He's an illusion-talent. Really strong. He needed a prism who could handle his power on stage. Said he didn't want to get someone from a focus agency. I found out why after I'd been working with him for awhile."

"He wanted you to do some work on the side, right?"

"Yeah. But he booked the outside stuff, y'know? I never even knew who hired us. Jink handled everything."

Orchid stirred in the shadows. "You tried to murder Rafe that night outside Theo's house."

"No, Founders' truth. We were just supposed to rough him up a bit. Scare him off. Least, that's what Jink told me."

"What was in the letter you took from Morgan Lambert's houseboat?" Rafe asked.

"Shit, I don't know. Jink found the letter. He never showed it to me."

"You deliberately overdosed Morgan on dirty-ice," Orchid said.

"No." Fear lanced through Crowder's voice. "Jink said he was only going to use enough ice to make Lambert forget a few things."

"He used enough to kill him."

"Oh, shit, I didn't know that. Honest, lady. It's not my fault. I was just supposed to help look for that damn letter. Jink fed the dirty-ice to Lambert. Used an illusion to make him think it was a beer. And then you arrived and screwed everything up."

Rafe released him and stepped back in disgust. "You're a waste of time, Crowder."

"I told you, I don't know anything."

"Let's hope you know enough to get out of town for a while. Because I have a hunch that whoever tried to kill you tonight will make another attempt."

Crowder flinched and edged sideways out of the doorway. "You think so?"

"Yes, I think so. What's Jink's schedule for this evening?"

"Why?"

"Because he's probably next on the shooter's list."

"Oh, shit. Oh, shit." Crowder glanced nervously over his shoulder as if he expected to see his attacker. "I gotta get out of here."

Rafe shifted position to block Crowder's path. "First tell me Mr. Amazing's schedule. When does he leave the Icy Dicey?"

"We've got another performance at midnight. He usually hangs around the club between shows. Got something going with one of the dealers, y'know? They get it on in his dressing room between acts."

"Maybe I'll be able to talk to him before his new employer gets to him." Rafe turned away. He reached for Orchid's arm.

"Wait." Crowder put out a hand as if to catch hold of Rafe's sleeve. At the last minute he thought better of it and snatched it back. He glanced at Orchid and then looked back at Rafe. "Why did you save me a few minutes ago?"

"I saved you because I'd hoped you could tell me a few useful things." Rafe smiled faintly. "But I was wrong. Which means that the next time I run into you, I won't go out of my way to do you any favors. So be careful, Crowder. Be very, very careful."

Crowder's face worked. He looked helplessly at Orchid. Then he turned and ran back down the street toward the lights of Founders' Square.

Orchid waited until he was gone before she spoke. "Do you think he was telling you the truth?"

"Yes." Rafe reholstered his pistol and adjusted the cuff of his trousers. "Come on. We've got to get back to the club."

"This whole thing is coming together." Rafe's hand tightened around Orchid's arm as he hurried her back toward the Icy Dicey. "If we move fast, we may finish it tonight."

In spite of her jangled nerves and the adrenaline that was still ripping through her system, Orchid grinned briefly at Rafe's intense satisfaction. It radiated from him in fierce waves. He was no longer riding the energy train of a focus link, but the strat-talent side of his nature was definitely in full bloom.

Well, maybe "full bloom" was not a good analogy, she conceded silently. There was nothing flowerlike about Rafe tonight.

He hauled her swiftly through the crowds toward the nightclub. The hunter in Rafe, never far from the surface, was what she saw in all its many aspects tonight. He was in full control, but the power that he held in check was strong enough to make the hair stir on the back of her neck.

She knew she was not the only one who sensed the presence of a hunter. She had seen the expression on Crowder's face a few moments ago before he turned and fled.

"I assume we are working under the assumption that it was Dr. Austen who just tried to kill Crowder?" Orchid realized she was breathless. If she was going to do this sort of thing on a regular basis, she had better start doing her meta-zen-syn exercise routine more than three times a week.

"Austen is definitely on the short list of possible candidates." Rafe slowed a little as the rambunctious crowd closed in on them. "He's trying to cover his tracks. But he's not a pro. He's screwing things up."

"You mean, we're screwing things up for him." Orchid studied the garish lights of the Icy Dicey up ahead. "This could be a little awkward if Crowder was right about Mr. Amazing's between show activities. Be sure you knock first."

"Afraid of seeing Mr. Amazing without his stage costume?"

Orchid thought about the overstuffed crotch of the magician's sparkling suit. "Let's just say that I wouldn't want to be disillusioned."

Rafe led the way into the alley beside the casino. Orchid followed, relieved to see that the narrow passage was not completely dark. A weak jelly-ice bulb glowing above a door kept some of the shadows at bay.

There was no one guarding the stage door entrance. Orchid concluded that Mr. Amazing was not overly troubled with eager fans. When Rafe turned the knob, it twisted easily in his hand.

She followed him into a dimly lit hall that stank of stale sweat and old booze. The muffled music of a torch singer could be heard through the wall together with the distant racket of gaming machines.

Rafe came to a halt in front of a closed door decorated with a sadly faded star.

He paused for a moment. Orchid sensed a fleeting pulse of familiar psychic energy, but Rafe did not seek a focus link. The small surge of talent vanished quickly. To Orchid's surprise, a new wave of battle-ready tension suddenly vibrated in the air around Rafe.

"Damn." He reached into his pocket, pulled out a pair of thin leather gloves and tugged them onto his strong hands.

"Why are you—?"

"Here, put these on, Ms. Private Investigator." He slapped a pair of thin plastic gloves into her palm.

They were not sexy leather gloves like his own, Orchid noticed. They were the kind of cheap, disposable gloves used in food preparation work. She made a note to buy herself some more stylish gloves at the earliest opportunity.

"I'll go in first," Rafe said quietly. "Wait here."

"You're always telling me to wait. How am I ever going to learn if I'm always kept waiting around in the hall?"

"Trust me on this. You don't want to go in first."

He was right, she thought. She did not have the vaguest idea of what she would do if she suddenly came face to face with Mr. Amazing.

Rafe did not knock on Mr. Amazing's door. He

opened it and went in very fast. Orchid noticed that no light spilled from the small room. There was no feminine shriek of surprise. No masculine yell of outrage. The room was empty.

Orchid realized she had been holding her breath. She relaxed fractionally and went to stand in the darkened entrance. She peered into the shadows but she could not see much.

"Guess Mr. Amazing isn't here after all," she said.

"He's here, all right. Come in and close the door behind you."

"What do you mean?" She wrinkled her nose as she obediently shut the door. "And what is that dreadful smell?"

"Brace yourself." Rafe flicked on a light. "Whoever tried to kill Crowder a few minutes ago got here ahead of us."

Orchid stared at the unnaturally still figure sprawled on the floor near the wall. Blonde hair concealed the handsome face. Bright red blood stained the front of the spangled blue body suit. She felt her stomach twist into a sickening knot.

"Oh, my God." She swallowed. "Is he . . . ?"

"Yes." Rafe scowled at the sight of her face. "Can you handle it for a few minutes? I want to take a quick look around and it would be better if you waited in here rather than out in the hall. I don't want to take a chance on someone seeing you near this dressing room."

"I can handle it." Only because she was dazed, Orchid thought. The peculiar sense of disorientation seemed to have the effect of temporarily shielding her from the reality of the crumpled body on the floor. "It must have happened only a few minutes ago."

"Yes. While I wasted time questioning Crowder." Rafe crossed the room to the dressing table. He crouched to peer underneath it.

"Quentin Austen has gone crazy," she whispered.

"Looks like it." Rafe ran his fingers along the bottom of the dressing table.

"What are you looking for?"

"Whatever it was the killer came here to find." He straightened and checked behind the mirror. "He was in a hurry. He had to know that we were only a few minutes behind him. He wouldn't have had time to do a thorough search."

For the first time Orchid realized that the small dressing room was in a cluttered, jumbled state. Someone had obviously gone through it in a hasty, perhaps desperate fashion.

Get a grip, she thought. *You can have a nervous breakdown later.* She took a cautious breath, willed herself to concentrate on the problem at hand. Gingerly, she went toward the open door of a small closet. She could see a row of glittering costumes inside.

"I'll check his wardrobe," she said in what she hoped was a businesslike tone.

Rafe paused long enough to give her a narrow look. Concern gleamed in his eyes. "You sure you're all right?"

"Yes." *For now, at any rate. Ask me again, later.*

She pushed aside the gaudy stage clothes and found a row of open drawers. The killer had already pawed through them. Wide belts studded with artificial gemstones, rakish scarves and stage jewelry had been carelessly tossed about like so much flotsam and jetsam on a beach.

Orchid grimaced as she pulled out a handful of masculine undergarments. She shuddered when she held up a pair of slinky black briefs that featured a large pouch in the front and a narrow silk thong in the rear.

"Mr. Amazing must have had a subscription to the *Syn-Sex Male* catalog," she muttered.

"The guy had class, all right." Rafe eased the dresser away from the wall to look behind it. "Got to admire the taste of a man who stuffs a sock in his crotch."

ORCHID

"You don't know that for certain." She stooped to examine a row of leather boots decorated with sequins and fake stones. There was nothing inside the footwear.

When she started to get back to her feet, her head brushed against one of the hanging costumes. She cringed when she noticed that she had collided with the bulging crotch section of a pair of form-fitting crimson trousers.

The large, codpiece-like lump in the front of the pants did not give beneath the impact. She gazed at it thoughtfully for a long moment. Then she steeled her nerves for the task of investigating the interior of the costume.

There was nothing inside the first one except a great deal of artfully arranged padding. The second costume revealed more of the same. But in the third one she discovered something else besides stuffing in the artificially enlarged crotch.

Very slowly she withdrew a piece of paper that had been rolled into a tight scroll.

"Rafe?"

"Yeah?" He did not look up from a floorboard he was exploring with the tips of his gloved fingers.

"You were right about Mr. Amazing. It was all an illusion." She unrolled the paper she had found.

"What are you—?" He paused, eyes slitting at the sight of what she held in her hand. "What is it?"

"A photocopy of the letter Theo sent to Morgan Lambert."

Chapter

15

❖❖❖❖❖❖❖❖❖

Morgan:

If you're reading this letter, it means that something has happened to me. Weird thought. At any rate, I'll keep this brief because I don't have much time. I'm on my way out of town. Better if you don't know where I'm going.

I've got to disappear for a while. I got involved in a really big mess. I can't explain it all but I know that I took one of the alien artifacts from the lab where I work. I don't remember much about the theft. It's kind of a fog. I only know that I took the thing with me one night. I remember giving it to my therapist, Quentin Austen. Now someone is trying to kill me.

I think Dr. Austen is somehow responsible for what happened to me. I can't go to the police. I have no proof. I can't even remember anything about this whole mess very clearly. I'm sure the bastard deliberately clouded my memory with his hypno-talent. He's strong enough to work for several seconds at a time without a prism. He gave me some medication, too. I think the stuff enhanced the effect of his hypnosis.

The artifact I stole for Austen is different from the others. I don't have time to go into details, but believe me, it's potentially dangerous.

Here's the zinger. Austen can't control the relic by himself. He needs a very powerful ice-prism. We both know there aren't many of us around. Now that I've broken free of his control, he may look for another strong ice-prism.

Be careful. Maybe you better warn Orchid. I didn't give him your names, at least I don't think I did. But you can't be too cautious. I have a feeling Dr. Austen's crazier than people say I am.

I'll call you as soon as I think it's safe.

Theo

Rafe slowly re-rolled the letter. He looked at the body on the floor and idly tapped the little scroll against the dressing table. "Mr. Amazing probably tried a bit of blackmail with this photocopy and got himself shot for his efforts."

"It looks that way, doesn't it?" Orchid rubbed her hands over her arms. The small room was warm, but she felt chilled. "Poor Theo. I knew he was innocent. If only he'd told someone what was happening."

"He was right about one thing. It would have been extremely difficult to prove anything. If he'd gone to the cops they would have taken one look at the situation and slapped him in jail for stealing a valuable artifact from a research lab." Rafe shrugged. "And dismissed the rest of his story out of hand."

"Especially if they talked to his helpful syn-psych therapist, Dr. Quentin Austen, who would have fed them a pack of lies about the state of his mental health." Orchid set her teeth. "That bastard, Austen. He's the one behind this whole thing."

"If he's looking for another ice-prism to help him control his stolen artifact, we'll have to conclude that he really does believe that crazy stuff about it being a thing of power. Which makes him a syn-psych head case."

"I can see how it happened. Theo innocently went to Austen for therapy. Probably mentioned his work at the lab in the course of his sessions. He must have mentioned that he thought one of the relics had some power and that an ice-prism could somehow control it. Austen evidently believed him."

"And then Austen hypnotized Willis so that he would steal the relic," Rafe concluded thoughtfully. "After that, things began to come apart. Willis somehow escaped Austen's mind control and fled in panic."

"I'll bet Austen probably arranged for Theo's death in that car crash."

"And then got worried that someone would connect him to Willis. He hired Mr. Amazing and Crowder to keep watch on Willis's house. Then he somehow learned that Willis had sent a letter to Lambert and sent the team to find it."

"And then Mr. Amazing tried to blackmail him with a photocopy of the letter." Orchid shivered. "So he set out to kill both Jink and Crowder."

Rafe tapped the little rolled up cylinder again. "Most of it fits."

She slanted him an uneasy glance. "Theo really did have some mental problems, you know. That stuff about being able to control one of the alien relics has got to be a fantasy."

Rafe looked thoughtful. "He obviously convinced Quentin Austen that it was true."

"I don't doubt for a moment that Theo really believed it. And I agree that he somehow made Dr. Austen believe it. Which proves that Austen is as unstable as jelly-ice. He's already killed at least two people, Theo and Mr. Amazing."

"And tried to do in a couple more, Morgan Lambert and Crowder." Rafe reached for the phone with a gloved hand. "All because he believes some wild tale about a still-functioning alien relic. You're right. The man is not normal."

"Who are you calling?"

"We finally have some hard facts and a body. Time to call the police. I've got a friend who works homicide. I'm going to give him what we have. And then I'll call Brizo at the lab and warn him that we can't keep the lid on this any longer."

"Quentin Austen must be found before he kills anyone else," Orchid said when they finally walked into Rafe's house two hours later. "But what about the missing relic?"

"The cops may find it when they find Austen. But there's a chance it's already disappeared into the underground collector's market." Rafe locked the front door and turned to face her. "Which means, we've still got a case."

She studied the hard lines of his face, saw the intensity in his gaze. The hunter in him would not quit until he had found what he had set out to find, she thought.

She gave him a wan smile. "You know something? I'm glad you're not after me."

"Who said I'm not after you?"

She did not move. Desire, power, and need thickened the atmosphere. She could not tell what portion of the heady, dangerous brew came from her and what emanated from Rafe.

"This is probably not a good time to talk about it," she said. "We've both been under a lot of stress lately. A bit too much excitement—"

There was perfect, if darkly brooding comprehension in his gaze. "Are you afraid of me?"

"Not exactly."

"That's not quite the answer I was looking for."

"What do you want me to say?"

"Just tell me the truth." He rose with fluid ease and crossed the short distance between them. He came to a halt in front of her, reached down, closed his hands over her shoulders, and hauled her lightly out of the chair. "Are you afraid of me? Does the fact that I'm a strattalent scare you?"

She gazed into the dark, shadowy places in his eyes and saw the secrets in him. "No."

"Am I a little too primitive for the daughter of a couple of Northvillers?"

"No."

"Then what did you mean when you said that you aren't *exactly* afraid of me?"

She framed his face between her hands, and smiled wistfully. "I meant that I'm afraid that I might be falling in love with you."

The stunned expression that flashed in his eyes would have amused her under other circumstances. But tonight she was trapped in the swirling waters of her own emotions. She could not take refuge in laughter. She had an uneasy suspicion that her entire future was at stake.

Rafe said nothing. He groaned, caught her close, and kissed her with a raging passion that left no room for words. Then he picked her up in his arms, carried her into the library, and pulled her down onto the carpet in front of the fire.

A long time later Orchid stirred, stretched, and opened her eyes. She smiled wryly when she saw Rafe crouched in front of the hearth. He was gazing into the flames as though he could see visions of Old Earth. He had refastened his trousers, but he had not put on his shirt. The firelight warmed his bare shoulders to a rich gold and etched the strong contours of his back. For a moment she simply savored the sleek, masculine strength in him.

"You know, this business of making love in front of a roaring fire works nicely in my novels," she said finally. "But in real life it causes rug burns. Next time let's put you on the bottom."

"Orchid, I want you to think about marrying me."

Orchid stared at him. He did not turn his head to look at her. Everything in him was focused intently on the images only he could see in the flames.

"Rafe—"

"Just think about it, okay? You said you thought you might be falling in love with me."

She licked her lips. "Any matchmaking agency counselor can tell you that sort of emotion can't be relied upon as a basis for a good marriage."

"What else have you got to go on?" he asked with frightening logic. "You said, yourself, that, because you're an ice-prism, you don't trust the matchmaking agencies to find you a good match."

"What about you?" she whispered. "Why would you want to take such a risk?"

"My counselor has assured me that I'm almost impossible to match. Odds are I'll have to find my own mate, I mean, my own *wife*. You and I make a good team."

Orchid did not know whether to laugh or cry. "I see." Perhaps she should be a little more direct. "Well, how do you feel about me?" *Do you love me?*

"I just told you, I want you. I wanted you the first time I saw you and I want you even more now that we've been together. You feel . . . I don't know, you feel right."

She wondered if that was as close to a declaration of love as he could get. "What happens if your marriage agency counselor does turn up a match for you?"

"I won't want her." There was absolute certainty in the words.

She sighed. "That sounds a little overly simplistic on your part."

"Why should it be complicated?" He did turn then. The flames on the hearth were nothing compared to the heat in his eyes.

"Rafe—"

"I know I'm not normal. I'm an exotic. The syn-psych experts don't even know how exotic I really am. But I know some things about myself. You don't have to be afraid of me. I would never hurt you. I could never hurt you."

She took a deep breath, let it out slowly. "I know that."

"Think about it. That's all I ask."

There was nothing to think about. She was in love with him. But he had said nothing about loving her. She had to make certain that he knew his own heart as well as she knew hers. She could not marry a man who did not love her, regardless of how committed or protective he felt toward her.

But she could think about it. She could even dream about it. At least for a while.

"All right, Rafe. I'll think about it."

Triumph gleamed in his gaze. He got to his feet, crossed to where she lay, and settled down beside her. He reached for her.

"That's all I ask," he said against her throat.

When he started to push her back onto the rug, she flattened a palm against his chest. "Hold it right there."

He stilled. "Why?"

"This time you get to be on the bottom."

His laughter was a dark, sensual force in the firelit chamber.

Rafe was still grinning to himself at odd moments for no particular reason the next morning. He first became aware of the strange, new mannerism when he looked into his shaving mirror. He quickly discovered that it was not easy to wield a razor while smiling like an idiot. After the second nick, he forced himself to pay attention to the job at hand.

It was not a done deal, he reminded himself. Things could still go wrong. But he had the edge now. Orchid wanted him. Of that he was certain. He could work with that.

He was still feeling remarkably cheerful when he walked into the breakfast room a few minutes later. Orchid was already there. She was hunched intently over the morning paper, a cup of coff-tea in her hand. She did not look up from the article she was reading.

He took a moment to appreciate the sight of her sitting here in his house in the morning light. Her denim-clad legs were tucked under her chair. The black T-shirt she wore emphasized the elegant curve of her throat. Her freshly washed hair was held back behind her ears with a headband. She looked fresh and vibrant and sexy as hell.

She looked right.

"Good morning." He started toward her.

She kept her attention fixed on the newspaper article. "You aren't going to believe this, Rafe."

"Don't bet on it." When she did not lift her face, he contented himself with kissing the top of her head. He did not need para-sharpened senses to enjoy the fragrant mix of her herbal shampoo mingled with her own enticing scent. "This morning I could believe in anything."

"Try this." She pointed at the article she had been perusing.

Rafe glanced at the newspaper. The headline was on page three of the front section of the *New Seattle Times*. An important story but not a major one.

**Syn-Psych Therapist Dead—
Possible Suicide**

"What the hell?" Rafe snatched the paper up off the table and read the article through very quickly.

> The body of Dr. Quentin Austen, a syn-psych therapist with a practice in New Seattle was pulled from the bay at approximately two o'clock this morning.
>
> Dr. Austen was last seen on board the ferry *Old Seattle*, which departed the downtown dock on its last run of the night at one-thirty this morning. He is believed to have jumped overboard somewhere en route. An autopsy will be conducted later today.
>
> Rumors that Austen had a history of periodic bouts of depression and that he had experienced recent financial setbacks and was facing an impending lawsuit from a former patient led authorities to speculate that he committed suicide. "We get a few jumpers every year," said a source who asked not to be named. "A man can't last more than twenty or thirty minutes at the most in the cold waters of the bay."

Rafe tossed aside the paper and reached for the phone.

"What do you think?" Orchid asked.

"I don't know yet. I've got to call my friend in homicide."

Fifteen minutes later he hung up the phone, picked up the coff-tea Orchid had poured for him, and propped his elbows on the table.

"Tallentyre says there won't be any formal announcement until the autopsy results are in, but the people who handled the case are definitely calling it suicide."

"Mr. Amazing was killed around eleven o'clock last night. Austen would have had plenty of time to commit the murder and make it down to the ferry docks to catch the last run of the night." Orchid frowned. "But why would he kill himself at that point?"

"I don't know. Who can say what a man with a history of syn-psych problems will do in a situation like that? Maybe the act of murdering Mr. Amazing put him over the edge. I know he was definitely panicking last night when he tried to shoot Crowder and missed."

"How do you know that?"

"I just know it."

"But *how* did you know it?" she insisted, curious.

He shrugged. "I sensed it during the focus link. By the way, Tallentyre says they did not find the relic when they searched Austen's house."

"So we still have a case?"

"Yes." Rafe put down his cup and got to his feet. "I'm going to go down to the station. I want to talk to Tallentyre in person. Maybe I can get some more information."

Orchid watched him pace out into the hall. The long, eager length of his stride told her more clearly than words that he was wholly intent on the hunt.

So much for a cozy discussion of their future.

Morgan Lambert looked toward the door when Orchid walked into his room shortly after nine. He managed a weary smile.

"Hi," he said.

"Hi, yourself." She leaned on the metal rails that framed the hospital bed. "How are you feeling?"

"Like I'll live. Barely." He rubbed a hand across his face. "They gave me something to blunt the withdrawal effects, but it can't mask all of them. I'm still twitching a bit. And I feel as if I'm going to throw up, but other than that I'm just dandy."

"You gave us quite a scare."

"Your friend, Stonebraker, was in early this morning. He said that he was on his way downtown to talk to the police. He told me what had happened. I guess I owe you my life."

"Do you remember anything?"

Morgan's face twisted in frustration. "Just bits and pieces. The doctor said a few hours of partial amnesia is a common side effect of dirty-ice. I seem to recall leaving a message on your answering machine. Something about a letter from Theo, wasn't it?"

"You said you'd received a message from him."

"Oh, yeah. I think I remember part of it. Some wild tale about being hypnotized by his syn-psych therapist."

"I've seen a copy of the letter. Theo claimed that a shrink named Dr. Quentin Austen forced him to steal an alien relic. He also said that Austen needed an ice-prism to control the thing. He wanted to warn you and me because we were the only other strong ice-prisms he knew."

Morgan sighed. "Poor, crazy Theo."

"It looks as though his therapist was even crazier. Dr. Austen must have believed that the relic really did have some power or he would never have sent those two men to your houseboat to find Theo's letter."

"Power?"

Orchid gave Morgan a quick rundown of events. When she was finished, he stared at her in amazement.

"So Austen killed Theo and another guy and then jumped off a ferry?"

"So they say. Rafe is checking into the details now, but apparently Austen had a history of mental problems."

"What a pair he and Theo made, huh? The crazy treating the eccentric."

"And now they're both dead," Orchid concluded. "And the firm of Adams and Stonebraker is going to find the missing relic."

"Adams and Stonebraker?"

"She means Stonebraker and Adams," Rafe said from the doorway.

Orchid turned. "There you are. How did it go with the cops?"

Rafe shrugged as he walked into the room. "They think it's pretty open and shut. Crazed syn-psych shrink manipulates equally nutty patient. Arranges to have a valuable artifact stolen and then tries to cover up crime by killing people. Eventually goes completely bonkers from stress of committing murder and kills self. Valuable relic missing."

"Hmm." Orchid eyed him thoughtfully.

"Precisely my conclusion," Rafe murmured. He looked at Morgan. "I'm told you're going to be discharged today."

"Right."

"I want you to do me a favor."

"What's that?"

"Get lost for a week. Take a trip to the Western Islands. Pretend you just won a contest."

Morgan gaped. "The Western Islands?"

"All expenses paid by the firm of Stonebraker and Adams," Rafe said.

"You're lucky," Orchid said. "Second prize was two weeks in the Western Islands."

Both men stared at her.

She blushed. "Sorry. My great-great grandmother told me that one when I was very little. She said it was an old Earth joke."

Orchid gave Rafe a long look as she got into the Icer. "What's wrong? Why are you still worried about Morgan?"

"I don't know," he admitted. "But something doesn't feel right about this case yet. It's not just the fact that the relic is still missing, either."

"Are the police satisfied?"

"Yes. The important part of the case, the murder of Mr. Amazing and the probable murder of Theo Willis, has been solved. That's all they care about."

"Don't they have any interest in the relic?"

"They assume that it disappeared into the underground collector's market. They'll keep an eye out for it, but it's not a big priority for them."

"So what's our next move?"

"I'm not sure yet, but we've still got a client. I talked to Brizo. He definitely wants us to find the relic." Rafe glanced at her as he drove out of the hospital parking lot. "In the meantime, we've also got a date to attend your cousin's wedding. It's tomorrow afternoon in Northville, right?"

Orchid groaned. "To tell you the truth, I'd almost forgotten about that."

"I haven't," he said a little too smoothly. "I owe you. I always pay my debts. Stonebraker tradition."

Orchid wondered why she was suddenly overcome with the old hunted feeling. "Rafe, I won't lie to my family. I won't introduce you as an agency date."

"Of course not. At this point I'm just a regular date. The kind of guy you go away with for the weekend."

Her face burned. "But I don't go away for weekends with guys."

"Until you met me." There was a wealth of satisfaction in his voice.

Chapter

16

❖ ❖ ❖ ❖ ❖ ❖ ❖ ❖ ❖

It was a typical meta-zen-syn wedding, Rafe discovered. The bride wore yellow. The groom wore blue. The majority of the guests wore white. Seated next to Orchid in a pew near her parents, he felt extremely conspicuous in his dark suit and tie.

He had been aware of the meta-zen-syn tradition of wearing white but he just could not see himself in a white suit. He was luckier than the groom, he thought. After the ceremony both the bride and the groom would change into green, the color that resulted when blue and yellow were combined.

The change of attire was symbolic of the power of synergy.

Meta-zen-syn was a philosophy, not a religion, but here in Northville many of its symbols had been grafted on to the far more ancient religious portion of the wedding ceremony.

Rafe was amused to see that Orchid did have some white in her wardrobe, after all. The dress she wore today was a breezy thing that fluttered and drifted with every movement. It was very meta-zen-syn, he thought as he studied it out of the corner of his eye. It somehow managed to reveal and conceal at the same time. Very modest by any standard, it nevertheless managed to make him salivate.

This was no time to turn primitive, he reminded himself. He was trying to make a good impression here in Northville.

When the vows had been exchanged, Veronica and her groom vanished into separate antechambers. The congregation meditated in silence while everyone waited for the couple to change into the formal green clothes that symbolized the synergistic result of the chromatic union of blue and yellow.

Synergistic principles were symbolized everywhere in Northville, Rafe noticed.

On the way into the austere little chapel he had seen North's three basic tenets carved in stone on the outside wall. Not that he and everyone else on St. Helens did not already know them by heart, he thought. Every schoolchild learned them in kindergarten.

North's Three Principles, after all, were the philosophical bedrock upon which any understanding of scientific and natural phenomena on St. Helens depended. It was the discovery and acceptance of that intellectual framework that had enabled the first generation colonists to survive. The principles were paradoxically both simple and profound.

> *The whole is greater than the sum of its parts.*
> *The struggle for balance and harmony governs*
> *all natural processes.*
> *Balance and harmony are achieved only when*
> *the synergistic contribution of each element is*
> *equal to that of all other elements in the whole.*

Rafe glanced at Orchid. She did not notice. Her attention was fixed on a tall, elegantly lean man dressed in a stylish white suit who was seated in another row. Preston Luce.

Rafe was relieved to see that Orchid's expression was thoughtful, not wistful.

At that moment Preston turned his head slightly and smiled at Orchid. She immediately switched her gaze, to the large, unframed canvas that hung behind the simple altar. The painting consisted of two lightning bolt slashes, one black, one white. Rafe recognized the picture as the work of Eldon Moss, a master of the Neo–Post Synergistic Abstract school. The minimalist approach of the painters of that school had made their work very popular with the meta-zen-syn crowd.

Rafe had been in Northville for only a few hours, but already he had seen a lot of art and architectural design that was clearly inspired by minimalism.

He had to admit that, in large doses, the austere style took on a bland, flat sensibility. He could understand why a young woman with a strong romantic streak might have had a little trouble fitting into the Northville milieu.

There was a small stir of anticipation in the crowd. Veronica and Terrence reappeared in their formal green attire and were introduced as husband and wife. The congregation rose to greet them with a solemn meta-zen-syn chant of welcome.

The new couple walked back down the aisle together. Row by row, the guests followed.

Rafe took Orchid's arm as she got to her feet. "Do we get to eat now?"

She gave him a fleeting grin. "Yes, but don't say I didn't warn you. At a classic meta-zen-syn wedding even the food is supposed to symbolize the Three Principles."

"I'm hungry enough to eat green hors d'oeuvres."

The afternoon was warm and sunny. The reception was held in a serenely austere garden that overlooked the heavily wooded hills of Northville.

To Rafe's relief, the canapés were not all blue and yellow or even green. The small pastries, skewered tidbits, and assorted delicacies were, however, artfully arranged in classic meta-zen-syn patterns on the trays. Most were decorated with meta-zen-syn designs, but the symbolism did not affect the taste. The intellectual elite of Northville were a sophisticated lot. They relished gourmet food and wine.

Half an hour later Rafe stood in front of an abstract minimalist stone sculpture that consisted of a large circle and a triangle and looked out across the low rock wall that surrounded the garden.

From his vantage point he could see most of Northville and the campus of the Patricia Thorncroft North Institute for Synergistic Studies. The town and the prestigious think tank were inextricably linked together. Everyone who lived in Northville was affiliated with the institute in one way or another. The connection was underscored by the manner in which the architecture of the homes and shops in the village echoed the meta-zen-syn elegance and simplicity of the institute's buildings.

The effect of an entire town built along meta-zen-syn principles was either profoundly serene or downright dull. It depended, he supposed, on one's philosophical orientation. The fact that he found the vista a little dull made him wonder about his own personal outlook.

"Enjoying the scenery, Rafe?"

Rafe turned to see Orchid's father, Edward Adams, coming toward him. The two men had been introduced earlier, but there had been little opportunity to talk before the wedding.

Edward was much older than Rafe had expected. The professor was in excellent physical condition, but his hair was completely silver. There was a calm intelligence in his green eyes.

Rafe recalled Orchid telling him that she was the youngest of the Adams' three offspring, but he had not realized until he had met her much older brothers that she had been born several years after them. She must have come as a surprise in more ways than one, he reflected. A rebellious romantic in a family of meta-zen-syn intellectuals.

"I've never seen a whole town designed by meta-zen-syn architects." Rafe munched a small cracker topped with minced, spiced aspara-cado and cheese. "It's interesting."

Edward chuckled as he came to a halt. "That's the word my daughter uses when she's trying to be polite about a work of art she doesn't like."

"Useful word." Rafe glanced across the garden to where Orchid was chatting with Veronica and her new husband. "I must remember to thank her for it."

Edward continued to smile but his eyes held a father's watchful, probing expression. "I understand that you and Orchid met through an agency?"

"Yes, sir." Rafe smiled.

"A *focus* agency, I believe. You hired her for a routine assignment?"

So much for the fleeting hope that he might be able to pull off a small misunderstanding here the way he had at Alfred G.'s birthday party. "It wasn't exactly routine."

"Few things are where Orchid is concerned. She's always marched to a different horn-drum."

"I figured that out right off."

"Because you also march to a different beat?" Edward studied him with a shrewd gaze. "Perhaps that is why you are drawn to each other."

Rafe reminded himself that he was talking to a full professor of metaphysics with a specialty in synergistic theory. One had to be careful what one said around people like Edward Adams. They put things together in a hurry.

"Orchid and I have quite a lot in common," Rafe said easily.

"Is that a fact?"

"Yes, sir, it is."

"She tells me you're a strat-talent."

Rafe braced himself. "That's right."

Edward spread one hand on the round form of the sculpture as if he found the texture of the stone fascinating. "You and Orchid both have highly unusual para-profiles."

"Yes, sir."

"Because of those profiles, neither of you has been successfully matched yet by your respective matchmaking agencies."

"Like I said, Orchid and I have a lot in common."

Edward's eyes met his in a level man-to-man stare. "I suspect that, being a strat-talent, you've concluded that you're quite capable of finding your own wife."

Rafe contemplated the keen scrutiny in Edward's eyes and decided there was no point playing games with him.

"I don't have much choice. I think my marriage agency counselor has given up on me."

Instead of the immediate condemnation that was the only appropriate response to such a shocking announcement, Edward merely nodded. "I see. I was afraid of this."

"Afraid of what, sir?"

"You're a romantic, too."

Rafe nearly choked on the last bit of the canapé. "Like hell."

Edward studied him for a long moment, but he did not respond. Instead, he turned to gaze out over the relentlessly tranquil view of Northville.

"I don't mind telling you that my wife and I have been somewhat concerned about Orchid's future," he said at last. "Ice-prisms are notoriously difficult to match properly."

"Yes."

"It's not as bad as it used to be," Edward said. "More research has been done on them in recent years. Orchid, herself, participated in one of the most significant studies."

"The ParaSyn project."

Edward frowned slightly. "You know of it?"

"She told me about it. The experience was not, I gather, a pleasant one for her."

"No." Edward sighed. "I can't understand what went wrong. ParaSyn is a first-class research center. Over the years the labs there have produced not only some groundbreaking research in the para-bio fields, they have also come up with some extremely profitable technical breakthroughs. I, myself, own stock in ParaSyn."

"So do I." A lot of it, Rafe added silently, thinking of the holdings in the Synergy Fund.

"Dr. Gilbert Bracewell, who is head of the research labs there, has done an outstanding job for nearly twenty years."

"I know."

"Orchid never fully explained why she and the other two research subjects quit the ice-prism project before it was completed. Nevertheless, a great deal was learned." Edward narrowed his eyes. "Some of that knowledge was used to help modify the Multipsychic Paranormal Personality Inventory and other syn-psych tools that are used by matchmaking agencies."

Rafe realized the very civil skirmish between himself and Edward was taking a dangerous twist. He marshaled his arguments carefully.

"That doesn't make up for the fact that there are very few ice-prisms around," Rafe said. "The agencies haven't had much opportunity to see how the new versions of the MPPI and the other para-profiling techniques actually work long term."

"Still, an agency match is always preferable to a non-agency match."

"This is an unusual situation." Rafe paused deliberately. "An agency marriage might carry as much risk for Orchid as an unmatched marriage."

"There is some risk in any marriage, of course. But logic and common sense indicate that an agency marriage stands a better chance of success than one contracted for, shall we say, old-fashioned reasons?"

"Is *old-fashioned* a polite meta-zen-syn term for *primitive?*" Rafe asked in his most polite voice.

"A student of meta-zen-syn comprehends that nature and human beings cannot be understood in terms of primitive versus sophisticated. Indeed, there is no such distinction to be made. What matters is the degree of balance and control individuals achieve over the synergistic forces that operate on both the physical and metaphysical plane."

"The struggle for balance and harmony governs all natural processes," Rafe quoted softly.

"Precisely. Perfect balance is never achieved. It is only a goal toward which the thoughtful person must continually struggle. Each individual must deal with a different set of synergistic forces within himself. Therefore the struggle takes different forms for all of us."

"I'm a businessman, not a philosopher. You're losing me here, Professor."

"On the contrary, I think you understand me very well." Edward's silver brows rose. "Orchid tells me that you are a very powerful strat-talent, but even if she had said nothing about your paranormal abilities, I would have known soon after meeting you that the synergistic forces of your nature are extremely strong. Yet you have achieved a very high degree of control over those forces."

"I like to think so. But just to be on the safe side, I try not to go out on nights when both moons are full."

To Rafe's surprise, Edward chuckled. Then his eyes grew solemn once more.

"I will be frank," he said. "It took my wife and myself considerable argument and, some might say, outright pressure, to persuade Orchid to register with a matchmaking agency last year. For her sake, we would very much prefer to give the agency process a chance to work."

"I understand there was already one screw-up."

Edward winced. "You know about Preston Luce?"

"Yes."

"That was—" Edward's gaze drifted across the crowd to where Preston Luce stood talking to another guest— "regrettable. I'm afraid it put Orchid off the matchmaking process entirely. She wasn't keen on it to begin with. I don't think it suits her romantic inclinations."

"How much longer do you think she ought to wait for Mr. Right to come through an agency?" Rafe asked softly.

"Another few months, at least."

Rafe's jaw tightened. "I see."

"You want her badly, don't you?"

In spite of his growing respect for Edward's savvy insight, Rafe was startled by the unexpectedly blunt question. "Is it your experience as a practitioner of metazen-syn that tells you I want her or are you just naturally intuitive?"

"It's my years of experience as a man and as a father that enables me to spot that particular expression in another man's eye," Edward retorted. "Trust me, if you ever have daughters of your own, you will develop the same kind of instincts."

Rafe grinned in spite of himself. "Sounds primitive."

"Oh, it is. Very."

There was a short silence. Rafe broke it first. "Will you change your attitude on this particular subject if a few more months go by without Orchid getting an agency date?"

"I may have no choice," Edward admitted. "But in the end, the choice must be Orchid's."

"On that point, we agree."

Edward examined the scene spread out below the garden for a long time. "You mentioned that you and my daughter had a lot in common."

"You mean besides our mutual inability to get an agency date?"

Edward did not smile at that. "Yes. What are those things, in your opinion?"

"Well, I've got to be honest and tell you that we don't share the same taste in poetry. But on the positive side, we both admire Later Expansion period architecture."

Edward groaned. "So terribly overwrought. Everything about it was designed to stimulate the emotions and arouse a sense of dark romanticism."

Rafe quirked a brow. "Your daughter does write romantic psychic vampire novels."

"True. And with some success." Edward's smile was rueful. "All I can tell you is that it doesn't come from my side of the family."

"She probably gets it from my side," Anna Adams said from behind Rafe. "I shouldn't admit it, but there is a wildly romantic streak in my branch of the family tree. It pops up from time to time no matter how hard we try to conceal it."

Rafe inclined his head. "Hello, Dr. Adams."

Orchid's mother was a few years younger than her husband but she, too, was older than Rafe had expected. Her once-dark hair was streaked with silver. She had the trim, lithe frame that characterized many of the other local meta-zen-syn practitioners.

"Is Edward grilling you, Rafe?" She smiled at him as she came to a halt near her husband. "How very rude."

"It's all right, Dr. Adams. I understand. In his shoes, I'd do the same."

"Please, call me Anna." Her eyes gleamed with the same mischievous light that appeared in Orchid's gaze when she was amused. "Two professors in one family can be a bit confusing."

Rafe shrugged. "I'm used to it. Both of my parents are on the faculty of New Seattle University."

Edward shot him a quick, searching look. "Is that so?"

"Yes. Department of synergistic theory."

A thoughtful expression appeared in Edward's eyes. "Indeed?"

ORCHID

Instinct made Rafe suddenly search for Orchid again in the crowd. He saw that she was no longer talking to Veronica. Preston Luce had gotten her off by herself near a large reflecting pool at the far end of the garden.

"Mr. Stonebraker was just telling me about the things he believes that he and Orchid have in common," Edward said to Anna. "Thus far it seems to be limited to a taste for Later Expansion period architecture."

"I'm sure that's not all they have in common, dear." Anna gave Rafe a speculative look. "Isn't that so?"

"What?" Rafe concentrated on the tableau near the reflecting pool. "Oh, yeah. Right. A lot more in common. We both like to eat leftovers at three in the morning."

"Hardly the basis for a lasting relationship," Edward observed.

"You'd be surprised." Rafe started to step around Edward. "If you'll excuse me, I just remembered something I wanted to say to Orchid."

"Where is she?" Anna glanced around. "Oh, yes, I see her." As she gazed at the couple standing near the pool, a faintly troubled expression marred the serenity of her brow. "She's chatting with Dr. Luce."

Edward frowned. "Why would she want to talk to him?"

"He probably didn't give her much choice," Anna murmured. "I do hope there won't be a scene."

That comment made Rafe pause. "You think Luce might make a scene in the middle of a wedding?"

Anna's mouth quirked with humor. "Of course not. Preston Luce is much too diplomatic to cause a scene. It's Orchid who worries me."

"Orchid?"

"She's never really forgiven him for the manner in which she believes he used her to get himself introduced into the right circles here at the institute. I've always had the nasty suspicion that she would not pass up an opportunity for revenge should it happen to come her way."

"Anna, you exaggerate," Edward said firmly. "Orchid would never do anything to upset the synergistic harmony of Veronica's wedding day." But he did not look as certain as his words indicated.

"I'll be right back." Rafe started down the graveled path that would take him to the opposite end of the garden.

"Wait, there was, ah, one more thing I wanted to ask you," Edward called after him. "On the off chance that my daughter never gets another agency date—"

Rafe stopped. He turned slowly. "What's that?"

"It's a very old-fashioned kind of question." Edward smiled wryly. "I'm sure you'll understand. What, exactly, do you do for a living?"

"I'm happy to be able to tell you, sir, that I have a pretty good job lined up. Nice benefits, excellent retirement plan, the works. I start in two months."

"And just what is this job?"

"I'm going to be the new C.E.O. of Stonebraker Shipping."

Edward's jaw unhinged. Comprehension lit his eyes. "Good lord. Do you mean to say you're one of *those* Stonebrakers?"

"Close your mouth, dear," Anna murmured. "That unfortunate expression implies a lack of harmonious balance in the alignment of your personal synergy."

Rafe did not wait around to see if Edward got his mouth closed. He was too busy making his way toward the reflecting pool at the other end of the garden, where Orchid stood with Preston Luce.

Some of his most primitive instincts had gone to red-alert status.

Preston did not smell right. The realization made Orchid curious. He certainly did not smell *bad*. He was as freshly showered and groomed as all of the other guests.

The herbal scent of soap and the faint tang of an expensive after-shave were pleasant enough.

But he did not smell right the way Rafe did.

She wondered if frequent focusing for a powerful strat-talent had sharpened some of her own more basic instincts.

She did not find Preston's scent compelling, but she had to admit that he was as handsome as ever. And as well dressed. The cuffs of his white trousers draped fluidly over his white shoes. The expensively styled white jacket was nipped in just enough at the waist to emphasize the physique he kept carefully honed with frequent meta-zen-syn workouts.

She suspected that Preston practiced meta-zen-syn because it was fashionable among the faculty of the North Institute, not because he had any real interest in achieving personal harmony. Nevertheless, he had a flair for the proper outward effect. The white turtleneck he wore under the white jacket added just the right meta-zen-syn touch. Simple, refined, classically balanced.

"It's good to see you again." Preston smiled his fallen-angel smile. "You haven't been around much during the past year. I've missed you."

"I doubt that," Orchid said. "I'm sure you've been much too busy securing grant money and climbing up the academic ladder at the North Institute to notice whether or not I was anywhere in the vicinity."

"Things have been going rather well." Preston had never seen any particular virtue in modesty. "I'm now an associate in the department of synergistic studies. In a couple of years I'll probably take over the department."

"I don't doubt that for a moment."

Preston sipped blue wine and shoved one hand casually into the pocket of his elegantly pleated white trousers. "I understand that your little psychic vampire novels have started to become rather popular."

She gritted her teeth at the condescension in his voice.

"I'm cautiously optimistic that I'll be able to make a living from my writing."

"I haven't read any of them myself."

"Somehow that does not surprise me."

"Tell you what. Why don't you give me one before you leave?" Preston winked indulgently. "I'll be glad to take a look at it when I have a chance and give you a critique."

"That's very magnanimous of you, but I'm afraid that you're operating under a totally false assumption, here, Preston."

"I beg your pardon?"

She gave him her brightest smile. "You're assuming I want or would value your opinion of my books. I don't and wouldn't. Besides, I doubt that you'd have time to read them."

Preston frowned as if vaguely baffled by the fact that the conversation was not going quite as he had planned. His expression cleared quickly, however. With his customary social adroitness, he shifted direction.

"You're right about the time factor. I have enough trouble just keeping up with the research literature and departmental memos. To say nothing of the time it takes to chase grant money."

"And heaven knows, seducing attractive new research assistants is practically a full-time occupation in itself, isn't it?"

Preston's fine brow furrowed briefly. He wanted something from her, Orchid thought. The fact that he did not find an excuse to end the conversation was a very big clue.

"And then there's the never-ending effort it takes to publish your assistants' work under your own name."

He scowled. "I publish the results of work performed under my direction. I have a right to put my name on those papers."

"And we mustn't overlook the amount of time you

invest in discreet ass-kissing in order to get funding for your projects."

Preston reddened. "Now see here, I pull in a hell of a lot of grant money for the institute and don't you forget it. Grant money is the life's blood of research."

"And you use a little para-hyped charisma to get it, not your research credentials. You should have been a politician, Preston."

Preston's eyes darkened furiously. He took a step closer to her.

A few more inches, Orchid pleaded silently. *You're almost at the edge of the pool. Just a teensy bit farther.*

But just when she was hopeful that his temper would make him careless on the wet stones at the water's edge, Preston's face relaxed abruptly into an expression of gentle concern.

Orchid felt the pulse of psychic energy and knew that he was trying to use his talent on her. He was limited by the lack of a prism, but even without someone to help him focus, she knew that he could project very strongly for a few seconds at a time.

She took a step back. "Save it for the next corporate honcho you plan to ambush for grant money. I'll admit that a little punch of charisma-talent makes your suit and your teeth look really shiny and bright, but the effect doesn't last long on someone who knows you well, Preston."

"You're bitter," he said gently.

"No, actually, I'm pissed off at you."

"Because of what happened last year?"

"Because you used me, damn it. I know you faked your marriage agency registration papers. Or maybe you even went so far as to bribe my counselor at Affinity Associates."

"You can't prove that."

"That doesn't mean I don't know it's the truth."

"What makes you so sure?" he demanded.

"Because there's no way you and I could have ever

been matched." She gave him a triumphant smile. "We don't have a single thing in common."

"Ah, now I understand what this is all about." Preston gave her a compassionate look. "You're jealous. You want me back."

"Are you crazy?" She broke off as she caught sight of Rafe coming toward her. Something about his long, gliding pace made her uneasy. She did not need to be any closer to him to feel the energy emanating from him. He was in a dangerous mood. She wondered if her father had grilled him.

Preston turned slightly to follow her gaze. His expression cleared. "Say, that's your friend Stonebraker, isn't it?"

The hastily concealed eagerness in his face answered one question, Orchid thought. Now she knew why Preston had sought her out this afternoon. He had wanted to get to Rafe. In his customary fashion, he had used her to accomplish his goal.

"I don't believe we've met." Preston put out his hand as Rafe came to a halt. "I'm Dr. Preston Luce. Associate professor in the department of synergistic studies here at the institute. I understand you're a friend of Orchid's."

Orchid felt more energy zap across the psychic plane. A jolt of high-powered charisma-talent hummed briefly in the atmosphere.

Preston's smile suddenly sparkled with enough warmth and charm to light up a dark room. Orchid noticed that Rafe seemed completely unaffected. Maybe strat-talent conferred some kind of immunity to charisma, she thought. After all, a hunter could not afford to be charmed by his prey.

"You wouldn't, by any chance be related to the Stonebrakers of Stonebraker Shipping, would you?" Preston asked ingenuously.

"Funny you should ask," Rafe said.

Orchid was alarmed by the low, baiting drawl of his voice. But before she could react, she sensed the stirring of another strong talent on the metaphysical plane. Strattalent this time.

"Oh, dear," she murmured.

Power shimmered, invisible and dangerous, in the air. Preston frowned. Then he blinked and froze for an instant, a moose-deer caught in the headlights.

Orchid knew the feeling. She swiftly ditched her own simple plans for revenge. It was one thing to arrange for Preston to fall into a reflecting pool. That sort of thing could be passed off as an accident. A full-scale brawl in the middle of Veronica's wedding, on the other hand, was another matter altogether. Her parents would never forgive her.

She moved quickly to head off disaster. She planted one slender heel squarely on the toe of Rafe's black leather shoe.

"Rafe's grandfather is the current president and C.E.O. of Stonebraker Shipping," she said glibly. "Isn't that right, Rafe?"

"Yes." Rafe cut off the small shockwaves of talent he had been projecting and eased his toe out from under Orchid's high heel. But he continued to gaze at Preston with the wistful expression of a hungry predator.

Preston blinked again, very rapidly, in apparent confusion. He shook his head and pulled himself together with a visible effort. Orchid was almost certain that he did not realize what had happened.

He managed another suave smile. "Your grandfather. Let's see, that would be Alfred G. Stonebraker, I believe."

"He'll be stepping down in a couple of months," Rafe said. "I'll be taking control of the company."

Preston's eyes widened ever so slightly. Then they immediately narrowed in speculation. "Is that so?"

"Yes," Rafe said. "That's so."

Orchid fixed Rafe with a determined look. "Time to mingle."

"You run along," Rafe said. "I'll join you in a minute. I want to have a little chat with Dr. Luce."

Orchid closed her eyes. Things were out of control. "Uh, Rafe, I don't know if that's such a good idea."

"Stonebraker's right," Preston said cheerfully. "Why don't you run along and let the two of us get to know each other."

"You don't know what you're doing here, Preston," Orchid warned.

"Of course I do." He waved her off. "Don't worry. I'll see you again before you leave."

He was prey at the watering hole, Orchid thought. Blissfully unaware of the predator sneaking up on him in the bushes. In any other circumstances, she would have been more than happy to leave him to his fate. But this was Veronica's wedding.

She gave Rafe a stern look. "No scenes. Think of the bride and groom."

"No scenes," he promised happily. "Much too primitive." He did not take his attention off Preston.

Orchid gave up. She turned away and hurried along the gravel path back toward the safety of the herd.

When she reached the main cluster of wedding guests she headed straight for the wine bar. She did not dare look back to see what was happening at the far end of the garden.

"What can I get for you, ma'am?" the waiter asked politely.

"A large glass of whatever is handy."

The young man glanced back toward the section of the garden where she had been a few minutes earlier. He studied the tableau of Preston Luce talking with Rafe. An expression of sympathy crossed his face. "Yes, ma'am."

He reached for a bottle of expensive champagne, poured a glass, and set it down in front of her.

Orchid heard the collective gasp of astonishment from the crowd just as she started to take the first sip. She cringed. She could only hope that Veronica would some-day forgive her. She took a long, fortifying swallow of champagne and braced herself.

Then with a sense of deep fatalism, she turned. Everyone was staring at the scene taking place at the reflecting pool.

Rafe stood at the water's edge. From Orchid's vantage point it was impossible to see the expression on his face, but his posture radiated mild concern and helpfulness.

Preston staggered to his feet in the center of the shallow pool. His white suit was drenched and stained with mud. He ignored the hand Rafe extended toward him.

As Orchid and the others watched, Preston splashed across the pool in the opposite direction and climbed out on the other side. He scrambled awkwardly over the low rock wall that surrounded the garden and disappeared in the direction of the parking lot.

No one laughed. That would have been very un-meta-zen-syn. The assembled faculty and staff of the North Institute were much too sophisticated for such behavior. But no one seemed very dismayed by Preston's accident. In fact, the murmur of conversation that went through the crowd sounded suspiciously cheerful to Orchid.

She waited with a stoic sense of inevitability as Rafe walked back toward the crowd of onlookers. She saw him pause here and there to answer questions.

As he drew nearer, she could hear what he was saying.

"He slipped and fell. The stones near the edge of the pool are wet. Got to be careful . . ."

When he reached her she saw the look of gleaming satisfaction in his eyes. He reminded her of a wolf-hound returning from the hunt with a rabbit-mouse to lay at its master's feet. Rafe's tongue did not actually loll out of the side of his mouth, but she could tell that it was firmly wedged in his cheek.

She was tempted to pat him on the head.

The waiter handed him a glass of blue champagne without waiting to be asked.

Rafe accepted the offering with a surprised nod. "Thanks."

"My pleasure." The waiter met his eyes. "Least I could do in exchange for the pleasure of seeing Professor Luce pick himself up out of that pond. Probably all of the revenge some of us will ever get."

Rafe looked politely interested. "Revenge?"

"I'm tending bar today to pick up some extra cash. But in my real life, I'm an assistant in Professor Luce's department at the institute. Last month he published a paper that summarized the results of a year's worth of my work in the *Journal of Synergistic Theory*. Didn't even put my name on the list of research assistants who contributed to the project."

"Hold on, here," Rafe said. "If you're implying that I deliberately tossed Luce into that pool, I assure you, it was an accident."

The waiter grinned. "Every student of meta-zen-syn knows that there are no true accidents." Without waiting for a response, he moved off down the bar to pour wine for another guest.

Out of the corner of her eye, Orchid saw her parents walking toward her. She leaned back against the edge of the bar and took another sip of champagne.

"An accident you say?" she murmured.

"He lost his balance and fell. Could have happened to anyone."

Orchid was suddenly absurdly pleased. "Preston did not fall into that pool by accident."

Rafe gave her a superior smile. "Remember North's Second Principle: *The struggle for balance and harmony governs all natural processes.*"

Anna appeared at Orchid's side. She smiled serenely at Rafe.

"And in a shining illustration of that important principle," she said, "it would appear that Professor Luce just lost the struggle to maintain his synergistic balance."

Orchid was startled to see the undisguised satisfaction in her mother's eyes. "Mom?"

"Yes, I know dear. It's not very meta-zen-syn of me to take such pleasure in seeing Preston fall into a pond. But we all have our little lapses. Don't tell your father."

"I don't think Preston fell into that pond." Orchid glanced at Rafe. "I think he may have had a little help."

"Nonsense," Edward said as he strolled over to join the small group. "Your mother is right. Preston just got a sharp lesson in synergistic realignment. Isn't that so, Mr. Stonebraker?"

Rafe shrugged philosophically. "Like they say, synergy happens."

Chapter

17

❖ ❖ ❖ ❖ ❖ ❖ ❖ ❖ ❖

Shortly after midnight, Rafe came awake with the sudden, all-over awareness that Orchid was not asleep. He turned on his side, automatically reaching for her before he remembered that she was not here with him. This was the guest bedroom in her parents' home. She was in another room down the hall.

Earlier in the evening Edward had explained that no two homes in Northville were precisely identical, but all were built along the same meta-zen-syn aesthetic lines. The principles of simplicity, harmony, and balance dominated. The Adams' house was a serenely designed structure built around a courtyard. Every room had windowed walls that opened onto the central garden.

Rafe pushed back the covers and got to his feet. He started toward the door and belatedly remembered his trousers. Something told him that it would be very un-meta-zen-syn to be caught wandering naked down the hall to Orchid's room at this hour of the night. There were those who might view such activity as downright primitive.

He pulled on his trousers, fastened them, and headed toward the door.

Halfway there, he paused again.

He could not feel her presence in the room down the hall.

He freed his senses with a short flash of para-energy, allowing them to absorb the vibrations of the sleeping house. *Two people in a single chamber at the far end of the hall. Mr. and Mrs. Adams.* But no sensations came from the other bedroom.

Orchid was elsewhere. He turned slowly, listening for her with all of his senses.

She was outside in the courtyard garden.

He walked to the windowed wall of his bedroom and looked out into the night-shrouded scene. Orchid sat in the hollowed-out seat of a moon-washed meditation rock. She had her arms wrapped around her up-drawn knees. The folds of a white robe flowed around her.

He smiled to himself. The lady did have an instinct for the romantic.

He opened the glass door and stepped out into the balmy night. Simultaneously he released a psychic probe onto the metaphysical plane. The brief sense of disorientation lasted only a few seconds. When things steadied he saw the clear crystal prism Orchid had crafted for him. He sent power through it, watched it shimmer as she tuned its various facets to focus his talent with perfect clarity.

The night opened up around him.

For a moment he savored the heightened awareness, knowing that through the focus link Orchid was able to enjoy some of the same sensations.

Then he cut off the flow of talent and walked across the meta-zen-syn garden to where Orchid waited for him. He wondered how much longer it would take her to understand that she was his true mate.

He knew she was aware of him, but she said nothing

until he reached the rock where she sat. Then she turned her head to look at him.

"You pushed Preston into that pond for me, didn't you?"

"Why is everyone so convinced that I pushed Luce into that pond? I keep telling you, he slipped and fell."

She ignored that. "How did you know that I very much wanted him to fall into that pond?"

"It came to me in a blinding flash." He took a seat on the rock beside her.

"I'm serious," she said. "How did you know?"

"Telepathy?"

She waved that aside with an irritated little motion of one hand. "Tell me how you knew."

He was surprised by the urgency in her voice. "It wasn't as if there were a lot of options. I mean, you had the reflecting pool no more than a couple of steps away and you had Luce almost within pushing distance. There was a certain sparkle in your eye that I have come to know very well. I already knew you didn't much like the guy. It didn't require telepathy to figure out what you were thinking."

"I see."

"But the synergistic result was very similar to telepathy." The meditation stones were more comfortable than they appeared, he discovered. He settled into the curved seat, leaned back, and rested his weight on his elbows. "Why does it worry you that we might be developing some kind of psychic connection that goes beyond a focus link?"

She was silent for a moment. "I've spent my whole life being different. I'm not sure I want to be any more different than I am already."

"I can see where you would have felt a little out of place here in Northville," he conceded.

"Don't get me wrong. I love my family. I value what I learned here. I even enjoy coming back to visit my relatives. Northville will always be a part of me, but this is not where I belong."

"I understand."

"I always knew that I disappointed everyone by failing to pursue a career at the North Institute the way my brothers and my cousins have."

"Hey, you want to discuss disappointing other people?" Rafe heard the glass door of Anna's and Edward's room open behind him, but he did not turn around. "Try walking away from Stonebraker Shipping when everyone in the family expects you to join the company the day you graduate from college."

"I can imagine what it must have been like for you. But now you're going back. You've completed the circle. I can't do that. I can't come back here. Not permanently."

"There's no need," Anna said gently from the shadows beyond the pool. "You are finding your own balance in life."

Orchid turned her head. "Think so?" She smiled faintly. "That's a very meta-zen-syn thing to say, Mom. You know, I always knew that stuff was good for something."

"The trick is to use it properly." Anna sat down on a meditation stone and glanced at Edward, who had followed her out into the garden. "Isn't that right, dear?"

"Precisely right." Edward lowered himself onto one of the smoothly shaped rocks. "Speaking of weighty philosophical questions, what is going on out here? It's nearly one o'clock in the morning."

"I couldn't sleep," Orchid said.

"I knew she wasn't asleep so I came out here to see what she was doing," Rafe explained.

Edward looked at him with unexpected sharpness. "How did you know that Orchid couldn't sleep?"

"Don't ask," Orchid said quickly. "Rafe thinks we're developing some kind of telepathy."

Instead of chuckling at the ludicrousness of that statement, Edward simply nodded. Rafe thought he looked oddly resigned.

"I was afraid of that," Edward said.

Anna's face was thoughtful in the moonlight. "One must accept the inevitable, dear. The forces of synergy balance themselves with or without our assistance."

Orchid scowled at her parents. "What the heck is that supposed to mean? Don't tell me you two actually believe in telepathy? Everyone knows it's nonsense. It's a metaphysical impossibility. Psychic energy doesn't work that way."

"Don't tell that to two people who have been married as long as your father and I," Anna said.

Orchid wrinkled her nose. "Okay, I'll admit that you and Dad can finish each other's sentences and you know all of each other's jokes. But that's not the same thing as telepathy."

"No, of course it isn't," Anna said soothingly. She looked at Rafe. "What made you push Preston Luce into the reflecting pond this afternoon?"

Orchid grinned.

Rafe spread his hands. "Why does everyone think that I tossed Luce into that pool?"

"Because," Orchid said with mocking patience, "we saw Preston climbing out of the pool, that's why. He was soaking wet. You can make all the meta-zen-syn comments you want about balance and harmony, but I know that he did not fall into that pond by accident."

Rafe studied the intelligent faces of the other three people who shared the night with him. "Did anyone actually see me throw, toss, or otherwise heave Preston Luce into the pool?"

Orchid exchanged glances with her parents.

"No," Anna said slowly. "I don't believe I actually witnessed the incident."

"Neither did I," Edward admitted. "That section of the garden is quite a way from where most of us were standing."

Orchid looked at Rafe. "Okay, I didn't actually see you do it, but it's the only explanation. Why are you arguing the point?"

"Because I resent the fact that everyone assumes that just because I'm a strat-talent, I would do something so gauche and tacky as to push a man into a reflecting pool at a wedding," Rafe said.

"Now, Rafe," Orchid began. "That's not quite what—"

"Your assumption about what happened between Luce and me only goes to show that even sophisticated, intelligent, well-educated people have some grave misconceptions about strat-talents. It's no wonder a guy like me can't get an agency date. Talk about being stereotyped as the primitive type."

A charged silence descended on the courtyard garden. Rafe enjoyed the expressions of chagrin that appeared on the faces of Edward and Anna. He gave everyone what he considered his most virtuous smile.

Orchid rolled her eyes.

"You may be right," Anna said. Her expression was somber, a little troubled. "I don't like to admit it, but I did leap to the conclusion that Preston Luce did not fall into that pool by accident. Not that I was complaining, you understand."

"He certainly deserved that and more," Edward agreed. "But you're quite correct, Rafe. We should not have assumed that you would do something so . . . well, so *physical* just because you're a strat-talent."

"It was your daughter who intended to push him into the pool," Rafe said. "Ask her."

Anna and Edward turned to her.

"Is that true?" Anna asked, eyes gleaming with amusement.

"Yep." Orchid exhaled deeply. "I figured it was the least I could do under the circumstances. I don't care how good Preston is when it comes to pulling in grant money, he's a nasty little user."

"In the past few months I have regretfully come to the same conclusion," Edward conceded reluctantly.

"What's more, I know he faked his para-profile on his marriage agency registration last year so that he could be matched with me. Or maybe he bribed my counselor. I'm still not sure which. Either way, his only goal was to get himself into the right circles here at Northville so that he could use his charisma-talent to land a good post. And darned if his plan didn't work."

"Your father and I have had a few suspicions along that line," Anna admitted. "Unfortunately, there is no way to prove that."

"I know." Orchid grinned. "Which is why I was left contemplating such a primitive sort of revenge as pushing him into a pond. But I never got the chance, thanks to Rafe. He interrupted things before I could finish. And now he's claiming that the final result wasn't even real revenge, just an accident."

"Deliberately pushing Luce into a pond would have been childish and immature," Rafe pointed out.

"But fun," Orchid said.

Anna shook her head. "So much for all those years of meta-zen-syn training." She looked at Rafe. "So you're going to stick to your story? Preston really did fall into that pond by accident?"

"Sort of," Rafe said.

Orchid pounced. "Ah-hah. I knew there was more to it than that. What, exactly, happened at the reflecting pool this afternoon?"

"If you must know, Professor Luce took a swing at me. He lost his balance when he missed. That's how he fell into the pool."

The other three gaped at him.

Orchid recovered first. "Preston tried to hit you?"

"Fortunately, one of the benefits of being a strat-talent is that I have fairly quick reflexes," Rafe murmured. "I was able to step aside."

"But why on St. Helens would Luce take a swing at

you?'' Edward stared at him, still astonished. "I've never noticed any violent tendencies in him. Besides, he never even met you until today."

"He was probably pissed-off because I told him that when I took control of Stonebraker Shipping I planned to review the portion of his grant funding that was derived from Stonebraker's corporate contribution to the North Institute."

Orchid stared. "You did *what?*"

"I strongly hinted that I had the power to see to it that any projects that listed him as primary analyst would be handed off to someone else on the institute staff."

A stunned silence descended. Rafe watched with amusement as the full impact of what he had just said hit the other three.

"My God," Orchid whispered. "You threatened to cut off a huge chunk of his grant money."

"I didn't exactly threaten," Rafe said carefully. "I pretty much promised I'd do it. I also warned him that as Stonebraker's C.E.O. I'll have a certain amount of influence with some of the other corporate heads who contribute to the institute."

"So much for being primitive." Edward's face screwed up into a strange expression. "What a perfect meta-zen-syn revenge."

"Thank you," Rafe said. "I like to think I'm not entirely a victim of my throwback genes."

The look on Edward's face got odder. And then he exploded with laughter.

Anna's eyes sparkled with humor. She clapped a hand over her mouth and dissolved into muffled giggles.

Orchid was the only one who did not look wholeheartedly amused. There was a distinctly wary gleam in her gaze. "I assume that just because you're cutting Preston's funding, you won't withdraw corporate financial support from the institute altogether?"

"No, I'll probably increase it. My grandfather has always been too tight when it came to funding basic research. My own view is that Stonebraker needs to spend more, not less in that area. Long term, the institute projects are extremely valuable to us and every other company on the planet."

Orchid grinned. "An excellent corporate philosophy. Very forward thinking. Guess that's why they'll be giving you the big office in a couple of months."

"I don't think it's my corporate philosophy that's going to get me that big office," Rafe said. "I think it has more to do with the fact that I won't let them give it to anyone else."

Orchid sighed. "There is that aspect of the situation."

Rafe looked at Edward. "I do have one question concerning Dr. Preston Luce."

Edward got his laughter under control. "What's that?"

"I understand that it was his connection to Orchid that got him into the right circles here at Northville. And I realize that he does have some charisma-talent. But I still can't see your personnel department hiring him without doing a basic background check."

"Oh, Luce had excellent references," Edward said. "He came to the institute with glowing recommendations from his former employer."

"True." Anna grimaced. "They were so good, that I wouldn't be surprised to learn that he wrote some of them himself."

Rafe looked at Orchid. "You said that he used you to get himself here."

Orchid shuddered. "Don't remind me."

"How did he meet you?"

Orchid blinked in surprise. "I explained that. We met through my marriage agency, Affinity Associates."

"No, I mean how did he find you? How did he know where you were registered? Hell, how did he even know that you were from Northville and that he could use you? He must have learned a lot about you before he even went to Affinity Associates to register."

"I see what you mean." Orchid shrugged. "He probably came across my file during the time he worked at ParaSyn. He was on the staff there for a while after I left."

"Well, *shit.*"

Edward gave him a faint frown of disapproval. "I beg your pardon?"

Rafe sat up swiftly. "It always comes back to ParaSyn, doesn't it?"

"What do you mean?" Anna asked.

"Here's my insider stock trading tip of the day," Rafe said. "Sell your ParaSyn shares first thing in the morning."

"Why?" Edward demanded, baffled.

"Because something tells me there's a problem there."

Edward frowned. "How do you know that?"

"I just know it."

Orchid did not press him for details until the next morning when they got into the Icer for the drive back to New Seattle.

"All right, time to explain the 'well, shit,' last night, Stonebraker," she said as she buckled her seatbelt.

"Sorry." Rafe eased the car out of the driveway. "Guess that wasn't a very meta-zen-syn thing to say, was it?"

"No, but we'll leave that aside for the moment." Orchid slid the passenger window down and leaned out to wave farewell to her parents.

She did not know what to make of the expressions on their faces as they stood watching the Icer pull out of the drive. A cross between acceptance and wistful concern, she decided. A very parental look.

It was almost as if they knew something about her future that she herself did not. Whatever it was, it worried them, but they had come to terms with it. She'd seen that look in their eyes on other occasions. The day she left Northville to find an apartment in New Seattle, for instance. She knew now that they had known then that she would never make her home in Northville.

Being the offspring of obsessive meta-zen-syn types could be trying, she reflected, not for the first time.

She finished waving and slid the window back into place. It sealed itself with a soft hiss.

"Why did you say it?" she asked as Rafe drove through the artfully arranged landscape of carefully situated homes and austere rock- and reflecting-pool gardens.

She realized she liked to watch him drive. He did it with the same fluid ease and controlled power that characterized all of his movements. It was probably some extremely primitive aspect of her own nature that caused her to savor such a simple and elemental aspect of a man.

"I said it because it suddenly struck me that everywhere I turn ParaSyn keeps popping up in our conversations."

"It pops up a lot because of me. If you hadn't hired me to focus for you on this case, you wouldn't have come across any references to ParaSyn."

"You're wrong," he said softly. "As soon as I started looking into Willis's background, I would have learned about the ice-prism project."

"Yes, I suppose that's right."

"Sooner or later, I would have made a connection to Morgan Lambert. That would have led me to the fact that Lambert and Willis had met at ParaSyn." Rafe smiled abruptly, as though he had just been struck by a very satisfying thought.

Orchid eyed him suspiciously. "Now, what?"

"It just occurred to me that even if I had never gone to Psynergy, Inc., to hire a full-spectrum prism, I would have met you eventually in the course of tracking down all of the people who had close ties to Theo Willis."

"Hmm."

"Funny how synergy works, isn't it?"

She made a face. "Must be destiny, all right."

"What? You don't believe in destiny? And here I thought you were the romantic type."

"Forget the destiny stuff. Tell me why you're concerned about the ParaSyn connection."

"I don't have anything solid yet." Rafe guided the Icer through the relentlessly serene village of Northville. "To get it, I'll need something that ties Quentin Austen to ParaSyn."

Orchid watched the last Northville speed limit sign slip past the window. Rafe accelerated rapidly.

"What would such a connection tell you?" she asked.

"I'm not sure. But it would certainly prove very interesting."

Orchid gazed out the windshield at the heavily wooded landscape. But she did not see the trees that marched down the hillsides to the banks of the North River. Other images filled her mind. Scenes of grueling focus sessions with mentally disturbed talents. Exhausting lab tests conducted by cold researchers who did not seem to notice or care about the stress they induced in their volunteer subjects. The eagerness of the experts to move from experiments with the mentally ill to focus sessions with the criminally insane.

With an effort she shook off the unpleasant chill. "If our search for the missing relic leads to ParaSyn we may need to get inside."

"We'll see."

She took a deep breath. "I've got the perfect excuse, Rafe."

Rafe shook his head. "Security at a place like ParaSyn is always very tight. I doubt that the authorities would grant a former research subject free run of the place. Especially given the fact that the project you were involved in was closed down three years ago."

"I'm not sure I'd get free run of the place." Orchid kept her attention on the serene view of the river. "But I know they'll let me back inside. They've been trying to coax me back for a follow-up project for weeks, remember?"

Rafe gave her a raking glance. "Forget it. You aren't going back there under any circumstances."

"But if it means closing our case—"

His jaw was stone. "You aren't going back to ParaSyn."

"Not even if it means finding the missing relic?"

"That damn relic is not worth sending you back to ParaSyn. Besides, odds are it's nowhere near ParaSyn, anyway."

"What do you mean? You just said there might be a connection. Maybe some researchers at ParaSyn arranged to steal the relic."

Rafe looked surprised by her suggestion. "Not likely. There would be no need to steal it. ParaSyn is a major company with a lot of clout. If the experts there wanted to conduct experiments on some of the alien artifacts all they would have to do is contract with the authorities at the university and the New Seattle Art Museum. No one would turn down a request from them."

"Good point." She sank back in her seat, briefly deflated but also secretly relieved.

"Even if the executives at ParaSyn had decided to engage in a little industrial espionage, they would have used a more efficient and more reliable agent than Theo Willis."

"I see what you mean."

"All I'm looking for is another lead on Quentin Austen. There's something a little too convenient about his suicide. But I can get the kind of information I need without sending you back to ParaSyn."

Orchid was touched by his vehemence. Smiling tremulously, she reached across the short distance that separated them and patted his hand. "Thanks."

"I missed you last night," Rafe said after a while.

"I was just down the hall."

"I'm getting used to having you in my bed."

She did not know what to say to that. The truth was, she was getting used to being in his bed, too.

Rafe said nothing for a time. After a while he glanced at her, eyes gleaming. "I guess pulling over to the side of the road, driving into that grove of trees near the river, and getting into the backseat would be a really primitive thing to do."

"Are you kidding?" She was horrified. "It would not only be primitive, it could be extremely embarrassing. This is a major highway. Someone might see us."

"Not much traffic," he observed. "And the woods look pretty thick. I don't think anyone would notice."

"That grove near the river is just the sort of place a family would choose for a roadside picnic."

"You know what your problem is, Orchid? You lack a spirit of adventure."

Orchid felt the Icer slow perceptibly. "You wouldn't dare."

It was fast and intense and in the end Orchid actually screamed. It was probably real primitive of him, Rafe thought, but he liked that part best.

"I can't believe you did that." Twenty minutes later, Orchid perched on the edge of the backseat struggling to pull on her jeans.

It was not an easy task, Rafe thought. There was very little room for her to maneuver because he was taking up most of the available space. He lounged in the corner, one leg stretched out behind Orchid's madly wriggling rear, and enjoyed the scene.

"Might be easier if you opened the door and got out," he said.

"I'm not getting out of this car until I'm dressed. We're not that far from Northville. What if some of my parents' friends happened along?"

"Suit yourself, but I really don't think anyone can see you from the highway."

"I'm not taking any chances." There was a soft snap

as Orchid managed to fasten the waistband of her jeans. "Isn't there some kind of law that says that no one over the age of eighteen is allowed to do it in the backseat?"

"I won't tell the backseat police if you don't." He sat up reluctantly and gingerly rezipped his pants. "If you'll excuse me for a moment, I believe I'll use the facilities."

"What facilities?" She peered through the fogged up windows. "This isn't a rest stop. We're in the middle of the woods."

"Right. The facilities." He cracked the door open and slid it up into the roof. "Be back in a minute."

"Oh, I see." She turned pink. Then she studied the river bank that was only a few feet away with a thoughtful expression. "Maybe I'll take the opportunity to wash up myself."

Rafe got out of the car. "Don't fall in. That water will be ice cold at this time of year."

"Don't worry. My balance is a lot better than Preston's."

"I believe it." Rafe turned and walked a discreet distance into the trees, savoring the after effects making love to Orchid always had on his senses. He felt relaxed and pleasantly aware of the sights, smells, and small sounds around him.

Life was good this morning.

He kept walking.

The morning sun filtered through the leaves, dappling the ground with spots of gold and shadow. The rich soil beneath his boots smelled of spring. The air tasted better than blue champagne.

He allowed his mind as well as his senses to wander as he chose a suitable tree and unzipped his jeans.

From out of nowhere he recalled the billing ledger he had found the night he and Orchid had searched Quentin Austen's office. He had a sudden memory of the pink sticky note attached to the back.

The synergistic possibilities hit him with the impact of summer lightning.

Energy pulsed through him as he hastily rezipped his jeans. The small burst of adrenaline took his already heightened senses up another notch for a few seconds.

Just long enough to alert him to the presence of another person nearby.

Not Orchid.

The sense of imminent danger crackled through him. He had to get back to Orchid. He shoved more energy out onto the psychic plane, instinctively seeking her through the focus link.

He saw the familiar prism take shape, clear and sharp even at this distance. He sent a warning crashing across the metaphysical realm even as he isolated the taint of the *other* and followed it.

He whirled, orienting himself. Through the trees he caught the unnatural glint of sunlight on steel.

He dove for cover just as the shot rang out. He landed on the ground behind a large tree.

"Rafe," Orchid's shout came from the river's edge. "That was a shot."

It was clear now that he was the target, not her. "Stay where you are."

"Hey, you in the woods with the gun," she yelled. "There are people here. It's illegal to hunt this close to the highway."

Rafe doubted that her warning would carry much weight with the shooter. Whoever he was, he was no ordinary hunter. But Orchid's words did provide a distraction.

Rafe sensed that the other's attention was divided now.

From the would-be killer's point of view, things were disintegrating rapidly, he thought. The first shot had missed and the intended victim was no longer in sight. To top it off, a woman who was invisible through the veil of trees was yelling.

Rafe flattened himself on the ground and made his way toward the shelter of the next large tree.

Another shot rang out, but this one went wild. The gunman had lost track of his quarry.

"There are people here, you idiot," Orchid shouted furiously. "What do you think you're doing?"

Rafe concentrated on sending more power through the prism. He knew exactly where the gunman was now. He began to circle toward him, using the heavy undergrowth as cover.

Apparently sensing the impending danger, the gunman abandoned his post. Rafe heard the rush of pounding footsteps in the distance. The man was plunging through the trees toward the road.

"Shit."

The bastard was going to get away.

Rafe broke into a charging run.

He heard the slam of a car door and knew that he was too late. An instant later came the whine of an engine. It was followed by the squeal of tires on pavement.

Rafe reached the edge of the road in time to see the tail of a white Phase 1000 disappear around the curve in the highway.

There were, he reflected, a lot of Phases in the world.

"Are you certain it wasn't some stupid hunter who thought you were a moose-deer?" Orchid asked for the third time as she refastened her seatbelt.

"Positive." Rafe started the Icer and backed out of the trees toward the highway. "Whoever he was, he must have been following us since we left your folks' house."

"He couldn't have known that we would stop here."

"No, but when he saw us pull off the road he probably figured he had a golden opportunity."

"To kill you? But who would want to do that? Dr. Austen was the only killer we've come across recently and he's dead."

"There's still the little matter of the missing relic," Rafe pointed out.

"But we don't know where it is."

"Someone may be worried that we're still searching for it."

She mulled that over for a moment. "I don't know. Even if we assume that there is someone else involved in this thing besides Austen, why would he or she consider you a threat? With Austen's death, the trail has gone cold."

"Not quite." Rafe glanced over his shoulder and then pulled out onto the highway. "Just before that guy took a shot at me, I had what you might call a small epiphany."

"An epiphany? While using the facilities?"

"While taking a leak against a tree, to be precise."

She grimaced. "What is it with men and trees, anyway?"

"It's a guy thing. You wouldn't understand. As I was saying, I suddenly recalled something we saw the night we went through Austen's office."

"What?"

"On the back of Theo Willis's chart there was a small sticky note, remember?"

"Sure. You said it looked as if the receptionist had jotted it down to remind herself to send a thank-you note for the referral."

"I think," Rafe said, "that it would be very interesting to find out who referred Theo Willis to Dr. Austen."

"Maybe," she said slowly.

"You sound unconvinced."

"I hate to say this, but I think you're reaching a bit here. We have nothing to indicate that there was anyone else besides Quentin Austen involved with the missing relic. But we can say, with some certainty, that there are a couple of other people who might take a potshot at you if they got the chance."

He raised his brows. "Such as?"

"Your cousin Selby."

Rafe looked briefly intrigued. "I hadn't thought of that."

"He's got a lot to lose if you take over Stonebraker Shipping."

"When, not if."

"I beg your pardon. *When* you take over Stonebraker. And there's someone else you have recently pissed-off, too, don't forget."

He frowned. "Who?"

"Preston Luce."

"Luce? Five hells, I cut off his funding, not his balls."

"With Preston, it probably amounts to the same thing. Grant funding is his raison d'être. Obtaining money for research projects is what he does. It's what gives him clout at the institute. If he can no longer play rainmaker, he won't last long. As a pure research analyst, he's a bust."

"I see what you mean."

"Let's face it Rafe. When you get right down to it, you are not the most popular man in the city-state."

"Okay by me," he said cheerfully. "I don't care what everyone else thinks as long as you'll still sleep with me."

Chapter

18

❖ ❖ ❖ ❖ ❖ ❖ ❖ ❖ ❖

"Yes, Mom. We got back to the city yesterday at about two o'clock. We, uh, stopped for a bite along the way." Carrying the phone in one hand, Orchid paced back and forth across the small living room. She had told her parents nothing about the incident on the highway. The information would only alarm them and there was nothing they could do about it. "Just wanted to let you know that everything's fine on this end."

"The wedding was lovely, wasn't it?"

"Beautiful. Veronica and Terrence were meant for each other."

"That," Anna said meaningfully, "is just what their marriage counselors said."

Orchid raised her eyes to the ceiling. "I know."

"Still no word from your agency?"

"No." Orchid suppressed a flash of guilt. She had not yet informed her parents that Affinity Associates had lost her file. She paused beside her desk, picked up a pen, and dutifully jotted herself a note.

*Call Affinity Associates. Find out what happened to
my file.*

"I must say, your Mr. Stonebraker was very interesting."

"Yes, he is that." *Interesting.* Orchid winced. Rafe was
a lot more than interesting.

She picked up the note she had just written to herself,
crumpled it in her fist, and tossed it into the waste can.

"Mom, I know this is going to sound like a dumb
question, but do you, by any chance, happen to know
what kind of car Preston drives?"

"I'm not sure what type it is. I don't pay much attention to cars. But as I recall, it's white."

White. Like a white Phase 1000? Orchid wondered.
She sat down heavily in her chair. "Does Dad know?"

"I don't know. Why?"

"Oh, nothing. I just thought I saw Preston pass us on
the highway on the way back to the city. I wondered if
he had left Northville because of what happened between him and Rafe."

"I don't know if he's still here or not. I'll ask your
father when I see him later today. About Mr. Stonebraker—"

"I'm sorry, Mom. I've really got to run. Love you.
'Bye."

Orchid hung up the phone before her mother could
continue the gentle cross-examination.

She sprawled in her chair and thought about the fact
that Preston Luce's car was very likely white. White was
an extremely common color in cars, especially in Northville, she reminded herself. It was so very meta-zen-syn.

The low, resonant bong of her front doorbell roused
her from her state of intense brooding. On the off
chance that it would be Rafe with news of his investigation into the white car and maybe some take-out pasta,
she got to her feet.

When she reached the door she automatically started
to open it. But the events of the previous few days had
taken their toll. She paused long enough to peer through

the peephole. She stifled a small groan when she saw Briana Culverthorpe standing in the hallway.

Taking a deep breath, she pasted what she hoped was a pleasant smile on her face and opened the door. "Hello, Mrs. Culverthorpe. What brings you here?"

"I should have telephoned first." Briana did not smile. "But I happened to be driving past your apartment and I thought I'd take a chance on your being home."

"Why?"

"I'd like to speak with you." Briana glanced past Orchid into the tiny entrance hall of the small apartment. "May I come in?"

"Yes, of course." Orchid stepped back.

Briana was the same patrician woman Orchid had met briefly on the night of Alfred G. Stonebraker's birthday. Her pale hair framed her attractive face in two elegantly curved wings. The beautifully tailored suit she wore was a pale, pastel blue.

The only difference was that today there was an air of tension about her that did not suit the look of wealthy sophistication.

Orchid watched, amused as Briana glanced around the small living room with ill-concealed curiosity. She took in the sight of the genuine yellow velvet covered Later Expansion period sofa and the assorted reproduction pieces in the same style. An air of faint disdain lit the cool blue eyes.

"We probably don't use the same interior designer," Orchid said.

"No," Briana sat down gingerly on the edge of the flamboyantly curved, high-backed sofa. She did not allow herself to sink into its depths. "I doubt that we do."

"Coff-tea?"

"No, thank you. I won't be staying long. I shall come straight to the point, Miss Adams. My husband made you an offer a few days ago. I wish to know if you intend to accept it."

Orchid saw the anxiety in Briana's eyes. She found

herself wanting to let the other woman down gently. But
she could not think of any graceful way to refuse a bribe.

"No. I can't accept it."

"I see." Fine lines appeared at the corners of Briana's
beautifully made-up mouth. "Perhaps Selby did not
make the offer high enough."

"Actually, he left it pretty open-ended. Told me I
could just about name my own price. But there is no
price, Mrs. Culverthorpe."

Briana gave her a level look. "I trust you do realize
that when this is all over, he won't marry you."

"Who? Stonebraker?"

"He registered at a marriage agency a few weeks ago
because he needed a creditable fiancée to parade in front
of his grandfather and the Stonebraker board of directors. Given his, shall we say, unusual nature, there
couldn't have been a lot of choice when it came to a
match. I suspect he grabbed the first one he was
offered."

"Me?"

"Yes. I also suspect that, even if it's a genuine match,
it's a very low-probability one. Take some advice, Miss
Adams. If you're going along with it because you think
it's worth the risk in order to marry into Stonebraker
Shipping, don't be fooled."

"Fooled?"

"Don't make the mistake of believing that Rafe will
actually go through with the marriage just because it's
an agency-arranged match."

"I already got this lecture from your husband."

"My husband was right. Rafe is not interested in marriage at this point." Briana stood up abruptly and
walked to the window. "All he cares about is seizing
control of Stonebraker. He will do anything to achieve
his goal. It's his nature. But when he has what he wants,
he will no longer need you."

"Mrs. Culverthorpe—"

"Eventually, of course, he will marry. But when he

does choose a wife, he will do it the same way he does everything else, with an eye toward how well she suits his purposes."

"You don't think I'll suit his purposes?"

"No, I do not. Even if the marriage agency that put the two of you together is convinced that you were a reasonably good match in syn-psych terms, I doubt that they understand the rest of it."

"What do you mean?"

"The agency probably didn't take into account the fact that people who come from a certain social strata frequently marry for reasons other than compatibility and mutual affection. They choose spouses for more pragmatic reasons."

"Was your marriage based on those kinds of reasons?"

Briana shot her a glare that could have frozen lava. "As it happens, mine was an agency match. But the counselors were careful to ensure that social factors were considered along with the syn-psych aspects of the match."

"I see."

Briana turned back to the view of the street. "I will be blunt. I understand the people in the Stonebraker world infinitely better than you ever will. I can promise you that you will never fit into that world."

"I'm pretty adaptable."

Briana's spine stiffened. She did not turn around. "Let's be honest here. A woman like you is not likely to fit into the environment in which Rafe Stonebraker will move if he succeeds in getting control of Stonebraker Shipping."

Orchid felt a ripple of tension go through her. "What do you know about my background?"

"My husband did some checking," Briana said. "You were raised in Northville. I think that says it all."

"Contrary to popular opinion, Northville has a great deal more in common with the real world than most people seem to believe."

"I'm not disputing the importance of the North Institute or the people who staff it. But everyone knows it's an ivory tower filled with meta-zen-syn types. Anyone who grew up there would have little to offer Rafe Stonebraker."

"What do you think Rafe will look for when he chooses a wife?"

Briana shrugged. "Someone who can bring him good business and social connections. A woman who will know how to entertain his friends and associates. A wife who moves in the right circles."

"I was never very big on going around in circles."

"Damn you." Briana swung around. "Don't you understand? He's *using* you."

"I beg your pardon, Mrs. Culverthorpe. I've known some real users, and Rafe is not one of them. I will admit he's single-minded and goal oriented, but he's not a user."

Briana's eyes widened. "You think this is some kind of game, don't you? Are you doing this because it amuses you?"

"No."

"Good. Because I assure you, this is no game. There is a great deal at stake here."

"I'm well aware of that, Mrs. Culverthorpe."

Briana's eyes narrowed. "I was afraid of this."

"Afraid of what?"

"You're sexually attracted to him, aren't you?"

Orchid said nothing.

"You're having an affair with him. That's obvious. Perhaps you've even convinced yourself that he's in love with you."

Orchid did not respond.

Briana smiled grimly. "I told Selby that if you had been so foolish as to fall in love with Rafe, the bribe would not work. But he was certain you weren't that stupid. He seems to think that, because you're a full-spectrum prism, you're too smart to miscalculate the risks of getting involved with a strat-talent."

"My relationship to Rafe Stonebraker is a very personal matter, Mrs. Culverthorpe. I'm sure you can understand that I don't wish to discuss it."

"You do know that he's a strat-talent, don't you?" Briana frowned. "He didn't find a way to conceal that from you by any chance?"

"I know he's a strat-talent."

"Yes, of course. The matchmaking agency would have told you that much. They would have been grossly negligent in their responsibilities if they'd kept the fact from you."

"Uh huh."

"Having been raised in Northville, you may not be fully aware of all the, shall we say, implications."

"I think I've got a pretty good handle on the subject."

Briana did not appear to hear her. "They call them hunters, you know. Throwbacks to an earlier evolutionary time. They're quite rare in the population."

"I'm aware of the misconceptions that surround them."

"Their talent is considered primitive. Potentially dangerous. Most of them become criminals."

"Not most of them, Mrs. Culverthorpe. Only some. Just as some psychometric-talents and some hypnotalents and," Orchid paused to give her words added weight, "some tech-talents do."

Briana whirled around. "Damn you, my husband is not a criminal."

"He's trying to destroy a family business that supports not only the members of his own clan, but a couple of thousand employees. Some people might see that as a criminal enterprise."

Briana's face tightened. "That's not true."

"Forgive me, Mrs. Culverthorpe, but I have to trust someone's version of events. I've decided to trust Rafe's."

"Then you're a fool."

"There is no doubt in my mind that Rafe is going to take control of Stonebraker because he genuinely believes that the firm is in danger of being destroyed by your husband."

Briana gave her an incredulous look. "Why would my husband destroy Stonebraker?"

"I gather the motive is revenge. Something to do with what happened to his father."

"Rafe fed you that old tale?" Briana gave a short, harsh, crack of laughter. "It's utter nonsense. An old family legend that has circulated for years. No one, least of all my husband, actually believes that Alfred G. murdered Perry Culverthorpe."

"Are you certain of that?"

"Of course, I'm certain." Briana turned very quickly back to the window. "Selby would never destroy Stonebraker. He's devoted to the family firm. And to our children. He would never do anything that would hurt their future."

Orchid watched Briana open and close her hand around the strap of her purse. "I have a hunch that your husband has planned the future of his own, immediate family very carefully, Mrs. Culverthorpe. When he tried to buy me off the other day, he made it clear that he expects to be very, very rich soon."

"Naturally, after he takes control of Stonebraker—"

"Stop it," Orchid said. "You're his wife. You know what he intends to do, Mrs. Culverthorpe. Who are you trying to fool? Me or yourself?"

Briana stared fixedly out the window. She looked so stiff and brittle that Orchid feared she might shatter.

"He won't destroy Stonebraker," she whispered. "He won't do it. He can't. When he gets control he'll realize—"

"I don't know what happened in the past." Orchid got to her feet. "As far as I can tell only two people know the truth, Rafe's grandfather and your husband's father.

One is dead and I suspect that the other will go to his grave sticking by his version of events."

"Just a family legend," Briana whispered.

"Which your husband believes."

"No."

"Yes." Orchid hesitated. "Briana, Selby was right about one thing. I'm a trained, full-spectrum prism. I've had a lot of experience with various kinds of talent. I know something about the para-profiles of people like your husband."

"I don't need your so-called expert opinion on Selby's para-profile."

"Too bad. You've given me a lot of unasked for advice this afternoon. I'm going to dispense a little of my own."

"I don't want to hear it."

"Tough. Pay attention here. Your husband is a tech-talent. That means he's good at engineering things, including revenge. But it also means he can be obsessive about his goals. He's been plotting revenge for so long, he's forgotten there's any other purpose in life. We need to find a way to remind him."

"We?"

"Well, you, for the most part," Orchid admitted. "After all, you're the one who's married to him. Maybe you should try to get him to a syn-psych therapist."

"Are you serious?"

"Look, we've got good material to work with here." Orchid clasped her hands behind her back and began to pace. "You just told me that you and Selby were agency matched. That means that fundamentally the two of you form a good team."

"My marriage is none of your affair," Briana said fiercely.

"Selby's gone a little off course because of his fixation with revenge. But if you can break through that fixation, you've got a chance to change everything."

"How dare you try to interfere in my life?"

Orchid met her eyes. "You have the nerve to ask me that after what you just did?"

"I've done nothing to you."

Quite suddenly, Orchid had had enough. "Who do you think you are? You treat me as if I were a fool. First, you and Selby try to buy me off. Then you give me lectures on how I shouldn't expect Rafe to marry me. You tell me I couldn't possibly become a good little Stonebraker because I don't have the right social connections."

"I'm only trying to warn you that you're involved in a situation you can't possibly comprehend."

"You don't think I *comprehend* what is going on here?" Orchid stopped pacing. She drew herself up and looked straight at Briana. "I was raised in the tenets of meta-zen-syn. Perhaps you are not fully aware of just what that means."

For the first time Briana looked uncertain. "I only meant—"

"I was trained from the cradle to analyze the synergistic forces at work in any situation. I comprehend things in ways that you can only guess, Briana. The ability to *comprehend* on the abstract level was bred into my very bones."

"I realize you had a very good education," Briana said weakly. "Especially in philosophy."

"A *good* education? When I graduated from high school I had an awareness of the confluence between the physical and the metaphysical planes that exceeded that of the average graduate student in synergistic theory."

"I only meant—" Briana broke off. She fell back when Orchid took a step toward her.

"When I reached the university level, my ability to comprehend the philosophical principles of synergism was superior to that of the average *professor* of synergistic theory. Do not presume to tell me that I am not capable of comprehending something as simple as the situation between Rafe and Selby."

"You call it simple?" ·

"We're talking about two men who have distrusted each other since childhood because one of them is hell-bent on revenge and the other one knows it. Nothing could be more simple."

Briana took another step back. She began to look desperate. "It's not that straightforward."

"Of course it is. The most powerful truths are always simple and straightforward. Have you forgotten the basic synergy lessons you learned in kindergarten?"

"This isn't about synergy."

"Oh, but it is, Briana. So far as Stonebraker Shipping is concerned, it can take two possible forms. Survival or destruction. You have power in this situation. Use it to help save the company and your husband."

Briana held up a hand as if to ward off an ill omen. "My God. Are you saying that Rafe will . . . will try to physically hurt Selby?"

"No. I'm saying that Selby will hurt himself and his family if he continues on his present course. Revenge never brings balance or harmony of a positive kind. It begets a downward spiral that ultimately results in destruction. Is that what you want for your family, Briana?"

"I won't listen to this. I don't have to listen to this."

Eyes bright with anger and anguish, Briana took a series of jerky steps toward the door. When she reached it she yanked it open.

"Briana."

At the sound of Orchid's voice, Briana halted on the threshold. She half-turned with the air of a woman bracing herself for a blow. "I've heard enough."

"Think about the future of your family, Briana. Think about what you can do to alter the synergistic forces so that the struggle for balance is weighted toward survival, not destruction. You love your husband. Use that love to try to make him see where he is headed. Make him understand that he will not find what he seeks if he is successful in toppling Stonebraker."

Briana stared at Orchid. "You're wrong. I don't have the power that you seem to think I do."

"We all have power, Briana. But not all of us are smart enough to use it. I'm betting that you are."

Briana stepped out into the hall and slammed the door behind her.

Orchid stood very still for a few minutes. Then she did some deep breathing to help shake off the effects of the tension and energy that flowed through her.

She walked to the window and looked out and down. She saw that Briana had practically flown down the single flight of stairs. The other woman had already reached the sidewalk and was running awkwardly toward a car that was parked at the curb.

A white car.

Orchid's stomach went cold. She peered more closely at the vehicle.

It was a Phase 1000.

"Dear God."

She whirled and ran to the phone. Punched out Rafe's private number and waited without breathing for him to pick it up. Her heart sank when she heard the familiar click of the answering machine.

"You have reached seven zero seven nine zero nine four. I'm either on the other line or away from the phone. Please leave a message after the beep . . ."

"Rafe, it's me, Orchid." She carried the phone back to the window. "I just had a visit from Briana Culverthorpe. Rafe, listen to this. She drives a Phase One-thousand."

Outside on the street, Briana sat behind the wheel of her car. She made no move to drive off.

"She doesn't like you very much, Rafe. And I think

she would go to great lengths to protect her husband. If she thought that getting rid of you would solve everything she just might . . . Oh, hell. She's getting back out of the car. I think she's . . . Yes. She's coming back upstairs." Orchid carried the phone back to the desk. "Got to go. I'll call you again as soon as she leaves."

The doorbell bonged. Orchid was so startled she dropped the phone. Briana must have run back up the stairs.

"Coming." She fumbled the phone back into its cradle and crossed the room.

She took a deep breath, composed herself, turned the knob, and opened the door. "Back so soon, Briana?"

"I've been thinking about what you said a few minutes ago." Briana clutched her purse very tightly. Her eyes held barely controlled desperation. "I want to talk to you some more."

Orchid felt the tension go out of her. It was going to be all right. Briana had made her decision.

Orchid smiled, stepped back, and held the door wide. "Come in. I'll make coff-tea."

Briana walked back into the apartment. Turned. Looked past Orchid and out into the hall.

And opened her mouth to scream.

Orchid heard the rush of footsteps behind her. Belatedly she spun around but there was no chance to run.

There were two of them, both dressed in the nondescript green work uniforms of the gardeners who serviced the apartment complex's grounds, and they were headed straight for Orchid's front door.

One of them pointed a small canister in her face. He pressed the button. Orchid was vaguely aware of the second man aiming a canister at a stunned Briana. She heard a hiss. A cold mist enveloped her.

The apartment began to whirl around her.

She leaned into the uniformed man in front of her, groping for the front of his shirt. She felt him take a sideways step to avoid her. She kicked his ankle out from underneath him.

"He said you might be difficult." The man pressed the button on the canister a second time.

More of the icy mist struck her in the face. A great darkness began to descend on her. She held her breath, but that did not stop the stuff from penetrating the membranes of her eyes, nose, and lips.

The world receded swiftly in a black haze. Her legs dissolved beneath her. Voices came to her out of the gathering shadows.

"What about the other one?"

"She saw us. Better bring her along. He can decide what he wants to do with her."

Orchid felt the texture of heavy twill beneath her fingertips. The fabric of a gardener's uniform. Someone was holding her while she sank into oblivion.

She fought the effects of the spray with meta-zen-syn concentration techniques while she reached out wildly. She searched for something, anything to leave behind for Rafe to find.

"She's not going under very fast. Still struggling."

Orchid's hand brushed against a pocket. The meta-zen-syn mental exercises could not keep unconsciousness at bay for more than a few more seconds. She had to find something, anything that would constitute a clue for Rafe.

There was an object inside the man's pocket. A pen? A small flashlight?

She got two fingers into the pocket. The man who held her captive did not seem to notice. She seized an object. Held on tight.

"Bat snake shit. What's it going to take to put her out?"

"The doctor said she was a loony, remember? You know how it is with the crazy ones. Takes more than it does for normal people. Give her another shot of the stuff."

More mist in the face.

And then she was being bundled through the doorway.

As she was dragged across the threshold, she vaguely remembered to let go of the small object she had taken from her attacker's pocket. She heard it roll lightly on the floor.

She drew a gasping breath.

The darkness closed in on her.

She hoped she would not dream.

Chapter
19

❖❖❖❖❖❖❖❖❖

"Take a seat, Mr. Stonebraker." Thelma Dorling waved him toward a chintz covered chair that was presently occupied by an overweight cat-dog. "Snooky won't mind." Thelma flapped her hand at the animal. "Go on, get off the chair, Snooky. Let the nice man sit down."

Snooky did not move. He watched Rafe with baleful yellow eyes.

"Just give him a little push," Thelma advised Rafe. "Snooky won't bite." She started toward the kitchen. "Can I get you a beer? I've got Old Earth Ale and Western Islands Lager."

Rafe glanced at her. Thelma Dorling was a pretty, young woman with a figure that resembled those of the models featured on the covers of the magazines Rafe had discovered in the bottom drawer of Austen's desk.

He concluded that she either could not find clothes to fit or else she liked her attire a size too small. Her pink blouse strained at the buttons. The skirt rode high on her thighs. It was stretched so tightly across her buttocks that it formed creases at her hips.

It had taken the better part of the day to track down Austen's former receptionist. When she'd finally returned his call, Rafe learned that she had been out interviewing for a new job.

"Thank you," he said. "I'll take the lager."

"Great. I'll be right back. Don't know about you, but I always need a couple of beers after a day of job hunting." She vanished into the kitchen.

Rafe heard the icerator open and close in the other room. He gazed thoughtfully at the plump cat-dog who was obviously comfortably ensconced with all six legs tucked under him. "That chair is not big enough for both of us, Snooky."

Snooky flexed some claws and bared his fangs. A low growl reverberated through the room.

"Very impressive, Snooky, but I've been told I'm a little on the primitive side, myself."

Snooky growled.

"Behave yourself, Snooky," Thelma called from the kitchen. "Don't mind him, Mr. Stonebraker. He's really quite harmless."

Rafe smiled at Snooky. "But I'm not."

Snooky blinked. His fangs disappeared.

Rafe continued to smile at him.

Snooky retracted his claws. The growl became a soft whine. He rolled onto his back, paws in the air, and exposed his throat.

Rafe sighed. "I hate it when that happens."

He walked over to the chair, reached down, and rubbed the cat-dog's furry belly.

"You know, you might want to take off some of that excess weight before you try to defend your chair from anyone else, Snooky."

Snooky slithered off the chair and took up residence on the sofa.

Thelma reappeared. "Here's your beer, Mr. Stonebraker. Now what was it you wanted to know about Dr. Austen?"

"Do you remember a patient named Theo Willis?"

"Willis? Oh, sure." Thelma kicked off her shoes, sat down on the sofa, and propped her feet on a footstool. "But I hope you don't want to ask me any real personal questions about him."

"Of course not."

"A syn-psych doctor's receptionist isn't supposed to talk about the patients."

"I understand."

"Just between you and me, Willis was a real nutcase, y'know? Dr. Austen said the guy was seriously paranoid. Real big on conspiracy theories and stuff like that. But he was harmless. I felt sorry for him. He seemed to be getting a lot worse toward the end. Real agitated, y'know? I wasn't surprised when I heard he'd killed himself."

"I see. I respect the fact that you won't discuss any personal issues concerning Mr. Willis's syn-psych diagnosis and history," Rafe said gravely. "Nice to know that there is still such a thing as patient-doctor confidentiality in this day and age."

"You bet there is. And it's up to people like us medical receptionists to maintain the standards."

"I, for one, am grateful. But as I said, this isn't a personal question about Willis. It's about a matter of office procedure."

"What about it?" Thelma took a swallow of beer.

"I'm trying to find out who referred Theo Willis to Dr. Austen."

Thelma tipped her head to one side. "How come you wanna know that?"

"It's a confidential matter, but given your responsible attitude toward this kind of thing, I'm sure it's safe to tell you the whole story."

"Oh, yeah." She watched him with eager interest.

Rafe cleared his throat and lowered his voice. "I've been hired by the New Seattle Association of Synergistic Psychologists to look into some problems that have cropped up with the standard practice of professional referrals."

"Referrals?" Thelma looked baffled. "You mean, like, when one doctor sends a patient to another doctor?"

"Yes. Apparently some unlicensed syn-psych therapists have been forging referrals for a fee."

"Yeah?" Thelma wrinkled her brow. "Why would anyone do that?"

"The association believes it's the work of certain, mentally disturbed individuals who like to masquerade as therapists." Rafe shook his head. "We see cases like this two or three times a year."

"Yeah? Weird."

"Now, then, I'm assuming that Dr. Austen sent notes to professional colleagues who referred patients to him?"

"Sure. I usually wrote the letters for him to sign."

"Do you remember writing one to whoever referred Willis to Austen?"

"No."

Rafe stilled. He had been so certain this was going to go somewhere important. "You mean you didn't write a letter?"

"Uh-uh. I mean Dr. Austen told me he'd take care of that one, personally."

"Why would he do that?"

Thelma rolled her eyes. "Because the little pervert was thrilled that such a major honcho in the syn-psych world had referred such a difficult case to him."

Rafe was briefly distracted. "The little pervert?"

"Between you and me and old Snooky here, Austen had a thing for some of his female patients. One of 'em was actually threatening to sue him. Claimed he'd hypnotized her into having sex with him in her office."

"Is that so?"

Thelma shrugged. "Probably the only way Austen could get any sex at all."

"I see. About the thank you letter Dr. Austen wrote—?"

"Oh, yeah, right. Well, he was really thrilled because the other doctor told him that he thought Austen was the only one in New Seattle who could handle the case."

Rafe felt the whole thing come together. Anticipation hummed in his veins. He did not realize he had allowed it to show until Snooky suddenly lifted his head off his paws and uttered a low whine.

Thelma patted the tense cat-dog. "Be a good boy now, Snooky."

Snooky paid no attention and stared at Rafe.

"Who was the doctor who referred Willis to Austen?" Rafe asked.

"Didn't I tell you? Dr. Gilbert Bracewell of ParaSyn Research."

Rafe knew then that he finally had the link he had been looking for from the very beginning of the case. He smiled.

Snooky howled. He scrambled off the sofa and ran madly down the hall.

Thelma's face crinkled into a perplexed frown. "Now what in the world got into Snooky? He hasn't moved that fast in ages."

An hour later Rafe stood in the center of Orchid's small living room. He was no longer smiling. He was engaged in a battle with the white hot fires of fury that threatened to consume him.

He knew that this kind of anger was useless. He had to get control of it. The only hope was to freeze the rage so that he could think.

So that he could hunt.

Selby stormed through the open door. "What in five hells is going on here?" He came to an abrupt halt and gazed around in confusion.

Rafe watched him closely as he examined the scene in Orchid's front room. Selby appeared genuinely bewildered by the sight of the overturned chair, the crumpled rug, and the shattered vase.

"I don't like being *summoned*." Selby's eyes narrowed as he switched his gaze back to Rafe. "I don't work for you."

"I'm aware of that. But I thought you might like to be involved in this."

"Involved in what?" Selby waved a hand at the disordered room. "What happened here? And what the hell is my wife's car doing parked at the curb out front?"

"Good question. What *is* your wife's car doing out front?"

Selby scowled. "I don't have time to play games."

"Neither do I. Someone kidnapped Orchid."

Selby's mouth fell open. "Are you crazy?"

"I think whoever took her may also have taken your wife. I have a hunch she was in the wrong place at the wrong time."

Selby stared at him with dazed, uncomprehending eyes. "But . . . but that's impossible. Why would anyone—?"

"It's a long story. I'll tell you on the way." Rafe started toward the door.

"On the way to where?"

"The headquarters of ParaSyn Research."

Selby took a hesitant step and then ground to a halt. "I don't understand."

"I know." Rafe paused in the doorway. "We'll have to make a stop at my house. I need to get some stuff off the computer. Are you coming with me?"

"Not until you explain some things."

"Such as?"

Selby gathered himself. "Such as why you insist on going to ParaSyn. If something has happened to my wife, we have to go to the police."

"I don't think we have time to call the cops. Orchid might survive for a while because Bracewell thinks he needs her. But he has no use for Briana. He may decide to get rid of her as quickly as possible."

Selby's face worked. "Oh, Christ. Oh, Christ. Briana. He wouldn't dare hurt her."

"Don't bet on it. He's already killed a couple of times."

"Oh, Christ." Selby took a hesitant step toward the door. "But how do you know he took Briana to Para-Syn?"

"I'm not positive that he did. But I think it's a good place to start looking." Rafe led the way outside into the darkening twilight.

Selby stumbled through the doorway, automatically closing it behind him. He followed Rafe downstairs to the Icer as if he were in a daze and got into the passenger seat.

He sat staring through the windshield while Rafe pulled away from the curb.

After a while Selby moistened his lips. "ParaSyn is a major corporation. A reputable laboratory. I've got stock in the company, for God's sake."

"You may want to think about dumping it." Rafe accelerated swiftly down the street. "I got rid of all the shares in the Synergy Fund this morning."

"What in hell makes you believe that someone at ParaSyn took Briana and Orchid?"

"Among other things, this makes me believe it." Rafe reached into his pocket and removed the small object he had found on the floor in Orchid's house. He handed it to Selby.

"It's a pen." Selby looked up, more puzzled than ever. "I don't get it. What's the big deal about a pen?"

"Take a closer look."

Selby peered at the pen as if it were a strange alien artifact. "Oh, Christ. It's got the ParaSyn logo on it. You think whoever took Briana and Orchid dropped it?"

"Yes."

"Ransom. They'll probably want money."

"I don't think so."

"Oh, Christ." Selby sagged back into his seat. "What can we do?"

Rafe whipped the Icer around the corner and increased speed. "We can find Orchid and Briana."

"ParaSyn's a huge lab." Selby shook his head, dazed. "How do we find them in a facility that big? Assuming they're even there in the first place."

"Like I said, we're going to stop by my place first. I've got a lot of details about ParaSyn on file in the Synergy Fund data base."

"Why would you have that kind of information available?"

"Because I never take a position in a stock unless I've researched it thoroughly. I've got all the details of the ParaSyn campus, including plans of the labs, mechanical layouts, the works. I've also got information on the security setup."

Selby blinked a couple of times. Behind the lenses of his glasses, his eyes narrowed. "My God. I see what you mean by thorough. Do you always do business that way?"

"Always."

"Not that it seems very important at the moment, but tell me something. Do I even stand a chance at the annual board meeting?"

Rafe hesitated. "No."

"I could have done it if you hadn't come back."

"Yes."

"Why did you?"

Rafe glanced at him. "It was time."

"I see." Selby gazed through the windshield at the gathering shadows. "It'll be dark soon. ParaSyn will be closed for the day."

"Don't worry," Rafe said. "I do my best work at night."

Orchid was aware of the smell of the place first. She remembered it all too well. That sterile, mechanical, clean-room smell that dominated the labs and halls at ParaSyn. Beneath it was the faint odor of chemicals and instruments. The heavily conditioned air had a stale, antiseptic taint.

Fear wafted through her. It was followed by the cleansing rush of anger. Strange how odors could trigger such strong emotions, she thought.

The next thing she noticed was the temperature of the room. A few degrees too cool for comfort. That, too, brought back unpleasant memories.

She hated this place.

Someone moaned beside her. Orchid opened her eyes. Her head swam. The after effects of the anesthetic gas, she thought.

Bright lab lights glared down on her from the acoustically baffled ceiling. To her right she could see a long lab bench laden with machines and instruments. She realized she was lying on a small, narrow gurney.

Fear pounded through her again, driving out even the anger for a moment. Some of the most severely disturbed talents had been brought from the locked synpsych ward on gurneys like this one.

She struggled wildly for a few seconds and managed to sit up. But when she tried to slide off the gurney she discovered that her right wrist was fastened to one of the metal rails with a plastic cuff.

A burst of adrenaline helped to clear her head a little.

Another moan drew her attention. She looked over her shoulder and saw Briana on a second gurney. She, too, was secured with a padded cuff.

"Briana?" Orchid kept her voice to a whisper. "Briana, wake up. We've got to get out of here."

Briana stirred restlessly, as though caught in a bad dream.

"Briana."

Briana's eyelids fluttered and then opened. She blinked several times, sluggishly. "Orchid?" Her voice sounded thick.

"Yes, it's me. Don't talk too loud."

"Where are we?"

"ParaSyn Research." Orchid studied the neat array of equipment on a nearby lab bench. "We've got to find something we can use to cut through these cuffs."

"I don't understand."

"We've been kidnapped." Orchid managed to slide gingerly off the gurney. She clung to the rail when her knees threatened to give way. "I don't think the bastard meant for them to take you. But you were there when they came for me."

"Who are you talking about?" Briana asked just as a door opened.

Orchid turned awkwardly. A familiar figure trotted into her range of vision. He had a clipboard tucked under one arm.

"Miss Adams is referring to me, I believe." Gilbert Bracewell smiled his jolly elfin smile. "Allow me to introduce myself. Dr. Gilbert Bracewell, director of research here at ParaSyn. At your service."

"Little sonovabitch." Orchid clung to the gurney. "I never did like you."

"Naturally, I'm crushed to learn that, but I'll get over it, I'm sure." Gilbert chuckled. "I'm delighted to have you back here at ParaSyn, my dear. When you and the others walked out on the ice-prism experiments you ruined a great deal of my research. Very naughty of you. But then, you always had that rebel streak, didn't you? Seems to be a basic component of the ice-prism para-profile."

Gilbert had changed very little in the three years since she had seen him. He was still round and bouncy and his white lab coat was artfully tailored to fit his portly figure. He was a malicious elf of a man. He should have been wearing long, pointy-toed shoes and a cap with a tassel on it, Orchid thought.

There was one small change in him, she noticed. The

gleam in his merry little eyes seemed a little too bright, a bit more unnatural.

Orchid shivered. She took a couple of meta-zen-syn breaths to steady herself. "You have done a very, very stupid thing, Gilly."

Annoyance flickered across his red-cheeked face. "You never did show the degree of respect appropriate for a man of my power and accomplishments. But before we have finished, my dear, you will learn to call me Dr. Bracewell. Oh, yes. You will learn."

"Hard to respect a man who has done something as dumb as this." Orchid waggled her hand in the plastic cuff. "What makes you think you can get away with kidnapping Briana and me?"

Gilbert's eyes sparkled. "This makes me believe it, my dear."

He reached into the pocket of his lab coat and removed a long, thin object that resembled a small flashlight. In the glare of the lab lights it gleamed with a strange, metallic sheen.

"Well, that answers one very interesting question," Orchid said. "You were the twit who arranged for the theft of the alien artifact."

"I did, indeed, Miss Adams." Gilbert glanced at the silvery relic with fascinated pride. "I learned about the relic's powers when I persuaded Mr. Willis to return to ParaSyn a couple of months ago for a three-year follow-up."

"Theo would never have come back here willingly."

"Poor Mr. Willis was in need of money. He had some silly dream about opening a focus agency specializing in ice-prisms. Utter nonsense, of course. But when I offered to pay him a considerable sum for a single, one-hour session, he reluctantly agreed to return."

"I still can't see him confiding data about the relic to you."

"To tell you the truth, I, too, did not trust him to be fully cooperative during the session. So while he was here I took the liberty of using some new medication that induced him to talk quite freely. He had just started his job in Dr. Brizo's lab."

"You mean you drugged him and that's when he told you that he thought one of the alien relics in Brizo's lab had some real power?"

"Yes."

"And you actually *believed* him? Sheesh."

Gilbert gave her a disapproving frown, as if she had disappointed him. "He was under the influence of the medication, my dear. He told me the truth."

"What he believed to be the truth, maybe. Theo had a few syn-psych problems, if you'll recall."

"Rest assured, it's the truth." Gilbert chuckled. "At any rate, he explained that while working with one particular relic, he had sensed that it contained some form of energy. He wanted to conduct further tests before he wrote up his report. He wanted to be very certain, you see, because he was afraid his new associates would think he was crazy if he simply told them what he suspected to be true."

"Theo Willis didn't like you any better than I did. Mind telling me how you got him to steal the relic for you?" Orchid gave him a derisive look. "You're only a low-range hypno-therapist, after all. Class two at best."

The barb stung, as she had intended. Gilbert's hand clenched violently around his clipboard. But he quickly recovered his composure.

"It was quite simple, my dear. I worked through a much stronger hypno-therapist."

"Quentin Austen," Orchid whispered.

"Yes, indeed. Once I discovered the value of the relic, I knew I had to have it. But I could not risk having ParaSyn connected to the theft. With the assistance of my new hypnotic enhancement drug, I convinced Mr. Willis that he would benefit greatly from therapy. He agreed to allow himself to be referred to Austen."

"Austen used hypnosis to get Theo to steal the relic."

"You've already figured that out, have you? Quite right. What's more, with the aid of the same new medication I just mentioned, Dr. Austen was able to instill and enforce an especially strong hypnotic suggestion in Mr. Willis."

"Why would Austen help you?"

Gilbert beamed. "Because he was about to lose his license to practice due to a pending lawsuit from one of his ex-patients. He needed the support and influence that I wield with the disciplinary committee of the New Seattle Association of Synergistic Psychologists."

"You told him that if he helped you use Theo to steal the artifact, you'd see to it that he got to keep his license, is that it?"

"Precisely."

"Once you had the relic, you arranged for Theo to be murdered."

Gilbert's brow furrowed. "I really had no choice. I assumed that getting rid of Willis would erase any trace of a link between ParaSyn and the stolen relic. Besides, I intended to use another ice-prism, not Willis, for my work on the relic. Willis was much too erratic for serious research."

Orchid felt suddenly very queasy. "You intended to use me, didn't you? That's why you kept sending me those letters urging me to return to ParaSyn for follow-up studies."

"Yes. I had hoped the influence of your Northville academic background would persuade you to return to the lab. But, as always, you proved extremely stubborn and uncooperative." Gilbert smiled. "Ah, well, you're here now and that's all that matters."

Orchid ignored that. "You hired Mr. Amazing and his prism to murder Theo, didn't you?"

"Actually the illusion-talent who called himself Mr. Amazing handled the car crash on his own. He had no need of a prism for such a simple job."

"But things started to go wrong after that, didn't they?"

"Things began to grow untidy." Gilbert's plump fingers tapped nervously on the back of his clipboard. "The attempt to discourage Mr. Stonebraker failed. It was really most annoying. Then Austen came to me. He was extremely distraught. He said that just before he died, Willis had written a letter accusing him of hypnotizing him and forcing him to steal the relic. In the letter Willis claimed he had arranged to have another letter sent to a friend, instructing him to go to the police if anything happened to him."

"The letter to Morgan Lambert," Orchid said softly.

"I employed Mr. Amazing again to retrieve the letter and get rid of Lambert. He and his prism found the letter, but the fool made a copy. He had the temerity to try to blackmail me with it."

"So you killed him and tried to kill the prism who had helped him. But you screwed up, didn't you, Gilly? You didn't succeed in killing Crowder."

"Things got a bit out of control," Gilbert admitted.

"And you got desperate. You tried to make it look as though Quentin Austen was behind the theft and the murders. Then you killed him, too. You wanted everyone to think that he had finally gone over the edge and committed suicide."

"It wasn't quite like that, but you're very close, my dear. Very close, indeed. The plan should have worked." A troubled expression marred Gilbert's cheery features. "It will work. I have you now."

"Not for long. Stonebraker will come for me." Orchid deliberately slipped into melodramatic tones that were more appropriate to an actor in a late-night horror film. "He's a strat-talent, Gilly. Do you know what that means?"

Gilbert frowned. "They're rather primitive, I believe."

"Very primitive, Gilly. Some people call them hunters.

Rafe will find me. And when he does, Gilly, he will hunt you down and he will *rip out your throat.*"

Gilbert's eyes widened. He took an involuntary step back. She did not write psychic vampire romance novels for nothing, Orchid thought.

Briana stirred on the gurney. "My God. I hope he does exactly that, you nasty little worm."

Gilbert's face darkened. "Mr. Stonebraker is no longer a threat. If he appears, he will be dealt with. Everything is under control in terms of security here at ParaSyn."

"Uh huh." Orchid looked at him. "If you believe that, Gilly, I've got a nice bridge in the Western Islands I can sell to you."

"Shut up," Gilbert hissed. "Shut up this instant. And don't ever call me Gilly again. I have had enough of your scorn and disrespect. You don't know what you're up against."

"You're no different now than you were three years ago, Gilly. You're still envious of people who have more psychic power than you do, aren't you? You're well and truly wacko if you think that alien relic is going to help you increase your talent."

"Damn you. I will show you what this relic can do." Gilbert tightened his grip on the artifact. *"Link."*

"Fat chance, Gilly."

Gilbert lifted his chin. Very methodically he put the clipboard down on the lab bench, reached into his pocket, and brought out a small pistol.

"Link, you stupid little ice-prism, or I will kill Mrs. Culverthorpe. You have until the count of three to make up your mind."

"Orchid?" Briana struggled to sit up on the edge of the gurney. Fear twisted her face. "Orchid, I think he means it."

"One," Gilbert hissed.

*   *   *

Selby stared at the slumped form of the guard who had just dropped to the ground with a dull thud. "Did you kill him?"

"No. But he'll be out for a while." Rafe went down on one knee beside the ParaSyn guard.

Working swiftly, he stripped off the snappy black uniform and boots. He removed the plastic restraint cuffs from the black leather belt and clipped them around the guard's wrists. Then he retrieved the two-way radio.

Thus far things had been easy. Too easy, perhaps.

The layout of the ParaSyn physical plant that he had retrieved from his computer had been accurate. He hoped the data on the security system was also.

Rafe and Selby had left the Icer parked on a side street and simply walked up to the front gate. Selby had distracted the guard with a string of questions about a friend who worked at ParaSyn. Rafe had taken care of the rest.

He got to his feet and tugged on the ParaSyn uniform. He attached the small radio to his belt.

"Where'd you learn how to do that?" Selby sounded both awed and shocked.

"Operate a two-way radio? It's not all that tricky. They're used a lot in Stonebraker warehouses and on the docks."

"I wasn't talking about the damned radio. Anyone can work a two-way. I meant what you did to the guard just now. The way you crept up behind him and put your arm around his throat. He didn't even make a sound. He just collapsed."

"It's no big deal, Selby. I just cut off the flow of blood to his brain for a few seconds. He sort of fainted."

"Fainted? Is that what you call it?"

"Actually, it's a meta-zen-syn exercise taken to its logical conclusion."

"I thought that meta-zen-syn stuff was all peace and harmony and synergistic balance."

"Balance is not always achieved with peace and har-

mony. Sometimes you have to give things a little push."
Rafe started to turn toward a stand of trees.

"Wait a second. We're inside the grounds, but what's
the plan here?"

"We find Orchid and Briana and we get them out."

"Just like that, huh?"

Rafe tapped the small radio. "With any luck, this will
make things a little easier. Come on, let's get moving.
We don't have much time. The guard has to check in
periodically. When he misses his next call from headquarters, someone will come looking."

Rafe led the way into the trees that darkened the
parklike grounds of the ParaSyn campus. Moonlight
splattered on the ground like so much spilled milk.

"Lucky they don't have any guard wolf-hounds,"
Selby muttered.

"According to the security data, Dr. Bracewell doesn't
like animals around except the ones used in the labs.
Too dirty."

"I still don't understand why this Bracewell character
would want to kidnap your friend Orchid."

"It's a long story." Rafe quickened his pace. He was
almost loping through the trees now. His senses were
jacked up as far as they could go without the aid of a
prism. Periodically he used a burst of psychic energy to
widen his awareness for a few brief seconds and to make
a sweep of the psychic plane in a search for Orchid.
Thus far he had gotten no response to his questing probe
but he was certain she was here somewhere.

The headquarters of ParaSyn functioned as Dr. Gilbert Bracewell's lair. According to the map in the Synergy Fund files, Bracewell actually lived on site. He had
a small apartment in the main building.

Bracewell would feel safe here, surrounded by his
guards and his unassailable prestige, Rafe thought. He
would feel in control here. A man who was slipping over
the edge would cling to a sense of control the way a
drowning man clung to a rope.

"Not so fast." Selby's breath quickened as he strained to keep up with Rafe. "I can barely see you, let alone where I'm going. It won't help matters if I run into a tree."

Selby had a point. Rafe knew he could not afford to risk leaving his cousin to wander aimlessly around the darkened grounds. Reluctantly he slowed his pace.

A few minutes later he halted at the edge of the woods. The main building of ParaSyn, Lab A, was so well lit with outdoor floodlights that it almost glowed. The annual report claimed that it operated around the clock but tonight it looked as if it had been shut down for a holiday weekend.

Rafe studied the two other, smaller labs. Both appeared equally quiet.

He could feel the trap. The only question was, who had set it? The Synergy Fund biographical data on Dr. Gilbert Bracewell had not painted a picture of a man who was a great strategic thinker. Yet Bracewell had to be involved in this somehow.

Selby stumbled to a halt beside Rafe and gazed at the brilliantly lit building in despair. "We'll never be able to get inside."

"Sure we will. All we need is another uniform."

"How the hell are we supposed to get one? Take out another guard?"

Rafe glanced across the service road. He watched a man in a blue work uniform walk out the side door of Lab B. The man headed toward a van parked in the lot behind the building. The sign on the side of the van read "ParaSyn Janitorial Dept."

"I think I see an easier way," Rafe said.

Chapter

20

❖ ❖ ❖ ❖ ❖ ❖ ❖ ❖ ❖

Orchid saw the wild glitter in Gilbert's eyes. He had already killed more than once. There was no reason to think he would hesitate to shoot Briana.

She felt the probing tendril of a low-range psychic power.

"Two . . ." Gilbert tightened his grip on the pistol.

She answered the probe with a brilliant, crystal clear prism.

"Ah, yes." Gilbert's face relaxed into an expression of approval. "I knew you would be reasonable about this, my dear."

Unwholesome waves of power began to flow through the prism. Orchid fought the instinctive impulse to dissolve the focus. The only thing that made the experience tolerable was the fact that Gilbert Bracewell was not a strong talent.

"Okay, you've got your focus link, Two-Watt. Now, what?"

"Now, this, my dear." Gilbert tightened his grip on

the relic. His face grew taut as though he strained to lift a great weight. "Now, you will understand—"

Without warning, his low-class hypno-talent surged. Out on the psychic plane, Orchid watched first in alarm and then in mounting horror as the power pouring through the prism intensified.

In a matter of seconds she found herself focusing a great, rushing, pounding psychic talent. Dark energy crashed through the prism in waves that grew stronger with every beat of her heart.

"The relic," she managed. "You're doing this with it."

"Indeed, I am." Gilbert's smile was tight and strained, but his eyes were bright with cheerful madness. "The artifact is some sort of mechanical device that can heighten the level of an individual's psychic power. But it only functions when that power is focused through a prism who can adapt to the odd wavelengths given off by the alien machine."

"An ice-prism."

"Yes, my dear. An ice-prism is the only kind of prism that can work with it. A very strong ice-prism. You see now why you are so important to me, Miss Adams?"

In the metaphysical realm the dark, unwholesome power surged to new levels. This time Orchid sensed that Gilbert was not simply exercising his new level of psychic talent. He was gathering it with a purpose.

Dread shafted through her. With the aid of the relic and her unique prism capabilities, Gilbert had become a hypno-talent of monstrous magnitude. A true psychic vampire.

"What are you going to do?" she asked.

"I believe this is an excellent opportunity to conduct a small demonstration of my enhanced psychic powers. By the Curtain, no one will ever call me Two-Watt Bracewell again."

He kept the pistol trained on Briana as he opened a drawer beneath the lab bench. Orchid tensed.

"Gilly, you don't know anything about this relic. There's no way to test it safely under these conditions."

"Give me some credit, my dear Miss Adams. After all, I am the director of research here at ParaSyn. I know what I'm doing."

Gilbert turned slightly to reveal the object he had taken from the drawer. The cold lab lights glinted on a pair of heavy shears. Orchid recognized it as a tool used for cutting wire and other hard objects.

Carrying the shears in the same hand he used to clutch the relic, Gilbert walked across the room to where Briana sat on the edge of the gurney. He freed her hand from the plastic cuff with a single snip.

"Take these, Mrs. Culverthorpe." He slapped them into her hand. "And look into my eyes."

Understanding dawned on Orchid. "Don't do it, Briana. Don't look at him."

Still dazed from the effects of the gas that had been used to stun her, Briana stared uncomprehendingly down at the shears. Then she raised her confused gaze to meet Gilbert's eyes.

Hypno-talent slashed through the prism. Briana's gaze went from dazed to glassy-eyed.

"What do you want me to do?" she whispered in an emotionless voice.

"Very simple my dear." Gilbert stepped back several paces. He smiled broadly. "Take the shears and plunge them into your chest."

"No." Desperate now, Orchid tried to dissolve the prism.

Nothing happened. The prism was locked in Gilbert's enhanced psychic talons. She could not cut off his mechanically augmented power surge.

"Please be quick about it, Mrs. Culverthorpe. I don't have all night, you know. Miss Adams and I must leave here soon."

"Briana, no," Orchid shouted. "Don't do it. Look at

me, Briana. Don't look at that stupid little elf. *Look at me.*"

But Briana continued to gaze steadily at Gilbert, who smiled fondly back.

Dark psychic energy whirled and slammed through the prism, intensifying the hypnotic effect.

Briana raised the shears and aimed them at a point between her breasts.

"You bastard." Orchid stared at Gilbert. "Don't do this. I'll go with you. I'll help you conduct your experiments. But only if you stop this right now."

"You'll help me regardless, my dear. I have you in my power now."

Orchid saw a strange expression pass through Briana's eyes. It was as though some part of her understood what she was about to do and resisted. But her muscles tensed in preparation as she aimed the shears at her own heart.

Orchid no longer had the ability to dissolve the glittering ice-prism. But there was still the possibility that she could manipulate it.

There was no point struggling against the alien-tainted power. But meta-zen-syn taught that all power was dependent upon the endless struggle for balance.

She concentrated on the brilliant crystal facets of the prism. She would have only one chance to alter the synergistic balance. If she failed, Briana would die.

Gently she began to shift the focus. The raging power followed, realigning itself.

For an instant Gilbert did not realize what was happening. He was too busy concentrating on the results of his terrible experiment.

"Orchid?" Briana's eyes cleared slightly. She blinked and stared at the shears she had aimed at her own breast. "Orchid, what's going on?"

Orchid did not answer. She was wholly occupied with the task of altering the focus of the prism facets.

Gilbert suddenly realized that something was wrong. He was slamming more power than ever through the prism now, but Briana had begun to lower the shears. Rage screwed up his gnomelike face.

"What's this?" he screamed. "What's happening?"

Orchid continued to manipulate the focus. Mirrors, she reminded herself. The facets were tiny psychic mirrors fashioned to focus energy waves the way a laser focused light waves.

"Stop it," Gilbert shouted. "Stop this at once."

But he was too late. Orchid sensed the exact instant when he frantically tried to cut off the flow of talent. But nothing happened. Power slammed through the refocused prism. Gilbert was as much a prisoner now as Orchid. The alien relic was out of control.

Slowly, inevitably, Gilbert turned the gun so that it no longer pointed at Briana. He aimed the barrel at his own chest.

His eyes no longer twinkled with evil glee. They widened in horror. More dark, raging hypno-talent surged through the refocused prism.

"No," Gilbert screamed. *"No."*

But it was too late. Overwhelmed by his own magnified hypno-talent turned back on himself, he squeezed the trigger of the pistol.

The blast echoed loudly in the cold, clean room. The gun clattered on the white tile floor. Gilbert toppled backward. Orchid watched, stunned, as blood welled in the center of his tailored lab coat.

On the psychic plane the flow of talent ceased with appalling suddenness. Orchid was free. She hastily dissolved the prism. There was no reason to think that the alien relic could function on its own without a talent to guide it, but there was no sense taking chances.

"Dear heaven," Briana stared at the fallen Bracewell. "He killed himself."

Orchid wrenched her attention away from the horrifying scene on the floor. "The shears. Give them to me so that I can cut off this restraint cuff."

Briana looked at her. "You made him do that, didn't you? Somehow you reversed the flow of his hypno-talent."

"Yes." Orchid pushed the gurney closer to Briana. "I'm an ice-prism." She reached for the shears.

Briana shook her head, dazed. "You saved my life."

"Least I could do under the circumstances." Orchid gently removed the shears from Briana's hand. "It's my fault you're here in the first place."

She snipped through the plastic restraint that bound her left wrist to the gurney rail. Then she freed Briana.

"What are we going to do now?" Briana slid off the gurney. She clung to Orchid to steady herself.

"Now we get out of here. Can you walk?"

"Yes." Briana made a visible effort to pull herself together. "Yes, I can walk if it means getting away from this place."

Orchid led the way to the door. She sensed the presence on the other side just as she opened it, but by then it was much too late.

A tall, ruggedly handsome man with sandy brown hair and sharp brown eyes smiled at her. He was dressed in a crisply pressed black uniform decorated with a great many epaulets, buttons, and snappy cargo pockets. His black boots gleamed.

He had a gun in his black-gloved hand.

"Hello, Orchid. It's been a while. I've missed you."

Orchid bit back a scream. It was not the gun in Calvin Hyde's hand that aroused the primal fear in her. It was the hunger in his voice.

"If I were you I'd get a new tailor, Calvin. That uniform makes you look like something out of a comic book."

He was unfazed. "You'll be happy to know that after tonight I'll be able to afford the best tailor in New Seattle."

*   *   *

"Now what?" Selby huddled in the shadows of the janitor's closet and struggled with the snaps of the blue uniform.

"Now we ask our friend here a few questions." Rafe smiled at the bound man on the floor.

The janitor, dressed only in his briefs and a T-shirt, stirred nervously. "Look, I just work here, okay? I don't know what you want, but I doubt if I can help you."

"Have you got the keys to the mechanical equipment room down the hall?"

"Well, yeah, sure. I've got the keys to all the rooms in the buildings except those inside the restricted zones."

"Then you can help me."

The janitor stared at him, bewildered. "But there's nothing in the mechanical room except a bunch of valves and switches. I don't even know what valve operates what kind of equipment."

"Don't worry," Rafe said. "That's not your problem." He glanced at Selby, who had just finished with the last snap on the blue uniform. "I've got a tech-talent with me."

Still smiling his feral smile, Calvin used the gleaming black steel pistol to wave Orchid and Briana back toward the gurneys. He caught sight of Gilbert's body on the floor.

"Well, well, well. You surprise me, Orchid. I thought you were much too meta-zen-syn for that kind of thing. How did you manage it?"

"Do you care?" Orchid asked.

"Not really." Calvin leaned negligently against the long lab bench. He kept the gun trained on Orchid and Briana. "I was going to have to get rid of old Two-Watt soon, anyway. He never was real stable, but he definitely went over the edge after Theo Willis told him about that damned artifact."

Briana looked from Calvin to Orchid and back again. "Who are you?"

"Allow me to introduce myself, Mrs. Culverthorpe." Calvin inclined his head with mocking formality. "Calvin Hyde. I'm the chief of security here at ParaSyn."

Orchid stared at him. "When did you get that job?"

"Shortly after you left. I convinced Bracewell that I could be of significant service to him. Made him see that he needed me."

"What did you get out of the deal besides a steady job?"

Calvin chuckled. "You know me so well, Orchid. The answer is that it was a very lucrative arrangement for me. I now own several thousand shares of ParaSyn stock, which I will, of course, sell first thing in the morning before anyone learns that the head of ParaSyn's research department is dead."

"Smart move," Orchid muttered.

"I'm a strat-talent, remember? We're good at making money."

"So they say."

Calvin glanced at Bracewell's body and shook his head. "It was a good gig while it lasted, but I knew it couldn't go on much longer. Bracewell was getting nuttier by the day."

"Nuttier?" Orchid repeated cautiously.

Calvin used one finger to circle his ear in the old gesture meant to indicate craziness. "He actually believed that stupid artifact could give him heightened paranormal power. He thought he could turn himself into a genuine off-the-chart talent if he could just get a strong iceprism to help him control it. What would you call that kind of thinking?"

"Definitely a wacko," Orchid said quickly.

"The man was certainly crazy," Briana agreed with an uneasy glance at the alien relic, which still lay on the floor.

Orchid decided it would not be wise to inform Calvin that Gilbert had been right about the relic. There would be no way to get past Calvin. Her only hope now was to buy time. It would not take Rafe long to figure out that something had happened.

"You've been involved in this from the beginning?" Orchid asked. Calvin had never been shy when it came to bragging.

"Unfortunately, no." Calvin grimaced with disgust. "If I had, things would have been handled much more efficiently. Bracewell was very secretive at first. He didn't want anyone, especially me, to know about the relic."

"Especially you?"

Calvin grinned. "Probably figured I'd steal it and become twice the man I am. As if I need any more talent than I've already got."

"The only thing larger than your talent is your ego, Calvin."

Briana's eyes widened in alarm.

Calvin merely laughed. "Your sense of humor was one of the things I always liked best about you, Orchid."

"Yeah, right. Go on with your story."

"I didn't figure out what was going on until the night Bracewell killed that illusion-talent in Founders' Square."

"How did you know Bracewell had shot him?"

"I was here when old Two-Watt returned that night. He was badly shaken because someone had very nearly caught him when he tried to shoot the prism. He knew he had lost control of the situation. He was terrified." Calvin snickered. "He said he felt as if he were being, and I quote, *hunted.*"

"You offered to take charge of the situation for him, is that it?"

"I promised him that, for a few thousand more shares of ParaSyn stock, I'd clean up the mess he'd made. He was desperate by then. He accepted the offer."

Orchid gritted her teeth. "So it was you who pushed Quentin Austen off that ferry."

"Sure. I realized immediately that we had to get rid of Austen."

"You're the one who tried to shoot Rafe in the woods outside of Northville, aren't you?"

"Yes. It was after I saw him move that day that I knew I was in a duel with another strat-talent." Calvin's golden brown eyes glittered with cold anticipation. "The only other hunter I've ever come across in my entire life. There are so very few of us, you know."

"I know," Orchid whispered.

"I've been looking forward to meeting up with him again."

"Why would you want to do that?" Orchid asked.

"You could not possibly understand. Only another hunter could comprehend the challenge of going *mano-a-mano* with a man who is my equal. It will be a duel to remember. The ultimate test of my talent."

Orchid blinked. "You're looking forward to the challenge of hunting Rafe?"

"Why do you find that so surprising? I assure you, Stonebraker will enjoy the game as much as I will. It's in his blood."

"How do you intend to set up a duel here at ParaSyn?"

Calvin gave her a mockingly pitying look. "Don't you understand yet? The arrangements for the duel have already been made."

"What are you saying?" Briana demanded.

Calvin gave her a brief, disinterested glance. "Stonebraker will follow Orchid here tonight because she is his mate. He will come alone because that is his nature. When he arrives, he will discover that he must do battle with me in order to reclaim Miss Adams."

"Talk about primitive thinking," Orchid muttered. "You know, Calvin, it's guys like you who give strat-talents a bad name."

"I told you, only another strat-talent can possibly savor the blood-rush of a life-or-death hunt when the quarry is as dangerous as the hunter." Calvin breathed deeply. "Only another strat-talent can know the primeval call of the wild. The exhilaration of the stalk. The elemental pleasure of the kill."

Orchid half expected to see steam jet out of his nostrils. She felt the invisible pulse of a deeply disturbed psychic talent. Energy hummed in the air around Calvin, unwholesome, monstrous, dangerous. He had definitely gotten worse during the past three years.

She was careful to keep her own psychic power securely battened down. She did not dare risk giving Calvin a prism to focus his talent. One experience with a psychic vampire tonight was enough.

Calvin smiled at her. It could have been a trick of the light, but she could have sworn she glimpsed fangs.

The hair on the nape of her neck stirred. Out of the corner of her eye, she saw Briana tremble. She understood the involuntary reaction. They were, after all, in the presence of a very dangerous beast of prey.

"You know something, Calvin?" Orchid said. "I think you may have overestimated Rafe's interest in the sport of hunting."

Calvin's smile held no humor. There was a terrible excitement in his eyes. "Stonebraker and I have never met except for that day in the woods outside Northville. But I know him better than you or anyone else ever could. We were both born for the hunt and the kill. Only one of us will survive this night."

"Don't rush me, damn it." Selby concentrated on the array of valve handles in front of him. "This isn't easy, you know."

"You're supposed to be a high-class tech-talent." Rafe aimed the small flashlight at the instrument panel. "Figuring out what all those widgets do should be child's play for you."

"I'm working without a prism, remember? It takes longer this way. I have to go more on intuition and gut reaction. Now shut up and let me think."

Rafe shut up. While he held the flashlight steady, he

tried another psychic probe, seeking contact with Orchid.

Still no response. But he knew she was here. He could feel it.

"Okay," Selby said after a while. "I think I've got most of these lines figured out. Fire suppressant, hot and cold water, and jelly-ice supply. But I don't recognize this red one." He tapped a valve. "It's a gas line, but I don't have any idea of what kind of gas it carries."

Rafe studied the symbols etched on the valve. "Chemistry is not my strong suit."

Selby frowned. "I can read the symbols. They just don't make any sense. Not in those proportions. If this were a hospital, they might indicate some type of anesthetic. But who would pump anesthetic gas throughout a big facility like this? There's no point in it."

Rafe recalled the security data he'd pulled from his computer. "I think it's an emergency system. Some kind of gas used to control the patients if they become violent. The stuff is piped everywhere throughout the facility. It's very subtle. Makes everyone euphoric and then puts them to sleep."

"That might make sense."

"Cousin Selby, I think you have just saved the day," Rafe said. "But before we use that stuff, we need to find out exactly where Bracewell and the other guy are and where they've got Orchid and Briana."

"Who's this other guy you keep talking about?"

"There's another strat-talent here somewhere."

Selby glanced at him sharply. "How do you know that?"

"I just know it, that's all."

"You used to say stuff like that when we were kids. It bugged me then, too."

"How do you think I felt when you always got your new some-assembly-required toys up and running before I could even get mine out of the box?"

* * *

Calvin nudged the alien relic with the toe of his shiny black boot. "You know, the really funny part is that this whole thing started because Bracewell actually believed this thing would give him some kind of super psychic power."

Orchid held her breath when he reached down to pick up the artifact. She glanced at Briana, who watched with agonized eyes as Calvin tossed the object lightly into the air and deftly caught it.

"Like you said," Orchid murmured. "Bracewell was crazy."

"Yeah. But I'm going to be a wealthy man because of the little bastard. Guess I owe him something." Calvin's mouth twisted slightly as he glanced at the body. "Too bad it's too late to repay him. But, hey, those are the breaks, right?"

"Right. Say, Calvin, have you given any thought to your own somewhat limited future?" Orchid asked.

"There won't be any limitations on my future after tonight. I just told you, I'm going to be very, very rich." He frowned at his watch. "Stonebraker should be inside by now."

Orchid chilled. "How do you know that?"

"Same way I know he'll come alone. Besides, I made it easy for him. I gave most of the security guards the night off. I left only a few on duty so that no one would be suspicious but the majority are assigned to B and C Labs."

"You're here in A Lab all alone?" Orchid said. "I don't believe it."

Calvin chuckled. "You do know me, don't you Orchid? You're right. I've got some backup. The two men who brought you and Mrs. Culverthorpe here tonight are still nearby. They're keeping an eye on the entrance to this lab. I gave them instructions to stay out of sight unless something goes wrong. I don't want them interfering in the evening's entertainment unless absolutely necessary, you see."

Full comprehension swept through Orchid. "You've set a trap for Rafe, haven't you? This whole thing was designed to lure him here so that you could hunt him down."

Calvin grinned. "You've got it, babe. I went along with Bracewell's plan to kidnap you because I knew that I could use you as bait to draw Stonebraker here where we could hunt on my turf. I know every hall, every underground tunnel, every nook and cranny in this facility. And I've got my two men waiting in the wings for backup if things go wrong. Stonebraker won't stand a chance."

"I thought this was supposed to be an equal battle between two strat-talents. *Mano-a-mano*. The blood-rush of the ultimate duel to the death between equals, etc., etc."

Calvin's laugh rang out. It bounced off the stainless steel lab bench and ricocheted off the white tile walls. "I'm a strat-talent, not a fool."

A frisson of awareness set up a tingle on Orchid's nerve endings. The questing probe of a clean, strong, strat-talent. Rafe was somewhere in the vicinity. The probe came and went but she knew he would seek her out again in a moment. She dared not give him a prism in case Calvin intercepted it.

"Don't be too sure of that," Orchid whispered.

Calvin continued to show his teeth in a cruel grin. "The only risk factor here is you, Orchid. I know you need to be in close proximity to a talent in order to focus for him. I intend to keep you out of Stonebraker's range. But if he gets near enough to use you for a prism, I'll have to take steps to prevent that from happening."

"Steps?" Orchid asked.

"The first step will be to shoot Mrs. Culverthorpe, here."

Briana groaned. "Not again."

"Step two will be to shoot you, Orchid. I really don't want to do that unless absolutely necessary. I've got plans for the two of us. We have some unfinished business, you and me. I'd really like to keep you alive for a while. I want Stonebraker to watch me take his woman on the floor in front of him."

Orchid braced herself against the sick hunger that swirled in the room. "Don't you think that's just a little bit on the primitive side, Calvin?"

"Primitive." Calvin savored the word. "Yeah. That's me."

Chapter

21

❖ ❖ ❖ ❖ ❖ ❖ ❖ ❖ ❖

Everything was going far too well. No guards inside the building. A convenient janitor who carried a lot of keys. No demands for a check-in from the gate guard's two-way radio.

The situation was just too dandy for words.

Rafe could feel the trap closing around him, but there was nothing to do but keep moving ahead. Orchid was close. He was sure of it. Why didn't she respond?

He looked at Selby, who was still fiddling with some dials in the mechanical equipment room. "Wait here. Give me ten minutes to locate them and then turn on the gas in all of the lab rooms at once. Remember, no gas in the hallways. Got it?"

"Got it."

"Leave the gas on for three minutes and then shut it off."

Selby squinted at him. "You sure you know what you're doing?"

"I'm a strat-talent, remember? I'm good at this kind

of thing. Hit the master switch for the building lights if anything goes wrong. Blink them once. Understand?"

"The lights? Why?"

"It's a nifty way of telling me that Plan A is no longer working."

"Is there a Plan B?"

"There is always a Plan B." Rafe retrieved the small pistol from his ankle holster. "I just have to figure it out, that's all."

"Great. How do you intend to avoid the effects of the gas, yourself? Some of it might seep into the hallways through the cracks around the doors."

Rafe frowned. "I'll put some cloth over my face or something."

"That sounds like a strat-talent sort of plan, all right. A little weak when it comes to the high-tech side of things." Selby reached for a triangular shaped device on an overhead shelf. He lifted it down and handed it to Rafe. "Maybe you ought to take one of these with you."

Rafe took the strange object from him. "What is it?"

"Gas mask," Selby said dryly.

Rafe grinned. "I always knew you tech-talents had your uses."

He opened the door and slipped out into the hall.

He tried once more for a prism, but again there was no response from Orchid. Alarm trickled through him. He had told himself that she was safe because Bracewell needed her alive. The same logic held true for the strat-talent, who no doubt viewed her as bait.

At the end of the hall, Rafe turned and started down another corridor. He used another small burst of talent to see if he could snag Orchid's prism. She was nearby. He knew it in his bones. He wondered if she was unconscious. Bracewell could easily have drugged her.

He rounded a corner, gun raised, and went along another passageway. He sent out a burst of strat-power. For a few seconds his senses opened wide.

Ice sleeted through his veins when he caught the unmistakable taint of blood and death. He knew that in that moment he was as close to losing control as he had ever been in his life. A searing rage howled through him.

But in the next second he knew that the blood was not Orchid's. A stranger lay dead somewhere up ahead.

Before the relief could set in, his jacked up senses caught the traces of two men.

Somewhere behind him.

It was almost reassuring. He had guessed right. This was a trap.

Rafe flattened himself against the wall at the end of the corridor and looked back down the long white hallway. There was no one in sight. But they were there. He could feel them. The strat-talent's backup team.

He tried another short rush of talent.

He caught a distant, fleeting sound. The clang of an object against a pipe.

The emergency equipment room.

"Damn."

He loped swiftly back down the hall. The overhead lights did not wink out. The guards had gotten to Selby before he could hit the master switch.

So much for Plan A.

Calvin was getting restless. Orchid was surprised. She was accustomed to Rafe's quiet ways and seemingly unlimited patience. But Calvin lacked that degree of self-control.

He no longer leaned negligently against the lab bench. He had begun to pace. Periodically Orchid caught the telltale whisper of his psychic energy and knew that he was testing the air, seeking a trace of Rafe.

Orchid traded glances with Briana and saw that she understood the mounting danger.

"He should have been here by now." Calvin reached the end of the lab bench, turned, and looked at Orchid.

"It would be a real joke on me if it turned out I'd under-estimated his interest in you, wouldn't it?"

"A real joke, all right."

"I'll give him another ten minutes and then I'm afraid I'm going to have to cut my losses." He smiled. "That will mean killing you both, of course."

Orchid said nothing. Neither did Briana.

We're getting numb to the threats, Orchid thought. Probably not a good sign.

"Shit." Calvin thumped the handle of his pistol on the stainless steel lab bench. He glowered at Orchid. "If only I could use you as a prism."

Orchid swallowed. "You know it won't work. We proved that three years ago. I can't focus your talent because you're too powerful."

"Yet Bracewell believed that you could focus his stupid artifact." Calvin glanced thoughtfully at the cooling body on the tile floor. "I wonder what convinced him you were strong enough for that?"

Rafe crouched above the mechanical room. He was perched on the edge of a section of the lowered ceiling that concealed the piping. He gazed down through the opening he had created when he had removed one of the three-by-five acoustical panels.

Below two men in ParaSyn security garb exited the emergency equipment room. One of them had a gun to Selby's head.

Rafe waited until all three were directly underneath him before he made his move.

Funny thing about quarry, he reflected as he dropped down onto the back of the man who held Selby captive. They were skittish of shadows. They peered cautiously around corners. They glanced frequently back over their shoulders.

But quarry seldom, if ever, looked up to see what might be waiting overhead.

* * *

The first indication Orchid had that something had altered in the situation was that Calvin had stopped pacing. He had started whistling, instead.

She looked at Briana. Briana smiled back.

A relaxed, decidedly *cheerful* smile.

Orchid suddenly became aware that she, herself, was feeling very good.

In fact, she was much too happy, considering that there was a dead man on the floor and another man was waving a gun about as if it were a toy.

She chuckled.

And then she remembered the gas in the ceiling. How it made everyone, even the most severely disturbed talents, unnaturally cheerful. How it made them want to take a nap.

Rafe had discovered the security system.

She started to laugh.

Calvin and Briana joined in.

When Rafe opened the door and walked into the lab a moment later, they all howled at the hilarious sight he made in his gas mask.

Calvin made one or two attempts to aim his gun at Rafe, but wound up dropping it on the floor. That sent him off into another gale of laughter.

He collapsed on the floor beside the fallen pistol and promptly went to sleep.

Rafe walked toward Orchid.

She was feeling very sleepy, but she had enough energy left to giggle again at the sight of him. "I knew you'd come for us."

"You were right." His voice was curiously distorted by the mask.

"He said you'd want to go *mano-a-mano* with him." She chuckled. "It was supposed to be a duel to the death between the two of you. A battle between equals to see who was top strat-talent."

Rafe caught her as she started to sink to the floor.

"Why would I want to do things in such a primitive way when there's a nice high-tech alternative available?"

"I always knew you were a lot more sophisticated than Calvin." She slipped blissfully toward sleep. "I really do love you, you know."

"I'm glad." Rafe lifted her into his arms. "Because I love you, too."

She smiled as she nestled against him. "That's nice."

"Marry me."

"Sure. Why not?" She closed her eyes, content, and went to sleep in his arms.

Chapter
22

❖ ❖ ❖ ❖ ❖ ❖ ❖ ❖ ❖

Rafe walked into the hospital room carrying a newspaper and a massive bouquet of rose-orchids. He put the flowers down on a small table and looked at Orchid.

"How do you feel?" he asked.

She had never been so happy to see anyone in her life. "Like I'm going to throw up."

"The doctor said that's a common side effect of one of the ingredients in Bracewell's anesthetic gas."

"Nice to know there's a logical explanation. How's Briana doing?"

"I looked in on her before I came here. She's fine. Selby is with her." Rafe crossed the room to stand at the foot of the bed. "I called your folks. They're on their way to New Seattle, even as we speak. So are your brothers."

"Just what I need."

Rafe grinned and unfurled the morning edition of the *New Seattle Times*. "Give 'em a break. You're on the front page. That's enough to worry any family, even an obsessive meta-zen-syn family."

"Let me see that."

Orchid propped herself up against the pillows. She snatched the paper out of his hands and scanned the headline of the front page story.

Executive and Fiancée
Stop Murderer

> *The future C.E.O. of Stonebraker Shipping, Rafael A. Stonebraker, and his fiancée, Miss Orchid Adams, were instrumental in catching two men whom police allege are responsible for at least two and possibly three murders. One of the victims, Dr. Quentin Austen—*

"You don't have to read the whole thing." Rafe gently retrieved the newspaper from Orchid's hands. "I can summarize it for you."

"What does it say about the relic?" she demanded.

"There is no mention of the alien artifact."

"How did you manage that?"

Rafe shrugged. "It was just lying there on the floor. I picked it up and put it in my pocket."

Alarm flashed through Orchid, temporarily taking her mind off her nausea. "Listen, that thing really works. It was so strong that when I reversed the focus, Dr. Bracewell's hypno-talent turned back on itself."

"I know. You woke up a couple of times on the way to the hospital. Told me all about it."

"Did I?" She frowned, unable to recall anything after falling asleep in his arms. "At any rate, Bracewell actually killed himself because of that thing. It's very powerful. And very dangerous."

"Not anymore. Whatever you did to it when you reversed the flow of energy through it burned it out."

She searched his face. "How do you know that?"

"I took it to Brizo. Told him what it might be capable

of doing. He called in an ice-prism on staff at another lab. They conducted several tests."

"And?"

"There's no trace of any power left in the relic. Brizo's theory is that it was never designed to work with human psychic energy. He suspects that in the few minutes it was activated, the combination of your paranormal power and Bracewell's talent destroyed the mechanism."

"That's a relief." Orchid relaxed back against the pillows. "But what if there are other artifacts that also retained some power?"

"Brizo thinks it's highly unlikely. His experts are convinced that the only reason that particular relic still had a trace of energy left was because it was frozen in jelly-ice for a thousand years. They think the ice somehow preserved some of the fuel in the relic. Whatever it is, it's gone now."

"I hope he's right."

"Just in case, Brizo is going to see to it that security around the artifacts is increased. From now on everything will be tested with the help of ice-prisms."

Orchid brightened. "That will certainly drive up ice-prism focus salaries."

The door slammed open. Rafe winced. He turned to see Clementine Malone stride into the room. She waved a copy of the *New Seattle Times*.

"They got it wrong," Clementine bellowed. "Again. I can't believe it. Where do reporters go to school, anyhow? I've got a call in to the front page editor of the *Times*. This kind of screw-up is excusable once, but not twice."

"What did the paper get wrong?" Orchid asked.

"The idiot who wrote the story says that you're a *marriage* agency date from Psynergy, Inc. This is the second time he's made that mistake. I told him the last time that we aren't a matchmaking agency. We're a focus agency."

"Things were still a bit confused last night when the journalists arrived on the scene," Rafe said.

"Hell, maybe you ought to call the *Times* yourself." Clementine scowled. "You probably want this mistake cleared up as much as I do. You've got more clout. Get on the phone and tell that dipstick reporter that you aren't marrying Orchid Adams. Tell him you hired her from a very *exclusive* agency named Psynergy, Inc. for her professional focus skills."

Rafe looked at Orchid. "But I am going to marry her."

Clementine stared at him. "What in five hells is going on here?"

Orchid went very still. She could not take her eyes off Rafe. "Did you mean what you said last night?"

"Unlike you, I was not under the influence of Bracewell's happy gas."

"Oh."

"What about you?" he asked softly. "Did you mean what you said? You may not remember—"

"I remember every word." She smiled. "And I meant every word."

"Now, hold on just a minute, here." Clementine planted her hands on her leather-sheathed hips and glared first at Orchid and then at Rafe. "Are you two saying what I think you're saying?"

"Yes," Rafe and Orchid said together.

"But you haven't been properly matched by a matchmaking agency," Clementine protested.

"We will soon be matched by the best matchmaking agency in town," Rafe said. "Synergistic Connections."

"How do you know that?" Clementine demanded.

Orchid raised her brows. "Yes, how *do* you know that?"

Rafe thought about the Affinity Associates file on Orchid that he had found when he had gone through Gilbert Bracewell's office shortly before the police arrived. The note attached to the file had made everything clear.

It was Bracewell who had arranged to obtain the file from Affinity Associates. He had requested it from Orchid's counselor on the pretext of requiring it for use in a very special research project. Awed by a request from such a prestigious lab and apparently intimidated by the demand for secrecy, the woman had sent the file to Bracewell.

Bracewell had kept the file hidden in his office. He'd had plans for Orchid. The last thing he'd wanted was for her to be matched while he pursued his scheme to obtain the relic.

The counselor who had supplied the file had expected it to be promptly returned. But Bracewell had never sent it back. The woman eventually took another job in New Vancouver. Apparently uneasy about the situation she had created and, perhaps, belatedly aware of the ethics violation she had committed, she had kept quiet about the status of Orchid's file.

"I just know it," he said.

Chapter
23

❖❖❖❖❖❖❖❖❖

It was a typical meta-zen-syn wedding. The groom wore blue. The bride wore yellow. When they reappeared after the ceremony to join their guests in the gardens of Stonebraker House, both wore green to symbolize the power of synergism.

The evening was balmy. The twin moons were full in the night sky. They cast a golden glow over the festive scene.

"I feel really stupid in green," Rafe said in a low voice as he walked through the crowd with Orchid.

"Okay, so it's not your best color." She waved to her cousin, Veronica, who was chatting with her parents. "Look at the bright side. You only have to wear it once in your life."

Rafe smiled with deep satisfaction. "True."

Hobart Batt popped up in front of them, dapper in a pale pink suit and tie. He saluted them with a glass brimming with champagne.

"All best wishes, etc., etc., from Synergistic Connections," he chortled.

It occurred to Orchid that Hobart had had several glasses of champagne. "Thank you, Mr. Batt."

"I know you'll both be very happy together." Hobart took a sip and winked. "In fact, I believe I can say that with ninety-nine-point-nine percent certainty. A near perfect match. Who would have guessed?"

Rafe swiped a canapé off a passing tray. "Not you, that's for sure."

Hobart contrived to look hurt. "Here, now, can't blame me for being a trifle concerned. Strat-talents are notoriously difficult to match. And ice-prisms are no easier. Used to make all sorts of mistakes in the old days. But the new techniques are much more accurate."

"Glad to hear that." Rafe wrapped his fingers around Orchid's wrist. "If you'll excuse us, I think my grandmother is trying to get my attention. She probably wants us to lead off the first tango-waltz."

"Of course, of course." Hobart shooed them away with a movement of the champagne glass. "Oh, before I forget, congratulations on your new position as the C.E.O. of Stonebraker Shipping, sir. Saw the news in the paper last week."

"Thank you, Batt." Rafe swung around with Orchid in tow and nearly collided with Selby and Briana.

Selby swept Rafe's suit with an assessing look. "Green is definitely not your color, cousin."

Briana looked pained. "Oh, for heavens sake, dear. You know perfectly well that Orchid was raised in Northville. Green is traditional at a meta-zen-syn wedding." She smiled at Orchid. "Pay no attention to him. You both look spectacular."

Orchid laughed. "Thanks." She turned toward Selby. "How are things going with the plans for Stonebraker's new transportation technology development facility?"

"Things are on schedule." Selby's eyes lit up with enthusiasm. "We've got the financing in place. The new computer system is set up. I hired two new department heads this past week. Personnel is recruiting young tech-talents at the university—"

"You had to ask," Briana said to Orchid. "He's been like this ever since Rafe made him a vice president and put him in charge of Stonebraker's technical development arm."

Orchid saw the happiness in Briana's face and knew that Rafe's decision had been the right one. She still did not know exactly what had happened between Rafe and Selby that night in the ParaSyn lab. Whatever it was, it had altered the synergy of their relationship.

"Now all I have to do is talk Rafe here into giving me some additional resources for a full-scale wind tunnel," Selby concluded happily.

"I don't want to hear about wind tunnels until after my honeymoon," Rafe warned. "Come on, Orchid. Grandmother is getting serious. I think she just sent Alfred G. to fetch us."

He guided her across the lawn to the terrace. The crowd gathered there moved back to make space. The band struck up a tango-waltz.

Orchid saw her parents standing at the edge of the circle. They smiled broadly when she stepped into Rafe's arms. Clementine and Gracie Proud and Byron Smyth-Jones grinned at the newly wedded couple.

On the other side of the ring of onlookers, Lucas Trent and his wife, Amaryllis, stood with Nick Chastain and Zinnia. They all raised their glasses in a toast as the music swelled.

Applause broke out as Rafe swung Orchid into a long, gliding turn.

"Just one question, Mr. Stonebraker," Orchid said.

"What is that, Mrs. Stonebraker?"

"Did you alter my marriage registration file so that Hobart Batt could match us?"

"It wasn't necessary. I just gave him the file I found in Bracewell's office. Untouched and unaltered."

"Things might have been a bit awkward if Hobart hadn't concluded that we were a perfect match."

"There was no chance that would happen." Rafe smiled into her eyes. "The first time I saw you, I knew we belonged together."

"Hah. I don't believe that for one moment. You needed a date and you were getting desperate."

"Ah, but deep down, I knew that you were the woman I'd been hunting for . . . uh, I mean *searching* for, all my life."

Happiness shimmered through Orchid in a sparkling wave. "What a coincidence," she said. "I knew it, too. About our little private detective hobby."

"What about it?"

"I know we won't have much time for that kind of thing in the future, but I'd hate for us to give it up altogether."

"No reason why the firm of Stonebraker and Adams can't continue to do a little business on the side when the mood strikes." Rafe smiled down at her, eyes brilliant with his love. "But not tonight."

"No," Orchid agreed. "Not tonight."

Discover love's magic with

a paranormal romance from Pocket Books!

Nice Girls Don't Live Forever
MOLLY HARPER

For this librarian-turned-vampire, surviving a broken heart is suddenly becoming a matter of life and undeath.

Gentlemen Prefer Succubi
The Succubus Diaries
JILL MYLES

Maybe bad girls *do* have more fun.

A Highlander's Destiny
MELISSA MAYHUE

When the worlds of Mortal and Fae collide, true love is put to the test.

**Available wherever books are sold or at
www.simonandschuster.com**